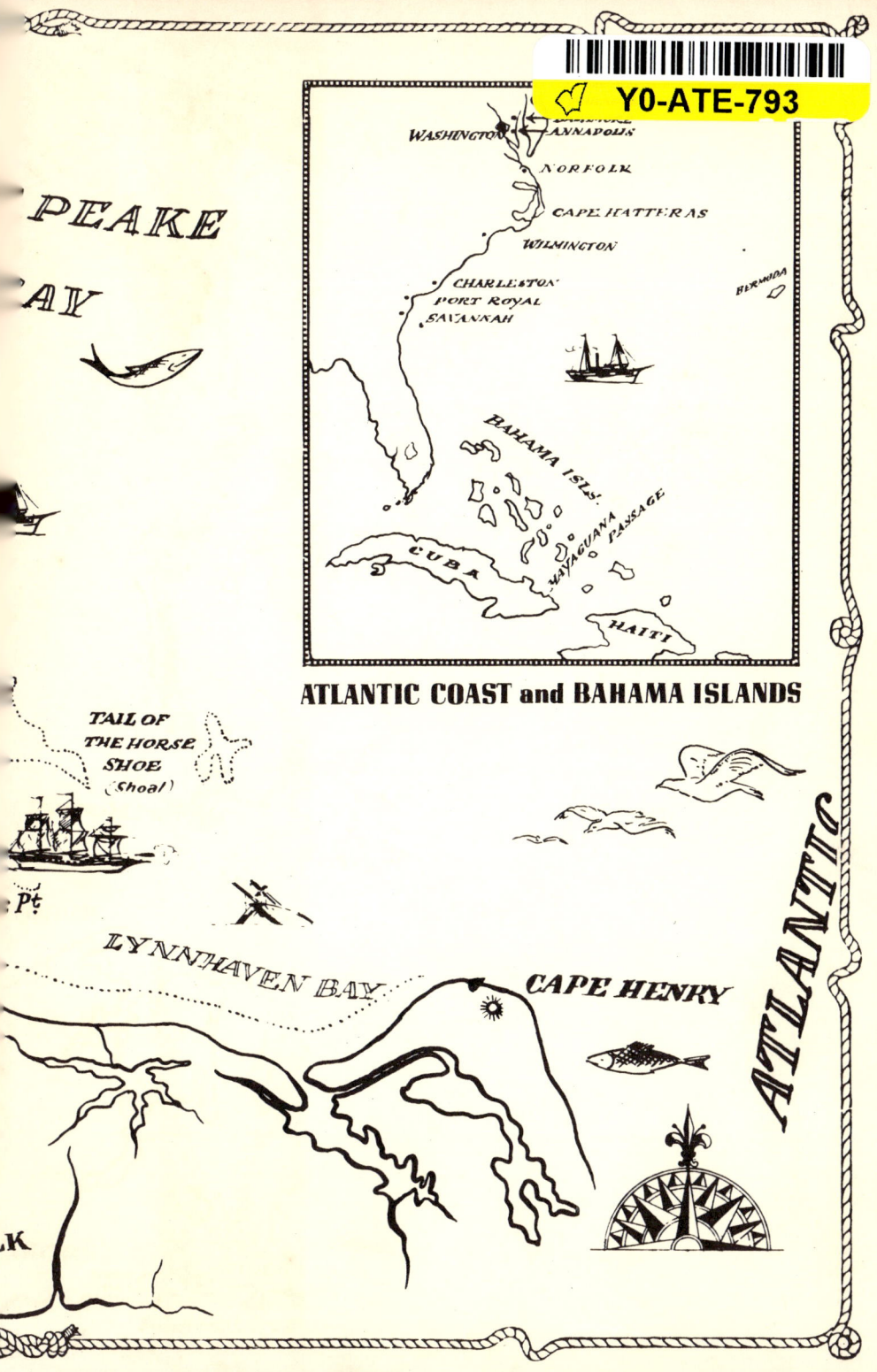

Caleb Pettengill, U. S. N.

GEORGE FIELDING ELIOT

CALEB PETTENGILL, U.S.N.

JULIAN MESSNER, INC.
NEW YORK

Published by Julian Messner, Inc.
8 West 40 Street, New York 18

*Published simultaneously in Canada
by The Copp Clark Publishing Co. Limited*

© George Fielding Eliot, 1956

Printed in the United States of America

The publisher wishes to thank the McCall Corporation for permission to use portions of stories which have appeared in Bluebook Magazine.

*To June, my wife
with love*

Caleb Pettengill, U. S. N.

Chapter One

Sailor voices came through the cabin skylight, beating at the ears of Master's Mate Caleb Pettengill in a yammer of gathering mutiny. He choked back the disciplinary roar that rose in his throat.

He wasn't eavesdropping on purpose, and he wasn't going to have the hands think so. He was standing with his head inside the skylight because it was the only place in the prize brig *Ranee*'s little cabin where all six feet two of his lanky frame could stand upright and shave in comfort. . . .

He'd have to hurry his shaving and get on deck. Two hours' waiting for a lazy swab of a quarantine doctor to put in an appearance was outrageous. He was going to do something about that. He had to or there'd be real trouble. . . .

His prize crew of sixteen were mad with woman-hunger. During five weeks of the homeward passage they had talked of nothing but women. White women. Day by day and in the long hours of the night watches, the pressure had steadily mounted; with the first glimpse of home shores, at daybreak that morning off Cape Henlopen, it had suddenly become unendurable. They had waited two years—two weary, blazing, fever-haunted years, chasing slavers off West Africa. Now they were home. The waters they sailed were no longer the green swells of the Atlantic, but the brown flood of the Delaware River. Tonight was the night, and they were in no mood to be balked by any dilatory pill-roller, quarantine laws or no quarantine laws.

Pettengill scraped at the last patch of stubble on his wind-seamed jowls. Above, on the poop deck, he could hear the hands of the afterguard still grousing as they cleaned their brightwork:

"Where's that goddam doctor?"

"Two hours ve vait alretty here at anchor! Py Gott—"

"Forty mile yet to Phillydelphy; tide's on the ebb, too. Sure an' it'll be sundown 'afore we fetch the Navy Yard!"

"No liberty tonight, then, less'n we're there in time fer Mister Pettengill t' report 'isself to the bloomin' commandant 'cordin' to orders."

"Listen to me, mates! There ain't no Pettengill, nor no orders, nor the whole damn Navy what's gonna stop my liberty."

"Stow that gab, y' pack o' born idjits!" Pettengill recognized the wheezy tones of old white-haired Quartermaster Aycock, thirty years in the Navy—he'd been wearing the uniform seven years before Pettengill had been born. "Turn to on that brightwork, an' git yer minds off them Front Street sluts!"

Defiance toned down to an angry mutter, amid which the last voice repeated: "Tonight's my night, fer all that!"

The breaking point wasn't far off.

"Not that I blame 'em," muttered Pettengill, scowling into the square of mirror that he had tacked inside the skylight coaming.

Deep within his own hard-muscled body, the same urge gnawed at his self-control. But, he informed the reflection in the mirror, Caleb Pettengill would always put duty first—women could be attended to when duty was done.

A faint flicker of instinct, like a momentary glimpse of white breakers from a storm-swept masthead, hinted that uncharted reefs might lie to leeward of that firm resolve. Pettengill, scraping now at his lower lip—"mustaches and imperials," said the regulations, "are not to be worn by officers and men on any pretense whatever"—peered at his mirrored face, snorted, and kicked instinct into the scuppers of his contempt.

He had no means of knowing that his contempt was based on sheer inexperience. The she-image in Pettengill's consciousness was a weird compound of the half-remembered bodies of unenthusiastic water-front prostitutes and of delightful dream-fancies about a wholly different race of female creatures classed in Pettengill's mind as "good women" or "ladies."

Common sense assured him that these creatures had bodies, too. But this remained, to Pettengill, an unproved assumption. During his service in the Panama steamers, he had heard some of his brother officers, on occasion, boasting loudly in the mess room about the delectable results of practical research among the female cabin passengers. Often enough Pettengill had meant to explore the matter for himself, but he had never been able to overleap the barrier of his own diffidence.

In his thoughts he was still the gawky boy at whom the girls of Miss Pierce's Academy in Litchfield, Connecticut, walking two by two to church of a Sunday morning under the eagle eye of their preceptress, had giggled unkindly.

The nine years that had passed since Pettengill had seen Litchfield—nine years spent mostly at sea, seven in the merchant service and two in the Navy—had changed him from a gangling ship's boy of fourteen into a tough, self-reliant officer, but they had taught him exactly nothing about women because the inner Pettengill remained a fugitive from the memory of girlish giggles.

Certainly the changes wrought in his appearance had not made him less likely to be giggled at. The long mahogany face that the mirror showed him, as he wiped away the last remnants of lather, had been homely enough before it had been splattered with smallpox pits, souvenir of the Aspinwall pesthouse, or before he had acquired a broken nose to remind him of the night William Walker's guerrillas had tried to take over the Pacific Mail steamer *Champion* during Fourth Officer Pettengill's watch. Other men could disguise their facial shortcomings under a heavy growth of whiskers. Pettengill had tried that: all he could produce was a potato-colored mat of hair which looked exactly like a deck swab no matter what he did with it. At the moment he was following a compromise: straggly sideburns that covered the worst of the smallpox pits.

He contemplated the sideburns with distaste. He didn't want to admit that he was trying, in vain, to emulate the close-clipped sideburns affected by Lieutenant Pendleton Banks, lately his executive officer aboard the U.S.S. *Sheboygan*. A dark flush of embarrassment beneath the sideburns acknowledged this hidden weakness.

Suddenly he chuckled. What a ninny to be worrying about his looks at a time like this. What could he do about them, anyway? He grinned, and the rugged contours of his face came alive with drollery. A cheerful twinkle drove the clouds from his gray eyes. No one had ever told Pettengill how completely his face changed under the stimulus of laughter. No woman capable of appreciating the change had ever had a chance.

His laughter faded, dissolved by the acid mutterings that still filtered through the skylight. Time was running out on Pettengill. He had to do something, he had known that for an hour. But what *could* he do? This wasn't a problem he could lick with his fists.

Navy Regulations dealt with other matters than the wearing of mustaches. For example: "Captains of ships on entering ports, foreign or domestic, shall comply strictly with all rules thereof respecting quarantine." Pettengill, as prize master of the captured slave brig

Ranee, was for the time being captain of a ship. As he ducked his head out of the skylight, his eye took note of the oilskin-wrapped package that lay on his berth: it contained, among other papers relating to the prize, his written orders from his skipper, Commander Henry Nicholl of the *Sheboygan,* which reinforced the regulations by specifically directing Pettengill to anchor the prize off this quarantine station and obtain pratique from the port doctor before proceeding up the Delaware River to the Philadelphia Navy Yard. If he failed to obey, he knew he would be subject to trial by court-martial and to the penalties of the civil law. Especially since he came direct from a fever coast.

As usual, regulations and orders didn't cover the actual problem. The *Ranee* had been lying at anchor for two hours with the yellow quarantine flag fluttering from her fore-topgallant yardarm—meaning "I desire pratique"; at the truck it would have meant "Contagious disease on board." There was no disease aboard, contagious or otherwise. In his package of papers Pettengill had the certificate of the fleet surgeon stating that on parting company with the flagship off Monrovia, all hands, both crew and prisoners, had been in good health. He had a clean bill of health from the Portuguese doctor at Porto Praya, where he had called for fresh water and oranges. He had kept the brig as sweet and clean as he could, bilges pumped out and windsails carrying fresh air to the 'tween decks. He had forced quinine down reluctant throats daily, as the *Sheboygan's* surgeon had advised. He had worked the prisoners on deck in the fresh air morning and afternoon, scrubbing, painting, holystoning, until the little brig looked more like a man-o'-war than some real ones Pettengill could think of. He had overseen the men's meals himself, and had made every man, prisoners included, eat an orange a day as long as the supply lasted. They had worked the fever out of their bones: yellowish skins were taking on the ruddy hue of health and not one death was recorded in the log—a record indeed for a prize homeward bound from the African Squadron.

Pettengill was proud of the condition of his command. There could be no reason for delay in granting him pratique.

Except—no doctor.

Meanwhile, minute by minute, resentment and frustration were building up in his men. They had done their duty, all of them. Now, to their way of thinking, they were being denied a just reward, long anticipated, tacitly promised. Of such scarlet threads the fabric of mutiny was woven. At best, there might be wholesale ship-jumping;

at worst, violence that might force Pettengill to use his weapons against men he knew and loved. In any case, it was Pettengill who would be held to account. Until he reported his arrival officially to the commandant at Philadelphia, he was responsible for whatever happened aboard the ex-slaver *Ranee,* prize to the United States steamer *Sheboygan.* If things went wrong—if anyone was killed, or if the prisoners escaped or the ship ran ashore—Pettengill would be blamed. They'd more than likely break him. Acting masters' mates were easily broken; a stroke of the pen would do it. Then good-by to Pettengill's hopes of a permanent warrant as the first step toward a lieutenant's gold stripe.

But the roots of his anxiety went deeper than mere self-interest. Part of the creed he lived by was a paragraph in a tattered pamphlet entitled "Advice to Young Officers on First Joining a Ship":

"To command men worthily, it is not sufficient to hold a commission or a warrant. An officer should acquire such influence over his men that they will be eager to do his bidding and to follow him anywhere. The possession of that influence is the mark of a good officer, and it cannot be acquired without a knowledge of the names and the individual characters of the men under his charge. Above all, it cannot be acquired without the cultivation of qualities in yourself which the men will consider deserving of their confidence."

Pettengill wasn't sure whether he possessed such qualities or not. He did know, from experience, that he could command sailors, that they seemed to like him and trust him.

He had been one of the *Sheboygan's* three watch officers. The other two were Lieutenant Renfrew, ten years in the service, starchy and unimaginative, and Acting Master Stanfield, lately promoted from passed midshipman. Both were Naval Academy graduates. Pettengill had run away to sea as a ship's boy aboard the steam packet *Georgia* because his Connecticut lawyer-father had refused to obtain for him an appointment to the Annapolis school. It had been a matter of fierce, unrelenting pride with Pettengill that he, the salt-horse seaman out of the merchant marine, should keep as smart a watch as his Annapolis colleagues. His gun division had been as well drilled as theirs, too, though it had cost him many hours sweating over the Ordnance Instructions and Ward's *Elements of Naval Gunnery* by the light of a stinking whale-oil lamp. He had to catch up with things Renfrew and Stanfield already knew by heart. In one matter he was decidedly the superior of either: he had a gift for getting the best performance out of a steamer in any kind of weather, a knack which

Renfrew disdained and which Stanfield had never had a chance to acquire. In part this proficiency was due to Pettengill's habit of spending some of his off-duty time in the engine room, gammoning with the engineers, studying the machinery, and picking up valuable knowledge on such points as the length of time it took for a bell-signal from the watch officer to be translated into action by the paddle wheels—and why. This curiosity was born of Pettengill's passionate belief that steam was the wave of the future. He was a steamboat man through and through: all his years at sea had been spent in steamers except for one early Pacific voyage in a clipper ship, an experience which lent acidity to his scorn for the old-timers who sneered at engineers as "grease-monkeys," complained about the smoke and cinders that fouled up their beautiful white decks, and worked their ships under sail, in preference to using the engines, whenever they had a decent excuse. No wonder they didn't know how to get the best out of steam.

No man of the *Sheboygan*'s company would be likely to forget the thick rain-swept night off Cape Lopez when, just as Pettengill had been relieved by Lieutenant Renfrew, the lookout at the fore-topmast crosstrees had suddenly yelled: "Breakers on the port bow!"—nor how Renfrew had shouted "Full astern!" and Pettengill shoving his senior aside, had roared "Hard aport!" at the helmsman even as he grabbed the engine-room bellpull and rang up "Full ahead."

There wouldn't have been time, as Pettengill explained afterward to the skipper, for the engine's reversing gear to operate: the only hope was to increase speed and use the way the little gunboat already had on her, with the helm hard over, to claw clear of the danger—which she had done by inches. The skipper had read young Mr. Pettengill a stern lecture, for the benefit of the outraged Renfrew, on interference with a senior in charge of the deck. Thereafter, however, it was observed that Renfrew and Stanfield spent a succession of sweltering hours in the engine room learning what could and could not be expected of steam engines in the hour of trial.

The crew understood perfectly the meaning of their attentiveness, so that whether the *Sheboygan* was under sail or steam, whether the order was "All hands to reef topsails!" in a gale-swept mid-watch or "All hands to coal ship!" in a sun-scorched harbor, they moved just a little livelier if the order came in Pettengill's booming sea voice.

Later, when it came to sending in a boat's crew to cut this slave brig *Ranee* out of what her captain thought a safe, snug berth in the Maigudu River, it was Pettengill, the junior watch officer, who was tapped for the job. The tapping hadn't been done by the skipper, who was down with a touch of fever at the time, but by the *Sheboygan's* executive officer, Lieutenant Pendleton Banks, a cool, softspoken competent Virginian who was the one man aboard the *Sheboygan* of whom Pettengill stood in awe. Banks had been shipmates with Renfrew earlier, and an instructor at the Naval Academy when Stanfield was a midshipman there. Pettengill couldn't have been more astonished, or more gratified, at being appointed Commodore of the African Squadron than he was at Banks' quiet order: "I'd be glad if you'd have the first cutter armed and called away, Mister Pettengill. I want you to go in and get that fellow."

All these remembrances were in the back of Pettengill's mind now, not consciously reviewed but there just the same, and they brought their obligations with them. Most of the men in the prize crew had followed Pettengill over the brig's gunwale that blazing afternoon, yelling, cutlasses aswing. He would not have been standing there in the cabin, prize master, with the skipper's warm letter of commendation to forward to the Navy Department, if they hadn't followed him then.

They had been his men that day. They had been his men during the stinking process of working the slave-packed brig to Monrovia, cleaning her lower decks and bilges after landing the poor blacks, bringing her home across the Atlantic. They would be his men again tomorrow, when this festering woman-madness had been drained out of them.

But today they had slipped beyond his reach.

The uniform he wore had suddenly become the symbol of official injustice, magnified, as the hours slipped by, into deliberate persecution, denying their manhood. While that idea fermented in their heads, they would be capable of any folly: they were beyond the reach even of appeal based on their own interests.

Pettengill had already tried to make clear to them how much they had at stake in the orderly delivery of this prize to the United States Court at Philadelphia for adjudication: then, and only then, could they be transferred to the receiving ship to be paid off. Every man aboard was time-expired: all had at least two years' pay on the books. All were entitled to a share of the prize money when the *Ranee* should be condemned and sold; all were entitled, as well, to a share in the bonus of twenty-five dollars a head which the law provided for the 400-odd wretched blacks who had been found stowed in the fetid gloom of the brig's slave-decks, and who had been duly landed in Liberia as "liberated Africans." Finally, they were all entitled to the honorable discharge which Congress had provided for, six years ago in 1855, and which carried with it a bonus of three months' pay on re-enlistment.

For an ordinary seaman, the total emoluments would run hardly less than five hundred dollars. For the petty officers and seamen, it would be considerably more. Pettengill had worked it all out weeks ago and carefully explained the details. Every man aboard understood and had been delighted at the prospect. Until now. Now, he knew, they would throw it all away rather than put off for even one more day the slaking of the fires that burned within them.

He had to save them from themselves if he could.

Damn and blast that port doctor. And all females.

Pettengill slid his long arms into the sleeves of his blue frock coat, a sleazy affair made of "summer cloth," which hung on him like a gunny sack. Cheap tailoring, of course, but all a master's mate at forty dollars a month and twenty-five-cents-a-day ration money could afford. He slammed on his cap, with its gold foul anchor, and crossed the cabin, head down in instinctive deference to the low-hung deck beams. Opening the door, he stepped over the brass-bound coaming into the morning sunshine that bathed the spar deck.

It was good to feel the fresh easterly breeze whip the skirts of his frock coat about his bony knees. Even with the tide on the ebb, that breeze would carry the brig up to the Navy Yard in six hours—if it held. She was riding now to the tide on a single anchor. Hodgson, the burly bo's'n's mate who was Pettengill's second-in-command, had already passed the messenger around the capstan and was hectoring a group of fo'c's'le hands as they lighted it forward to the manger. It wasn't going to be Hodgson's fault if the brig didn't get underway quickly as soon as the miserable lazy scut of a port doctor showed up. But the customary heartiness was absent from Hodgson's voice; it cut like the lashes of a cat-o'-nine-tails; the hands moved sluggishly under its bite, finding new fuel to feed their smoldering sense of outrage.

Pettengill glared angrily at the reeds and sand dunes which, except for the small whitewashed quarantine station with its rickety wharf and a rowboat bobbing peacefully alongside, were all that was visible along the State of Delaware's shore line. Not a human being was in sight. Above Pettengill's head, on the poop deck, the ship's bell clanged twice. Nine o'clock.

Some of the hands looked over their shoulders at Pettengill as they labored with the heavy manila messenger. At the full length of the spar deck he could feel the angry impatience in their eyes. Seaman Jackson, pacing by the main hatch with cutlass and pistol at his belt, leaned over suddenly and bellowed:

"Pipe down below there! Ye'll come on deck when ye're told."

So the prisoners were getting restive, too. Those twenty-seven prisoners, formerly the crew of the *Ranee*, weren't the least of Pettengill's worries. An even sharper worry was their captain, Edward Harris, now locked up in the cook's cubby at the forward end of the deckhouse next to the galley, where he would be separated from his men and the sentry at the main hatch could keep an eye on him without leaving his post. Harris was as dangerous as a barracuda and as resourceful as a Malay pirate: twice he had come within an ace of making his escape, once at Monrovia and once at Porto Praya. Pettengill was going to feel much more comfortable after Harris and his gang of slave runners were safely in the custody of the United States Marshal at Philadelphia.

But he had to get them to Philadelphia first.

This idle waiting at anchor couldn't last much longer without an explosion.

"Hodgson!" he roared.

"Sir!"

"Get the whaleboat in the water! Lively, now."

"Aye aye, sir!"

Hodgson's pipe shrilled.

"Away-y-y whaleboat's crew! Hands to the falls!"

He drove them aft at a reluctant trot.

Pettengill said, loud and clear:

"I'll rouse out that blasted doctor if I have to start him with a rope's end!"

The hands moved a little faster, stirred by a spark of hope, but it was a spark Pettengill found hard to keep alive in his own mind as the whaleboat neared the quarantine wharf. The closer he came, the more utterly deserted the place looked. He hailed, hands cupped around his mouth. No answer, no sign of life. The boat's stem slashed through the reeds.

"In bow!" rasped Pettengill. "Way enough. Toss."

He leaped to the rotting planks of the wharf as the whaleboat rounded to alongside the dock and the bowman caught the stringpiece with his boathook. Half-a-dozen strides took Pettengill across the wharf to the roofed porch at the front of a building that was really little more than a shack.

There were one door and one window, and the door was secured with a large rusty padlock. A locked padlock.

Pettengill hammered on the door.

Silence: no stir within. He put his face to the window. He could see a round-backed chair, a table with a scattering of papers and books, a brass cuspidor, and a cupboard with a chart of Delaware Bay tacked to its front. Nothing else. He hammered again.

"Reckon Marse Doctor's done gone," said a quavering voice from the end of the porch. An elderly Negro in a hickory shirt and blue jeans stood there, blinking at Pettengill with watery eyes.

"Gone where?" Pettengill barked.

"Down to Virginny to see his folks, ah reckon," the Negro answered. "Foh good, maybe. He talk like he right put out wif Marse Linkum after dis shootin' dey had las' week at Fo't Sumter."

"What!" exclaimed Pettengill in quick excitement. The Negro cringed, drawing back a step. Pettengill controlled his excitement: if he yelled at this poor old fellow he'd scare all the sense out of him. Fort Sumter was in Charleston Harbor. Shooting there could mean big trouble. The last home newspapers Pettengill had seen, aboard the commodore's flagship off Monrovia, five weeks ago, had been dated early in February. They had been filled with disturbing news: Southern states seceding from the Union, troops drilling, a conspiracy in Washington to keep President-Elect Lincoln from taking office, state authorities in the South seizing Federal forts and arsenals and the Pensacola Navy Yard. Fort Sumter had been mentioned, something about an attempt to send reinforcements to the garrison in a merchant steamer, which had been driven away by South Carolina shore batteries. That had been some time in January.

Four thousand sea miles away, off the coast of Africa, news like this had seemed detached from reality. All during the fall of 1860 and the first month or so of 1861, there had been a flurry of excited talk in wardroom and steerage after every mail, but the news was always three weeks or a month old when it arrived, and somehow the knowledge that other things might have happened in the interval relieved the pressures of anxiety. No politics in the Navy. Do your duty, obey orders; the politicians will work out some sort of compromise as they've done before. Whether of Northern or Southern birth, most officers subscribed heartily to this comforting formula. Pettengill remembered the day when news came that South Carolina had actually seceded from the Union, and how young Stanfield had turned pale under his tan as he muttered: "Pray God Virginia doesn't follow suit." It was then that Pettengill had had his first inkling of the terrible problem that might face the Southern officer: loyalty to flag and oath or loyalty to home and family? He recalled the agony he had glimpsed in the dark eyes of Lieutenant Pendleton Banks, also Virginia-born, as Banks had given him two letters to be carried to the States: one addressed to Banks' younger brother, the other to a lady in Virginia.

Maybe things were worse now instead of better: so bad that even quarantine doctors were forced to make a choice. April 15, 1861, was the date at the top of the log-page this morning. Anything might have happened since February, and it was happening here in the United States, not an ocean away. The old Negro was edging off the porch.

"How long's the doctor been gone, Uncle?" Pettengill asked, as steadily as he could manage.

"Since day befoh yes'day, suh," the old man quavered. "Got aboahd a schooneh, he did, boun' down de coas' to No'folk. Took his trunk wif him."

"Isn't there any other doctor on duty at this quarantine station?"

"No, suh. Ain't nobody but Doc Simmons an' me. Guess Ah ain't got no mo' job heah, either."

"All right, Uncle," said Pettengill gently. "Here, buy yourself something to eat."

He tossed a half dollar; the Negro caught it with expert hand.

"Thank yo' kindly, Cap'n," he said, and vanished around the corner of the shack.

Pettengill rushed after him.

"Hold on!" he demanded. "Tell me about this shooting at Fort Sumter."

The old Negro looked back over his shoulder, his eyes rolling.

"Whar y'all been, Cap'n?" he asked. "Ain't yo' heered how de country's all busted to hell?"

Pettengill turned and walked slowly back to the boat. Four pairs of eyes stared at him: the men in the boat had heard every word.

Sand grated under his shoe soles. That sand was the soil of his country—this was the first time he'd set foot on it in well over two years.

All busted to hell, is it? Somebody's going to know they've been in one hell of a fight before that happens. . . .

"Hurray-y-y!"

Not until he heard that cheer, saw the flushed excited faces of the four oarsmen, did Pettengill realize he had spoken his fighting words aloud.

He dropped into the stern sheets of the whaleboat.

"Shove off!" he barked. "Up oars. Let fall. Give way together. Put your backs in it, bullies! I want to be off Philadelphia Navy Yard by six bells in the afternoon watch!"

They cheered again as they bent to the long ash oars.

Decision hardened in Pettengill's mind.

For the moment, almost by chance, he had lifted these men out of themselves, lifted them high on the wave crest of his own angry resolve that the Union should not be broken before the heads of some of its enemies were broken too.

He held them now in the grip of that idea, and the word they brought would be known to every man of the prize crew in seconds after these four set foot on the brig's deck.

This was something much bigger than the desire for women's bodies, or Master's Mate Pettengill's chances of getting a permanent appointment.

He jerked his right hand in a tossing motion. Seaman Reilly, pulling stroke, stared. Pettengill grinned as the whaleboat came round under the brig's stern.

"I've just thrown the blue book overboard," he chuckled.

Reilly laughed, and his laughter ran forward from thwart to thwart.

Pettengill was roaring orders even as he scrambled up the Jacob's ladder.

"Hands to the falls! Run that whaleboat up! Hodgson! All hands up anchor!"

Minutes were suddenly precious.

"Jackson! Rouse a dozen of the prisoners on deck. Man the capstan bars with 'em!"

Sending prisoners to the capstan would give him full use of the crew for making sail. But he didn't dare leave the rest of the prisoners, especially Harris, unguarded.

"Yoakum! Get pistol and cutlass from the arms rack and relieve Jackson as sentry on the main hatch."

Hodgson was piping madly: the crew of the whaleboat had hooked on the falls and were tumbling over the side; as they mingled with the others, excitement woke and flamed along the deck, then steadied to disciplined activity.

The prisoners came out of the main hatch, herded along by big Jackson, a length of lead line looped in his hand. They shivered as the breeze bit through their cotton rags: this northern sunshine held small comfort for men long accustomed to the blazing heat of the Slave Coast and the Middle Passage. Somebody laughed. The sight of suffering men, with no better prospect ahead of them than a cold stone cell, seemed to give the crew a certain satisfaction. On the voyage they had been sorry for the captured slavers. Now the prisoners were no longer just fellow seamen who had come upon misfortune. The word the boat crew had brought aboard had transformed these slave runners into enemies, meeting their proper fate.

Although two-thirds of them were foreign-born, the men of the prize crew had a simple, unswerving loyalty to the flag they served and the uniform they wore. Pettengill was proud of them.

"Man the bars!" he roared, standing spraddle-legged at the poop rail. "Heave 'round to a short stay! Clear away the jib! Let go the jib downhaul. Hoist away!"

The prisoners trudged around the capstan, the irons on their ankles clanking dismally. The jib would help bring the brig up over her anchor.

"Aloft sail-loosers!" bawled Pettengill. The hands were swarming up the rigging before the order was half uttered. "Lay out and loose! Tops'l sheets and halyards!"

"Let fall! Lay in! Sheet home!"

The wind filled the topsails, and the brig began moving upstream against the tide.

"Lay down from aloft! Haul taut! Reilly, get the spanker hauled out to port!"

"Up and down, sir!" yelled Hodgson from the cathead.

"Heave 'round!" The prisoners began again their weary tramp.

"Anchor's aweigh, sir! Clear anchor!"

Pettengill eyed the channel buoys.

"Port two points," he said to Aycock. The brig was slipping through the water smartly by this time.

Not quite half-past nine. He had had a busy half-hour.

He felt the inner freedom that comes from having made an irrevocable decision, however it may turn out. He was going to enter the port of Philadelphia without having obtained quarantine clearance—in defiance of the laws of two sovereign States, the Navy Regulations, and the written orders of his own captain.

When he reported to the commandant what he'd done, he would

find out what it was going to cost him, he supposed. But until then—
His eye caught a flash of yellow in the rigging.

"Hodgson!" he yelled. "Haul down that yellow jack!"

He nodded with grim satisfaction as he watched the scrap of saffron bunting come down from the yardarm.

His crime was complete.

Chapter Two

Behind the pall of smoke that overlay the Navy Yard, the chimney pots and roof tops of Philadelphia crowded against the afternoon sky.

The men of the prize crew, waiting for the final order, danced on the deck and cheered:

"Hooray fer ol' Philly!"

To them, those chimney pots were the outward and visible symbols of a city full of women—soft-bodied white women. But there was an edge of excitement in that cheer that wasn't born of the desires of the flesh. Pettengill recognized it and was glad. If he could just hold them a little longer, the danger might be over.

The brig was well within the buoyed limits of the Navy Yard anchorage. She had almost lost way—the spanker, the only sail still fully set, was pushing her stern around, bringing her to the wind.

"Stand clear of the cable!" Pettengill yelled. The brig hung motionless in the water, began to drift with the current. "Stream the buoy! LET GO!"

Buoy and anchor splashed into the brown flood of the Delaware: the cable rumbled out through the hawsehole.

"Man the spanker brails!"

The cable snubbed the brig gently as the anchor bit the ground.

"Brail up the spanker! Lay aloft and furl! Skin 'em up smooth, *Sheboygans,* the whole Navy Yard's watching."

They scampered up the rigging handily enough. Keep 'em busy, thought Pettengill—that's the trick. While it lasts.

He pulled his worn brass watch out of his vest pocket. Only a quarter of three.

That breeze had served him well. He might be able to dispose of the red tape and hand over prize and prisoners to the United States Marshal before the day ended. Then the commandant might let him give the crew immediate liberty, even if there wasn't time to transfer them to the receiving ship to be paid off. He thought most of the hands had a few dollars about them, enough at least for this first night ashore. . . .

And if he couldn't get the formalities straightened out in time? He'd have to ask the commandant to put a guard of Marines aboard the brig for the night, to make sure there would be no ship-jumping or other stupid nonsense when the hands heard the bad news. They'd regard that as a dirty trick, even a betrayal. But they would thank him for it afterward, when the paymaster on the guardo was counting out the gold pieces. . . .

He had thought this all out as he conned the brig upriver following a well-marked channel.

As for flouting the quarantine laws, that was something that had to be done and the consequences, whatever they might be, accepted. Maybe the fact that Doctor Simmons, apparently a Southern sympathizer, had deserted his post might be taken as a satisfactory excuse. . . .

"Veer to sixty fathoms, Hodgson," he ordered. "When all's shipshape aloft, turn to, clear up the decks."

"Aye aye, sir!" Hodgson's bad temper had gone over the side with the rest.

"The Yard looks kinda' busy, sir," said old Aycock, lowering the telescope from his eye. Something in his tone caught Pettengill's attention. "Let's have a look," he said, reaching for the telescope.

The Navy Yard was certainly humming.

Smoke poured from the brick chimneys of the blacksmith shop and the foundry. Loaded drays moved along every roadway, and gangs of men worked around the stacks of cannon and the piles of round shot and empty shells. The great wooden ship-houses were empty and deserted; no ships were then under construction at Philadelphia. Three steamers lay alongside the docks, and all were ant hills of human activity. Men were all over them, setting up rigging, mounting guns, swaying stores aboard, refitting, hammering.

Pettengill knew one of the steamers: she was the U.S.S. *Water Witch,* an old paddle-wheel gunboat, smaller than *Sheboygan* and the only regular Navy ship of the three. One of them, also a sidewheeler, looked like a coastal steamer: she was wearing a commission pennant now, and had 32-pounders mounted fore and aft. The third was a mere tug: a bronze howitzer gleamed on her foredeck. Pettengill's telescope came back to the *Water Witch.*

There was something more than queer about her. The red powder flag fluttered from the gunboat's foretruck: the sun glinted on copper as a sling-load of stores swung inboard over her hatch. That was a sling-load of powder tanks. She was taking powder aboard at a Navy Yard dock! There was no more rigid safety regulation in the Ordnance Instructions than the one which required that powder should never be loaded alongside a dock, but only in the stream, from a lighter, "unless upon some great emergency, the nature of which shall be reported to the Navy Department in writing." What great emergency could have moved the Commandant of the Philadelphia Navy Yard to risk both the consequences of possible carelessness and the displeasure of the Navy Department?

Pettengill shoved the telescope at Aycock. The old quartermaster's rheumy eyes blinked cheerfully.

"Trouble for sure, sir," he said. "Big trouble. I'd kinda' like to ship out with you, sir, wherever they send ya."

Pettengill grinned.

"I could do worse, Aycock," he said with conviction. "I'll see about that when I find out what's in the wind. Right now I've wasted five minutes gawking. Hodgson! I'll have the whaleboat alongside!"

He ran down the poop ladder and ducked into his cabin, warmed by Aycock's loyalty and simple conviction that if there was "big trouble," then as a matter of course he would be "shipping out" somewhere. He hoped Aycock was right.

He hoped, too, that the commandant might be so preoccupied with what was going on that he wouldn't bother asking troublesome questions like "Where's your certificate of pratique, Mr. Pettengill?" He took his sword from its becket above his berth and began attaching it to the slings of his sword belt. He had better take Captain Harris ashore with him now and hand him over to the commandant to be securely confined until the marshal came for him. That might mean some delay, questions, talk. But Harris was nimble-witted; he could think rings around Hodgson or Aycock, and he had undoubtedly hatched a dozen plans for making his escape. It occurred to Pettengill suddenly that a commandant who was talking about Harris might be a commandant who wouldn't be talking about other things, such as quarantine regulations. He opened his sea chest, took out his heavy Navy cap-and-ball revolver, and slipped the end of his belt through the loop of the holster; then he buckled the belt around his waist, settling it as smoothly as he could over his rumpled frock coat.

Six bells were striking under Aycock's practiced touch as Pettengill emerged again on the spar deck, his package of papers under his arm. Jackson was just relieving Landsman Briggs as sentry at the main hatch.

"Stay at your post, Briggs," Pettengill ordered, striding forward. "Jackson, open the door of the cubby and stand by."

"Aye aye, sir."

The original cubby door had been replaced by one made out of a wooden grating borrowed from the flagship; keys rattled as the big seaman unfastened the padlock, lifted the bar from its sockets, and opened the door.

"If you please, Captain Harris," said Pettengill, noting with satisfaction from the corner of his eye how Jackson stood back a couple of paces and laid hand on pistol butt.

Out into the sunlight stepped a slender, dapper figure, a man of medium height, with swarthy skin, black hair and mustache. He was dressed in a fashionably cut gray suit, with a flowered waistcoat and a snow-white shirt, a gay cravat, and patent-leather shoes. A cream-colored beaver hat was in his hand. As he emerged, he set it carefully on his head at just the slightest of angles. He could well have graced a fashionable club or the lobby of Philadelphia's best hotel—except for the glint of iron links at his ankles. Dark eyes, flat and expressionless as a reptile's, fixed their unwinking stare on Pettengill's face.

"Good afternoon, Mister Pettengill," said Harris in a voice without any intonation whatever. "I presume this is Philadelphia?"

"That's right. I'm taking you ashore now."

"Indeed," said Harris. "I am your debtor, sir, for allowing me soap and razor, proper clothes and fresh linen for my homecoming, though I must admit that shaving with a pistol muzzle a yard from one's back is rather trying on the nerves. But may I ask whether these irons were affixed to my ankles by your orders?"

"Certainly, Captain Harris," said Pettengill. "I ordered all prisoners to be ironed as soon as we came on soundings early this morning. I saw no reason to make an exception in your case."

"It is an order you may live to regret, Mister Pettengill," said Harris. The threat lost nothing of its venom from its toneless delivery.

"Boat's alongside, sir," reported Hodgson.

"Very good," said Pettengill. "Hodgson, take charge of the brig and the other prisoners until I return. I'm going ashore to report to the commandant. I'll be back within the hour. I don't want to find this brig looking like a dago coal barge if I bring any official visitors aboard with me."

"Aye aye, sir," said Hodgson cheerfully.

Pettengill was deliberately suggesting that the formalities of handing over the prize would be settled away that afternoon, with liberty for all hands as the natural consequence. He knew he might not be able to make this good, but it was important for the hands to go on thinking so for the present.

"Get your prisoner into the boat, Jackson," he ordered. "Put him in the stern sheets and stay right with him."

"In these?" Harris gestured toward his irons.

"In those," retorted Pettengill. "You can go down the ladder under your own power or I can secure a whip to the main yardarm and lower you into the boat. Make up your mind."

Harris shuffled across the deck to the gangway without another word. His descent into the stern sheets of the whaleboat was only a matter of a few feet, but it wasn't dignified. The boat pulled across the short stretch of water toward the nearest landing-steps, and with every stroke of the oars, the voice of the Navy Yard grew louder: the rumble of drays, the clatter of hoofs on cobblestones, the shouts of men, the clangor of hammers, and the creak of straining gear. A Marine sentry appeared at the top of the steps, saw the boat, and yelled: "Corporal of the guard, post number seven!" Three more Marines arrived on the double as Pettengill came up the steps. The corporal shouldered his musket and slapped the butt in salute at the sight of Pettengill's uniform, but he didn't move aside.

"Your pass, please, sir?" he demanded.

"Where'd I get a pass?" snapped Pettengill. "I'm just in from the African Squadron. My orders are to report to the commandant immediately on arrival. I'll thank you to show me the way to his office."

The corporal was staring at Harris, who had been helped out of the boat by Jackson, none too gently, and was slowly making his way upward, step by step.

"Who's this, sir?" he asked.

"A prisoner," Pettengill told him. "That brig's a captured slaver, and this man was her captain. Take me to the commandant, I haven't all afternoon to stand here arguing."

"Aye aye, sir," said the corporal doubtfully. "Here you, Schultz and Taylor, come along and help guard the prisoner."

The corporal wasn't taking any chances with strangers.

The little parade attracted attention on its way across the Yard. The two Marine privates led the way, followed by Harris, shuffling along in his leg irons with Jackson beside him. Pettengill brought up the rear with the corporal. Workmen stopped to stare and offer comment:

"Must 'a' kilt somebody!"

"They goin' t' hang 'im, y' reckon?"

"Jee-rushaphat Jones! Y'ever see a dude like that in irons 'afore?"

"Dang'rous man, must be. Takes three Marines 'n' a sailor t' guard him—say nothin' of the officer wit' th' sword 'n' pistol."

"Maybe he's a Rebel spy!"

"Spy! Spy! Hey, Mac, come lookit th' Rebel spy they caught!"

Pettengill was glad when the outer door of the commandant's office closed behind him. The commandant's anteroom was jammed with people; every clerk had half-a-dozen clamoring visitors around his high desk.

"I tell you this contract has to be signed today. I've got fifty men standing by. . . ."

"The commandant wants to see me immediately. I'm a friend of Secretary Cameron. . . ."

"Now see here, young man! Don't tell me to sit down and wait. Don't you know there's a war going on?"

Nobody paid the smallest attention to Pettengill and his escort.

"Guess you won't see the commandant today, sir," muttered the corporal.

Harris looked at Pettengill with malicious amusement.

"Stand him against the bulkhead there, Jackson, and don't take your eyes off him," Pettengill ordered. He pushed through the crowd toward a table in the far corner; behind it was a small door which he guessed must lead into the commandant's private office. The clerk who sat at this table was an elderly man wearing a green eyeshade and a certain air of authority. Pettengill shouldered aside a red-faced fellow in a loudly checked suit.

"I've just brought a slaver in from Africa," he said. "Please tell the commandant I'd like to report according to orders. Master's Mate Pettengill. Prize master."

The clerk stared, blinking.

"A slaver!" he exclaimed.

The red-faced man echoed:

"A slaver, d'you say? You mean you've captured a slave ship? Hooray fer you, young feller!"

The clerk was on his feet.

"This way, please," he said to Pettengill. "Captain Du Pont has someone with him, but I'm sure he'd want to see you at once."

Pettengill edged around the table and followed the clerk through the door. There was carpet under his feet as he stepped over the threshold, the smell of good cigar smoke came to his nostrils.

A deep voice was saying:

"I can't perform miracles, Ronckendorff. You're off for Pensacola in the morning with the *Water Witch*. I don't know what the Department imagines I can do about Norfolk. The *Keystone State* won't be ready for three days, say what you will. The tug might help a little, but I haven't a single reliable officer to put in command of her unless I'm to leave the *Keystone State* shorthanded."

The deep voice was booming forth from a thicket of magnificent whiskers. The officer to whom voice and whiskers belonged stood beside a carved walnut desk in the center of the room, a leonine figure of a man, broad-shouldered and nearly as tall as Pettengill himself. It scarcely needed the three gold stripes of a captain on his sleeves to inform Pettengill that this was the commandant. Samuel Francis Du Pont bore the stamp of one born to command.

He turned now as the clerk spoke quickly in an undertone; then he looked over at Pettengill, waiting by the door.

"From the African Squadron?" he exclaimed, his eyes lighting. "What ship, sir? What ship?"

Pettengill, cap in hand, took a step forward.

"Brig *Ranee*, sir. Prize to the *Sheboygan*," he reported. "Master's Mate Pettengill, prize master. My orders, sir."

"Only a prize, eh?" The commandant eyed the thick package of papers that Pettengill laid on his desk. "I wish you might have brought me the *Sheboygan* herself. Another steam gunboat would be worth her tonnage in gold just now. But it's not your fault." He held out his hand. "Welcome home, Mr. Pettengill. I'm Captain Du Pont, and this is Lieutenant Commanding Ronckendorff of the *Water Witch*."

Pettengill shook hands with Du Pont and a thick-bodied, weather-beaten lieutenant who acknowledged the introduction by a grunt.

"Sit down, gentlemen," Du Pont went on. "Mr. Pettengill, you'll find some reasonably decent cigars in that box, I think. You'll pardon me keeping you waiting, I hope, Ronckendorff. I'll just run through Mr. Pettengill's papers."

Pettengill sat down, trying hard to recall all he had heard about Captain Du Pont. He had heard a great deal; probably no officer was the subject of more conversation in the Navy of 1861. Du Pont had been the most active member of a board of officers which had been appointed to rid the Navy List of the infirm and incapable old gentlemen who could no longer perform their duties but who blocked the promotion of those who could. He had done a good job. He hadn't endeared himself to the old gentlemen and their many friends, but on the other hand, almost every officer and man who had ever actually served under Du Pont was completely devoted to him. Lieutenant Pendleton Banks was one of these, and for Pettengill's money a captain who could inspire whole-hearted devotion in Pendleton Banks was somebody to take rank with Decatur or John Paul Jones.

Certainly few officers holding the highest rank in the Navy would have bothered to welcome a lowly master's mate home from Africa, or to ask him to sit down in their presence, much less offer him a cigar. Pettengill found himself hoping he might have a chance to serve under Captain Du Pont. He puffed his cigar and anxiously watched Du Pont thumb through the papers.

Du Pont became suddenly absorbed in reading one of the papers, then looked again at Pettengill:

"How long have you been in the Navy, Mr. Pettengill?"

"Two years, sir."

"As master's mate?"

"Yes, sir. They gave me an acting appointment to fill a vacancy for a watch officer in the *Sheboygan* when she was on the point of sailing for her African cruise."

"You've had other sea service, of course?"

"Seven years in merchant ships, sir, mostly in steamers. Three years before the mast. Four with a mate's ticket: third and fourth officer in the Panama packets."

"Why the devil should you have left a snug berth as a merchant officer to ship as master's mate in the Navy at half the pay?"

Pettengill blushed.

"I've always wanted to be a naval officer, sir," he muttered.

"But with no chance of promotion, all commissions reserved for Naval Academy graduates—ah, young men must have their fancies, I suppose. You seem to have done well aboard *Sheboygan:* my old shipmate Henry Nicholl writes of you most warmly. Did they teach you anything about gunnery?"

"Boned it up myself, sir. I had the nine-inch pivot gun in the *Sheboygan;* but I know the drill for broadside guns too, and for boat howitzers."

"Good. Where were you born?"

"Litchfield, Connecticut, sir."

"Connecticut, eh? Are you acquainted with Mr. Gideon Welles?"

"I've heard my father speak of him, sir. I've never met him."

"H'm. He's Secretary of the Navy now. Hope he'll be a better one than the last; God help us if he isn't." Du Pont sounded a trifle relieved: the commandant wasn't anxious for officers with political connections.

Du Pont went back to the papers.

"Do you consider yourself qualified for command, Mr. Pettengill?" he demanded suddenly.

Caution stopped an unqualified "Yes sir!" on the tip of Pettengill's tongue: caution and a memory of something Pendleton Banks had once said about Du Pont: "Never let him find you biting off more than you can chew. He hates overconfidence."

"I think I'm qualified to command small steamers, sir, gunboat types," he said quietly. "I'd be the better for some experience as executive officer first, of course."

Du Pont's eyebrows really went up at that.

"God bless my soul!" Du Pont murmured, and looked at Ronckendorff.

"Sounds like an answer to prayer, sir," the lieutenant said. "I rather like the cut of Mr. Pettengill's jib; I'd be glad to have him in *Water Witch—*"

"None of that, Ronckendorff! You'll make do with the officers you have. I'll be in hot water enough with Woodhull when he finds I can't give him even one junior watch officer for *Keystone State*."

"Very well, sir. But there'd be some good hands in the prize crew, I suppose?" Ronckendorff said, persisting.

Du Pont looked at Pettengill.

"Sixteen men, sir," Pettengill said. "One bo's'n's mate, one quartermaster, five seamen, three ordinary seamen, and six landsmen. All time-expired."

"And r'aring to hit the beach, I imagine," chuckled Du Pont, with another glance at Ronckendorff.

"They'll be wild to get at the women if they're anything like the lads I brought home from Paraguay last year," the lieutenant said.

"Sailors and women!" grumbled Du Pont. "The sea's a jealous mistress, Mr. Pettengill. She lets the harpies of the shore have her sons for a day or two, but she always wants to reclaim them. Will any of your men re-enlist after they've had their fling?"

"Most of 'em, I think, sir. Especially if there's a prospect of active service."

"There's that in plenty!" Du Pont slammed his hand down on the scattered papers. "In any case, Mr. Pettengill, it's yourself I'm thinking about at the moment. I need your services. I'll write a letter at once, relieving you temporarily of responsibility for the prize proceedings and assuming that responsibility myself. It's highly irregular and probably illegal, but in wartime—"

"Wartime, sir!" exclaimed Pettengill, not realizing that he had committed the enormity of interrupting his superior officer.

"I forgot. You won't have had the latest news," said Du Pont. "Secession has turned into open rebellion. Three days ago the Rebel batteries began bombarding Fort Sumter in Charleston harbor. Yesterday the news came that the garrison had been forced to surrender. This morning President Lincoln issued a call for seventy-five thousand volunteers to suppress this rebellious combination and enforce the authority of the Federal Government. That means war, Mr. Pettengill. War in its most terrible form—civil war. A long war and a bloody one."

"But the Navy, sir!" cried Pettengill eagerly. "We can blockade the southern harbors, cut off their cotton trade. They can't support a rebellion without money."

"Spoken like a true sailor," said Du Pont. "It's what will be done in the end, of course. But right now the Navy's scattered from China to Africa. The only effective steam warship in commission between here and Florida at this moment is the *Pawnee*, and she's anchored in the Potomac with her guns trained on the Long Bridge to defend Washington, in case Virginia goes out of the Union. Meanwhile we're doing what we can to find men for ships in ordinary, like the *Water Witch*, and to charter or buy merchant steamers that can be converted for fighting purposes. *Water Witch* has to go to Pensacola, where there's an Army garrison in danger: now I'm ordered to send help to the Navy Yard at Norfolk, for which I'm preparing two steamers, the *Keystone State,* which can't be ready before Thursday, and the armed tug *Brother Jonathan*. I want you to take command of the *Brother Jonathan,* Mr. Pettengill, and proceed to Norfolk with her as soon as possible, in the morning, I hope. The mission is one of vital importance, as you'll see when you read your orders. I'll say frankly I'd send a more experienced officer if I had one to spare. As it is, I'm gambling on you."

Command, a wartime command—even if it was only command of a tug—and an important mission, too. Pettengill glowed.

"Aye aye, sir!" he cried. Then he remembered something. "But, sir—"

Du Pont's brows drew together:

"Did I hear you say *but*, Mr. Pettengill?"

"My men, sir, out on the brig. And the prisoners. . . ."

"Quite right, Mr. Pettengill," said Du Pont. "My apologies. An officer who isn't conscious of his responsibility to his men won't be conscious of his responsibility to his government. I'll have your brig warped alongside the dock and put a Marine guard on board her. Then you can transfer your crew to the receiving ship: I'll see they're paid off at once if the paymaster has to sit up till midnight to do it. And you might use what influence you have with 'em on the subject of re-enlistment later on. But what's this you say about prisoners?"

He was shuffling through the papers again.

"The prisoners, sir," Pettengill explained quickly, "are the former crew of the *Ranee*. Twenty-seven of 'em are under hatches aboard the brig. I brought the skipper ashore with me. He's in your outer office now, with an escort of course. Name's Harris, Edward Harris."

"Edward Harris!" exclaimed Ronckendorff. "Excuse me, Captain, might I ask Mr. Pettengill if that isn't the rascal they call the crown prince of the slave trade?"

"So I've heard, sir," said Pettengill. "There's a man named Francis Bowen who's known as king of the slavers, because of the fortune he's accumulated, and this fellow Harris is next in line."

"Why, dammit, the man's notorious!" said Du Pont. "Wait till the newspapers get wind of this! You'll find yourself something of a hero, Mr. Pettengill, the temper of this city being what it is just now. Bring Harris in, I'd like to have a look at him."

Pettengill went happily toward the door. Du Pont had been diverted from those papers again.

Jackson was on the alert: a flick of the finger was enough to tell him that his prisoner was wanted. Harris shuffled past, iron links jingling: Jackson followed and took station just inside the door.

Halfway across the room Harris stopped and made the commandant a courtly bow, sweeping the carpet with his high-crowned beaver.

"Sir," he said, "I am immensely relieved to find myself at last in the presence of a gentleman. I am also happy to have the opportunity of bringing to your attention—I trust before it is too late—the reckless manner in which this person"—he gestured toward Pettengill—"has endangered your command and the whole city of Philadelphia by bringing the brig *Ranee* into port without quarantine examination."

"What!" said Ronckendorff sharply. "From Africa?"

Du Pont looked at Pettengill and waited.

Pettengill stood there, horrified. Harris was a master mariner, he'd been in and out of seaports all his life. He knew very well that no quarantine doctor had come aboard, and all he had to do was to listen to the chatter of the crew, ear at grated door, to learn the details. Now he had his revenge for the irons, and for the deeper hurt Pettengill had done to his pride in capturing his precious *Ranee*.

"Sir," Pettengill said, "when I arrived off the quarantine station I found the place deserted except for an old Negro, who told me that Doctor Simmons, the quarantine officer, had left his post and gone to Virginia, taking his belongings with him. There seemed nothing to be gained by waiting there at anchor, and my men were getting restive. I therefore proceeded, since I had no disease aboard and a clean bill of health from my last port of call."

"No disease aboard!" cried Harris. "How about that yellow gal you threw overboard three nights ago, Mister Pettengill, after she developed symptoms of plague? I heard her screaming with my own ears."

"That's a goddam lie!"

The same words were on Pettengill's lips, but Jackson had uttered them. The big seaman's face was scarlet with outraged indignation.

"Belay that, Jackson!" Pettengill shouted.

"Plague!" Ronckendorff exclaimed. "My God! Plague!"

"It's not true, sir," said Pettengill. "I had no girl aboard, and there were no symptoms of plague or any other contagious—"

"I've heard enough," interrupted Du Pont, rising to his feet. "Quite enough. Call the guard, Ronckendorff."

There was no friendly sparkle in his eyes now; they were ice-hard as they met Pettengill's.

"But, sir—"

"I said that I'd heard enough, Mr. Pettengill."

At the door, Ronckendorff was calling to the Marines who still lingered outside:

"This way, corporal. On the double."

[36]

The corporal of Marines, musket at trail, came through the doorway and halted beside Jackson.

A malicious smile lifted the corners of Harris' mouth.

"Corporal," ordered Du Pont, "take this person to the Marine Barracks and tell the officer of the day, with my compliments, that he's to be locked in a cell and a close watch kept on him until my further orders."

He pointed at Edward Harris.

"D'you take me for a fool, Harris?" he roared. "These papers show the prize brig *Ranee* took her departure from Monrovia on March thirteen, thirty-four days ago. That was her last port of call. I take note she left there with a clean bill of health. Yet you tell me that a female aboard that brig developed symptoms of plague only three days ago; that is, twenty-two days after leaving the last place where she or anyone else on board could have become infected. D'you suppose I've been at sea for nearly half a century without learning that a person infected with plague invariably develops the unmistakable symptoms within ten days at the latest, and usually much sooner? So, as Jackson says, your story is a goddam lie—unless you're suggesting that this yellow girl of yours caught the disease from a stray albatross."

Jackson snickered. A broad grin spread across Ronckendorff's face. Pettengill, spinning in a whirlpool of mixed emotions, looked from one to the other and back at Du Pont.

"Get him out of here, corporal," Du Pont ordered.

"There will be another time, Mr. Pettengill," murmured Harris, and shuffled toward the door. Jackson held it open and followed Harris out.

"I make no doubt he'll hang," Du Pont growled. "This administration can't afford to be tender with slave captains just now. They'll try him as a pirate. Well, Captain Ronckendorff, I suppose—"

He paused.

"I'll be getting along to look after *Water Witch*, sir," said Ronckendorff. "Good luck, Mr. Pettengill."

The door slammed behind him. Du Pont's eyes came back to Pettengill.

"Mr. Pettengill," he said, "I don't want you to take me for a fool, either. I was already aware that the port doctor had deserted his post and gone South. Therefore your arrival here told me you must have taken the law in your own hands: the first thing I looked for was your clean bill of health from your last port of call. I intend

[37]

to have the present condition of your crew and prisoners examined by the surgeon before they come ashore. Subject to the result of that examination, about which I have small doubt, I consider you justified in your action: but you should have reported it to me at once instead of hoping that I'd overlook it. Don't try that again, Mr. Pettengill."

"No, sir," said Pettengill.

"Very well. You may return to the brig now and make ready to take her alongside. I'll order a yard tug to go out to you. The surgeon will report aboard as soon as she's made fast to the dock. When he's satisfied, I'll send you the Marines to take charge, and you may march your men, with their bags and hammocks, to the receiving ship and turn them over to the executive officer to be paid off. Their pay accounts are here, I see: I'll have them in the paymaster's hands before the men arrive. Including your own. When you've drawn what money you need for the present, you'll doubtless want to have a look at your new command: you'll find her lying just astern of the *Water Witch*."

"Thank you, sir," Pettengill managed to say.

"I'll be glad to hear what you think of her," Du Pont said. "I'm having some friends at my quarters after dinner this evening. Perhaps you'll join us for a glass of wine, Mr. Pettengill, and a bite of supper later on? Any time after seven. Supper at nine."

Supper at the commandant's quarters!

"Th-thank you, sir," Pettengill said again.

Du Pont nodded.

"Very well, Mr. Pettengill."

It was dismissal. Pettengill tucked cap under arm, hitched up his sword, and marched toward the door.

"Oh, Mr. Pettengill."

"Sir?"

Pettengill turned around.

"I've been delegated certain powers by the Secretary of the Navy during this trying period," said Du Pont. "One of those powers relates to the appointment of officers. I do not consider your present rank adequate for the mission being entrusted to you. Chiefly for that reason, you may consider yourself an acting master as of today's date. You'll receive a warrant from the Navy Department in due course."

Pettengill heard himself saying "Thank you, sir" for the third time.

This time he got through the door and closed it behind him.

Jackson was waiting in the outer office, his ruddy face creased with anxiety.

"I hope all's well with you, sir," he said.

"Jackson," said Pettengill, grinning, "do you suppose you could get that fire in your innards shaken down enough tonight so's you could ship out with me in the morning—on active service?

"Because if you can, Jackson," Pettengill went on, "you'll be shipping as quarter gunner."

"Thank you, sir," Jackson said.

Chapter Three

"Yoakum, Benjamin, ordinary seaman," droned the paymaster's clerk.

"Here, sir." Yoakum's blond hair glistened in the lamplight as, hat in hand, he stepped up to the pay-table on the spar deck of the receiving ship *Princeton*. His round boyish face was a mirror of happy anticipation.

"Two hundred sixty-seven dollars, twenty-nine cents," the fat paymaster read off in his monotonous voice. That was two years' pay at fourteen dollars a month, less advances and various deductions. The prize money would come later.

"Check," said the clerk, and looked up at Pettengill.

Pettengill nodded. His duty was simply to identify each man and to witness the "marks" of those who couldn't sign their names. Yoakum could write: he was scrawling his signature already. He'd had some schooling: aboard *Sheboygan*, he'd been a loblolly boy in the sick bay for a while, and Pettengill had found him both helpful and ingenious in carrying out the surgeon's advice about sanitary measures during the *Ranee*'s homeward voyage.

Gold coins clinked under the paymaster's practiced fingers. "Two hundred—two hundred twenty—two hundred forty—two hundred sixty"—he pushed the stack of double eagles across the table to Yoakum, added a five-dollar goldpiece, two small gold dollars, a silver quarter, a three-cent piece, and a bright copper cent. Yoakum swept his wealth into a small canvas bag and dropped it inside his blouse.

"Good luck to you, Yoakum," said Pettengill, holding out his hand. "I've made a note on your discharge paper recommending you for sick-bay duty if you ship over. The Navy'll be needing men with sick-bay experience; I wouldn't be surprised to see you a surgeon's steward one of these days."

[40]

"I'll think on't, sir, I'll think on't," bubbled Yoakum, and headed for the gangway on the trot.

The paymaster's chair creaked as he hoisted his bulk out of it. "Listen to the lad," he jeered. "He'll think on't, he will. Ha! All he's thinking on is laying a course for the nearest bawdyhouse." He yawned and began buttoning his vest over several rolls of flesh. "Thank God that's the last of your African rascals, Pettengill," he went on. "I must say you wasted your pains trying to get 'em to re-enlist. If you'd paid off as many as I have, you'd know that before the week's out most of 'em will be right back aboard this guardo anyway, stony broke and bleary-eyed from rotgut. Women are the sailor's curse, Pettengill. Never forget it."

"Don't know but you're right about that," muttered Pettengill. He was depressed by the failure of his efforts: he'd shaken each man by the hand, wished him well, and spoken of the advantages of shipping over. He'd had only two takers; except for Jackson and Aycock, he would be steaming down the Delaware tomorrow with a green crew at his back and war on the horizon.

"Of course I'm right," the paymaster said. "Look at poor Oliphant—the man whose gear you bought. Why'd he resign and shove off in such a tearing hurry, asking me to dispose of his uniforms for what they'd fetch? Between you and me and the dolphin-striker, I'd say he's gone South. Damn shame. He's a New Yorker-born, same as me. But he married one o' these li'l honey-chile Ah-do-declare gals from Savannah, and she's addled his wits. You steer clear of half-pint females, my lad: they're poison for big horse-built fellers like you and Oliphant. Pure poison."

"I can take 'em any size when I need one," Pettengill said, with a hoarse chuckle which he hoped was suggestive of a vast experience. Inwardly he was profoundly shocked. A Northern officer "going South"? Turning his back on his flag and his duty because of a woman. Out of the corner of his eye he caught a glint of gold—the gold border of a shoulder strap which, unbelievably, was perched on his own shoulder. Those were Oliphant's shoulder straps he was wearing, Oliphant's broadcloth frock coat, Oliphant's gold-banded cap with its wreathed anchor in front.

"Stick to the fat ones, they're at least grateful," the paymaster was saying. "I'm for a snort before turning in. I've a bottle of Demerara that has some real authority. You'll join me, I hope? Rum's a better friend for a sailor than women, any day of the week."

"Much obliged, sir, but I'm overdue to pay my duty call on the commandant. I'll hope for another opportunity."

"My pleasure," the paymaster said. "You'll find a neat assortment of females at Du Pont's, I'll gamble. Pick yourself a nice plump squab for your first night home from Africa. But when you're finished with her, leave her where she lies and forget her. 'Night, Mr. Pettengill, and good hunting."

He waddled off in the direction of the wardroom companion. The clerk had long since cleared up the litter on the pay-table and departed. Pettengill stood there alone, staring after the paymaster.

Did that tub o' lard take him for a born fool, suggesting that Captain Du Pont would have loose women as guests in his house? . . .

Pettengill strode briskly toward the gangway, his steps echoing under the high peaked roof of the housed-in deck.

He didn't want to call on the commandant. He resented every minute that kept him from the *Brother Jonathan*. He had barely had a chance to look her over and he wanted to spend the night making a thorough inspection: engine room, boiler, steering gear, pumps, bilges, bulkheads, everything. Even a little screw tug needed careful attention when she was being fitted out for war service: and there might not be much time in the morning, with Du Pont in such a tearing hurry to get him off for Norfolk. Maybe he could just have a glass of wine and slip away without bothering with supper. His stomach immediately reminded him that he hadn't eaten since noon, and then only a biscuit and a pannikin of coffee. Maybe he could snatch a quick bite and leave.

A tingle of excitement stirred in his mind. Would there really be women there? He loathed the idea, but an inner tingling of excitement persisted as his long legs carried him across the dark Navy Yard toward the gleam of lanterns at the main gate. His fingertips strayed over the sleek broadcloth of ex-Lieutenant Oliphant's frock coat. He had paid a hundred dollars in good hard gold for it, with a blue service jacket and two suits of whites thrown in. Not a bad bargain, even counting the ten dollars he had given the ship's tailor of the *Princeton* to rush the needed alterations. It had needed some fitting; the single gold stripe of a lieutenant had to be removed from the cuffs and replaced by the three large-size Navy buttons which were proper for a master, and the silver foul anchor in the center of the shoulder straps had to be carefully picked out, leaving an empty blue field within the gold borders. Considering his size he had been lucky to find uniforms ready to wear. A regular naval outfitter would have taken two weeks to make clothes like these, and charged him a fancy price. Now, he still had nearly four hundred dollars in back pay on the books, with his prize money still to come. And from now on he would be drawing a hundred a month in sea-pay instead of a master's mate's pittance of forty dollars.

He jingled the coins that remained in his pocket after paying for his new gear. He had twenty or twenty-five dollars left over—more than enough to enjoy a bottle with a lady in some quiet wine-parlor.

His face grew hot. That idiot of a paymaster had certainly infected him with some crazy ideas. Pettengill strode under the archway of the gate, gave the countersign to the Marine sentry, and emerged on the gas-lit sidewalk. He turned left along the wall; ahead of him he could see a splash of light and carriages at the curb. That would be the commandant's front entrance. He felt the tingling of excitement again.

Under the wall, a shadow stirred: heels clicked on the brick sidewalk close at his elbow, a hand caught at his sleeve.

"Where you going in such a big hurry, honey?" a woman's voice demanded. Perfume tickled his nostrils. He checked his stride, looking a long way down, to the face that was turned up to him; the gaslight across the street just enabled him to see that it was a pretty face, even with all the paint.

"Come on, honey, buy me a drink?" She tugged at his arm. "I'll show you a good time. You won't be sorry."

Fiercely the frantic desire to take her at her word surged up in Pettengill's body. She felt his response and laughed happily. The gaslight showed him blackened stumps of teeth between her lips. He had accepted worse often enough in water-front dives, but now he jerked away from her touch.

"Shove off," he growled. "Women your size are poison to me. Pure poison."

He quickened his step. Behind him, he heard the girl's shrill curses.

The commandant's white-jacketed steward opened the door for him. Hospitable noises flowed out to welcome him: the soft laughter of women, the rumble of men's voices, the tinkle of glass. He paused in dismay. The place was full of people: women in stiff taffetas and heavy silks, their skirts vastly extended by hoops; men mostly in dark coats relieved by patterned vests and gay cravats, though here and there white neckgear marked acceptance of the new English fashion for evening wear. There were half-a-dozen officers in uniform. To his horror he noted that the nearest of these was wearing epaulettes. Captain Du Pont ought to have warned him; he was entitled to wear epaulettes now, but his miserable Connecticut cheeseparing economy had balked at the price of Oliphant's full-dress rig.

He swallowed with relief at the sight of Du Pont himself, towering above the crowd as he plowed through it like a stately ship-of-the-line passing through a fleet of fishing smacks. Du Pont, God bless him, was in service uniform: frock coat, shoulder straps, plain pantaloons, sword belt and slings without the sword.

"Happy to see you aboard, Mr. Pettengill!" Du Pont said loudly. "You'll have a glass with me, I hope? Then I must abandon you to the tender mercies of the ladies. They're all agog to meet the officer who brought in the slaver. It's the talk of the town by this time." He was steering Pettengill expertly toward a gleaming buffet, with a word here, a laugh there, which somehow avoided the need for introducing Pettengill to anyone. "You'll have had small experience with the press, I suppose," he said in a lower tone. "The young man in the brown coat over there is Gaffney, of the *Public Ledger*. He'll be at you presently, too. Champagne, Mr. Pettengill? Or do you prefer a still wine?"

"Champagne by all means, if you please, sir," said Pettengill. He had never tasted champagne in his life, but Du Pont's nod approved his choice. He lifted the glass the commandant poured for him.

"Your health, Mr. Pettengill, and good fortune in your first command." The last words were spoken very softly. Du Pont leaned forward a little, his eyes stern with warning. "Remember this carefully, Mr. Pettengill. You are at liberty to discuss with Mr. Gaffney, or anyone else, your experiences in Africa and the capture of the *Ranee*, but you are not, under any circumstances, to discuss your new orders, or so much as mention the word Norfolk."

"Aye aye, sir," said Pettengill.

"I'm not just being super-cautious, Mr. Pettengill. I've no time to explain, and this isn't the place for it if I had, but I've received telegraphic instructions which render secrecy imperative. So much so that you'll sail under sealed orders tomorrow, and— Ah, Mr. Gaffney! Anxious to meet the lion of the hour, eh? Permit me to make you acquainted with Mr. Pettengill."

Gaffney's bright brown eyes matched the warm velvet of his coat collar and his liberal sprinkling of freckles. He grinned at Pettengill.

"Just in from Africa and promoted already, I see," he cried. "You were a master's mate when you arrived, according to my legion of trustworthy spies in the Navy Yard. Off for Southern waters, I suppose?"

He grinned slyly at Du Pont.

"You forget how long prize proceedings can drag themselves out, Mr. Gaffney," Pettengill said. "I've heard of prize masters being kept hanging about for months while the lawyers argued."

"Ah, yes," said Gaffney. "No doubt you were promoted to give greater dignity to your appearance before the honorable court?"

"You might be right," said Pettengill innocently. "But maybe there's more to it than that. I don't know any more than a Krooman boat-boy about how politicians think, but couldn't somebody have had a notion that to promote an officer who brings home a slaver might be one way to remind the public, through the medium of the press, of course, Mr. Gaffney, that the new Administration means to be a lot tougher than the last one about slave trading?"

"Of course," agreed Gaffney. "But to get back to—"

"I'm just coming to that, Mr. Gaffney," said Pettengill. "I can understand how anxious you are to know the details. Now let me try to refresh my memory."

"Permit me, Mr. Pettengill," murmured Du Pont. Champagne creamed into Pettengill's glass. "And you, Mr. Gaffney? A pleasure."

"Thank you, sir." Pettengill gulped a swallow and went on talking. "The story really begins when we raised this slaver's royals on the horizon. Let me see—that must've been March the second. I had the mid-watch; it was just turning daylight when the lookout on the fore-topmast crosstrees hailed the deck: 'Sail ho!' he sings out. 'Where away?' I asked him. 'Broad on the larb'd bow,' says he. I had a word with him later about that, I can tell you, Mr. Gaffney. You've no idea how hard it is to break these old salts of saying 'larboard' instead of 'port,' as regulations require. The reason is, of course, there's too much chance of confusion between 'larboard' and 'starboard,' and confusion in executing helm orders, say on a dark night off a lee shore, can mean disaster in five minutes, as I'm sure you can imagine. Well, to get back to my story, I sent the messenger below to call the captain, and pretty soon Captain Nicholl—Henry Nicholl is his name, Mr. Gaffney, in case you want to make a note of it. He's really a commander, but all officers in command of naval vessels are called captain by courtesy. Well, Captain Nicholl and the executive officer, Lieutenant Pendleton Banks, came on deck. 'What d'you make of the strange sail now, Mister Pettengill?' the captain asks. So I hailed the lookout again. 'She's a brig, sir,' says the lookout. 'She looks to be under all plain sail to the royals, steering nor'-nor'east.' As for us, we were just plowing along, running the engine half speed and using the tops'ls and jib to help the paddle wheels—I suppose you know, Mr. Gaffney, that a side-wheeler under sail alone is almost impossible—"

"Excuse me just one moment, Mr. Pettengill," interrupted Gaffney. "A gentleman whom I must have a word with is just leaving. I'll hustle right back."

Pettengill drank his champagne and looked around for the commandant. Du Pont was on the other side of the room, talking to the white-haired officer in epaulettes. His booming laughter filtered through the clack-clack of voices. Pettengill was suddenly penned against the sideboard by a semicircle of half-a-dozen people, two of them women. By their expressions they had been listening and were avid for more.

"Do go on, Mr. Pettengill!" said one of the women. "It's *so* exciting!"

"Andrew, you might fill Mr. Pettengill's glass before he's required to do any more talking," said the other lady. She was a tall woman, well enough shaped for all he could see above the billows of her crinoline. He guessed her to be about twice his own age. Her brown hair was gathered into a severe bun at the nape of her neck; a pair of gold-rimmed spectacles perched on her nose, with a black ribbon depending from them. She reminded Pettengill of a schoolteacher under whose stern rule and ruler he had suffered long ago. She had the same crisp habit of biting off her words, a habit that didn't invite discussion.

"I'm Mrs. Harrifield," she informed him. "This is Mrs. Carruthers, and the gentleman fumbling for the champagne bottle is Mr. Carruthers."

The three other men sidled away: Pettengill muttered acknowledgment of the introductions, wondering how he was going to make his own escape.

"For my part, Mr. Pettengill," Mrs. Harrifield proclaimed, "I might as well tell you that I'm not nearly so interested in nautical narrative as I am in the fate of the poor Africans you found aboard this slaver. Captain Du Pont was saying there were four hundred of them. What became of those four hundred human beings, Mr. Pettengill?"

Brass-buttoned blue broadcloth topped by a dark spade-shaped beard appeared between the portly Mrs. Carruthers and the slender Mrs. Harrifield.

"Hope I'm not interrupting," the officer said in a deep-South drawl. Mrs. Carruthers sniffed. Mrs. Harrifield glared. "I'm Commander Steedman, Mr. Pettengill. Happy to make your acquaintance. The commandant tells me you can give me news of a former shipmate of mine, Pendleton Banks. He was midshipman of my division in the old *St. Mary's* at Vera Cruz during the Mexican War."

"I've heard him tell of those days often, sir," Pettengill said. "I left him as well as a man can expect to be after two years on the African station. He's hoping to be home shortly, the *Sheboygan's* cruise is about over."

"Looking forward to it, I suppose?" suggested Steedman. "Home, friends, dear ones—all that? Oh, of course."

"Andrew—" said Mrs. Carruthers.

"Yes, dear," her husband replied meekly.

"So charmed to've met you, Mr. Pettengill," said Mrs. Carruthers. "Andrew—Emma—"

They moved off amid a rustling of hooped fabrics.

"Damned fools," Steedman said contemptuously. "They won't believe a Southern-born officer can put his country above his State. Count yourself lucky you're a blue-nosed Yankee, Pettengill. You've no idea what it means these days to have 'South Carolina' alongside your name in the Navy Register, as I have. Or even Delaware. Some of these fanatics actually mistrust Du Pont, just because Delaware's a slave State. Talk about Caesar's wife—but that's the reason I wanted news of Pendleton Banks. You understand?"

"Yes, sir. Only I don't know the answer. Banks isn't gabby about what he feels inside."

"Never was," muttered Steedman.

"Virginia's his State," Pettengill reflected. "She's not out of the Union yet, is she, sir?"

"Teetering on the brink," said Steedman. "This militia call of Lincoln's may tip the scales the wrong way. But I don't see what else the President could have done. The Union's got to be preserved, Pettengill, if not by persuasion, then by force."

His dark eyes were sad, but his face showed resolve that rose above pain and accepted sacrifice. Pettengill had seen a kindred misery in Pendleton Banks' eyes one African morning not so long ago. "Of course, Pettengill," Banks had said, "you may not have the opportunity, but if duty or good luck takes you anywhere near Norfolk, I'd deeply appreciate your delivering these letters in person instead of by the mails. I—I fear they may not be answered; I'd be grateful to hear from you how they were received, that is, if any message—"

"I have an idea, Commander Steedman," said Pettengill, "that Lieutenant Banks might agree with you about sticking by the Union, come what may. God knows I hope so."

"We'll drink to that hope of yours," cried Steedman. "For such a noble purpose bubble water's too weak, here's a Pellevoisin that'll mix comfortably with it." The twin stripes on his cuff gleamed in the light of the gas chandelier as he poured the brandy into two thin-stemmed glasses. Standing there in a captain's house, drinking a toast with a commander, Pettengill was conscious of what a world of difference there was between being a master, a wardroom officer, and a poor slob of a master's mate swinging his hammock in the steerage.

"Here's to our friend Banks. May we three be shipmates soon!" said Steedman, and emptied his glass at a gulp. Pettengill dutifully followed suit.

"Captain Du Pont was saying this afternoon that he fears we're in for a long civil war, sir," he said. "Do you agree with him?"

"I'm afraid I do," Steedman answered. "The die's cast. The Northern politicos kept talking compromise and offering concessions until Southerners became largely convinced the North would never fight to save the Union. So the hotheads had their way. But the first gun that was fired against Sumter was like a spark in a magazine. I've never seen such a change in so short a time. Look at these men here. Half of 'em are bankers and merchants and manufacturers. A week ago they were muttering against Lincoln, demanding more compromises, puling about their lost southern business. Listen to 'em now. They're red hot for coercion and damning him because he hasn't asked for twice as many troops. Fire and sword for rebels, the gallows for traitors! It won't be that easy. The North'll fight, all right: but so'll the South, and it's my guess that it'll be the slow strangulation of blockade rather than fire and sword that'll bring the South down to defeat in the end. I only hope Lincoln has a better idea of how to make proper use of his Navy than Madison had in 1812."

"Steam will mean a tighter blockade than in the days of sail, won't it, sir?"

Steedman nodded, reaching for the brandy bottle.

"I've had little service in steamers myself, but you're right," he agreed. "The South has no industry, depends on exports: it's as vulnerable to blockade as any country on earth. Their one hope is to win enough early successes to gain 'em foreign recognition. Bottoms up, Mr. Pettengill! We're being piped to supper."

The chattering throng was flowing toward a huge pair of double doors, now hospitably flung wide open, at the rear of the room.

"The drill is," Steedman explained, "you load up a couple of plates, find a lady who looks hungry and give her one, steer her to a seat and sit down and eat with her. When Mrs. Du Pont's here, there's a proper station-bill made out, with partners duly ticked off, but she spends most of her time at home in Delaware; her health's never been what it ought to be, poor lady."

Find a partner and eat with her! Make small talk! Answer more stupid questions!

"'Ware boarders," muttered Steedman.

A hand slid inside Pettengill's elbow.

"I haven't forgotten those poor martyred black men, Mr. Pettengill," said Mrs. Harrifield. "You're going to get me some supper and tell me all about them while we enjoy our repast."

"I—uh—Commander Steedman—"

"Has abandoned you to your fate," said Mrs. Harrifield.

Steedman's blue back confirmed this. He braced up and filled away at the first sign of the enemy, the coward, thought Pettengill.

"I'll thank you for a slice of turkey breast, Mr. Pettengill, cranberry jelly, and a little of whatever salad you find," Mrs. Harrifield was saying. She sounded like Captain Nicholl: "I'll thank you to take in the quarter-deck awning and have it spread again properly, Mr. Pettengill. Where d'you think you are—in the Portugee Navy?"

Pettengill just managed to substitute "Yes, ma'am" for an instinctive "Aye aye, sir."

Mrs. Harrifield didn't let him get too far away from her: all the time he was working his way through the crowd around the heavily loaded dining table, she was standing near, vigilant against flight or interference. Pettengill obtained what she wanted, and two large slices of roast beef for himself, with plenty of soft white bread and fresh butter. People seemed to know him by this time and spoke to him cordially:

"Grand work, catching that rascal slaver, Mr. Pettengill!"

"Hope they make an example of that man Harris: hanging's too good for him."

"Hear! hear! A firm hand and no nonsense! I was saying to General Patterson just this afternoon—"

"It'll all be over in three months, now Old Abe's got his dander up. Don't you agree, Mr. Pettengill?"

"My boy's in the City Troop. He came home to dinner in uniform, and his mother—"

Pettengill drew clear of the crowd with a last grab for knives and forks. Mrs. Harrifield steered him to a brocaded settee, settled her surging crinoline, took off her spectacles, and attached them to a small hook on her bodice.

"Now, then, if you please?" she said, smiling up at him.

Without the distortion of glasses, her wide hazel eyes were attractive; in fact, Mrs. Harrifield was a handsome woman, and with artifice she might have been more so. Her features were regular, her complexion cream-soft and clear of blemishes. She was younger, too, than Pettengill had first thought.

"I'm waiting, Mr. Pettengill," she reminded him.

He managed to sit down beside her. There was suppressed laughter in the hazel eyes, but her words were as crisp as before.

"Now then, Mr. Pettengill. I'd like to get back to where you found these four hundred black men imprisoned in the brig's hold. Were they in chains, Mr. Pettengill?"

"Nope," said Pettengill indistinctly through a mouthful of beef and bread. "Harris just struck 'em below and clamped the hatch gratings on 'em."

"Struck them? You mean he beat them to drive them below, of course?"

"Prob'ly he did, but tha's not what I meant. 'Strike's' a sailor's word for 'take' or 'send' below. It was close stowage down there, of course. Harris had rigged temporary decks—all these slavers do—that allowed the poor devils only about four feet o' headroom. Slaves couldn't stand up: they had to lie on the deck all jammed together."

"But four hundred people in that cramped space?"

"You wouldn't want the details, ma'am. Make you sick." Pettengill stowed away more beef, spread another slice of bread thickly with that wonderful butter.

"And what happened when you captured the ship? To the poor Africans, I mean?" Mrs. Harrifield demanded. "Were any of them killed by the cannon balls?"

"We didn't use any cannon balls, ma'am. We took the *Ranee* by boarding from a small boat. Harris and his people showed fight, a couple of 'em got killed, but no slaves."

Mrs. Harrifield's eyes widened. They seemed lighter in color, almost tawny, like the eyes of a leopardess Pettengill had seen in a cage at Saint Paul de Loanda.

"Killed, you say? Two of those villains killed? Did you kill them yourself, Mr. Pettengill?" she half-whispered.

He stared at her.

"I shot one of 'em," he told her brutally, "to keep him from sticking a boarding-pike into my stomach. Seaman Jackson cut the other one down; he died of his wound after the brig was taken."

He waited for the gasp and the shudder of revulsion. Instead the tip of her tongue slipped into view for just an instant above her lower lip. Her tawny eyes were very bright.

"Were you hurt at all yourself, Mr. Pettengill?"

"A little nick across the ribs with a knife, ma'am," he answered. "Nothing to speak of. Some of the other lads were hurt a lot worse."

Mrs. Harrifield's hand touched his wrist. It was a hot hand, vibrant, almost electric.

"Emma! Andrew and I think it's time we were leaving."

Mrs. Carruthers had arrived.

Mrs. Harrifield looked at her friend through drooping eyelashes. She did not remove her hand from Pettengill's wrist.

"Mr. Pettengill is seeing me home, Frances," she announced.

"Indeed," said Mrs. Carruthers. "I might have guessed. Good night, Emma."

"You don't mind, I'm sure," Mrs. Harrifield said. "It's only a few squares, and there'll be plenty of hacks at the door." She spoke with authority again.

"Certainly," muttered Pettengill. "Honored, of course."

Mrs. Harrifield was signaling to a colored servant to take away the supper plates.

"There's dessert, of course," she said to Pettengill, "but I find dessert a trifle heavy after a late supper."

Pettengill nodded agreement. He didn't want to waste more time than necessary.

"Then," said Mrs. Harrifield, rising, "I'll just get my cloak—no, don't bother, you'd never find it. You may attend me at the door, if you will."

Trailing humbly in her imperious wake, Pettengill made his way to the wide hallway where Captain Du Pont was now receiving the farewells of the early departers.

"Ah, Pettengill. Leaving already?"

"It was kind of you to let me come, sir, and I've enjoyed the best supper I've had in years, but I think I ought to be turning in before long."

Du Pont nodded.

"I hope they gave you quarters for the night in the *Princeton*."

"No, sir. I had my gear taken aboard—" He stopped short, knowing that he must not mention the *Brother Jonathan*.

Du Pont's nod conveyed approval.

"Quite right," he said. "You handled Gaffney well, Mr. Pettengill," he added. "Why, Mrs. Harrifield, do I see you in your cloak? Surely you're not going so soon? I'd promised myself the pleasure of taking a glass of wine with you."

She gave him her white-gloved hand.

"You are too kind, Captain Du Pont. But I came with the Carrutherses, and they had to leave before I'd finished supper, so I've induced Mr. Pettengill to see me to my door. Thank you so much for a delightful evening."

"It was gracious of you to come, Mrs. Harrifield," Du Pont said. "In these difficult days an old sailor is always grateful for such small glimpses of beauty as his duties permit. As I was remarking to Mr. Pettengill only this afternoon, the sea is a jealous mistress."

"As a young sailor, I'm sure Mr. Pettengill is always grateful for such small crumbs from the table of your experience, Captain Du Pont," said Mrs. Harrifield. "Thank you once more, and good night."

She didn't actually add "Come, Mr. Pettengill," but the way she swished toward the door was an order as clear as Pettengill had ever heard given on a quarter-deck.

"I'll expect you in my office by six bells in the morning watch, Mr. Pettengill," Du Pont said. "Good night."

"Good night, sir."

Pettengill took his cap from the hovering steward and followed Mrs. Harrifield through the vestibule and down the steps to the sidewalk. A hack was at the curb, a closed carriage, to whose driver Mrs. Harrifield gave an address which Pettengill didn't catch. He held the door for her in silent disapproval: it was a lady's place to tell her escort where she wished to go and allow him to instruct cabbies.

The cab jounced along over the cobbles. Mrs. Harrifield's scent wasn't as pronounced as the little street-walker's, but it was still disturbing. He hadn't noticed it before. He sneaked a cautious glance at her as they came to a well-lighted corner. She had her glasses off again. Her face seemed paler than it had been. She turned and saw that he was looking at her. She leaned toward him: he thought she was smiling.

"Ex-try! Ex-try! Read all about the slave ship!" shrilled a voice on the sidewalk.

"You're famous, Mr. Pettengill," said Mrs. Harrifield softly. "And you deserve to be."

Her hands were on his shoulders, pulling his head down. . . .

Through the red turmoil in his brain, Pettengill heard the driver say "Whoa!" and felt the carriage wheel grate against stone.

Instinctively his grip relaxed. Mrs. Harrifield tore free of his arms, shrank back into the darkness of the far corner as the door opened.

Pettengill got out.

He had no idea where he was: all he could see was a row of quiet-looking brick houses, side by side and looking exactly alike, with white doors facing the street and short flights of white steps leading up to them. Here and there a gleam of light showed behind discreet curtains: a gas lamp shone dully at the corner.

Mrs. Harrifield was maneuvering her crinoline through the carriage door; the hood of her cloak was close about her face.

"Will you ask the driver to wait, please, Mr. Pettengill?" she said. The tone of command was back again.

"But—" he began.

"I'll wait, mister," put in the driver. "Long's you like."

Pettengill fumbled in his pocket, found one of the gold dollars.

"Here's something to keep you company," he muttered.

"Thanks kindly, mister."

Mrs. Harrifield moved closer to Pettengill as they crossed the sidewalk: her hand found his, pressed something into it.

"The keyhole's just below that brass knob. Don't fumble," she whispered.

She drew him inside, closing the door behind them. He could see a low-turned lamp with a flowered globe; beyond, antimacassars showed ghostlike in the gloom. Mrs. Harrifield's skirts rustled as she slipped out of her cloak.

"You're sure it's all right for me to come in?" he whispered.

"What on earth are you whispering for now?" demanded Mrs. Harrifield in her normal voice. "Oh, because of that key business? I just didn't want the driver to imagine that I'd brought a strange gentleman home; cabbies are great gossips."

"Bu—your family—your husband—"

"There's no one in the house except one maidservant, who knows enough to mind her own business," interrupted Mrs. Harrifield.

"Oh," said Pettengill. Understanding was slowly seeping into his incredulous mind. He took a step toward her. . . .

She was picking up the flowered lamp.

"Take this lamp, if you will, Mr. Pettengill." As she held it toward him, its light gleamed on the polished newel post of a staircase.

"Just under these stairs," she informed him, "you'll find the cellar door. The wine bins are directly opposite the foot of the steps. Would you mind fetching two bottles from the third bin in the second row—the one labeled Madeira?"

"Of course, ma'am."

"And you might bring the bottles right up to my little sitting room, Mr. Pettengill," Mrs. Harrifield directed. "It's more comfortably furnished than these lower rooms."

Her skirts were whispering up the stairway. Pettengill swept a hand across his eyes as though to recover his equilibrium. Above, the rustle of taffeta died away. He walked slowly toward the cellar door.

Presently, lamp in one hand and bottle-necks gripped in the other, he climbed the carpeted staircase. A faint rectangle of light indicated an open door. His heart thumped against his ribs as he approached it. Mrs. Harrifield's voice came out to greet him:

"Leave the lamp on the hall table, if you will, Mr. Pettengill," she directed. "And the wine, too. For the present."

Pettengill set down lamp and bottles, and was through the door in one quick step. A candle burned dimly inside a cone of dark-blue glass: it gave just enough light for him to see a vast expanse of white, with something darker at its farther end.

The white expanse was the coverlet of a bed, and the dark something was Mrs. Harrifield's hair adrift across a pillow. . . .

Later, she spoke in a small voice, hesitantly, like a child who fears reproof:

"Tell me your first name."

"It's Caleb."

"Just Caleb? No middle name?"

"Just Caleb."

"Where were you born, Caleb?"

"Litchfield, Connecticut."

Bit by bit, she drew out the tale of his early years: how his first memories were of the clang of steam hammers and the yarns of the retired sea captains whose affairs were in his father's care; of how his dream had been born and grew, the dream of conquest of the sea by Yankee-made steam warships; of the grizzled master mariner who'd patted him on the head one night and told him that some day the teamwork of Yankee engineers and Yankee seamen would wrest the trident of Neptune from the grasp of England and make it their own; how the old man had given the boy Caleb a colored lithograph of the new steam sloop-of-war *San Jacinto,* and how his father had taken it from him later, saying that he'd have no son of his getting wild notions into his head.

"I reckon," mused Pettengill, "it was right about then I made up my mind I was going to run away to sea. Father wouldn't get me an appointment to Annapolis, though he could've. He was hell-bent I should follow the law, take over his practice some day. If Mother'd lived, it might've been different. As it was, I worked at odd jobs in the summer till I had enough money to ride the cars to New York. I tried to ship as a boy in the Navy, but they wouldn't take me without my father's consent. So I shipped out in a Havana packet—and I've been a sailor ever since."

"How old were you then, Caleb?"

"Fourteen." He kept on talking, opening up his heart as he hadn't done in years. "That packet was the *Georgia:* her skipper was a naval lieutenant on leave. They used to allow naval officers leave of absence to take such jobs so's they could make enough money to keep their families instead of starving on waiting-orders pay. Porter was his name, David D. Porter. He was a tough little man with a black beard something like Commander Steedman's and the most piercing dark eyes I ever saw. He was old Commodore Porter's son. You've heard of *him,* Porter of the *Essex?*"

"Of course." She added quickly, "You thought a lot of this Captain Porter of yours, didn't you, Caleb?"

"Yes. He didn't keep me waiting on table and swabbing out the galley like the other ship's boys. He said I was born to be a sailor, and he had me rated ordinary seaman when I'd made only two round trips to Havana with him. He lent me books, too."

"Tell me about the books."

"They were wonderful books. There was Dutton on navigation— that's the text they use at the Naval Academy—and Bowditch's *American Practical Navigator,* and Captain Totten's *Naval Text Book and Dictionary,* and Pierce's *Plane and Spherical Trigonometry.* I don't know what I'd've done without those books and the paper and pencils and all. You see, the *Georgia* was a steamer, and

Captain Porter wasn't one of your old shellbacks who only uses his engines when he hasn't got a wind. Kept a taut hand on his engine room, too, he did. No engineer could make a monkey out of D. D. Porter about coal consumption or leaking condenser tubes: he wanted to know why, and God help the engineer who tried to feed him a lot of slumgullion in the hope he didn't understand engine-talk. I've known him to log an engineer for neglect of duty more'n once for trying that. A proper steamship captain, he was. Well, anyway, he used steam all he could or as much as the owners'd let him, always squalling about coal bills like they used to, so we weren't laying aloft to reef tops'ls or set stuns'ls two or three times in a watch. I had time on my hands, and those books just about kept me from going crazy."

There seemed to be tears in Mrs. Harrifield's eyes. To cover his embarrassment he refilled the wineglasses.

"So that's how you became an officer," she said.

"Not right away. I went out to Australia with Captain Porter in the *Golden Age*. Fifty-three, that was," Pettengill told her. "Time we made Melbourne, Captain Porter said I was ready to stand for my mate's ticket, but I was too young. Nearly the whole crew jumped ship and headed for the new gold fields. I wanted to stick with the skipper, but Porter said no, I needed more experience than I'd get in the Melbourne and Sydney coastal traffic he was going into. So he made me ship for Frisco in a clipper. I was an A.B. by that time, and they were glad to have me. That voyage taught me to stay out of windjammers; we were becalmed for a week once, and da— mighty near bilged on a coral reef when our anchors wouldn't hold. Steam would've made all the difference. Anyway we got to Frisco at last, and I shipped A.B. in the steam packet *Champion* on the Panama run. I passed for my mate's ticket the next year, but I didn't get a berth till fifty-five, fourth officer in the *Champion*."

"There were gold fields in California, too, weren't there?"

"Sure were. But I wasn't interested. I wanted to be at sea."

"And how did you get into the Navy, Caleb?"

"That was pure luck," he gloated. "I'd had smallpox in Panama; after I got well they put me on the Atlantic side, running between New York and Aspinwall. One day in New York, two years ago, who should I meet up with but Captain Porter. He'd just come from the Navy Yard, where he'd been calling on an old shipmate of his, Captain Nicholl of the *Sheboygan*. The *Sheboygan* was on the point of sailing for a two-year cruise on the African station, and she was short a watch officer: there weren't enough passed midshipmen to go around, what with the frigate captains gobbling up the young fellows as fast as they could lay hands on 'em and the Paraguay expedition needing so many on top of that. Nicholl had asked authority by telegraph to appoint an acting master's mate to fill the vacancy: he'd got the authority, but he couldn't find a capable man to take the job at forty dollars a month. 'Would he take me, d'you suppose, sir?' says I to Captain Porter. 'Take you? He'd grab at you,' says Porter. 'But don't be a blasted fool. What's your pay now?' 'Ninety dollars,' I told him. 'But I want to be in the Navy.' Porter did his best to talk me out of it, but he finally took me with him to the Navy Yard and introduced me to Captain Nicholl—and here I am. Acting Master Pettengill, U.S.N."

"You appear to have what people call a single-track mind, Caleb."

"I've heard people say that before," he admitted. "All I know is, being an officer in the Navy, the new steam Navy, is what I've always wanted. Now I've got it. Only I haven't really got it yet. I'm just a master with an acting appointment. The law still says that only 'masters in the line of promotion' can be given commissions as lieutenants, and to be appointed a 'master in the line of promotion' you have to be an Annapolis graduate. Maybe, if we're really going to have war, that'll make some changes, open the way: they'll need more lieutenants than they can get from the Academy. That's my hope, anyway."

"Is that all you'll be fighting for?" demanded Mrs. Harrifield.

"Of course not!" What was the matter with her all of a sudden? "I'll be fighting because it's my duty—and—and to keep this country from being all busted to hell."

"Not for the right? Not to free your brothers from bondage? To rid our land forever from the shame of slavery?"

"I don't like slavery," he told her. "Where I come from, we don't hold with it. But it's been here for a couple hundred years and nobody's gone to war over it. I reckon most folks in the North will fight to save the Union, though: and a lot of 'em who'll fight for that wouldn't risk their skins to smash slavery."

"John Brown did," she cried. "My husband did, too. They gave up their lives for the sacred cause."

"Your husband, ma'am?"

"My husband," she said, "was murdered a year ago by a slave-owning ruffian in Kentucky because he tried to protect a poor terrified black man from recapture and the lash."

Her white teeth clicked on the last word.

"But why—"

"My husband and I were humble workers for the Underground Railroad. You may have heard of the Underground Railroad, Mr. Pettengill?"

"Of course. But I still can't see why you and your husband—"

"From conviction. Heart-felt conviction of the righteousness of our cause. Hatred of the evil thing against which we fought. Acceptance of the fact that it was our duty to destroy it. Would you understand such feelings, Mr. Pettengill?"

"I don't know," he said. "I'm a naval officer. My idea of duty is obeying orders and—"

"You were cruising off the coast of Africa for two years. How many slave ships did your vessel capture?"

"Just this one I brought in this afternoon."

"Did you meet no others?"

"We overhauled a dozen of 'em, first and last," he admitted. "But the law requires that there be unmistakable evidence, evidence that'll stand up in court, before a vessel can be seized for trading in slaves. A captain can be dead-sure of the facts, but if he can't prove 'em— Anyway, the government, at least in Buchanan's time, has been pretty lukewarm about the prizes our ships did send in."

"Exactly my point!" she flared. "Obeying orders is your idea of duty, Mr. Pettengill. It's the Navy's idea of duty. Do as you're told and win promotion. So you let villains go free, you let the Lord's vengeance go unfulfilled, because weak men or wicked men holding a little temporary authority command you to act against God's will. I say to you, Caleb Pettengill, that if you and all the other warriors of the North fight this war under any such false conception of duty, only defeat, shameful defeat, awaits our nation."

Pettengill sprang up and stood glaring down at her.

"Let me say something to *you*, Emma Harrifield," he roared. "When the officers of the United States Navy start holding prayer meetings to decide whether they're going to obey their orders or not, that'll be the day our nation'll be facing defeat. God keep us from ever seeing its dawn!"

"You—you—" she gasped. "I thought of you as a hero, a champion of the helpless, one sent me as a sign, a command for the fulfillment of my vow."

"Your vow?"

She threw back her head, looking Pettengill straight in the eye.

"When my husband was murdered by a slave driver," she said, "I registered a vow in Heaven that I would give my body to the first man who came to me with the blood of such a one on his hands."

"My God!" Pettengill stared at her for one incredulous instant, while the shreds of his foolish pride withered into the dust of self-abasement.

Without a word he left the room.

He cursed her, half-sobbing, in the darkness of the lower hallway. He had turned his back on an honest whore because she had bad teeth and had taken this creature instead, this devil who made her body an altar for a rite of vengeance.

He lurched toward the door. Just as his hand touched the knob, he heard a whisper from the head of the staircase, "Caleb—Caleb—"

The cab driver roused from his slumber, rubbing his eyes. "Y' took long 'nough, mister."

"I'll pay for your time," Pettengill snapped. "Take me to the Navy Yard gate on Front Street."

From somewhere nearby, as the vehicle jerked into motion along the dim-lit street, a church clock began to strike: one — two — three — four — five — six — seven — eight — nine — ten — eleven — twelve. There were seven hours before he was due at the commandant's office. He had seven hours to devote to the *Brother Jonathan*, his new command.

He had neglected his ship, his duty, for a woman. It would never happen again.

Chapter Four

Against the dull gray shadow that was Fortress Monroe, orange flame throbbed briefly in the dawn-mist. The flat thud of a 32-pounder echoed across the oily waters of Hampton Roads.

In the pilothouse of the Navy tug *Brother Jonathan*, Acting Master Caleb Pettengill muttered, "Goddam all nervous soldiers" and gave his engine room a slow bell.

That had been a blank charge by the sound of it. The next one might be shotted if he didn't make a satisfactory reply to the challenge, but he had no means of doing it. . . .

Not for forty-six years, since 1815, had there been any need for recognition signals between United States naval vessels and United States harbor forts. Like many another young officer suddenly confronted by the desperate emergencies of a new war, Pettengill had about thirty seconds to come up with an answer to a problem that no one had bothered to work out during the comfortable years of peace when there had been plenty of time.

"Do those fools think I'd come barging up right under their guns with all my running lights burning if I was an enemy?" Pettengill growled.

"Dunno, sir," said Quarter Gunner Jackson, who was standing a wheel trick because the water-front scourings who made up the bulk of the crew didn't include any dependable helmsmen. "Mebbe the Rebs got the fort now," he added brightly.

They might, at that. Monroe had been in Union hands thirty-six hours before, when Pettengill had pushed off from the Philadelphia Navy Yard: while in Washington the politicos clung to a fading hope that the Old Dominion would stand by the Union, after all. By this time, however, the whole situation might have changed for the worse. Virginia might be out of the Union and her troops might be grabbing at all the Federal posts within her borders, as the cotton States had done already.

Pettengill doubted whether a fort as strong as Monroe could be stormed by raw Virginia militia. It might have been surrendered by an irresolute commander, or one confused by weasel-worded orders as Major Anderson had been at Fort Sumter.

The lighthouse was dark. That could be a bad sign. Another blank charge! The next one'll be pushing a solid shot ahead of it for sure. . . .

Pettengill made up his mind. He was not going to admit the possibility that the most important military position on the whole Atlantic seaboard had been tamely handed over on demand.

He leaned out of the pilothouse window.

"Aycock!" he yelled.

A shadowy head appeared in the little square hatch just abaft the 12-pounder bronze howitzer which was the tug's only gun.

"Sir?"

"Go burn a blue light in the bows before those idiots in the fort knock us to smithereens."

"Aye aye, sir."

Quartermaster Aycock hoisted his body out of the hatch and trotted to the signal locker, his bare feet flapping on the wet deck.

Behind Pettengill, the door of the pilothouse slammed open.

"Was that gunfire I heered just a minute ago, Cap'n Pettengill?" a whining voice said.

Pettengill groaned. Another of Engineer Canty's endless complaints was not what he wanted to hear just then.

"Yes, Mr. Canty," he said, wearily, turning from the window to face the lumpy man whose bulk filled the narrow doorway. "That was gunfire. A signal gun from Fortress Monroe, which lies right over there. We'll be going alongside the dock in a few minutes, so I'll thank you to get back to your engine and stand by for bells."

The sweat on Canty's face glistened in the rays of the chart-board lamp.

" 'Twasn't neither no signal gun," he complained. "I heered you say they was goin' to knock us to smithereens. There's a war goin' on here, that's what, an' me'n the boys never signed on for no war!"

That was what came of going to sea with a black gang that hadn't a man in it who'd ever been out of the Delaware River in his life before. Civilians, hired by the day because the sudden strain of mobilizing for war hadn't left so much as a Navy coal heaver available on the Philadelphia receiving ship, let alone an engineer officer or a fireman. . . .

[61]

"You and your men signed on for thirty days, Mr. Canty, unless sooner replaced by Navy people," Pettengill said with what patience he could command. "You're being well paid, and you're in no danger."

The glare of the blue light suddenly filled the pilothouse with ghastly radiance. Canty yelled and tried to shove his way into the pilothouse. Pettengill took two quick strides, grabbed him by the front of his filthy sweat shirt, and hurled him back outside.

"Lay below to your throttle, damn you!" he snarled, and slammed the door in the man's frightened face. Jackson laughed.

"Fort's signalizing, sir!" shouted Aycock from the fo'c's'le.

Through the glare of the blue light, Pettengill could see a winking spot of yellow above the dark ramparts.

"Can you make anything of it, Aycock?"

"Not me, sir. Army signal, I reckon."

"Then we'll take a chance it means 'Welcome, little tugboat.'" He yanked the bellpull for full speed; the beat of the tug's propeller livened at once. Canty was back on the job.

Pettengill applied himself to the business of conning the tug in to the fort's dock. The blue light was fizzling out, but the light of morning was growing by the minute. Pettengill could see the sharp outline of the masonry bastions; the upthrust finger of the darkened lighthouse gave him a reference point. He thought his present course would bring him up to the dock and by that time he could see well enough to lay the tug alongside without trouble.

If he wasn't steaming into a trap.

Suddenly it was almost daylight. Far to the eastward beyond the capes, a golden glow was pushing up out of the Atlantic, bright-edging the clouds on the horizon. Details of the fort became visible: the black square of the sally port in the curtain wall; the long dock thrusting out into the water; the serried embrasures where the great guns lurked; the thin sliver of a flagstaff.

A muffled thud came from the fort, not nearly as loud as the earlier signal guns, then a brassy wail of bugles. Something was climbing up the flagstaff—up, up, until the breeze caught it and spread it on the morning air.

"By the dawn's early light," muttered Pettengill, relieved and grateful.

"Hoist the colors, Aycock, and send a couple of hands aft to stir up our passengers."

He would be glad to be rid of the fifty Army recruits he had brought down from Philadelphia to reinforce the Monroe garrison. They cluttered his deck and were a serious responsibility. And the instant he had landed them and pushed off for the Norfolk Navy Yard, he could open the sealed orders and find out what he was supposed to do when he got to Norfolk.

The recruits would be happy to be rid of him and the *Brother Jonathan* too. Little wonder, after two nights huddled on the wet afterdeck with nothing to eat but hardtack and with no protection from rain and spray after the lashings of the last tarpaulin had yielded to the fury of gale-force winds. They were still desperately seasick, poor devils. He could hear them retching and moaning as Aycock and their sergeant kicked them to their feet. The tug was coming up to the dock. Soldiers came running, ready to handle the lines. An officer strode out of the sally port and over the wooden bridge that spanned the moat. The morning light gleamed on his polished scabbard. He looked very trim and smart.

Pettengill stared anxiously down at his own threadbare blue jacket and rumpled pantaloons. He hadn't been out of them for two nights and a day. They were his old clothes, not the handsome new gear he had acquired. The only change he had made in them was to tack a pair of hastily purchased gilt shoulder straps to the jacket. But what could the Army expect a sailor to look like, coming in from a rough passage with three hours' sleep out of thirty-six? Let this blue-and-scarlet sprig of an artilleryman laugh if he wanted to.

Pettengill eased the tug alongside the dock, saw her made fast.

"Stand by," he said into the engine-room voice tube. "We won't be here long." He went out of the pilothouse and walked to the rail of the little superstructure. The recruits were staggering ashore over a rickety gangplank. Some carried bags, others were just able to move themselves. A raw-voiced sergeant urged them to greater speed.

The officer who had come down from the sally port was saying something to the sergeant. He turned, saw Pettengill, and came over to the edge of the pier, snapping hand to visor in smart salute. Just in time, Pettengill returned the courtesy by lifting his cap, Navy fashion. It was hard to remember that he was no longer a mere master's mate, junior to everyone who wore shoulder straps. There weren't any hard and fast regulations about the relative rank of junior officers in the Army and Navy, but it was generally assumed that masters ranked with Army first lieutenants, and passed midshipmen ranked with second lieutenants like the pink-cheeked youngster on the dock.

Pettengill's gilt shoulder straps shone bravely: they weren't real gold lace, as the ones on his frock coat were, but they were good enough to rate him his first salute from an Army officer.

"Morning, sir," the young lieutenant was saying. "I'm Graham, Second Artillery. We'd be proud to have you at the mess for breakfast, if you've time, and I know Colonel Dimick will be happy to see you."

"Sorry, Mr. Graham," said Pettengill. "Please present Acting Master Pettengill's respects to the colonel and say I am under the strictest orders to leave here for the Norfolk Navy Yard the instant I've landed these recruits. I wish I could have breakfast at your mess. Army bacon would be a nice change from Navy salt pork, ten years in cask."

"It might if we had any," Graham replied, laughing. "We're on short commons as well as being shorthanded. We'd have fed you johnnycake and coffee. Anyway, thanks for the recruits; even fifty men are a godsend. I doubt if we have two hundred fit for duty at the moment."

Two hundred men weren't a tenth of the garrison the big fort ought to have at a time like this! Even Virginia militia, if there were enough of them, might overwhelm such a handful.

"Hell's bells, man!" Pettengill cried. "What are they thinking of in the War Department? The whole North's swarming with State troops and volunteers; they ought to have at least a couple of regiments here by this time. This place is the key to Chesapeake Bay and the Potomac River. If the Rebels get Monroe, they'll get Baltimore and Washington too!"

"Oh, there's help on the way," said Graham airily. "We had a wire last night to tell us that a Massachusetts regiment's coming by sea from Boston; it ought to arrive tomorrow or next day at the latest. Seven hundred men. We can hold this fort till hell freezes over with that many."

"Your wire connection with Washington runs by way of Richmond, doesn't it?" asked Pettengill. Graham nodded.

"Then," said Pettengill, "if it's still open, Virginia hasn't seceded yet."

"That's just what we don't know. Folks in Hampton and Newport News, we hear, are all excited about reports that the State convention passed the ordinance of secession yesterday. Nothing official yet. The colonel thinks they may be playing possum till they can get a big force of militia together to attack this fort and the Norfolk Navy Yard at the same time."

And since they can sit in Richmond and read all the messages, they know those Massachusetts troops are coming, so they'll hurry things along as fast as they can. . . ."

"Recruits all ashore, sir," reported the sergeant at that moment. He handed the lieutenant a clip-board and a pencil. Graham ran his eye down the paper, scrawled his name at the bottom of it, and stepped up on the stringpiece to pass it to Pettengill.

"There's your receipt for fifty bodies," he said. "We'll try to put a little life into 'em later."

Pettengill leaned over the rail and stretched out a long arm to reach the paper. As he did so he became aware of Canty's pale moon-face and bulging eyes in the engine-room gangway just below; the man must have been listening to every word that he and Graham had spoken. He pretended not to have noticed Canty.

"Good-by and good luck, Mr. Graham," he said.

"The same to you, sailor. Watch your step with those Rebel gals over yonder. I hear tell there's a bright-eyed little rascal in Portsmouth they call Terry the Terror 'cause she boasts she breaks a Yankee's heart every day and three on Sundays."

"Hope she tries to break mine," boasted Pettengill. "I'll take Miss Terry for a walk in the moonlight and show her the facts of life."

"Wish you luck," chuckled Graham, starting to turn away. Then he swung back, serious again. "Say—almost forgot to tell you—there's a report the Secesh have sunk barges in the channel leading up to Norfolk and are building batteries at Sewell's Point and Craney Island."

"That's a goddam sight more important to me than all the trollops between here and Texas!" snapped Pettengill. "How solid is your information?"

"Just a rumor, like everything else we get. Probably all hogwash. Thought I better mention it, though."

"Thanks," said Pettengill drily. "Mind having your men lend a hand to cast off those lines and run the gangplank ashore?"

"Wait! Wait a minute! We're gittin' off this boat!" It was Canty's voice, shrill with panic. The engineer came waddling and panting out of the engine-room door, a canvas sea-bag over his shoulder. Right behind him crowded his firemen and coal heavers.

Pettengill hit the deck in one jump, grabbed the collar of Canty's dungaree jacket, and flung him back against the first of the firemen.

"You'll stay right here and do your duty, Mr. Canty," he rasped. "You and your gang. Get below, the lot of you."

Canty was gripped by a terror that took no heed of anything else.

"I'm goin' ashore—ashore!" he babbled, striving to regain his balance. "I ain't goin' up no river to git blown up by no masked bat'ries! C'mon, boys!"

Pettengill's hamlike fist crashed against Canty's jaw as the engineer took the first mutinous step. He went down like a bag of blubber, his head cracking against the brassbound coaming of the engine-room door.

Graham called, "Need any help, Pettengill?"

"No thanks." Aycock was beside him now, pressing a Navy pistol into his hand. Canty moaned and stirred. "A bucket of water here!" Pettengill ordered, and Aycock was happy to oblige. Canty sat up, spluttering. There was blood on his head, and the side of his face was swelling, but Pettengill judged he wasn't hurt badly.

"Get below, Mr. Canty, and stand by your engine!" Canty stared up at him with eyes full of fear and hate, then lifted himself to his feet.

"Better do's the cap'n says 'fore he kills ya, chief," muttered the fireman. Canty cursed him, and turned toward the engine-room door.

"I'll have the law on ye fer this, Cap'n Pettengill, if ever I see Philly ag'in," he snarled as he started heavily down the iron ladder.

Pettengill didn't like the sound of that last phrase.

"Mr. Canty!" he called sharply. Halfway down the ladder, the engineer paused.

"Keep in mind, Mr. Canty," Pettengill said, slapping the pistol barrel against his left palm, "that this tug is proceeding to the Norfolk Navy Yard, and I'll consider any mishap to her machinery that may occur before she gets there as being a willful and malicious injury to a naval vessel within the meaning of the Articles for the Government of the Navy. In time of war, Mr. Canty, the penalty for violation of that particular article is death. If anything whatever goes wrong in your department before we reach Norfolk, Mr. Canty, I'll see you hanged for it."

"Nothin'll go wrong, Cap'n," Canty muttered. Pettengill nodded and turned away. In his heart he was sorry for the man. It wasn't Canty's fault that he was a coward.

But he was the only engineer Pettengill had, and if he wouldn't do his duty willingly he must be made to do it. Pettengill wasn't at all sure that the Articles for the Government of the Navy applied to civilian employees, or that this was legally "a time of war": he might find himself in trouble for what he had done. But for the moment he had Canty thoroughly cowed, and that was what counted.

"Cast off, Aycock," he sang out. He swung himself up the short ladder into the pilothouse, rang for slow astern. The engine responded, water boiled under the tug's fantail as she sheered out from the dock.

Pettengill forced himself to stand quietly beside the helmsman until he had conned the tug clear of the dock and had her well out in Hampton Roads headed up the main ship channel toward Sewell's Point. Not until then, after calling Aycock to take over the conn, did he retire into his tiny cabin behind the pilothouse to open the sealed orders.

The envelope was inscribed, in the round hand favored by navy clerks, "Sealed Orders for Actg. Master C. Pettengill, commdg. U.S. steamer *Brother Jonathan,* from Captn. Saml. F. Du Pont, U.S. Navy, Commdt. Navy Yard Philadelphia, Pa. NOT TO BE OPENED UNTIL DEPARTURE TAKEN FROM FORTRESS MONROE."

Pettengill slit the envelope neatly with his pocketknife. Inside were two sheets of official paper.

The first, written in that same round hand except for the signature, was a formal order:

> Commandant's Office, U.S. Navy Yard,
> Philadelphia, April 16, 1861

Sir:

You are hereby assigned to the command of the U.S. steamer *Brother Jonathan.* When ready for sea, you will proceed to Fort Mifflin, Pa., and take aboard fifty Army recruits now awaiting embarkation. You will then proceed with all dispatch to Old Point Comfort, Va., and deliver the said recruits to the Commanding Officer, Fort Monroe, taking proper receipt therefor.

Immediately upon delivery of the recruits, the Hon. Sec'y of the Navy directs that you proceed to the Navy Yard, Norfolk, Va., where you will report to the Commandant, Commodore Chas. S. McCauley, for such duties as he may assign you in connection with the removal from that Navy Yard to a place of safety of the U.S. steam frigate *Merrimack.* You will afford every assistance to such officers as may be designated by the Navy Department to prepare the *Merrimack* for sea and to take charge of her when ready for movement.

Upon completion of this duty, or when your services are no

longer required by the officers referred to, you will report with the steamer *Brother Jonathan* to Flag Officer G. J. Pendergrast, Commander in Chief, Home Squadron, for duty as tender to his flagship, the U.S.S. *Cumberland*.

Very respectfully, yr. obdt. svt.,
S. F. DU PONT
Captain, U.S. Navy, Commandant

Actg. Master Caleb Pettengill, USN,
Commanding U.S. Steamer *Brother Jonathan*

The first paragraph of this order was virtually identical with the verbal orders under which Pettengill had sailed from Philadelphia. All the rest was new, although he had known that he was to go to the Norfolk Yard after delivering the recruits. He turned eagerly to the other paper. It was covered with Du Pont's own forceful handwriting. Headed by the word CONFIDENTIAL, triply underscored, it went on:

To Acting Master Pettengill:

Officers detailed by Dept. to remove *Merrimack* from Norfolk are Comdr. Jas. Alden and the Engineer in Chief of the Navy, Mr. B. F. Isherwood. You are required to render them every assistance, but should circumstances arise compelling you to act on your own responsibility, you will consider it your first duty to prevent govt. property and arms falling into hands of illdisposed or treasonable parties and to give such protection to loyal persons as may be in your power.

You will bear in mind that instructions given while the hope persists of keeping Virginia in the Union may not apply to conditions which might arise should this hope prove illusory.

You may show this confidential note to Comdr. Alden and Chf. Engr. Isherwood, and to any other officer *of whose full loyalty you are properly assured*, if in your judgment the public service so requires.

Yrs., etc., in much haste,
S. F. DU PONT, Captain

Plainly the Navy Department had little confidence in the commandant at Norfolk, or Pettengill wouldn't be told to "afford every assistance" to other officers detailed specially by the Department to carry out a duty which properly belonged entirely within the sphere of the commandant's responsibility. He wasn't very familiar with official forms, but it seemed unusual for an order to a mere acting master in command of a tugboat to include the words "the Hon. Sec'y of the Navy directs" unless they wanted to make clear to Commodore McCauley that he wasn't to interfere with whatever Alden and Isherwood might want Pettengill to do.

But Du Pont's private note was the real sockdolager. It implied that a situation might well arise in which Pettengill would find himself on his own, though his orders were to proceed to a navy yard at which, besides the commandant, there were regularly stationed probably a dozen or more officers senior in rank to an acting master. It practically said that he might find among these officers some whose loyalty he could not take for granted. It came very near to providing him with cover for acts which under normal circumstances would bring him before a court-martial for insubordination. Never, save in the direst emergency, would such reliance be placed on the judgment of a junior officer of barely two years' service. Or—

In Philadelphia—probably all through the North—the public was wildly excited. They had faced at last the grim reality of civil war. Once they had done that, they wanted action—successful and immediate action. They demanded miracles, and they would be savagely intolerant of mishap, especially in these early days before they had learned by bitter experience that in war mishaps are inevitable. The politicians would be nervous, too: if mishap occurred now, even a very junior goat might be a convenience to a harassed government. He didn't even have the protection that went with holding a commission; his whole bright bubble of acting rank could vanish at the first breath of official disapproval as though it had never existed.

But Du Pont had trusted him to act on his own responsibility if he had to! Du Pont had gambled on him, admittedly because he had no better choice, but he must prove to Du Pont that no mistake had been made in appointing a commanding officer for the U.S. steamer *Brother Jonathan*.

One thing was certain: Du Pont had written off Virginia as lost to the Union. The Secretary may have thought so too. The *Merrimack* was to be removed "to a place of safety"; therefore the Norfolk Navy Yard was no longer considered a place of safety. And urgent as Pettengill's mission seemed to be, he had been delayed in performing it for the purpose of delivering a mere fifty recruits to Fortress Monroe! They were worried about Monroe too.

No wonder his orders had been given him under seal, to be opened only after clearing the dock at the fort. A careless word, even an attitude or a tone of voice, might have conveyed to the garrison some hint of the uncertainties and anxieties which were besetting the leaders of the Navy. And Fortress Monroe was wholly dependent on the Navy for reinforcements and supplies.

Knuckles rapped sharply on the cabin door.

"We're coming up to Sewell's Point, sir!" warned Aycock.

Hastily Pettengill stuffed his orders back into the envelope, buttoned his jacket over it, set his cap at what he hoped would be considered a jaunty, carefree angle, and went through the door into the pilothouse.

Sewell's Point was close aboard on the port bow, distant perhaps a thousand yards. No smooth-bore fieldpiece could do anything at such a range. Pettengill doubted whether the Virginians would have any heavy coast-defense guns in their possession: nevertheless he searched the shore with his glasses for traces of freshly turned earth or any other sign indicating the construction of batteries. Nothing of the sort appeared. Pettengill had hardly expected it. Whoever was directing the military affairs of Virginia was playing a deep and cautious game—a game for far bigger stakes than the destruction of a tugboat.

The tug was chugging along steadily, the uninterrupted beat of her propeller attesting Canty's complete subjection to Pettengill. She was making perhaps six knots. The water was smooth, and his glasses showed him that the buoys which marked the ship channel leading into the Elizabeth River were still in place: flat-topped red can buoys to starboard, conical black nun buoys to port. Then he saw something else.

A little beyond Sewell's Point, where the channel came closest to the shore, there was a flurry of white water just at the shoreward edge of the fairway. The chart showed no shoal or other obstruction there so it might be one of the sunken barges of which Graham had warned him. There was another one, maybe three or four hundred yards beyond the first. But they didn't seem to obstruct the channel.

He directed his glasses over the open water ahead and to starboard. A dozen small sailing craft were in sight; a schooner was beating over from the direction of Newport News; dead ahead, coming down-channel directly toward the tug, was a white side-wheel steamer, her walking beam teetering away behind her high funnel. Pettengill gave her his careful attention. Her decks were crowded with people, women and children among them, and there was no sign of guns. One of the regular boats running from Norfolk to Hampton or Newport News, Pettengill guessed.

The tug was coming up to the sunken barges. They were just barely awash now, at low tide. They might be much harder to see at high water, might perhaps be some danger to a deep-draft vessel bearing a little too far inshore if her skipper didn't know they were there. But once located, they were no obstruction at all. Pettengill marked them carefully on his chart, taking bearings on the beacon at Sewell's Point and on the numbered channel buoys. If they were part of a secessionist scheme, this information might be helpful in bringing out the *Merrimack*, a huge first-rater of thirty-two hundred tons which certainly must draw 22 or 23 feet of water.

By the time he had finished, the steamer was close at hand. Gay with flags and the bright colors of women's clothing, she wore her house flag at the fore, a string of bunting between her masts and down her after-stay, and a big blue flag at her stern. Suddenly he realized that nowhere did she show the Stars and Stripes. That blue flag flew in the place of honor. It had a device in the center. Pettengill focused his glasses on it. It was a gold wreath enclosing a heroic female figure trampling on something. There seemed to be some kind of lettering under the female figure, but he couldn't make it out. It must be the Virginia state flag flying where the flag of the United States belonged!

The sight of the Stars and Stripes fluttering smartly from the tug's pole mast or perhaps the dull bronze gleam of the howitzer on the foredeck seemed to be creating some excitement among the steamer's passengers. They were crowding to the rail, pointing and waving. Then he saw that they weren't waving. They were shaking their fists. Every face was contorted with hate. Yesterday that flag had been their own. Now they hated it as the flag of an invader, because it was being carried into Virginia waters aboard an armed vessel.

Virginia no longer was a part of the United States. Pettengill was steaming into enemy waters.

"Take the helm, Aycock," he said, re-entering the pilothouse. "Jackson, load the howitzer with grape; six charges of grape and three of canister to be handy on deck."

"Beg pardon, sir," said Jackson, "but that's one o' them newfangled rifled howitzers we got."

Rifled guns were something of a novelty. The Ordnance Instructions dealt with them in a very sketchy fashion. But Pettengill knew you weren't supposed to use grape or canister in them because they injured the rifling.

"Right you are, Jackson," Pettengill said. "Bring up six rounds of shrapnel instead. And, Jackson, cut the fuze deep on the one you load into the gun so's to get a muzzle burst. See the cutting-tool's kept handy if we have to cut the others."

"Aye aye, sir," said Jackson, and went to carry out his orders.

He was interested in gunnery. A promised promotion to quarter gunner had weaned him away from the Front Street girls after only one night ashore. He had been second captain of Pettengill's pivot gun aboard the *Sheboygan*, and would have made quarter gunner that cruise if there had been a vacancy.

"Aycock," Pettengill said, "call the best one of those receiving-ship farmers to the helm. I'll keep an eye on him for the time being. Then wash down the deck and pipe to breakfast. Tell Jackson I'd like all the muskets and pistols in the rack loaded before he secures the magazine. See that each man knows where his weapons are. After breakfast, all hands will be on deck ready to repel boarders. But I want no nonsense. Pass the word that the first man who answers back anything that's sung out from a passing boat will spend thirty days in double irons."

"Aye aye, sir," said Aycock calmly. After thirty years in the Navy, Aycock just obeyed orders, the responsibility was his captain's.

The responsibility of invading a hostile harbor with one small steam tug, one 12-pounder howitzer, and twelve men, only two of whom had seen any previous naval service except a few days on the guardo, and not counting the civilians in the engine room as fighting assets, was Pettengill's.

But it was only the Southern firebrands that worried him. He didn't think he would be attacked by any organized force. Even if the ordinance of secession had been passed yesterday, the Virginia leaders would need time to prepare for action: time to mobilize their militia, time to move it to positions where it could strike hard and suddenly against worthwhile objectives of strategic value, such as Fortress Monroe and the Norfolk Navy Yard.

Pendleton Banks had once told Pettengill that he possessed "military imagination." He hoped Banks was right.

The *Brother Jonathan* plowed on with no change in the steady beat of her propeller. Craney Island went by to starboard, then Lambert's Point to port. Now Pettengill could see the pillared façade of the naval hospital, and on the other bank, the roofs and spires of Norfolk.

The blue Virginia flag was everywhere. There was no sign of the Stars and Stripes, except on the staff above the portico of the naval hospital. The tugboat rounded the point on which the hospital stood, and ran up the harbor toward the channel of the Elizabeth River leading past Portsmouth to Gosport and the Navy Yard, with the crowded water front of Norfolk to port. There was plenty of water traffic here: small craft of all sorts, steam ferryboats plying between Norfolk and Portsmouth, ships of various sizes at anchor. From many of them the tug was greeted with yells and menacing gestures.

Aycock came into the pilothouse.

"There's the Yard, sir," he announced happily. "See them two big ship-houses? An' there's the old *Pennsylvania*, moored in the stream. She's the guardo here; they say she's hard an' fast on a shoal o' coffee grounds. Been right at those moorin's since way afore the Mexican war."

"What's the ship lying just astern of the *Pennsylvania*, Aycock?"

"Looks like a big sloop-o'-war, sir, jackass frigates they call 'em. *Cumberland*, I'd guess."

Just then Pettengill's eye was caught by a small white sailboat that was darting cross-channel, lying well over, lugsail filled by the breeze. Obviously whoever was at the tiller was going to try to cross the tug's bow. And obviously wasn't going to make it.

Pettengill yanked at the whistle cord. Short shrill blasts of warning split the air. The sailboat held her course.

"Starb'd! Hard over!" roared Pettengill, grabbing for the bellpull. The stop-bell down in the engine room rang, and Jackson, who was back at the wheel, spun it furiously. Pettengill snatched at a window-frame to keep from being thrown off his feet. The short-bodied propeller tug could turn on a dime. He clawed his way up the steep incline of the tilted deck to the hooked-back door. The little sailboat was zipping past, not ten feet away, serenely holding her course.

Two men were aboard her; one sat on the gunwale, well forward, and stared stolidly at the tug. The other was at the tiller. Pettengill was about to tell them in sailor's language a sailor's opinion of their boatmanship when he realized that the person at the tiller was a woman. Her honey-blond hair was blowing about her piquant face, and one slender bare arm was lifted toward Pettengill as though warning him to be more careful.

High and clear her words came across the widening strip of water: "Tear down that Yankee rag!"

She wasn't pointing at him, but at the colors fluttering above his head.

Pettengill lifted his cap politely. She pursed her lips and spat in his direction.

"Get back on your course, Jackson. Aycock, ring slow ahead."

Two prompt Aye aye, sirs did not erase Pettengill's impression that both Aycock and Jackson had just barely managed to wipe broad grins off their weather-beaten faces as Pettengill turned around.

He went out to the rail to get a better look at the shipping off the Yard. Sweeping his glasses casually over the Portsmouth water front, he saw the sailboat just going alongside a black two-masted schooner moored to one of the docks. Pettengill could read the name under the schooner's stern—*Sea Sprite*. Somebody was giving the girl a hand up the side. On the dock a gang of men was loading fresh-cut yellow pine timber aboard the schooner. She was as neat as a pin; the sun winked on polished brightwork; her paint was new, her rigging taut as a man-o'-war's. She was no lumber boat.

The huge bulk of the old line-of-battleship *Pennsylvania* was only a quarter of a mile ahead now, her three stumpy masts sticking up through the wooden roof that covered her main deck. Her topmasts had been sent down long ago; she was in commission only as a receiving ship. Beyond her towered the spars and rigging of the *Cumberland*, with Flag Officer Pendergrast's square blue flag fluttering from her mizzentruck and the ensign at her gaff.

Pettengill's attention shifted to another ship, one even bigger than the *Cumberland*. She lay alongside the dock near the two ungainly wooden ship-houses. She was full-rigged, too, but she had something the *Cumberland* didn't—steam. There was a tall funnel between her fore- and mainmasts. Smoke dribbled from it to mix with white vapor from an exhaust pipe. Pettengill had never seen the *Merrimack* before, but he had seen two of her sister frigates, *Colorado* and *Wabash*, and he knew her instantly. She was one of the most powerful men-o'-war afloat: only now, poor thing, she looked neglected. Her paint was peeling, not a sail was bent, her twin rows of gun ports were closed tight; she wore neither ensign nor commission pennant, which meant she wasn't formally in commission, though she had steam up. Astern of her, there was a landing place with stone steps, above which towered a huge set of shears.

"We'll go alongside that landing, Aycock," said Pettengill. "I don't see a soul ashore. We'll have to handle our own lines, I suppose."

"Fair gives me the creeps," muttered Aycock.

The great Navy Yard seemed utterly deserted. Not even a workman was in sight. No one appeared as Pettengill laid the *Brother Jonathan* alongside the sea wall and made her fast to the stone bollards. Having already had breakfast, he went into his cabin to shave and put on his new frock coat. He made sure his orders were placed in the envelope so that on reporting for duty he could pull them out without pulling out Du Pont's confidential note at the same time. He buttoned his coat over the envelope and went back to the pilothouse.

"Take charge, Aycock. Nobody goes ashore."

"Aye aye, sir."

Pettengill jumped to the landing and trotted up the stone steps. To right and left towered the ungainly ship-houses in which new ships were built directly on the launching-ways. No sound of hammering and sawing came from them now. The space between was occupied by the lofty shears: several guns lay near the sea wall, just beyond the landing. Two of them were fairly new short 32-pounders; the others were older and heavier. The shears could be used for swaying guns in and out of ships alongside the stone dock.

He was oppressed by the deserted silence of the place. The steam puffing from the *Merrimack*'s exhaust was the only sign of activity in the biggest and most valuable Navy Yard on the Atlantic coast.

Brisk steps crunched on the gravel along the sea wall. Around the corner of the nearer of the two ship-houses came a young officer, dark-haired, very slender and spruce in frock coat and gold-banded cap. He wore no sleeve stripes, and his shoulder straps were empty, like Pettengill's.

"Morning!" said Pettengill. "Could you tell me where I'll find the commandant's office?"

The young man's eyes flicked over Pettengill haughtily, shifted to the tug, came back to Pettengill.

"Might I ask where you've come from?" he inquired.

"Philadelphia," Pettengill said. He didn't like the other's manner and saw no reason to explain himself further. But he still tried to be polite. "My name's Pettengill," he went on. "Acting master, commanding tug *Brother Jonathan*." He held out his hand.

"We don't need any Philadelphia tugs here!" the other snapped, putting his hands ostentatiously behind his back. He had pronounced the word "heah."

"Mister," grated Pettengill, "I'm reporting to the commandant and not to you. I'll thank you to direct me to his office."

"It'll do you no good," said the young man angrily. "He'll never let you tow out the *Merrimack!* You and the rest of the Yankees that've come down here where you've no business—"

"My business as an officer of the Navy is where my orders send me. And it's no business of yours."

The blood drained from the other's face. His eyes blazed, his fists clenched. He took a step toward Pettengill.

"I'll make it my business!" he screamed. "We'll all make it our business—to get every damned sniveling Yankee sailor and soldier out of Virginia. This time next week, by God, there won't be one—"

"Mister Banks! That will do!"

The voice was crisp with authority. A tall handsome officer with the single stripe of a lieutenant on his sleeve, and a mouth firm-set with anger under his neatly trimmed brown beard, strode toward them.

Pettengill lifted his cap.

"Good morning, sir," he said. "Acting Master Pettengill, from Philadelphia, with orders to report to Commodore McCauley."

The lieutenant extended his hand.

"Happy to know you, Mr. Pettengill," he said courteously. "My name's Spotswood. I'll be glad to show you the commandant's office."

"Mr. Spotswood," the young officer began.

"Report to me in ten minutes, Mr. Banks," interrupted Spotswood. "That'll be all from you just now."

"Banks?" repeated Pettengill. "Excuse me, sir, but this young gentleman wouldn't be Passed Midshipman—I mean Master—Farnifold Banks, would he?"

"Farnifold Banks is my name," the young officer muttered sullenly.

"Would you by any chance have a brother in the Navy? Lieutenant Pendleton Banks?"

"Yes, if that's any affair of yours!"

"Not especially," Pettengill said. "Except that Lieutenant Banks was my executive officer in the *Sheboygan*, on the African station, from which I've just returned, and he asked me to bring you a letter. The mails being rather uncertain in these difficult times, I thought it better to fetch it along when I was ordered here."

He took two letters from the side pocket of his jacket, both inscribed in Pendleton Banks' precise handwriting. He handed Farnifold Banks the one addressed to him and put the other back.

"Thanks," muttered young Banks ungraciously.

"A pleasure," murmured Pettengill, and half-turned toward Spotswood. "At your service, sir?" he said on a slightly rising inflection.

"Oh—ah—yes, of course." Spotswood had been thinking hard about something. "This way, Mr. Pettengill, if you please."

He steered Pettengill past the shears and between the ship-houses, leaving Banks standing there turning his letter over in his hands as though not quite willing to open it.

"I hope you'll overlook young Banks' shocking discourtesy, Mr. Pettengill," Spotswood said. "Everyone in Norfolk and Portsmouth has been in a terrible state of excitement for the past three days, since word came of Mr. Lincoln's call for troops. Banks is a Portsmouth lad, as of course you know, having served with his brother Pendleton. It's natural for a young man to be influenced by the attitude of family and friends."

"Natural indeed, sir," said Pettengill. "I don't suppose his uniform makes him too popular just at the moment, what with the State convention voting for secession only yesterday."

"Quite so," Spotswood agreed. Then he added, a little too carelessly, "That is, if the rumors to that effect have any truth in them."

Pettengill tried to keep his face quite expressionless; Spotswood was looking at him sharply, but when he spoke again, all he said was, "We turn to the right here, it's only a step farther."

They had reached the end of the ship-house. Instinctively Pettengill turned his head for a last look at his little steamer.

Master Farnifold Banks was standing at the edge of the sea wall listening attentively to a fat man who had climbed on top of the tug's pilothouse. Whatever Canty was saying to young Banks was being said with gestures. The corner of the ship-house shut off the view, and Spotswood was saying:

"There's the commandant's office, Mr. Pettengill, that two-story brick building inside the picket fence, just beyond the flagstaff."

There was no Marine orderly at the commandant's door, no one in the hall inside, no aide or clerk in the anteroom, just empty desks. It was a relief to hear a human voice, rather high-pitched and harshly vigorous, which came from a partly open door marked COMMANDANT —PRIVATE. Pettengill could hear the words very plainly:

". . . call your attention, Commodore, to the peremptory nature of the Secretary's orders, that the *Merrimack* be removed from this Yard with the utmost dispatch. She has steam up, her engines are turning over, the engine-room crew is aboard."

Spotswood was listening too. He pushed past Pettengill, strode across the anteroom and through the half-open door without bothering to knock or ask permission to enter. Nothing could have been more significant of the total collapse of discipline in the Norfolk Navy Yard.

Pettengill followed him into the spacious room lighted on two sides by high windows. He had never seen so many old men in uniform in his life. The place was full of graybeards. Behind a big desk in the middle of the room sat the patriarch of them all, a bald-headed old gentleman with a half circle of pure-white whiskers framing a very red face, out of which pale watery eyes blinked uncertainly. He glanced around the room as though pleading for someone to tell him what to do.

The harsh voice hammered at him, "All that's needed, Commodore, is for you to endorse Commander Alden's orders and give him the word to cast loose and go!"

The speaker was a big burly man in civilian clothes who stood in front of the commodore's desk. He was no doddering relic; his smooth-shaven face might have been that of a man little older than Pettengill, except for the lines of authority deep-graven from nose to mouth-corners.

Spotswood was whispering urgently to a group of three elderly officers who stood to the Commodore's right. They all wore the double stripes of commanders. One of them, whose side whiskers and pouched eyes gave him the look of an unhappy Saint Bernard, glanced over at Pettengill.

"I haven't decided," the commodore was mumbling. "I'll let you know later, Mr. Isherwood. I don't think it's safe to take her out. The channel's blocked. Isn't that true, Commander Tucker? The channel's blocked, isn't it?"

"Yes, sir," said the Saint Bernard promptly. "I'm informed that unknown parties have sunk some barges in it."

"You hear that, Mr. Isherwood?" The Commodore's rheumy eyes shifted back to the big man in civilian clothes. On the farther side of his desk another group of grizzled officers, two captains and a commander, with a sandy-haired lieutenant hovering in the background, stirred uneasily. The commander spoke up:

"Lieutenant Murray here reconnoitered the channel clear out to Sewell's Point just before daybreak, sir. He tells me I'll have no trouble getting *Merrimack* past the obstructions."

"That's not my information, Alden," Tucker retorted.

"Commodore McCauley may have the fullest confidence in any report made by Lieutenant Murray," rasped an eagle-beaked captain.

"With great respect, Flag Officer Pendergrast," said Tucker, "I could not recommend that the Commodore rely on observations made under conditions of predawn visibility."

He looked hard at the Commodore, who blinked and said:

"No, no, of course not."

Over the top of the Commodore's bowed head, the officers on either side of his desk eyed each other in uneasy and reluctant hostility. For years they had worn the same uniform, served in the same ships, cursed the same stewards at the same wardroom tables, gone ashore together in search of wine and women in the same far-flung foreign ports. It was not easy for any one of them to think of any of the others as an enemy.

Whatever the convention at Richmond might have done, war had not yet come to Virginia. The first shot had not been fired, the first blood had not yet soaked the soil of the Old Dominion. There was still a chance that these things might never happen. If they did, there was not a man in that room who had not already made his choice. But every one of the older officers in his heart clung to that last expiring hope, though there was not one of them who did not at the same time try furtively in advance to secure advantage for his side should hope prove futile. They tiptoed toward the brink of war, none willing to assume the burden of responsibility for an act that might precipitate disaster while disaster might—just barely might—yet be avoided.

Isherwood alone saw his duty clear. The engineer in chief was determined to save the *Merrimack*, come what might. But he was an engineer, not a line officer. He dared not go too far in urging his views upon the others lest he prejudice his cause not only with his opponents but his friends.

Stalemate! Pettengill read it in their faces: in the faintly satisfied expressions of the Virginians, the troubled distress of the Northerners, the black anger of Isherwood. Anger flared in Pettengill too. It was a trick, a dirty sham. Those barges had been placed there to create an illusion in the mind of old Commodore McCauley.

"The channel's *not* obstructed!"

Every eye in the room turned instantly on Pettengill. He had done it again! Appalled at having piped up uninvited in the midst of such company, Pettengill plunged recklessly ahead, speaking directly to the Commodore. "Lieutenant Murray's report is entirely correct, sir. I came up-channel just an hour ago in full daylight. I noted the sunken barges and marked their position on my chart, which I'll be happy to hand over to Commander Alden. The barges are just at the edge of the fairway, not in the main channel. Commander Alden can get the *Merrimack* past them without the least difficulty once he knows where they are."

There was a moment of astounded silence, then a half-dozen officers started talking all at once. Through the babble cut the vigorous cry of Engineer in Chief Isherwood:

"Then, by God, now's the time to take *Merrimack* to sea before any more obstructions can be placed in that channel!"

The Commodore was staring at Pettengill.

"Who are you, young man?" he demanded.

Pettengill reported himself with due formality, presented his orders. The Commodore set his spectacles on his nose, read the orders, pushed them back across the desk to Pettengill.

His head came up, and in his watery eyes for a moment glittered the light of decision.

"You may take the *Merrimack* out, Commander Alden," he said in a voice that for the first time held the zing of the quarter-deck. "And by God! if you can't get her through the channel, burn her!"

Amid the excited buzz that followed, Pettengill heard Spotswood's voice, clipped and angry:

"I warned you, Tucker! That man Pettengill's dangerous."

Pettengill glowed with pride. He braced his shoulders as he followed Alden and Isherwood out into the April sunshine. He paid no attention to Farnifold Banks, who went hurrying past him into the anteroom, calling Spotswood's name in an urgent tone.

Chapter Five

The *Merrimack* was ready. Down in her engine room, steam hissed in the two six-foot cylinders as their double piston rods beat slowly back and forth. The crankshaft was not yet connected to the propeller shaft; that would be done as soon as the order came—"Stand by to get under way." The great 17-foot two-bladed propeller, which could be hoisted up under the ship's stern to avoid "drag" when the *Merrimack* was using sail alone, had been lowered into the water. Fires were spread: the safety valves of all four boilers were sputtering. The assistant engineers, firemen, and coal heavers moved quietly about their duties under the chilly eye of Chief Engineer Danby.

On deck, Lieutenant Murray with thirty seamen borrowed from the *Cumberland* had cast off the chain cables that bound the *Merrimack* to the dock, singled the remaining lines, and waited only for the word to cast them off too. Pettengill had the *Brother Jonathan* alongside, ready to help "wind" the big ship and get her headed down-channel.

All that was lacking was one final scratch of the Commodore's pen on Alden's orders, and Alden had gone ashore with Isherwood to get that now. They should be back in five minutes.

Pettengill, waiting at the door of the tug's pilothouse, was neither excited nor even mildly impatient. He had helped Murray in the final preparations; he had seen the *Merrimack*'s engines turning over. Now he was oppressed by a sense of anticlimax.

They were going to save the *Merrimack*. That was what he was here for. But he knew, too, that it wasn't just the *Merrimack* that had been in Captain Du Pont's mind as he scribbled those anxious words about preventing "govt. property and arms falling into the hands of ill-disposed or treasonable parties." *Merrimack* was government property, of course. Valuable property, considering the shortage of steam warships available for duty on the Atlantic seaboard right now. But she was just one big steam frigate, underpowered for her tonnage, too slow to chase, and drawing too much water to enter most southern harbors or keep a close inshore blockading station. Her value to the South as a military prize was nothing to the Navy Yard itself—the only fully equipped Navy Yard in all the Southern states—where more effective vessels could be built; or to the thousand-odd cannon piled up in the Yard and across the river at St. Helena. And the whole Navy Yard and all its contents would not be as valuable to the South as Fortress Monroe, the big fort with its scanty garrison. The Virginians weren't fools. Once they had Monroe they could take the Navy Yard at their leisure, secure from any immediate interference. . . .

"Mr. Pettengill!" It was Lieutenant Murray, hailing from the *Merrimack*'s poop rail. "Mr. Pettengill! Come aboard—quick! There's hell to pay!"

Pettengill grabbed his revolver belt, buckling it on as he ran aft. He leaped to the iron rungs of the frigate's side ladder, swarmed up and over the horse block to the deck, to read disaster on the stern faces of Alden and Isherwood, standing with Chief Engineer Danby in the starboard gangway.

"The Commodore's changed his mind," Isherwood told him. "He won't sign the order. Says he's decided to keep *Merrimack* here to help defend the Yard."

"With not a gun on board?" cried Pettengill. He knew that Alden had begged for the two new 32-pounders that lay so handy on the dock; Tucker, as ordnance officer of the Yard, had refused, saying they were "already requisitioned."

"No matter for that now," Alden said gloomily. "Robb and Tucker and Spotswood have been at the Commodore ever since we left. They've got him convinced that if he tries to move the ship, the local militia companies will attack the Navy Yard."

"Then why doesn't he have *Cumberland* drop down the river, and send word to the town authorities that he'll lay Norfolk and Portsmouth in ruins at the first sign of armed rebellion?" roared Isherwood. "Her nine-inch Dahlgrens could tear those towns apart."

"*Cumberland*'s under Flag Officer Pendergrast's orders, not the Commodore's," Alden answered. "Suppose the Commodore wanted to do anything like that—which I'm sure he doesn't—Pendergrast would never take such a responsibility on himself."

"Take this ship out anyway, Alden!" cried Isherwood. "Who's to stop you? Cut the lines and go! The Secretary'll back you up, my word on it."

Lieutenant Murray, running down the poop ladder, looked eagerly at Alden. But Alden plucked at his chin and slowly shook his head.

"No," he said. "My orders are to act under the Commodore's direction. I can't go beyond them, much as I'd like to. I'm going to catch the Baltimore boat this afternoon, go straight to Washington, and report to the Department. They'll have to decide if stronger measures are needed. You'd better come too, Isherwood."

"I may join you on the boat," said Isherwood in a dull voice.

Alden nodded and went briskly down the gangplank.

"I'd like to take her out for you, Mr. Isherwood," said Murray, "but I'd have to get the flag officer's permission first. Which I doubt would be granted. After all I'm first lieutenant of the *Cumberland* and that's where my duty lies."

"I'll try it if you like, sir," offered Pettengill. "I think I can handle her, anyway as far as Fortress Monroe. My orders are to render you every assistance."

"You're a good lad," Isherwood said. "But it won't do. You'd be acting under orders directing you to assist me: you'd be justified, but the responsibility for invoking your help would be mine. The old salts would never forgive me, an engineer officer, specifically barred from exercising military command, for taking a ship out of a navy yard without the sacred blessing of the commandant's authority, indeed in direct defiance of his instructions. Alden might have done it if he'd dared: he's a line officer, and his orders covered him. But for an engineer to do such a thing—to assume command of a vessel of the Navy—could churn up such bad blood between the line and the Engineer Corps, for which I'm responsible, that it could easily mean the ruination of the steam navy that's going to win this war. I've got to build that navy. One ship's not worth such a risk."

Pettengill nodded.

"You're right, sir," he agreed.

Feet clattered up the gangplank.

"Here comes trouble," muttered Murray. "Spotswood and that young spark of a Banks."

Spotswood, sword at side, strode straight across the *Merrimack*'s littered deck to Pettengill.

"Mr. Pettengill," he announced, "you're under arrest. By order of Commodore McCauley."

"What's the charge, sir?" demanded Pettengill.

"Maltreatment of a civilian employee subject to your orders," retorted Spotswood. "You'll have it all in writing by tomorrow. Meanwhile I'll thank you to deliver me your side arms. You're to be confined to quarters on board the *Pennsylvania* for the present. Mr. Banks will conduct you."

That damned Canty! But Pettengill remembered something else.

"Do I understand, Mr. Isherwood," he asked, "that you have no further need for my services or those of the tug *Brother Jonathan?*"

"That's correct."

"Then, Mr. Spotswood," Pettengill announced, "I'm no longer subject to the Commodore's powers of arrest, because I hold written orders, by direction of the Secretary of the Navy, to report to Flag Officer Pendergrast for duty in the Home Squadron the moment Mr. Isherwood no longer needs me or my tug."

"May I see those orders, Mr. Pettengill?" Spotswood asked.

"No need for that, sir," urged Banks. "He hasn't officially reported to the flag officer yet."

"Quite so," Spotswood agreed. "So your arrest stands—"

Murray cleared his throat. Looking at a spot on the mainmast about five feet above Spotswood's head, he remarked:

"I've been acting as fleet captain to the flag officer in addition to my other duties."

To report to the fleet captain, or chief of staff, was of course exactly the same as reporting to the flag officer in person.

Instantly Pettengill raised his cap.

"Sir," he said, "I report with the tug *Brother Jonathan* under my command for duty as tender to the flagship *Cumberland*. My orders, sir."

He whipped them out and passed them to Murray, who glanced at them, nodded, and smiled at Spotswood.

"Sorry, Spotswood," he said, "but I'm afraid that any charges the Commodore may have been—ah—induced to prefer against Mr. Pettengill will have to be sent to Flag Officer Pendergrast for such action as he may think proper."

"That's wholly irregular, Murray, and you know it!" Spotswood cried. "No engineer can relieve a line officer of one duty to permit him to report for another. Once admit that, and you have engineers exercising command, which is forbidden by law and by regulation. No disrespect, Mr. Isherwood."

"You gentlemen of the South," Isherwood rasped, "have nothing but disrespect for engineers. You've despised the mechanical arts and sciences as beneath your notice. But I tell you now, it is by those arts and sciences that your cause will be brought to ruin."

"That's as may be," Spotswood said coldly. "It does not affect the matter I'm discussing with Mr. Murray."

"There's no discussion," snapped Murray. "I don't know why you're so anxious to have Mr. Pettengill out of circulation, Spotswood, but in my view he's now an officer of the Home Squadron and any disciplinary action concerning him will have to be taken through the flag officer."

"Very well," said Spotswood. "We'll see what the Commodore thinks of this defiance of his orders. Come along, Mr. Banks."

Banks boiled over into furious speech:

"I'm warning you, Pettengill! If I catch you outside this Navy Yard I'll teach you to keep your filthy Yankee tongue off decent women!"

He marched down the gangplank behind Spotswood.

"Gal trouble, eh?" said Murray, one sandy eyebrow lifted.

"No, sir!" cried Pettengill earnestly. "I never saw young Banks before in my life till this morning. I was shipmates with his brother in the African Squadron, but that's nothing to do with him. I just don't know what he's talking about."

"The young fool has some silly bat in his belfry, a female bat, apparently," Murray remarked. "Well, gentlemen, I fear there's no more to be done here. I'd better be getting my men back to the *Cumberland*. You run 'em over in your tug, Pettengill, and you can tie her up alongside the flagship for the present, where you'll be handy if the Old Man wants you for anything. He's been begging Washington for a steam tender, so he'll probably be delighted to see you. If you're going to the Baltimore boat, Mr. Isherwood, may I offer you our gig to deliver you safely to the wharf?"

Isherwood hesitated, loath to say the final words that would acknowledge defeat.

Pettengill burned with sudden impatience. He had just realized that Farnifold Banks with his quick tongue might be a source of information about the enemy and that he had in his pocket the potential means of exploiting this possibility.

"You're very kind, Mr. Murray," Isherwood was saying. "I suppose I might as well accept your offer. As you say, there's nothing more to be done here. Not your fault—you've done all you could. So have you, Mr. Pettengill. I'll see the Secretary's so informed." He looked up at the steam still puffing from the exhaust pipe alongside *Mer-*

rimack's great funnel. "Finished with the engines, Danby," he growled. "Shut her down and draw the fires."

They stood on the deck of the fated *Merrimack,* listening to the slowing beat of her engines, until at last the sound faded into silence.

Chapter Six

"Dis de street, suh," said the ancient Negro on the driver's box of the ancient carriage. He guided the creaking vehicle around a corner. It was too dark for Pettengill to see anything at all, and the afternoon spent, on Murray's orders, at the coal dock, replenishing the tug's bunkers, had dampened his earlier excitement. There was no reason to believe that there might be a connection between Farnifold Banks and Miss Virgilia Seabright, to whom Pendleton Banks' letter was addressed.

Standing on the *Merrimack*'s deck his idea had seemed a real inspiration. Now, in this dark quiet street, it began to seem silly, and perhaps treacherous to Pendleton Banks, for Pettengill didn't really know how Pendleton Banks felt about the South and secession. However, it was Pettengill's duty to seek all the information of military value that he could get. Murray hadn't wanted him to go ashore in uniform. "You haven't sensed the temper of these people as I have this past week, Pettengill," he had warned. Pettengill had taken precautions for his personal safety, there was a slight bulge in the breast pocket of his frock coat. And there *was* trouble in the Portsmouth air. It wasn't evident here in the silent residential section, but over by the water front the sidewalks had been crowded; there were lights in most of the windows and blue State flags everywhere; Pettengill had seen a cheering crowd following a militia company in the middle of one street, and on the next corner a man had been making a speech to another crowd from a second-story window: "Shall we send our brave lads to coerce our sister States? Never! Up, Virginians, and strike a blow for freedom!" Rebellion was lifting its head. Behind the clamor, warlike plans were surely in the making, warlike acts might be no more than hours away.

That Spotswood and Banks, as well as the other Southern officers at the Yard, knew of those plans, Pettengill was convinced. But spying on Pendleton Banks' brother, using a letter written by Pendleton

Banks to a lady as the means of doing so, when he wasn't sure Pendleton Banks would stand by the Union, was an act of treachery, like firing on an enemy under a flag of truce.

"Whoa-a-a, Pompey," wheezed the driver. "Heah we are, suh. Dis yere de Seabright house."

"Wait for me, I won't be long," Pettengill said. The springs of the rattletrap carriage groaned under his weight as he jumped out.

Gaslight spilled between half-drawn curtains across a narrow front yard. Pettengill strode briskly along the path and mounted wooden steps to the veranda. Vines brushed his cap; the odor of honeysuckle was in his nostrils. The light gleamed on a polished brass knocker. Pettengill rapped twice, more and more embarrassed and oppressed by an uneasy conscience.

He heard quick, light footfalls approaching. He hastily wiped sweat from his face. The door swung open, to reveal a colored maid in a black dress.

"Good evenin', suh. Come right in," she invited.

"Is Miss Virgilia Seabright at home?"

"Yassuh, yassuh, Miss Virgie she's home eve'y evenin' these days. Come right in the pahlah and make yo'se'f comf'table. Who'll I tell Miss Virgie is callin', suh?"

As she spoke, she was ushering Pettengill through a door to the right of the narrow hallway into the room from which the gaslight shone. From a painting on the opposite wall, fierce eyes glared at him above a long black beard; on the shoulders were epaulettes of a colonel of artillery.

Pettengill mumbled his name. The maid gave him a glance bright with curiosity and took herself off. He laid his cap on a marble-topped table and sat down gingerly in a patent rocker, but finding himself directly under the disapproving gaze of the black-bearded colonel, he shifted to the horsehair sofa underneath the portrait. He could hear the maid running up a flight of stairs, calling out, "Miss Virgie! Miss Virgie! There's a Navy ge'mman in the pahlah!"

There was a confused murmuring of female voices, then steps coming down the stairs and along the hall.

"I'm Miss Seabright," said a cool voice from the doorway. "Mr.— Mr.— I don't think Bella quite caught your name."

Pettengill was on his feet, aware that his miserable face was turning bright pink. The simple cotton dress the girl was wearing was not extended fashionably on hoops. Eyes as gray as Pettengill's own looked at him in grave inquiry from beneath a coronel of ash-blond braids. She was a tall girl, taller even than Emma Harrifield, but much younger.

"My name's Pettengill," he said. "Caleb Pettengill. I'm just back from the African Station." He started to fumble in his pocket. "Lieutenant Pendleton Banks asked me to bring you a letter." He held the letter out, sadly crumpled. Her eager hand snatched at it.

"Thank you, Mr. Pettengill. Thank you so much," she breathed, speaking hardly above a whisper. "But I'm keeping you standing. Do sit down, please do, and forgive me. I'm not quite myself."

He sat down again in the patent rocker. The colonel regarded him with steely distaste.

"You left Mr. Banks well, I hope, Mr. Pettengill?"

"Yes, ma'am. He was in fine health when I left the old *Sheboygan* about six weeks ago. March fifth."

"And—and happy, Mr. Pettengill?"

"Well, ma'am, I guess he was about as happy as anybody can be cooped up in a little ship off the west coast of Africa. But of course Mr. Banks wouldn't complain, like the rest of us did. Not ever. As I guess you know, ma'am."

"Yes," she said. "I know. Indeed, I know. Mr. Pettengill, will you think me very rude if I read my letter now?"

"Of course not." Pettengill was on his feet again, but so was she, one hand fluttering at him pleadingly; her gray eyes were pleading too.

"No—please! Don't go. Just let me read my letter. Then I have so much to ask you. Please, Mr. Pettengill?" She was not to be denied. Pettengill dropped back into his patent rocker.

Paper ripped under eager fingers. Pettengill gave the colonel stare for stare.

"Oh!" There was heartbreak in her cry.

Pettengill forgot the colonel. He was suddenly four thousand miles away on the sun-drenched quarter-deck of the *Sheboygan,* his boat waiting at the ladder. He was listening to the quiet voice of Pendleton Banks. "This letter, Pettengill—I—I'm afraid it may not be answered. So if you'd write me, when you have time, to let me know how it was received—"

"Mr. Pettengill."

"Yes, ma'am."

"Do you know—did Mr. Banks talk to you about—what he writes in this letter to me?"

"No, ma'am."

Feet scampered up the steps and across the porch, the front door slammed back against the wall, a girl's voice cried, "Virgie! Virgie!" A small female in white and green whirled into the room, honey-blond hair flying in every direction about her head. "Virgie, I can't believe it, but Farny Banks had it in a letter this very morning. Pendleton Banks has turned Yankee! Who'd ever've thought that Pendleton Banks would turn out to be a dirty Yankee-loving abolitionist traitor! Why, I could spit on him! Oh, Virgie! I didn't know you had company."

Pettengill was on his feet again, moved by the sight of Virgilia Seabright's stricken face. Pettengill on his feet was not readily overlooked. He glared at the small honey-blond intruder. Wide mouth, snub nose, bright brown eyes—it was the girl he had come so near sinking that morning, the girl who had invited him to "Tear down that Yankee rag."

"Young woman," snarled Pettengill, "I don't know who you are, but you have the finer feelings of a mud turtle."

She went white with rage.

Virgilia Seabright said:

"Mr. Pettengill, allow me to present you to my younger sister, Miss Terentia Seabright."

"Pettengill? Did you say Pettengill, Virgie?" The brown eyes appeared to be giving off brown sparks. "Mister Pettengill is an authority on finer feelings, Virgie. Mister Pettengill boasted only this morning in front of the whole Yankee Army that the first time he met me he'd take me for a walk in the moonlight and show me the facts of life! Didn't you, Mr. Pettengill?"

"So you're Terry."

"Terry the Terror," she announced complacently. "That's what some folks call me."

"No wonder," snapped Pettengill.

Of course Canty had told Farnifold Banks. Canty had probably told him everything else that Pettengill had said to Graham at Fortress Monroe.

But Pendleton Banks was standing by the Union.

Virgilia Seabright was saying:

"Terry dear—please—try to understand."

"Oh, Virgie!" Terry's arm was around her sister's waist. "I *am* sorry, dear. I didn't mean all I said. Only it's so awful for you! How could he shame you so? Why—"

"Terry!"

"But Virgie! To turn on his own State! To fight against the South! Maybe come right here to Portsmouth and blow us all up, like they say the Yankees are going to do tomorrow! How can you ever live down having *known* such a creature?"

"What do you think I care for the South, or this war you're so excited about?" cried Virgilia. "All I know is that stupid and wicked men are starting a war in which Americans are going to kill each other—a criminal war—a war that's breaking the heart of the man I love. I hate the very thought of such a war! I hate every uniform, every gun, every brass button— Forgive me, Mr. Pettengill. You have been kind." She lifted her chin, looked Pettengill straight in the eyes. "If you see Lieutenant Banks again, Mr. Pettengill, will you do me one more kindness? Tell him that I love him, and that when he can send for me I shall go to him at once."

Pettengill bowed.

"I shall be honored to deliver your message, Miss Seabright," he said.

"Virgie!" Terry shrieked. "How can you!"

"If you'll excuse me now, Mr. Pettengill?" Virgie said and went out through the door into the hall, closing it behind her.

"You see what you've done?" Terry stormed at Pettengill. "You and your foul tongue—and your fouler letters."

"I thought this morning," said Pettengill, "that I'd never seen a female brat who was more in need of a damned good spanking. Now I'm sure of it."

He took a step toward her.

"You wouldn't dare," gasped Terry.

Once more feet clattered up the steps, across the porch, into the hall.

"Terry! Terry darling!" Farnifold Banks' voice—he ran past the closed door along the hall toward the stairs. "Come down quick, Terry! Wonderful news! General Taliaferro and Lieutenant Catesby Jones are here from Richmond. We've all resigned and we'll be commissioned in the Virginia Navy this very night! The guns have gone down to the *Sea Sprite* and come sun-up I'll—"

Terry screamed.

"Terry!" shouted young Banks. "Terry!" He came charging back through the hall, flung open the door into the parlor—stopped short. Terry stood there, arms akimbo, looking at him with flashing scorn.

"Terry! You screamed! What—" He glared at Pettengill.

"I had to do something to keep you from spilling everything you know out of your silly mouth in front of a Yankee officer!"

"How dare you come to this house, you Yankee scum?" Farnifold Banks shouted.

"At least I'm not here in a uniform I no longer have the right to wear," Pettengill observed. "But since I've outstayed my welcome, I'll withdraw."

"Farny! Don't let him go! Not after what he's heard! Haven't you got a gun?"

"Indeed I have. Stand right where you are, Pettengill." He reached for his hip pocket.

Pettengill's right hand moved fast. Then Banks was staring with unbelieving eyes into the twin muzzles of the little French double-barreled pistol which Pettengill had stowed away in his breast pocket.

"Never try to get the drop on an old-time mate from the Panama boats, friend Farnifold," he said. "Fact is, that's where I got this little gun. Pin-fire cartridges. Twelve millimeter. Bullet that size puts quite a hole in a man's stomach. Now, now, keep your hand away from that hip pocket. You'd never make it, Farnifold. Just turn around and let me relieve you of your shooting iron before I take leave of you and the, ah, lady."

He picked up his cap with his left hand and put it on.

Slowly young Banks was turning as he had been ordered.

"Coward!" spat Terry.

Too late Pettengill heard the crunch of hoofs on gravel. Banks dived through the door, slamming it behind him, and was out on the porch yelling:

"Spotswood! This way—quick! Pettengill's here! Knows everything!"

There were answering shouts from the sidewalk. Pettengill's retreat was cut off.

His hand flashed to the gas chandelier over his head, twisted the valve. As the light went out Pettengill scooped up Terry, tossed her shrieking over his shoulder, and charged for the door, shifting his gun to his left hand. He turned the gas jet in the hall as he went past it. The front door was open. Outside Spotswood was yelling:

"Guard the window, Banks. We'll go in the door after him. Shoot on sight, no chances now."

"Don't shoot!" screamed Terry. "He's got me—don't shoot!"

Two carriages stood at the curb. Dark figures were moving against their lights, figures that stood still, checked by Terry's anguished cry. Pettengill fired a shot over their heads, saw them duck for cover. He plunged down the steps with Terry kicking, pounding at his back with futile fists, yelling like a madwoman.

Pettengill dumped Terry into the first carriage. It was the one he had come in.

"Navy Yard!" he barked at the driver. "Lay on the whip!"

The whip cracked, the carriage jolted forward as Pettengill threw himself into the seat beside Terry and pinned her fast with his left arm just as she was almost out the other side.

"Hold it, lady," he said. Her nails slashed at his eyes, but he knocked her hand aside, got one long arm around her and pulled her close, clamping both her arms and leaving her helpless to do anything but kick and scream.

Behind he could hear shouting and the thump-thump of pursuing hoofs.

The carriage took a corner on two wheels, straightened out along a narrow street. Yellow carriage lamps followed around the corner.

Pettengill, still holding Terry with his left arm, twisted around and took careful aim. His purpose was to put his bullet close enough so that the driver could hear it zip. Apparently he succeeded, for a yelp of terror mingled with the echoes of his shot; the pursuing lamps swerved aside and stopped.

Pettengill shoved his empty gun back into his pocket. He had no more cartridges, but he had no intention of shooting anyone. Terry opened her mouth to scream. Pettengill clamped his hand over her mouth just in time to reduce a howl to a sputter. There were lights in some of the houses on the narrow street; at one or two windows heads appeared. A screaming girl might have brought excited citizens swarming into the street. Terry tried to bite his hand.

"You, there, driver! Ten dollars in gold if we make the Navy Yard gate ahead of those people in the other carriage."

The yellow lights were coming on again, but they were far behind.

"Yassuh, Cap'n, yas—SUH!" agreed the driver. "Iff'en this yeah contraption hol' togetheh that long. Giddap, Pompey."

Terry had stopped trying to bite. She had stopped squirming, too. She lay quietly inside his arm.

"Leggo my mouth," she gasped in a muffled voice. "Can't breathe. You' chokin' me."

"If I do as you ask, will you give me your word of honor not to yell or try to get away before we get to the Navy Yard?"

The blond head nodded emphatically.

Fool, warned New England caution. Trusting a girl's word—and a wild piece like this one.

Pettengill took away his hand.

"You—did you shoot—?"

"Over their heads. Just to gain time. Your precious Farnifold's not hurt. Don't fret."

"That ol' Farny Banks's going to be singing mighty small for a while," Terry remarked.

She moved a little in his arm. Almost any man but Pettengill would have thought she was cuddling.

The carriage rocked from side to side, bouncing over stones, jolting in and out of mudholes. Terry made no effort to brace herself; every time the rickety vehicle jounced into a hole, she squeezed a little closer to Pettengill. She felt soft and warm and exciting.

He twisted round for another look at the pursuit. The yellow lights were coming on, but not gaining. The driver of the pursuing carriage wouldn't get within pistol-shot again if he could help it. There were fewer lighted houses along the street now, more substantial-looking business buildings. They were getting close to the water front. There were more people on the sidewalks, too. Some of them turned to stare as the carriage rattled by.

"Stop that carriage! Stop thief! Stop thief!"

Farnifold Banks' voice rang clearly along the walled-in street.

Three men walking in a group halted to listen.

"Stop thief!"

One of the men suddenly darted out from the curb and flung himself at the horse's head. Pettengill leaped forward into the front seat as though propelled by a spring. Kneeling there, hanging to the back of the driver's box with his left hand, he flung his little pistol at the man. It hit him on the back of the head as he grabbed for the bridle, and he went down. Two of his companions dashed at the carriage and tried to climb in. Pettengill kicked one of them in the stomach, knocking him back into the other, who fell against the oncoming mudguard and was knocked sprawling on the stones.

The carriage lurched round another corner into a much wider street.

"Crawfohd Street, suh," gasped the terrified Negro on the box. "Straight run now foh the Navy Yahd bridge."

He lashed his horse into a hard gallop. Pettengill sank back, panting, beside Terry, who hadn't budged or let out a single cry.

"You could've got away then," said Pettengill.

"I gave my parole, didn't I?" said Terry. "In wartime, when you give your parole, it's not honorable to break it."

Instinct warned Pettengill not to laugh.

"So we're at war, are we, Terry?" he asked.

"Of course," said Terry. "Didn't you know that? The South has to fight to be free from you damned abolitionist Yankees, just like we all fought to be free from the British. I'm a Southern girl, you're a Yankee. You're the enemy. My enemy."

She had pressed close to him again and seemed to find it quite natural that he should hold her tightly, even though she was already bound by the chains of honor.

"I wish you weren't a Yankee," she said. "You surely can handle yourself in a fight." And then, quite irrelevantly: "Poor Virgie. How terrible to be in love with—with an enemy."

"Your sister doesn't think of Lieutenant Banks as an enemy."

"I know. But I'm—"

The rest of her answer was lost in the sudden thunder of hoofs and wheels on planks as the carriage hit the long bridge over the marshland that lay between the town of Portsmouth and the Navy Yard in Gosport.

Pettengill put his lips close to her ear.

"I'm not going to think of you as an enemy, either, Terry," he said.

"You'd better," she warned.

"Why, Terry?"

She shook her head, cuddled closer.

The thunder of iron on wood stopped abruptly; they were off the bridge, jouncing through muddy ruts. Behind, the pursuit still clattered over planks.

"Navy Yahd gate right ahead now, suh!" called the driver. "Lawd be thanked."

Leaning out, Pettengill could see a spot of light twinkling at the end of the street and a domed bell tower looming high against the stars. There would be a Marine sentry at the gate, and Murray had told him the Marines were loyal men.

"Good luck, Mister Pettengill," murmured Terry.

"Good luck to an enemy?"

"No. Just—good luck to you."

The driver was reining in his wearying horse. The spot of light was a lantern hanging under a dark archway. Beneath it, bayonets glittered. The guard was doubled. Somebody was nervous in the

Navy Yard tonight. The carriage stopped in front of the gate. Pettengill jumped out. So did Terry. Marine heels clicked as the rays of the guard lantern gleamed on his shoulder straps. Marine muskets snapped smartly to the carry. Pettengill tossed a gold half eagle toward the driver.

Then, without hesitation, as though it were the most natural thing in the world, he took Terry the Terror in his arms and kissed her. She clasped her hands behind his neck and pulled herself up in order to kiss him back properly. Her half-open lips were very soft and warm under his.

"Good-by, Terry," whispered Pettengill.

"Good-by—good-by. Oh-h-h! I don't even know your first name. Good-by." The other carriage was very near. Terry gave a little push, freed herself from Pettengill's arms. "But you're still the enemy!" she cried. With that she turned and ran toward the oncoming carriage, legs flashing in the lantern light beneath skirts high held, and her voice rang shrill, "Here he is! Right here at the gate!"

"What the flaming hell—" began a Marine.

"That'll do," snarled Pettengill, fighting for self-command. For one wild instant he had been on the point of running after the little devil. He spun sharply on his heel, and strode under the archway, ignoring the grins of the sentries. A corporal in the guardroom door came to attention.

"Sir?" It was a request for identification.

"Acting Master Pettengill, commanding flag tender, Home Squadron."

The corporal saluted. Keys jingled as he unlocked the postern in the big iron gate. The other carriage had just come to a stop outside the archway.

Pettengill stepped through the postern, heard it clang shut behind him and walked briskly into the dark and silent Navy Yard.

Would they follow? No—he heard the creak of departing wheels. Spotswood and Banks were officers and gentlemen. They could not use, as passports to enter the Yard where they no longer served, the uniforms they were taking off forever.

Pettengill quickened his pace in sudden desperate urgency. He knew what those men meant to do next.

They had sent guns down to the black schooner *Sea Sprite,* and they were going out with her that night to intercept the troopship that was due at Fortress Monroe tomorrow.

No other explanation fitted all the facts. They had not known

[96]

about that troopship until they had heard from Richmond of the telegram that had gone through. They had immediately started loading timber aboard *Sea Sprite* to strengthen her decks for gun mounts. They would have to prevent the fort's being reinforced by sea until they could collect troops for the attack. And Banks was boasting about every Yankee sailor and soldier being out of Virginia in a week. Spotswood had tried to get Pettengill out of the way by having him put under arrest for maltreating Canty. Of course Canty had blabbed every word that had passed between Pettengill and Graham. Spotswood didn't want a Yankee officer prowling about who knew the troopship was coming, knew the Virginians knew it, and had already expressed anxiety about the fort's scanty garrison.

You gave me too much credit for brains, friend Spotswood. I had to have young Banks practically draw me the plan before it was clear in my stupid mind. . . .

He had reached the landing.

To his right, the abandoned *Merrimack* loomed dark and silent. Out in the stream, the lights of the *Cumberland* were reflected on the water. The queer notion came to Pettengill that one day these two ships might be blazing away at each other in deadly combat. Then he noticed that the two 32-pounders which had been lying by the sea wall were no longer there. He knew where those guns had been taken: the guns that Tucker had denied to Alden as being "already requisitioned." It was the last confirming detail.

"*Cumberland* ahoy-y-y!" he hailed and was promptly answered. As he stood waiting for the boat, fear lest the flag officer might not believe his story shut out the bitter-sweet memory of Terry's soft mouth.

Chapter Seven

Flag Officer Pendergrast was not impressed by Pettengill's story about the *Sea Sprite*. He was not interested in assumptions. He was only interested in getting definite instructions from higher authority so he could stop worrying about doing the right thing. He had not heard a word from Washington for three days; he didn't even know whether there was peace or war in Virginia.

He was not even interested when Murray, who was inclined to take Pettengill's story more seriously, sent Lieutenant Selfridge in a boat to the Norfolk harbor master's office and got the information that the schooner *Sea Sprite*, F. Banks owner and master, had cleared for Charleston in ballast. Time of departure was not stated. That was a perfectly legal procedure, old Eagle-beak insisted. He had no authority to interfere with coastwise commerce. He had no proof that the *Sea Sprite* intended an attack on peaceful shipping. He had no proof even that she was armed.

Finally, the best Murray could do, with infinite tact, was to persuade the old gentleman to send Pettengill over to Fortress Monroe to find out if the telegraph line was still open, and if the Army had any news, and, more important, if any messages had come through from the Navy Department for Flag Officer Pendergrast. And even for that errand, Pettengill had not been able to get final permission to shove off until long after daybreak.

An armed Rebel schooner was loose at sea, the lives of seven hundred United States troops were in danger, and the commander of the only U.S. war steamer in the vicinity was tied down to carrying messages for a crotchety old man. Pettengill was savagely pleased that he had found only one message waiting for the flag officer at Monroe, some long-winded nonsense from Washington about a Presidential proclamation. The line had gone dead after it had come through, just a little while before Pettengill had arrived, so Flag

Officer Pendergrast would get no relief that day from the Navy Department.

A rain squall blowing out of the northwest was lashing the waters of Hampton Roads to yeasty foam as the *Brother Jonathan* pulled away from the dock at Fortress Monroe.

Visibility to seaward, out toward the Capes, was virtually nil. However, it didn't matter to Pettengill.

Murray had hinted that any U.S. naval officer who actually saw an armed attack being made on an American ship would be not only authorized but duty bound to take protective action. In Hampton Roads, under the guns of the fort, there would be no attack. The *Sea Sprite* might be lying in wait for the troopship in Lynnhaven Bay, seventeen miles east of Monroe; there the quarry could be intercepted as she came in past Cape Henry after making her landfall. Pettengill had worked it out on the chart. He had even toyed with the idea of running down to Lynnhaven Bay, despite the fact that he would have to use up five or six hours of time that he would be called to account for: but even if he found *Sea Sprite*, he couldn't touch her unless he caught her in the act of attacking another ship. He had no way of knowing when the troopship might appear, and there was no point in risking the flag officer's wrath for nothing.

Pettengill picked up the three sheets of closely written telegraph flimsy from the chart-board and leafed through them. At first glance they seemed to be about an insurrection going on in South Carolina and the other cotton States, so that the revenue couldn't be collected. The message seemed to contain nothing of the slightest interest to a naval officer.

The rain lashed wildly at the pilothouse windows.

Suddenly, from the second sheet, words leaped out at him:

> Now therefore I, Abraham Lincoln, President of the United States . . . have further deemed it advisable to set on foot a blockade of the ports within the States aforesaid, in pursuance of the laws of the United States and of the law of nations in such cases provided—

A blockade! Pettengill turned back to the first sheet: "South Carolina, Georgia, Alabama, Florida, Mississippi, Louisiana, and Texas." Virginia wasn't included.

But the *Sea Sprite* had cleared for Charleston; therefore her papers showed her as being bound for a blockaded port!

The proclamation required that ships proceeding to blockaded ports be warned off; those failing to heed the warning were subject to seizure in prize, and Farnifold Banks wasn't the type to give heed to warnings. And if Banks' hotheadedness should drive him to open fire when he saw Pettengill's tug approaching, the proclamation had a little paragraph about that, too, on page three:

> If any person, under the pretended authority of the said States, or under any other pretense, shall molest a vessel of the United States—such person will be held amenable to the laws of the United States for the prevention and punishment of piracy.

The proclamation was a vital circumstance of which Pettengill was aware, but the flag officer was not. That entitled Pettengill to act on his own responsibility, and look to results for justification.

The rain was slackening. He could see a little better. He was well away from Monroe, out in mid-channel. The dark object looming up ahead would be the Rip Raps. He took a last look at the chart.

"Course east-nor'east," he called.

"East-nor'east, sir," said Aycock, who had the helm. There was a trace of question in his response. He had expected the opposite order.

Pettengill looked at the chart again. This course would bring him out into the lower end of Chesapeake Bay directly on the inbound steamer track from Cape Henry. Then an ESE course, or perhaps a half-point south of that, would take him down into Lynnhaven Bay. What he needed now was better visibility, and as though in answer to his need, the wind drove the rain squall out to sea, leaving tail-end clouds behind. Pettengill swept his glasses over the expanse of dancing Chesapeake whitecaps, but there was nothing in sight, nor smoke nor sail. To seaward, vision was still limited, but improving fast.

The fresh nor'wester he was so pleased about would be dead foul for a sailing vessel lying in Lynnhaven Bay waiting to pounce on a steamer coming in past Cape Henry. Banks would realize that he hadn't a chance of overtaking a steamer once she got past him, if he had to beat up against that wind. He might not be anywhere near as far east as Pettengill had first thought.

Pettengill grabbed his glasses and climbed up the iron ladder to the top of the pilothouse. Already the visibility to seaward was what he would log as "good"—about ten miles. But he was more interested in the coast line to the south and southeast, where the *Sea Sprite* might be lurking behind the shoals or perhaps in some creek. Two miles due south he could see gentle surf breaking on the low sand spit of Willoughby's Point. He braced himself against the pressure of the wind, swinging his glasses slowly to the east along the shore line, and then to seaward. There were no craft to be seen. War, or the fear of war, had swept this great commercial waterway as clear of its usual busy traffic as though its shores were still inhabited only by Indians.

The remnants of the rain squall were tumbling toward the horizon. Then he saw something else, far out, bearing almost ESE, right on the steamer track. Smoke. It looked as though it was more than ten miles away, maybe twelve, but it was very definitely smoke from an inbound steamer. She must be past Cape Henry already. Pettengill's heart beat faster. She could be the troopship from Boston, and if Banks had a lookout aloft he would have made her out by this time. Pettengill turned his glasses back to the hazy southern shore. He thought he detected a flicker of movement. He rubbed his eyes, looked again. He saw a triangle of white—another—a schooner's tops'ls. She seemed to be coming out of a creek, which was why he hadn't seen her earlier. She was the *Sea Sprite* for a certainty, no fisherman or coasting schooner would have sails of that dazzling white.

Pettengill hit just one rung of the ladder on the way down from the pilothouse. He had a good chance of cutting the *Sea Sprite* off if he could bear a little south of east, through shallow water. The *Brother Jonathan* drew about eight feet, and the tide was out. Still, the chart showed nothing less than two fathoms on the course he wanted to follow. He gave Aycock the new course, lifted his glasses again. He could see *Sea Sprite* plainly now, black hull and all. She wasn't more than three miles away, running free with the wind on her port quarter and all sail set. The course she was steering was obviously intended to intercept the steamer somewhere south of the shoal called the Tail of the Horseshoe, set squarely in the mouth of Chesapeake Bay.

And though Banks must have seen the tug by this time, he wasn't changing course to try to avoid being intercepted himself. He must think that with two 32-pounders at his disposal, he wouldn't have to worry about a tug with only one little 12-pounder howitzer. Pettengill grinned, remembering the range table he had read only that morning.

The excitement of the chase was spreading through the ship by now: most of the crew were on deck.

"Jackson!" Pettengill sang out.

"Sir!" The quarter gunner's face was eager; he scented action.

"Draw that round of shrapnel that's in the howitzer," Pettengill ordered. "Open the magazine, get up a dozen rounds of shell. Provide the gun, have the crew stand by."

"Aye aye, sir!"

It was a good thing he had ordered Jackson to run the crew through a little gun drill during the trip over to Monroe. Not much, not nearly enough: they were still ham-handed. Not a man of them had ever handled a rammer or hauled on a gun-tackle before. But it was a lot better than nothing, and Jackson was a whole gun crew in himself. . . .

"If it comes to shooting, Aycock," Pettengill said, "I'll be at the gun. You'll handle the ship."

"Aye aye, sir."

Pettengill blew into the engine-room voice tube and said in an offhand tone:

"I'll want all the speed you can give me, Mr. Canty. It's a matter of overhauling a schooner I want to speak."

Canty grunted ungracious assent. Presently the beat of the propeller quickened.

The steamer was still hull-down. She was carrying no sail, coming in on steam alone. If she and the *Sea Sprite* held their present courses, Banks would be within gunshot of her in about an hour. The light 32-pounders of 27 hundredweight weren't much good beyond a thousand yards. Pettengill had an extra five hundred yards to count on, and as his course and the *Sea Sprite*'s converged, the distance between the two ships narrowed swiftly. The arrogant fashion in which Banks ignored the approach of a United States war steamer, even if she was only a tug, began to annoy Pettengill. Banks was sticking to his job with grim persistence.

It's what I'd do in his place, thought Pettengill suddenly.

If Banks had begun to bear away, Pettengill could have gradually edged him down into Lynnhaven Bay. With every point he yielded, his chances of intercepting the steamer would have been that much less.

The range to the schooner was now about twenty-five hundred yards. Pettengill focused his glasses on the steamer again. Her upper works were beginning to appear: she was almost certainly an ocean liner with tiers of cabins, just what they would have grabbed to carry troops.

He would be within distant range of the *Sea Sprite* in another fifteen minutes.

The time had come to deal definitely with Canty before he could panic, as he would at the first unexpected gunfire.

Pettengill walked aft along the narrow gangway to the door of the engine room.

"Let your oiler relieve you a minute, Mr. Canty. Come on deck."

Canty came puffing up the ladder, face streaming sweat, eyes glaring with suspicion.

Pettengill pointed out the distant steamer, the white-sailed *Sea Sprite*.

"Mr. Canty," he said, "that steamer out there is carrying seven hundred Union soldiers. The schooner you see yonder is armed and manned by Rebels. They mean to sink the steamer. I mean to prevent it if I can. But I can't do that without steam. The lives of those seven hundred young men, Mr. Canty, depend on your faithful performance of your duty for the next hour."

Canty swallowed. For an instant Pettengill thought he was going to faint.

Then he said, unsteadily:

"I ain't no hand fer fightin', Cap'n. Ain't built fer it, inside ner out. I ain't no friend o' yours, neither. But when it comes to drownin' seven hunnert boys in this here ocean, that's jest plain murder. I guess I aim to give ye all the steam ye need to stop them goddam Rebels from doin' such as that."

"Thank you, Mr. Canty," said Pettengill. He didn't make the mistake of holding out his hand. But for this occasion, Pettengill thought he could depend on Canty.

He went back to the pilothouse. There were dark clouds in the northwest again, these rain squalls were apt to be recurrent. For the moment the visibility was all he could wish.

Sea Sprite still held her course. As Pettengill's glasses focused on her, he saw the blue Virginia flag go soaring aloft to her mainpeak and an instant later flame-centered smoke puffed out at her stern. Pettengill counted seconds: three—four—five. A spout of water jumped skyward well ahead of the tug. A good line shot, fired at extreme elevation, but about a quarter of a mile short. Banks couldn't have hoped to reach the tug. The shot had been meant for a warning. The thump of the report came dully to his ears. He leaned out from the rail:

"Jackson! Fire a blank charge!"

An instant later the bronze howitzer banged smartly.

As the smoke cleared, Pettengill saw answering smoke and flame leap again from the schooner's quarter. He watched for the waterspout, saw instead a broken line of leaping foam coming straight for the tug.

A ricochet shot—fired with the gun level instead of elevated. No telling how far a roundshot would skip over reasonably smooth water. Banks was no fool as a gunner. It was going to hit! . . .

Crash! Splinters flew from the tug's gunwale, just to port of the stempiece. One of Jackson's gun crew was down, blood spurting from his arm. The cook came running with bandages and a tourniquet. The rest of the gun crew stood stolidly at their posts.

"Sponge!" barked Pettengill. He was suddenly very cool. A ship flying the flag of Virginia had fired on a United States ship.

"Load!" Into the rifled muzzle went the powder charge in its merino-wool bag. Pettengill automatically took note that the mark on the rammer staff came flush with the muzzle, showing that the charge was fully home. Jackson brought over the fuze, screw-threaded on one end. It was the duty of the officer in charge to tear off the soft metal patch so as to expose the fulminate cap, and to keep it in his pocket as a record of the number of rounds fired. Jackson screwed the fuze into the base of the queer-looking shell. Pettengill knew all about ordinary spherical shells, but he had never seen one like this before, an iron cylinder tapering at one end and thickly coated with grease. Jackson thrust it into the muzzle of the gun.

"Handsomely with that rammer now. Push her well home; don't let her stick in the bore," warned Jackson. "That's well."

"Prime!" ordered Pettengill. Jackson drew back the hammer of the lock and thrust the quill of the percussion primer into the vent.

"Ease off those compressors," he ordered. "A half-turn's plenty. Run out!"

The gun crew laid hold of the little gun and ran it forward as far as the slide would permit.

"Now heave taut on those compressors again," Jackson directed. Two men twisted at the brass handles, binding the gun to its slide.

"Ready, sir," Jackson reported.

Pettengill was already behind the gun. Naval gunnery was certainly getting to be a scientific business. He had seen adjustable back-sights before, but not like this one with a lateral adjustment for windage as well as a vertical adjustment for range. He guessed the range at eighteen hundred yards now, that called for only 5-

degree elevation. The man who made that range table was an optimist; he'd better make it 6 degrees. . . .

Lockstring in hand, Pettengill peered through the eyepiece of the rear sight, bringing the front sight into line as Jackson twirled the elevating screw in obedience to his circling finger.

"Haul a little left, you at the training rope. Foot of the mainmast's the best aiming point. There!"

Pettengill yanked the lockstring, the hammer fell. Cr-rack! The splitting report wasn't like any cannon shot Pettengill had ever heard; it fairly ripped at his eardrums.

The wind whipped away the smoke just in time for his unbelieving eyes to see a flicker of white water leap up beyond the dark hull of the *Sea Sprite*.

"Sponge!" In went the dampened sponge to extinguish any smoldering fragments. "Load! Prime! Run out!"

The raw crew was doing very well indeed.

"That's a rammer staff you've got in your hands, you farmer, not a hayfork!" Jackson was saying, but there was pride in his tone. These lads were doing him credit.

This time Pettengill, chastened by experience, adjusted the eyepiece of the sight according to the range table's instructions.

Cr-rack! The water column leaped just this side of the black hull. Missed her by less than five feet.

"Sponge! Load! Prime! Run out!"

Smoke and fire from the schooner's stern again, another ricochet shot, this one a little wide. Pettengill let the bronze tip of the foresight slide just a trifle higher in the eyepiece. Cr-rack!

An instant later smoke leaped up from the schooner once more, not the grayish-white smoke of cannon powder, but the clear white of the musket powder with which shells were filled. Through his glasses Pettengill could see fragments of debris fly into the air just at the foot of the mainmast. A hit!

"Look alive, hearties!" he yelled. "The enemy's hurt. Let's hurt him worse. Sponge! Load! Prime! Run out!"

Cr-rack! White smoke again.

"His mainmast's gone, by God!" screamed Jackson, dancing on the deck.

The proud mast was over the side in a horrible tangle of canvas and rigging, the schooner yawed, her stern was lower in the water.

Her fo'c's'le gun spat fiery defiance just the same.

"Sponge! Load! Prime! Run out!"

"She's sinking!" yelled Aycock from the pilothouse.

Pettengill's eye was at the sight. On the wings of that northwest wind, a new rain squall enveloped tug and schooner, blotting out all vision. Through the hammering rain, Pettengill heard a dull explosion somewhere out in the murk—another hit.

"Half-speed, Aycock! A lookout in the bows!"

The red mist of battle was clearing from Pettengill's mind.

"Well done, all of you!" he said to the gun crew. "Jackson, secure the gun and get those cartridges under cover."

Drenched, exultant, he climbed up into the pilothouse.

"Aycock, where was that steamer when the squall hit?"

"Hull-up, sir, and comin' fast, a point on the port bow as we head now. Four-five miles off. Big black funnel, looks like a Collins liner. Full o' sojers, blue with 'em topside."

The first Union victory at sea! Pettengill could see the headlines: TROOPSHIP RESCUED FROM REBEL RAIDER! TUG SAVES SEVEN HUNDRED MEN! HEROIC CONDUCT OF ACTING MASTER CALEB PETTENGILL. Only by then he would be Acting Lieutenant Pettengill. He'd seen what public excitement was like on the brink of war. No matter now whether he had exceeded his orders. The roar of acclaim that would greet the news from Hampton Roads would sweep away all thought of such trifles.

He stood there in the rain-pelted pilothouse and tasted the heady wine of fame.

"Boat ahoy-y-y!" It was the forward lookout. Pettengill flung an oilskin round his shoulders as he rushed out again into the savage fury of the rain. A faint cry came from somewhere out on the water.

The lookout's arm was pointing to starboard.

There was a boat. Pettengill could just see it, very low in the water, full of people. Only three oars.

"Stop!" called Pettengill to Aycock. "Slow astern!"

The tug shuddered as her backing screw checked her way. The boat was pulling toward her, was almost alongside.

"Throw 'em a line, Jackson," Pettengill shouted unnecessarily, for half the tug's crew were at the rail with lines and boat hooks. The rain beat viciously into the pale, upturned faces of the men in the boat, and upon two still forms in her stern sheets covered with a piece of tarpaulin.

Pettengill ran aft, his exultation gone.

"Please, Lord, please!" he whispered. His heart would break if he had to tell Pendleton Banks he'd fired the shot that had killed his brother.

A slender form rose in the boat's stern. Choking with relief and gratitude, Pettengill could hardly speak.

"Come aboard, Mr. Banks," he made himself say. "You'll be needing dry gear and some hot coffee."

"I'll thank you to see my wounded cared for first, Mr. Pettengill," said Farnifold Banks stonily.

Chapter Eight

"If you'd fought us fair," cried Farnifold Banks, "instead of standing off out of reach and tearing us to pieces with that damn rifled gun, there'd've been a different story to tell."

He was huddled in a blanket in Pettengill's cabin while his clothes dried down in the boiler room. He sipped at his black coffee and eyed Pettengill accusingly.

"It wasn't only the rifled gun, Banks," Pettengill said. "It was those mechanical arts and sciences that Mr. Isherwood spoke of yesterday. I had steam, I could choose my course; you were constrained by the wind. I had explosive shells and percussion fuzes; you had solid shot. You didn't have a chance, Banks, because your superiors hadn't given you the right tools. There's no reason why I should throw away a military advantage that was the product of better preparation by my superiors."

"Superiors, hell," muttered Banks. "If my superiors could lay hold of me they'd hang me to the yardarm. But I reckon I'm to regard myself as a prisoner of war?"

"I don't know," Pettengill admitted. "I'm not even sure there's a war going on."

He thought uneasily about the paragraph in the President's proclamation that mentioned the penalties of piracy.

Banks had fought under the flag of Virginia, and Virginia would stand by her son. The politicos in Washington were probably still trying to conciliate Virginia, so there would be no question of hanging. But his uneasiness didn't subside.

"What d'you mean, your superiors would hang you at the yardarm?" he demanded.

"A bunch of doddering old graybeards came down from Richmond last night," Banks told him. "They got to hemming and hawing and finally decided they wouldn't go along with what Charley Spotswood and I were planning. Told me I was free to go to Charleston and apply to the Confederate government for a letter of marque, but I wasn't to attack that troopship or do any other act of war under the Virginia flag. When you saw me at Terry's house, I thought it was all approved; it was later they crawfished on me. So I started for Charleston, but I just couldn't stomach it—Yankee soldiers landing in Virginia!" His dark eyes flashed. "I was going to stop 'em or die trying! Only you stopped me first."

"You damned young fool!" cried Pettengill, leaping to his feet. "What d'you think comes next? The Washington authorities'll demand an explanation from Virginia as to why a schooner flying the Virginia flag opened fire on a United States war steamer in Virginia waters. If Richmond says it was no doing of theirs, that Master Farnifold Banks of the Virginia Navy was specifically ordered to commit no act of war under the Virginia flag, what'll happen to you?"

Banks stared at him.

"You'll hang for a pirate, that's what'll happen!" Pettengill screamed. "Here—read this!"

He fished the telegraphic copy of President Lincoln's proclamation out of his pocket and shoved it under Banks' nose, his finger jabbing at the fateful paragraph.

Banks turned paler as he read.

If Banks' own people turned their backs on him, there would be no reason why the Washington government shouldn't gratify the mob by giving it a victim. Once that proclamation was widely known, voices would be raised to demand that an example be made of this first "pirate." The same wave of public excitement that would make Pettengill a lieutenant and a hero might send Farnifold Banks to the gallows.

Banks had done exactly what Pettengill had done in disregarding his orders and acting on his own responsibility for his cause. Pettengill would be lionized and promoted because he had succeeded. Banks would hang because he had failed. In a way, when Pettengill handed Banks over as a prisoner, he would be sending the youngster to the hangman in order to cover up his own transgressions amidst a blaze of glory.

How could he ever face Pendleton Banks again?

Banks crumpled the flimsies between hands that were shaking, but his voice was quite steady:

"Looks pretty bad for me, I reckon."

"Maybe I—" began Pettengill. There was a double rap at the door; Aycock's white head appeared.

"Troopship's comin' up astern, sir."

"Back in a minute, Banks," snapped Pettengill, and ran out to the rail beside the pilothouse.

The sun was filtering through the clouds; the second rain squall was blowing out to sea. The tug was bearing up for Fortress Monroe, which lay a mile or so ahead: astern, a huge steamship was rapidly overhauling the *Brother Jonathan,* smoke belching from her towering funnel. She was barkentine-rigged, but from the look of her it was clear that she was primarily a steamer, with sail power only for emergencies. This was just the reverse of the Navy's attitude toward steam. Her decks were jammed with blue-uniformed soldiers.

The steamer came slowly up to the tug's quarter; she would be within hail in a minute, and then he would know whether there was any hope for the plan that had suddenly come to him. It all depended on how much the people aboard that steamer had seen of what happened between the *Brother Jonathan* and the *Sea Sprite.* Pettengill had to find out before he could chart his course.

The steamer's bowsprit was level with the tug's pilothouse; high on the bridge a bearded man in uniform leaned over the rail, speaking trumpet raised.

Pettengill cupped hands around his mouth:

"Steamer ahoy!" he roared. "What steamer's that?"

It was the Navy's privilege to hail first and be answered first.

"Steamer *Kennebec!*" came prompt answer. "Parkinson master, Boston to Fortress Monroe with the Fourth Massachusetts Regiment on board."

"This is the U.S. steamer *Brother Jonathan,* Acting Master Pettengill," Pettengill shouted back. "Tender to flagship, Home Squadron."

"Hooray for the Navy!" yelled somebody, and then the whole regiment was cheering. The *Kennebec* was slowing down, just keeping pace with the tug.

The skipper had his trumpet at his mouth again. "Thought I saw gun flashes back there just before that squall came down," he called.

"You did, sir," Pettengill answered. "I was practicing my gun crew with this new rifled howitzer they've given me."

He saw the skipper turn and speak to the officers gathered behind him.

"Didn't I see a black schooner, too, Captain Pettengill?" the trumpet-booming voice demanded.

"You sure did," Pettengill replied. "Came out of a creek over there."

He gestured vaguely. "Guess he didn't like the weather and ran back in."

The skipper flourished his speaking trumpet.

"Thank you and good luck!" he bawled.

The steamer began to gather way again, slipping ahead toward the waiting fortress. Pettengill turned from the rail to meet Aycock's astonished eyes.

"Tell the Army nothing," he said. "I'll save my report for the flag officer."

Aycock laughed. That was a sentiment he heartily approved.

"Set a course for the Navy Yard, Aycock," Pettengill ordered, and ran for the cabin where Banks waited in white-faced silence. The port was dogged shut; he had heard nothing of what had passed between Pettengill and the *Kennebec*'s skipper.

"You're clear of the shoals, Banks!" cried Pettengill, clapping him on the back. "They didn't see enough to count."

"What? What are you talking about?"

"The people on the steamer! They were too far off to see anything but gun flashes. I told 'em I was practicing: they seemed to believe me. So now we won't have that transport skipper and the colonel of the Massachusetts regiment sending in reports about the big sea battle in Hampton Roads. And that leaves me free to do what I think right. About you, I mean."

"Which is?"

"I'm going to land you and your men at the naval hospital dock on my way up the harbor. I understand the surgeons have all gone over to your side, so you'll find plenty of help for your two wounded men."

For the first time there was a look in Farnifold Banks' eyes that reminded Pettengill of his elder brother.

"That's a mighty decent thing to do, Pettengill," he said. "But look here, what are you going to tell your Old Man?"

"Simply that your schooner was struck by a squall and was dismasted; that you left her in a sinking condition and I picked you and your crew up, brought you to Norfolk and landed you—shipwrecked mariners, naturally. All of which is strictly true. As far as it goes."

It also, he realized, accounted neatly for his delay in returning from Monroe.

Banks was laughing. The two young men fell comfortably into the familiar pattern of junior officers conspiring to outwit an unreasonable senior.

"But your crew'll blab," said Banks.

"I suppose they will, when they get a chance. But they won't know what I report to the flag officer. I'll see to it none of 'em gets aboard the *Cumberland* with any yarns for a few days. By that time a lot of other things are likely to have happened to occupy their minds. I'd suggest you go home and stay out of the way of any of your own superiors for the present. Suffering from exposure, let's say. See that your men do the same. Can you trust 'em to keep their traps shut?"

"For a while, I reckon. 'Course, I'll have to report for duty some time or other. I'll be asked questions. But as long as nobody was killed, I won't be in too much trouble. As you say, a lot of other things, maybe much more important, will be happening from now on. And *Sea Sprite*—" his voice softened—"wasn't a public ship, she was mine. Mine and Pendleton's. 'Bout the only thing Father left us. So I won't have to account for what happened to her."

He had been making war in his own ship, without even a letter of marque! Pettengill shook his head. They would surely have hanged him.

"You're a white man, Pettengill," Banks said. "You could've had a lot of credit out of saving that troopship."

"It would turn sour in my stomach next time I met your brother Pendleton."

"Or Terry?"

"It's not likely I'll be seeing Terry again." Pettengill was conscious of a little glow of pleasure. If Banks was jealous, Terry must have said something to make him so.

"I shouldn't've said that," Banks acknowledged. "Considering what you're doing for me. I hope I get a chance to pay you back one day."

"Who knows?" said Pettengill. "Might be a long war. Well, duty calls. I'll send a hand below to see if your clothes're dry. You'll be wanting to visit your wounded lads, I imagine. Make yourself comfortable meantime, there's another swig in that bottle."

There were plenty of matters that clamored for Pettengill's attention. He should make sure Jackson and the cook had done everything possible for the wounded sailors; he should see to patching the splintered gunwale and painting it over; he should have the howitzer cleaned. Ordnance Instructions were imperative about cleaning rifled guns after firing. But first he stood for a moment in the sunshine with the fresh breeze whipping his jacket about his lanky body and tried to make sure in his mind that there weren't too many holes in the report he was going to make to the flag officer.

Murray would be suspicious, that was sure. After all the hurrah Pettengill had made about Farnifold Banks and the *Sea Sprite*, a report about her getting conveniently dismasted in a squall and sinking just when he was handy to pick up her crew would be a little too thick for that smart officer. But he saw no good reason why Murray wouldn't be willing to let sleeping dogs lie. Fortress Monroe was safe. That was the main thing. . . .

Banks' superiors would certainly have taken advantage of his enterprise if it had succeeded. Denied reinforcements by sea, Fortress Monroe would almost surely have been lost to the Union. . . .

I saved it; I'll always have that to think about. Even if nobody else thinks about it. Of course young Banks'll think about it sometimes. Maybe Terry'll think about it too; he'll tell her and she'll think I let him go just to please her: she'll find that very romantic. I hope I see her again, just to tell her how wrong she is.

"Cap'n Pettengill!" Canty stood in the gangway by the engineroom door, his fat face creased in a thoroughly self-satisfied smirk. "Say, Cap'n Pettengill! You'n me sure whipped them Rebels to a frazzle, didn't we?"

"We sure did, Mr. Canty," Pettengill said heartily. "You stood by your engine like a hero."

"Proud to have you say so, Cap'n. Dad-dog it! Blew 'm sky high, we did! Goddam Rebels!"

Pettengill might never get another chance to be a hero, but Canty would be a hero for the rest of his life after he got back to Philadelphia! Pettengill leaned against the pilothouse and laughed and laughed until the tears ran down his face.

Chapter Nine

In the ornate writing room of Willard's Hotel, at the corner of Pennsylvania Avenue and Fourteenth Street in Washington City, Pettengill was writing a letter. The corroded pen sputtered at almost every stroke; the spindle-legged chair creaked ominously under Pettengill's two hundred pounds of solid bone and muscle each time he shifted his weight. But he persisted. This was a letter which had to be written, and written now, while he had the chance.

He took time out to read over what he had written so far:

> May 20, 1861. Dear Father: It is just a month today since I helped burn the ships and buildings at the Norfolk Navy Yard; we could not burn the Cannon, more than a thousand, so we had to leave them for the Rebels. That was a great Pity since they need Guns and they can't make many for themselves as they have no foundries like we have in Conn. We tried to knock the Trunnions off some of the Dahlgren guns with hammers, but the iron was too tough. If it ever comes to real fighting, we will find those guns shooting at our ships. That is what I am writing about, I mean real fighting, because it don't look like any. I wrote you about what happened at Norfolk, and I said, The War is On. I must tell you now, maybe the war isn't on. Everybody here in Washington does a lot of talking, but nobody does anything else. For a while they feared the Rebels would come from Virginia and put their flag on the Capitol, but now there are plenty of troops here, I guess maybe fifty thousand. All the soldiers do is drill and dig Latrines and raise H—

Pettengill made a blotchy job of changing a capital *H* into a capital *D*—Father didn't care for salty language—and went on:

> —Disturbances all night and fight with the Provo Guard. If it wasn't for the Navy, maybe the Rebels would be here in-

stead. It was the Navy kept Fort Monroe supplied so we could hold the entrance of Chesapeake Bay, and it was the Navy kept the Potomac River open, so the Army could come here when the Secesh in Maryland burned the R.R. bridges. My little Steamer goes up and down the River, protecting our shipping and trying to stop the Rebels from going back and forth between Maryland and Virginia, though they do it all the same because there are not nearly enough of us to stop them, just my Steamer and three river Steamers with a few guns. Then there are two sea-going sloops-of-war, the *Pawnee* and the *Pocahontas*, but they will be taken away for the Blockade any day now that Flag Officer Stringham has hoisted his flag as Commander in Chief of the Atlantic Blockading Squadron and is at Hampton Roads in the old *Minnesota* writing letters to the Dept. about how he needs more ships. We can only catch a few of the boats that sneak back and forth across the River every night. Everybody says the Rebels know everything that is done and said in Washington the next day and what's the Navy doing that they can't stop the Rebel courier service, which is a fool thing to say when anybody can get a pass and walk right across the Long Bridge into Virginia and tell the Rebel officers any thing he knows. If the Army would get up off its—

Pettengill checked his wretched pen again. He was all for progress and modern inventions, but these newfangled steel pens were a trial. Quill pens like those the Navy used might be old-fashioned but they didn't corrode. He scratched out the beginning of a word he had started to write. This letter was getting too long anyway.

—back sides and go over to Virginia and occupy Arlington Heights and Alexandria, this City would be safer but oh, no, nobody must do anything that might hurt the Rebels' feelings. I was down to Alexandria today with dispatches for Captain Rowan of the *Pawnee*, and I can tell you it made my Blood boil to see the new Rebel flag, the one they call the Stars and Bars. It looks something like our dear old Flag. There it was flying from a flagstaff in Alexandria.

Captain Rowan looked a little happier after he had read the dispatches I brought him, so maybe he got his orders for the Blockade. Of course he didn't tell me what was in the dispatches; the Navy keeps everything very secret these days so nobody knows what is really going on except the Rebel sympathizers who are all over town and get to know more than most of us do in the Navy. Especially the women, they are into everything. Captain Dahlgren says that Pres. Lincoln calls them the Secesh dames and declares they are more dangerous than the Rebel army.

Captain Rowan was at Norfolk the night we burned the ships. I helped him tow the *Cumberland* out of the harbor afterward, and you should have heard what he said when he found out the old commodore had scuttled the *Merrimack* so we couldn't tow her out too. He would be a good Captain to serve under in a fight, but he is not a deep thinker like Captain Du Pont who I saw when I went up to Philadelphia to give testimony at the prize proceedings on the *Ranee*. The Judge condemned the *Ranee,* so our lads will get the prize money, all right. Captain Harris got away scot-free, though. The Judge let him out on bail, but the newspapers made such a rumpus the Judge decided to cancel the bail, because the Government wanted to hang Harris instead of just letting him go with a fine like they used to do. Harris jumped bail and I guess he's gone South where he'll be safe. I didn't stay long in Philadelphia—

Once more he stopped writing to take a bandanna out of his pocket and wipe sweat and ink from his hand. He could have stayed another day in Philadelphia. He had wanted to see Mrs. Harrifield again. He had even tried. It had taken him an hour to find her house, but when he finally did, no one had answered the bell. Shame curdled in his belly. The pull of the flesh had torn away the bulwarks of outraged pride, and he had sought her out. In vain. Terry's face had haunted him that night, her brown eyes wide with reproach. That was stupid. Why should he be beholden to Terry? He'd never see her again.

His pen stabbed at the paper as his mind recoiled from the thought of his father's face if he told him about Mrs. Harrifield.

—but I did go down to the receiving ship and got two more of my *Ranee* lads who'd shipped over, Reilly and Yoakum, so I have four good men in my crew now. They've given me an officer, too, a young fellow from the merchant marine, Casson his name is, and I have three Navy firemen and two coal heavers but no engineer yet, though I'm promised one, and I've been given another howitzer for a stern chaser.

So you see all is well with me, though I wish I could get appointed to a sea-going ship on the Blockade, where if there is going to be any active service and Promotion, that is where to find it. But the prospects are not bright, which is what I really wanted to tell you because I know you must be reading an awful lot of Bilge Water in the newspapers, but down here on Potomac there is no war going on at all. I thought you ought to know, because maybe my other letter gave you the wrong idea.

I expect you will be wanting to hear about the Pres't, but I have never seen Mr. Lincoln, though he often comes to the Navy Yard to talk with Capt. Dahlgren, so I hear. They say the Pres. can see that Rebel flag over Alexandria from his study window. I wish I knew what he thinks about when he looks at it. Well, I must close now, and remain, Your dutiful and affectionate son, Caleb Pettengill,

Acting Master, U.S.N., Comdg. U.S. Str. *Brother Jonathan*.

Address as above, care of Commandant, Navy Yard, Wash'n City, D. C.

Pettengill scrawled his father's address on an envelope and thankfully laid the pen aside. His father probably wouldn't answer him. Pettengill had had only a half-dozen acrid notes from him in the nine years since he had left home: none at all during his African cruise, though he himself had written faithfully every month or so. When he had been given an officer's berth in the Panama steamers, he had detected a slight softening of tone in his father's correspondence, such as it was: a son who was on his way to becoming a master mariner and the recipient of fat bonuses might be acceptable, after all. But the change from merchant marine to Navy had dried up the letters from Litchfield at once. Pettengill sealed his letter without reading it over. He would never find words to make his father understand how he felt about the Navy, not if he filled a hundred sheets of the Willard brothers' paper. But the letter was one more duty done. Pettengill headed for the bar.

The bar was roaring, as always at Willard's in the late afternoon. There were civilians in every sort of dress, from broadcloth to Western homespun, but they were far outnumbered by officers in Army blue, relieved here and there by the gaudier uniforms of some of the State regiments, such as the gray-blue-scarlet Zouave costumes of the Eleventh New York, known as the Fire Zouaves because they had been recruited from the volunteer fire companies of New York City. They'd wish they were less conspicuous when they got under fire, thought Pettengill. If they ever did. He caught sight of a gold-banded Navy cap amidst the Army flood and set his course for it, hoping it was somebody he knew well enough to stand a drink: he hated to drink alone. The Navy cap turned around as Pettengill drew alongside: under it was the face of Lieutenant Glendy Sproston, skipper of the river steamer *Mount Vernon*, just in from patrol that morning. Sproston was a lieutenant of six years' seniority: Pettengill knew him fairly well, but he was careful not to overstep the line.

"Afternoon, sir. I see your glass is empty. Will you join me?"

"Why, hullo, Pettengill!" cried Sproston, cheerfully. "Happy to hoist one with you, only belay that 'sir.' Aren't we both bold captains in the world-famous Potomac Flotilla?"

Pettengill chuckled.

"So we are, come to think of it," he agreed. "What's your pleasure?"

"Kentucky whisky, straight."

"Mine's Barbados, with a dash of lime," Pettengill told the bartender.

"You were too long in Africa," chuckled Sproston. "Rum ruins a man's taste for real liquor. Here we are. Lift a glass to my new billet, Pettengill. I've just got my orders to the *Colorado*, fitting out at Boston for the Gulf blockade."

"No wonder you're looking so happy," said Pettengill, envious. "A good cruise to you, and a barrel of prize money!"

They drank to that.

On second thought Pettengill found his envy less acute. *Colorado* was one of the big steam frigates, a sister of *Merrimack*. Sproston was too young to be her first lieutenant: third or fourth was more like it. So he'd have considerably less play for initiative—of which he had plenty—than was afforded by his present command. If Pettengill were ordered to sea in a big ship, he'd be even worse off.

"Who'll be your new skipper?" he asked.

"Theodorus Bailey," Sproston answered. "He's all right. He's a fighter and has a sense of humor to boot. Of course we might get some old crab of a flag officer to cramp Bailey's style. I'll admit I'd rather have been ordered to a sloop-of-war than a first-rate— Oh, well, anything to get out of this bushwhacking flotilla business. But before I go—"

He glanced quickly to right and left, set his glass on the bar, and leaned closer to Pettengill.

"We're going to have a little fun right here. You've heard the news?"

"Nothing special."

"I'd better tell you, you'll get your orders when you get back to your ship anyway," Sproston went on. "This is Monday. On Friday we're going across the river and help the Army take Alexandria. My *Mount Vernon* carries troops, so does Howison's *Baltimore*. *Pawnee* covers the landing, with you standing by for any inshore work that comes along."

"Great day in the morning!" exclaimed Pettengill. "So we're getting ahead with the war at last!"

"And about time." Then Sproston's smile faded as he half-whispered: "The orders are secret, of course, Pettengill: you'll find there's an injunction that they're for commanding officers of vessels only, you can't even tell your executive officer till Thursday evening. Mind you remember that: this town's spy-crazy, and the Department's got a bad case of the disease. They'll keel-haul the man who blabs."

Pettengill nodded. The dispatches he had taken to Rowan must have been concerned with this same matter: they must have mentioned Pettengill's part in it, since he was to support Rowan, but Rowan hadn't said a word to him on the subject. Maybe that was super-caution, since Rowan knew that Pettengill either already had, or soon would have, his own orders. In a way Pettengill admired that attitude; he didn't quite like Sproston's whispering this secret in a crowded bar. Probably Sproston wouldn't have done it if he hadn't been in such high spirits over his sea orders.

If the Rebels got the word, they could bring up troops and guns from their main army at Manassas Junction and make the Union forces pay a bitter price in lives for Alexandria. For once, let a secret be kept until the blow fell. Sproston was signaling to the bartender. Pettengill, looking carelessly around, was fairly sure no one could have heard what had been said. There was too much noise in the big barroom.

Through the uproar Pettengill heard a voice which bawled:

"I've said it before and I'll say it again! What this country needs is a little bloodletting!"

The voice belonged to a bushy-whiskered man wearing a fawn-colored coat and a vest of the loudest plaid Pettengill had ever seen. He was leaning over a table at which two other men were sitting, hammering on the marble top with his fist.

"That's Senator Zach Chandler of Michigan," said Sproston. "A big gun in the Administration, I hear tell. The others are Senator Wade of Ohio, he's the bushy-head with the tight mouth and shoe-button eyes. The skinny one with the long nose is Senator Crossmore from—oh, some other Western state, I can't remember. All red-hot abolitionists."

Pettengill could scarcely hear his friend for the racket of approval that had greeted Chandler's words. Army officers, mostly half-seas over, were crowding around to shake the great man's hand and congratulate him on his sentiments.

"Look at 'em," grunted Pettengill. "Three months' militia, the whole pack. You don't see any Regulars joining the chorus; they know what bloodletting amounts to."

He downed his second rum-and-lime.

"I expect I'd better be getting back to my ship, Sproston," he went on. "If you're coming along, maybe we can share a hack."

"Good idea," agreed Sproston. "I'll be glad to be clear of this lot. Those three statesmen over there went down to Hampton Roads the other day to visit Old Man Stringham: Ward brought 'em back upriver in the *Freeborn*. From what he says, they don't think much of the U.S. Navy."

His voice was lowered again because they were passing close to the senatorial table.

"I tell you our boys are r'arin' to go, Senator!" a red-faced colonel was insisting. "On to Richmond, I say, and the sooner the better! Let's show these Rebels what war is!" He caught sight of the silver anchor on Pettengill's cap and lurched around, grabbing Pettengill by the arm. "What d'you say to that, my seagoing friend?" he demanded.

"Go ahead and God be with you," snapped Pettengill, jerking his arm free.

"I'm afraid, Colonel," said Senator Crossmore in a tone that was an open sneer, "you'll find our Navy is a very cautious service. Very prudent and careful when it comes to bloodletting. God help our country if it's left to the do-nothing Navy to stamp out this wicked rebellion!"

"Why, you—" began Pettengill.

Sproston laid a hand on his shoulder.

"Sheer off, sailor," he muttered. "The man's drunk."

Pettengill took more careful note of the pale, supercilious face with its curly beard. The eyes were bloodshot, the thin lips hung loose in tipsy derision.

"Better talk about something else, Crossmore," suggested Chandler.

"Tut-tut, Senator, you know I'm right; didn't you see our bold Navy in action just the other day?" giggled Crossmore. "Yes, indeed. Listen to this, gentlemen. Two big Navy ships, well armed, fully manned, opened fire on a Rebel battery at Sewell's Point, and what do you think happened? Why, when the Rebels fired back the Navy ran away."

Several Army officers laughed. Pettengill had no idea what had happened at Sewell's Point, a reconnaissance probably to test the Confederate defenses. Sproston was still tugging at his shoulder. After all, this man was a Senator. Pettengill took a step toward the exit.

"Prudent to the end," laughed Crossmore. "I hope you brave gentlemen of the Army won't find the Navy elsewhere on Friday morning when—"

Pettengill lunged sideways against the table, driving the marble edge of the table top into Crossmore's stomach. The breath went out of the Senator's body as the table pinned him against the wall. His hands clawed at his belly as he gasped for air.

Pettengill thrust Chandler aside, pulled the table away from Crossmore, and got an arm around his shoulders.

"My fault, Senator! My clumsiness!" he cried, trying to sound distressed. "I slipped on those damned wet tiles. You're not hurt, I hope?"

Sproston was right beside him, shouldering the clamorous mob of Army people away.

"He's not hurt," said Senator Wade grimly, speaking for the first time. "But, by God, he should've been. Leave him to me, young man. You've done your part. I'll do mine. I'll take care of him. Now shut your mouth, Len Crossmore."

Crossmore, sick and still clutching his belly, stared at Pettengill with a dull light of comprehension dawning in his eyes. His white lips moved.

"You did that apurpose," he whispered.

"Nonsense," rapped Wade. "It was an accident. Come on, Len. Get up. I'll see you to your hotel. Lend a hand here, Zach."

Crossmore staggered to his feet.

"Can't," he muttered. "Can't go hotel—yet. Got to meet lady."

Wade and Chandler linked arms with him.

"My sincere apologies, Senator Crossmore," lied Pettengill.

Crossmore wasn't looking at him. Wade turned his gray head far enough for Pettengill to see one jet-black eye close in a quick wink.

The Army contingent was melting away.

"I never saw anything so neatly done in my life, Pettengill," chuckled Sproston, as the two naval officers followed the Senators toward the door. "That son-of-a-bitch would've blurted out the whole business about Friday morning in another two seconds. You shut him off just in time. He won't talk now. Wade understands, and Wade's honest and a true Union man. I'm from Ohio myself, my family knows him. He'll keep Crossmore quiet, for long enough at least. But you've made yourself an enemy in Crossmore, Pettengill. He knows you did it on purpose, and he'll remember. He's the nasty type. If he ever gets on the Naval Committee—"

They were crossing one of the big parlors. Just ahead of them, Crossmore and his two companions were walking slowly.

"Len! Len, what's happened?" The sound of that voice froze Pettengill's feet to the flowered carpet. A woman in a dress of blue watered silk was running toward Crossmore. She gripped his sagging shoulders with both hands.

"Len, darling! Are you ill? Who— Oh!"

Too late, Pettengill started to turn toward the side door that led to Fourteenth Street. Too late to avoid looking straight into the tawny eyes of Emma Harrifield.

He kept on going, but he knew those widening eyes followed him until the door closed behind him.

He knew, too, where Senator Crossmore had acquired his low opinion of the Navy.

Chapter Ten

Surprise had been complete and overwhelming.
Both Alexandria and Arlington Heights were in Union hands, with scarcely a shot fired in their defense.

Colonel Ellsworth's Fire Zouaves had landed on the wharves just at dawn, less than an hour ago, and had pushed forward rapidly under the leadership of their dashing young colonel to meet the First Michigan, crossing by the Long Bridge: other regiments followed the Michigan outfit, still others crossed by the Aqueduct Bridge farther up the river. The small Confederate garrison had fled just in time to avoid capture, except for a few luckless cavalrymen, left behind as rear-guard, who had been caught by the Fire Zouaves and now stood huddled under sentry's charge on the wharf.

"Not much of a show for the Navy," grumbled Pettengill. He stood at the edge of the wharf, looking at the unhappy prisoners and their swaggering, baggy-trousered Zouave guards.

"The *Pawnee* had two boat crews ashore ahead of the Zouaves," said Master's Mate Casson. "That's something."

"Just Rowan's Irish bounce, trying to do the Army in the eye," retorted Pettengill. "I'll bet he'll hear from it when the Army people run hollering to the Secretary of War. That young Colonel Ellsworth didn't look pleased when he found Lieutenant Lowry waiting for him here on this wharf."

"All the same, Captain, the Navy was ashore first," insisted Casson. He was a bright young man, shorter than Pettengill, with a wiry, slender body that was much stronger than it looked. He had had no naval experience; his mate's ticket was only a year old, and he had spent that year in the Fall River steamers. But he had a quick mind: Pettengill was already teaching him the elements of gunnery, and was secretly proud of the way the boy caught on. It was a sort of fatherly feeling; Casson could hardly have been more than twenty-one, a full two years younger than Pettengill. Besides, Pettengill was delighted to have someone he could refer to as "my executive officer"; that was almost more satisfying than being called captain.

"Wonder how long they're going to keep us hanging around here doing nothing?" Pettengill grumbled.

The *Brother Jonathan,* by Commander Rowan's order, was tied up to the wharf, of which Pettengill was presumed to be in charge. The wharf itself was piled high with boxes of hardtack and rifle ammunition. Army officers came and went, all seemingly on pressing business: occasionally wagons creaked up, loaded stores amid a flurry of profane argument as to whether this stack of boxes belonged to the Seventh New York or the First New Jersey, and creaked away again.

The townsfolk had been much excited at first: now they were cooling off, some going about their usual business, others standing around staring at the Zouaves and seamen on the wharf. A few women came with food for the prisoners, which the Zouave officer good-naturedly allowed them to receive. There seemed to be very little rancor against the invaders: even a feeble cheer had been heard when Lowry had hoisted his boat ensign on the Custom House.

Alexandrians, take them by and large, didn't favor secession as strongly as the folks around Norfolk, though that Confederate flag was still flying above the Marshall House. Why didn't the Zouaves haul it down? Never mind. This was a beginning. . . .

In fact, as Pettengill dimly realized, the Army's capture of Alexandria, supported by the Navy, set a pattern for the future: the seizure, one by one, of the seaports of the South by amphibious operations. Storm from the sea, supplementing and relieving blockade. A harbor held by the Union Army didn't have to be blockaded by Union warships. A harbor held by the Union Army could also become a base of operations for the blockade of neighboring harbors, so that blockading steamers wouldn't be running back north for coal every few days. Commander Rowan had been saying something like that just the other day, growling about *Pawnee* being a big coal eater.

At the moment, the *Pawnee* wasn't eating much coal. She swung to her anchor a cable's length from the wharf. Her half-ports were out, the muzzles of her heavy shell-guns grinned through the five square openings in her side. Her launch and cutter were at the boom, ready. But there would be no need for guns or landing parties again today. Pettengill's own gun crews were at their quarters, armed and alert, manning the rifled howitzer for'd and the smooth-bore aft. He considered securing from quarters and turning to on ship's work, there was plenty to be done: no, better not until word came from

General Mansfield, the Army commander, that Alexandria was officially pronounced clear of the enemy.

Some of the Fire Zouaves had started a game of leapfrog.

"Full of steam, aren't they?" Pettengill muttered.

"Full of the Old Nick," Casson remarked. "They're tough lads, they'll try anything once. I know 'em, I was born and brought up in New York City. Most of these fellows were in the volunteer fire companies—about the roughest hell-raising lot of rowdies in the world. I hear tell their kid colonel's the only man can handle 'em; they just roll over and play dead like old dog Tray when he tells 'em to. They think he's God or something. Hello—we've got visitors."

An open carriage, escorted by two troopers of the District of Columbia cavalry, was coming down the street: there were four or five people in it, all civilians in stovepipe hats. No, one was a woman: Pettengill could see flowers among the stovepipes.

"Come to see the battle, the fools," said Casson.

"The officer who gave 'em a pass to cross the bridge ought to be cashiered," declared Pettengill.

His annoyance was tempered by the disappearance of the Confederate flag from the Marshall House flagstaff. Now maybe he would get permission to shove off. He hoped he could have the rest of the day alongside the Navy Yard wharf; there were a dozen things he wanted done to the *Brother Jonathan* before he went on patrol again.

Far up the street men were yelling. A horseman, galloping madly, came tearing around a corner headed for the wharf. He was an officer of the Fire Zouaves, a captain by the trefoils of gold lace on his sleeves.

"Colonel Ellsworth! Colonel Ellsworth!" he shouted.

He flung himself from his saddle at the wharf's edge, ran toward Pettengill, still shouting, his face scarlet with excitement or rage.

"Colonel Ellsworth's not here, Captain," Pettengill told him.

"I know goddam well he's not here!" howled the Zouave officer. "He's been murdered! Murdered by a dirty bastard of a Rebel because he hauled down that Rebel flag!"

A roar of fury went up from the throats of the Zouave guard. Other Zouaves were running along the street, shouting: "Kill the Rebels! Kill every Rebel rat! Burn the town!"

The officer of the guard jerked his sword from its scabbard, glaring at his prisoners. The captain joined him.

"Mr. Casson!" said Pettengill sharply. "Take the for'd gun crew and get those prisoners aboard the *Brother Jonathan*. Lively, now."

He strode over to the gibbering officers.

"I'm taking charge of your prisoners, gentlemen," he snapped.

The two Zouave officers both started yelling at once, half insane with grief and rage. Pettengill backed away from them, placing himself so that any Zouaves who tried to get at the prisoners would have to get past Pettengill first. Casson, cool and steady, was directing Aycock and six seamen who were herding the prisoners toward the tug. The frightened prisoners went eagerly enough.

"Don't let those villains get off scot-free!" shouted a loud angry voice. Three or four Zouaves started forward, sword-bayonets advanced—and halted as the steady muzzle of Pettengill's revolver confronted them.

"That's far enough, boys," barked Pettengill. "The Navy's in charge here on the wharf."

"The Navy's protecting Rebels and murderers as usual!"

It was the loud angry voice again. A man in a stovepipe hat was shouldering his way through the screaming mob of Zouaves, brandishing a gold-knobbed cane over his head.

Pettengill knew the voice now—and the face under the hat: the face of Senator Crossmore.

"Vengeance on murderers! God's vengeance!" howled Crossmore. He scrambled up on a pile of hardtack boxes; the Zouaves bayed about him.

Pettengill, flicking a quick glance over one shoulder, saw that all the prisoners were aboard the tug. Casson, wisely, was herding them down into the stuffy little fo'c'sle. They would be badly crowded, but they would be out of sight.

"Mr. Casson!" Pettengill sang out. "I'll have both gun crews on the alert, ready to fire on my order."

"Aye aye, sir!"

"Aycock! Signal the *Pawnee:* Need immediate assistance, send armed boats."

"Aye aye, sir!"

Crossmore was bawling about God's vengeance from his crackerbox pedestal, but his words were drowned in a rising chorus of lamentation mixed with fury. A great mass of gray, blue, and scarlet was coming down the street, gathered close about a group of men who were carrying something.

The Fire Zouaves were bringing the body of their dead colonel down to the waterside.

"There he lies, your gallant leader, slain by a Rebel's hand!" screamed Crossmore. "Are you going to let him die unavenged, brave Zouaves?"

"No! No!" cried a hundred furious voices.

In another minute it would be too late. Pettengill was working his way along the side of the wharf shed toward that pile of boxes.

"Then burn every—" began Crossmore.

Pettengill's long left arm snaked out past the shaven head of a screaming Zouave; his left hand closed like a vise on Crossmore's ankle and his feet braced themselves on the planks as he heaved with all his strength.

Crossmore came down with a crash on top of the hardtack boxes.

Pettengill grabbed him by the coat collar, yanked him erect, swung him toward the *Brother Jonathan*.

A dozen Zouaves were clawing at Pettengill's arms and shoulders. Pettengill, propelling the dazed Crossmore ahead of him, broke free: and there was Jackson, with Reilly at his side, leaping from gunwale to wharf to receive the prisoner.

"Lock him up in my cabin, he's under arrest!" Pettengill ordered.

"Burn! He said burn!" somebody shouted.

"Smash this shed! Make torches! Burn the damn Rebels in their nests!" The cry was spreading, but there was no commanding voice to keep it alive now. Pettengill saw the braided sleeve of the Zouave captain.

"You!" he seized the man by one shoulder. "Get up there! Stop those fools! You want your regiment disgraced forever?"

The captain stuttered something like "What can I do?"

The angry Zouaves eddied around Pettengill and the captain, eddied and broke away suddenly, leaving a little cleared space where other Zouaves were reverently putting down their burden on the planking.

The slight body of the little colonel in his brilliant uniform might have been the body of a tired boy, resting after playing soldier, except for the dark-stained jacket that hid his head and shoulders.

A woman was bending over him, a woman in a flowered hat.

She was dipping her handkerchief in the clotted blood.

Now she swayed erect, turned, and saw Pettengill staring at her with unbelieving eyes.

"Traitor!" spat Emma Harrifield.

Pettengill stood paralyzed, unable to find words to fit his feelings.

"When I show them this," hissed Mrs. Harrifield, "they'll make this town a funeral pyre in honor of their colonel!"

"That's it!" cried Pettengill, and jumped for the pile of crackerboxes on the wings of inspiration.

"Zouaves!" His great voice beat down the howls and sobs of the anguished men. "My orders are to take your colonel's body to Washington. President Lincoln himself is waiting to mourn beside it!"

There was a sudden silence. Faces that had been twisted with the lust to kill and burn became intent on Pettengill's words.

"It's not fit that he go alone with the Navy," roared Pettengill. "I want a guard of honor from his own regiment to attend him! Captain, fall in your companies! Tell off the two oldest soldiers in each company to go with the colonel!"

"He's lying!" screamed Emma Harrifield. "He's never—"

But her words were lost as a dozen officers and sergeants took up the cry: "Fall in! Fall in by companies! A Company, this way! D Company! F Company!"

A bugle blared the Assembly; the bayonets that had been threatening Pettengill were forming up in serried ranks of steel. The Zouave captain, finding his voice at last, took charge and began to make himself obeyed. There would be no fire and sword for Alexandria now.

Pettengill hopped down from his crackerbox rostrum, lifted his cap to Colonel Ellsworth's body, and started toward the *Brother Jonathan*.

Emma Harrifield said in a strangled voice:

"Mr. Pettengill, in the day of His wrath, the Lord will smite you."

He kept on going.

Lieutenant Lowry of the *Pawnee* came running along the wharf, sword in hand; seamen and Marines from his boats were swarming ashore behind him.

"What's happened here, Mr. Pettengill?" panted Lowry.

"Colonel Ellsworth's been murdered, sir," Pettengill told him.

"Who did it?"

"Some Rebel hothead. I haven't had time to learn the details. Senator Crossmore's been trying to get the Zouaves to burn the town and massacre the inhabitants. I had to stop that."

"I was watching some of it through my glasses," Lowry said. "You mean to tell me that was a United States Senator you heaved off that pile of boxes on his ass?"

"Yes, sir," said Pettengill.

Lowry stared at him, appalled.

"Lord help you!" he muttered.

"According to what I hear," Pettengill informed him, "that's not too likely."

Get it over with, thought Pettengill.

The big office in the Ordnance building at the Washington Navy Yard, which Captain Dahlgren preferred to the office provided for the commandant, was silent now, waiting. Secretary of the Navy Gideon Welles in person, looking like a bad-tempered Santa Claus, sat at Dahlgren's desk; Mr. Fox, the chief clerk of the Department, bent over the Secretary, whispering to him and glancing occasionally at Pettengill. At one end of the desk, Senator Crossmore brooded; his gloating eyes never left Pettengill's face. He had spoken his piece, with embellishments. Pettengill had tried to speak his, and had been cut short by a curt word from Welles. The Secretary was in a cold rage. Captain Dahlgren, blond-whiskered and scowling, stood behind the Secretary with half-a-dozen other officers. Pettengill could look for no help from any of them. Commander Rowan of the *Pawnee* might have said a word for him; he'd given verbal approval to what Pettengill had done, but he was still off Alexandria.

Unhappily, Pettengill had no proof of the frightful urgency that had laid such imperative compulsion on him at the moment he had yanked Crossmore off that pile of boxes. Crossmore had denied that he had intended anything more than the burning of the Marshall House, whose proprietor had been the murderer of Colonel Ellsworth. The killer himself was already dead, slain at the scene of his crime by Private Brownell. That his property should likewise perish as a grim reminder of the price of murder seemed to all present a just retribution.

Pettengill's eyes strayed out through the window to the rusty smokestack of his little *Brother Jonathan*—no longer his, in all likelihood. Just astern of her lay a much larger vessel, a long low black-painted screw steamer which had arrived yesterday from Philadelphia to be fitted out as a blockading cruiser. *Valiant*, her name was. Pettengill had dreamed, yesterday, of seeking transfer to her. That dream was dead, too. He was as good as out of the Navy right now.

Secretary Welles looked up at Pettengill and cleared his throat.

Here it came. . . .

There was a stir at the door. Fox looked around, muttered a quick word. Secretary Welles was rising to his feet.

"The President, gentlemen," said Captain Dahlgren sharply. The officers snapped to attention.

A tall, gaunt man in a suit of shapeless black came slowly across the room, hat in hand. He was taller even than Pettengill, and had much the same awkward carriage. The deep-lined face looked kind. Hope stirred in Pettengill's heart—and died again.

For close behind the President marched Emma Harrifield, her eyes alight with vengeful triumph.

"Mr. Welles," said the President in his resonant voice, "I have come here to pay homage to the remains of my poor young friend Colonel Ellsworth, the first Union officer to give his life for his country in this war."

"His body lies in the next room, Mr. President," said Welles.

"I have been told so," nodded Lincoln. "I shall go there at once. But this lady has a story I think you should hear. She informs me that my name was wrongfully invoked on the wharf at Alexandria to prevent Colonel Ellsworth's men from, as I take it, doing justice on his slayer. Invoked, Mr. Welles, by one of your officers, who also assaulted Senator Crossmore for intervening in the matter."

Welles gestured toward Pettengill.

"Acting Master Pettengill here is the officer in question," he said. "His conduct is now under consideration, as a result of Senator Crossmore's allegations."

Pettengill found the President's steady eyes looking straight into his: they seemed to hold more of sadness than of anger. They also seemed to hold a question.

He had nothing to lose by answering it.

"Mr. President," he said, "I did use your name. I also applied what seemed to me to be reasonable and necessary force to Senator Crossmore's person. I did so to stop Senator Crossmore from inciting Colonel Ellsworth's Zouaves to lay the town of Alexandria in ashes and massacre the people in revenge for the murder of their colonel. I don't know if it was the Senator's own idea or if he was being egged on by this lady."

"Well, of course—" began Crossmore, taking note, as had Pettengill, of the increasing gravity of the President's expression.

"Stand up like a man for what you know is right, Len Crossmore!" interrupted Mrs. Harrifield. "Fire and sword for Rebels and murder-

[130]

ers! Purge the sins of the nation in the cleansing flame of God's wrath!" Her voice mounted to a scream.

"Emma!" cried Crossmore. "This is no time—" He was at her side now, gripping her arm, talking on in a hurried whisper.

"Son," said Abraham Lincoln, looking at Pettengill, "you seem to've done some fishing in your life. Anyway you know how to bait hooks."

Secretary Welles cleared his throat again, running his hand over the flowing locks of his wig.

"The lady's remarks," he said in the driest of tones, "don't quite jibe with Senator Crossmore's earlier account."

Lincoln's deep-set eyes moved from Welles to Crossmore and came back to Pettengill. The question was still there.

"It seemed to me, Mr. President," said Pettengill, "that to carry fire and sword through the first Southern town to be occupied by our forces would rouse every Southerner to madness and dishonor our flag in the eyes of the world."

Lincoln nodded.

"There's something in that, Mr. Pettengill," he observed, "as the girl said when she put her leg in her stocking. Just exactly what did you do?"

"Senator Crossmore was making a speech to the Zouaves from a pile of crackerboxes, sir," Pettengill said. "So I pulled his leg out from under him and got up there and made a speech myself."

"Indeed," said the President, with careful solemnity. "And what was the subject of your speech, Mr. Pettengill?"

"Sir, what I said was suggested by a remark of Mrs. Harrifield's about making Alexandria a funeral pyre to do honor to Colonel Ellsworth's memory," said Pettengill. "I told 'em they shouldn't let the Navy have full charge of his body. They ought to form an honor guard to escort it here, where you would be waiting, sir. Of course I wasn't sure of that, but they seemed to think it was important. Anyway it distracted 'em."

"You were quite right in anticipating my presence," said Abraham Lincoln as Pettengill began to falter in embarrassment. "Mr. Welles, it'd be my view that this young man did the best he could under very difficult circumstances. Naturally I don't want to interfere with discipline."

"I appear to have been, ah, inaccurately informed, Mr. President," said Welles. "Mr. Pettengill seems to have had considerable justification." He glared at Crossmore.

Emma Harrifield stood in white-faced silence.

Crossmore said:

"Either we are going to put down this rebellion by ruthless force or let it grow until it destroys us. This I say now, Mr. President, and this I will say on the floor of the Senate as occasion offers."

"But the end, Senator," murmured Lincoln, "must be the restoration of the Union, with our Southern brethren returning to the fold. War is bad enough. If there is to be murder and rapine as well, then let the guilt not be ours. And speaking of murder, may I see—"

"This way, Mr. President—if you will honor me," said Dahlgren quickly. The President nodded to Pettengill and started toward the door that led to the room where Ellsworth's body lay.

Welles would have followed, but Crossmore was at his elbow, talking angrily in a low voice.

The room had become packed. Every officer in the Navy Yard must have jammed his way in as soon as the word was passed that the President was here: not only naval officers but quite a few of the Seventy-first New York, who garrisoned the Yard.

"Mr. Pettengill," said Secretary Welles.

"Mr. Secretary."

"Senator Crossmore has been making a study of our regulations," observed Welles acidly. "Including my recent order that every vessel of the Navy must be commanded by a regular officer. I gather from Mr. Fox that your status in that respect is somewhat, ah, anomalous."

"I have had two years' service, sir," Pettengill offered.

"So I am informed," said Welles. "But you still hold only an acting appointment as master. You are not a master in the line of promotion and hence, under existing orders, not entitled to command. I fear—"

Chief Clerk Fox looked up, his square-cut chin whiskers thrust out.

"The case is unusual, Mr. Welles," he suggested. "Mr. Pettengill is hardly a regular naval officer; but he has been serving as master's mate under an acting appointment since 1859, on the African station. I recall that he came home last month as prize master of a captured slaver, and was well reported on by his captain: he cut the slaver out himself with a boat's crew. Captain Du Pont appointed him acting master and gave him his present command. He was at the Norfolk Navy Yard during that terrible business: you'll recall Mr. Isherwood spoke well of him, and he helped Rowan tow out the *Cumberland* when the other ships were burned. I'd say Mr. Pettengill is considerably more valuable to the Navy than any fresh fish right out of the merchant marine."

Fox was an ex-naval officer and he seemed to have a sailor's sense of values.

"Nevertheless he isn't entitled to command a vessel of the Navy unless Mr. Welles wishes to change his present standing order," insisted Crossmore. "In which case, when Congress meets in special session on July fourth, I shall take the matter up with the Naval Committee of the Senate. I don't consider it safe to allow untested young men to hold naval commands."

Welles shook his wigged head.

"I don't want to be unjust, Fox," he said, "and of course there's no question now of Mr. Pettengill's not retaining his appointment as acting master. But perhaps he could be more suitably employed for a time."

It was plain that Welles wanted to throw Crossmore some sop of appeasement.

"Mr. Secretary, may I say a word?"

An officer in a lieutenant's uniform came pushing forward through the crowded room.

Unbelievably, but unmistakably, he was Lieutenant Pendleton Banks.

"Well?" barked Welles.

"Mr. Pettengill and I were shipmates in the *Sheboygan* these past two years," said Banks in his cool, detached way, his tropic-tanned face very serious in its frame of close-trimmed, dark side whiskers. "I can bear testimony to his worth as an officer. You have been good enough to appoint me to the command of the steamer *Valiant*, sir. If Mr. Pettengill's services are available, I should regard it as a privilege to have him as my executive officer."

Welles' face cleared. A faint suggestion of a smile wriggled in the Santa Claus beard.

"That is quite satisfactory," he said. "I trust Mr. Pettengill agrees?"

"Indeed, sir," cried Pettengill.

Welles' eyes twinkled under the fringe of his wig as he surveyed Crossmore's angry face.

"I insist—" Crossmore began.

"Senator Crossmore!" said Welles sharply. "It is your privilege to invite my attention to infringements of the regulations and standing orders of the Navy. It is not your privilege to dictate the appointments to be given to officers within the letter and spirit of those regulations. Mr. Fox, I shall be glad if Mr. Pettengill's orders to the *Valiant* are on my desk for signature this afternoon."

Pettengill, wringing the hand of his friend Pendleton Banks and trying to find words to express the gratitude that filled his heart, heard Crossmore say:

"You have not heard the end of this matter, Mr. Secretary Welles."

"I don't doubt that," said Banks to Pettengill. "But damn him! We'll do a job together that'll be more than all his malice can besmirch. Him and his feline female friend. Who the devil is she, anyway?"

"Name's Harrifield. I met her once at Captain Du Pont's house," Pettengill answered, taking note that Mrs. Harrifield was nowhere to be seen. "She's a dame with a mission, sir."

"Lord deliver us from all such," shuddered Banks. "Du Pont spoke well of you, Pettengill. He's coming here shortly to head up a board of strategy; he's the best man they could pick for that job. But tell me what you've been doing besides assaulting senators? Du Pont said something about your distinguishing yourself at Norfolk."

"I wrote you, but I suppose you haven't—"

"I've had no mail at all from home since I last saw you," Banks interrupted. "The *Sheboygan* arrived at Philadelphia three days ago to pay off; I applied for immediate sea service and was ordered straight to the *Valiant*."

"Then," said Pettengill, "I have news for you."

He watched the sun of a great joy rise in Banks' dark eyes as he repeated Virgilia Seabright's message.

Maybe some day—

No. He'd never hear such news from Terry.

Chapter Eleven

The U.S. war steamer *Valiant* lay alongside the Ordnance dock in the Washington Navy Yard, preparing for sea.

The sun of the hottest summer in the memory of the capital's oldest inhabitants beat down on her cluttered deck, and on her executive officer, with twenty things to attend to all at once. But he had known a hotter sun in Africa, and his heart was too full of happiness to worry about personal discomfort.

This time the orders were going to stick. Fox and Du Pont, now on duty in the Navy Department, had both given Banks their personal assurance that there'd be no more last-minute foul-ups. Three times the *Valiant* had been on the point of sailing to join Flag Officer Stringham's Atlantic Blockading Squadron. Three times her orders had been countermanded to keep her in the Potomac: once early in June because of a wild rumor that the Rebel army was going to cross into Maryland, once late in that month after Commander Ward had been killed trying to capture the Confederate position at Mathias Point, and once last week after the shattering defeat of the Union Army at Bull Run.

But the determined demands of Stringham for more ships and the urging of Du Pont that the blockade was more important than a few extra guns in the Potomac had prevailed at last. The day after tomorrow the *Valiant* would be steaming down the Potomac River on her way to report to Stringham at Hampton Roads, and Pettengill hoped that her keel would never plow muddy Potomac waters again.

No more Potomac Flotilla ("Mr. Casson, I'll thank you to sway those powder tanks aboard two at a time: four's too much of a strain on that purchase"). No more mosquitoes, sand bars, Rebel bushwhackers like the scoundrel who'd shot down poor old Aycock as he stood at the wheel. Why couldn't a shield of boiler iron be rigged to protect helmsmen in river craft? An iron gun-shield would have saved Commander Ward, too. What was the use of Yankee ingenuity and industrial capacity if it wasn't to be applied in such obvious ways? ("New draft from the receiving ship? Very well, have 'em stow their gear on the berth deck in charge of the master-at-arms, and turn 'em to at once. We're shorthanded as it is.") No more boat expeditions up stinking creeks, no more swamp fever ("Get those fenders over, Hodgson! Don't you see the shear-barge coming alongside?"). . . .

Now here was Yankee ingenuity in practice—that beautiful sleek new 60-pounder Parrott rifle that lay in its chocks on the shear-barge. What a hell of a time he and Banks had had, convincing the Ordnance people in the Yard that the old X-inch smooth-bore which the Parrott was to replace simply didn't have range enough to be the chase gun for a blockading cruiser. . . .

Lord, it would be good to be at sea again, with salt spray on face and a heaving deck under foot: and Lord, *how* good it would be to get away from the city of Washington and its mess of troubles, to get out from under the pall of gloom that had settled down over the capital since the terrible shock of Bull Run, to listen no more to prophets of doom and dark whispers of treason and betrayal. ("Boy, my compliments to Mr. Hurlbut and he can knock off stowing the hold and rouse his people on deck to bear a hand with that gun."). . . .

That would be the best of all, getting away from the clack-clack of tongues, especially the jeers and bragging of the Southern sympathizers, male and female, who still swarmed in Washington's streets and public places, openly predicting that the Rebel flag would be flying above the unfinished dome of the Capitol before that summer of '61 was over. The women were the worst—Lincoln's "Secesh dames"—not only those who shrilled their triumph and spat in the faces of wounded soldiers being carried past on litters, but those who made it a practice to lure officers and seamen into brothels and worm from them bits of information which somebody, somewhere, might weave into a pattern. . . .

Yes, it would be good, damned good, to be at sea again where the Atlantic gales could sweep away all the filth, almost too good to be true. Of course Banks didn't quite agree that females were an unmitigated curse to sailors, considering that he was getting married tomorrow. . . .

Pettengill had a good crew. More than half of them had had prior service in the Navy. He had brought along Jackson and half-a-dozen others from the *Brother Jonathan;* Banks had gathered up twenty or thirty old *Sheboygans,* including Bo's'n's Mate Hodgson and Cox'n Quinn. . . .

"There's an Army officer come aboard, sir. Asks to have a word with you."

"Very well, quartermaster."

Pettengill disliked the visitor at sight: a short, stub-bearded fellow in a major's fatigue uniform, with the too-clever face of a weasel and the sharpest blue eyes Pettengill had ever seen.

"My name's Allen," he introduced himself. "I understand your captain isn't aboard?"

He made it sound like an accusation.

"Not at the moment," said Pettengill shortly. "I'm the executive officer—Acting Master Pettengill. What can I do for you?"

A rush of men from forward, swaying up the next sling-load of powder, almost took the little major off his feet.

"A private word with you, perhaps?" he suggested. His harsh voice held a hint of a Scots burr.

"I can't leave the deck just at present, Major Allen," said Pettengill, liking less and less the way those gimlet eyes bored into him. "The powder flag's flying, we're about to hoist in a new gun, and—yes, chief, what is it?"

"The Yard workmen haven't come aboard to put the felt and sheet-iron casings on my cylinders," complained the chief engineer, wiping sweat, grease and engine oil from his face with the sleeve of a filthy dungaree jacket. "If we don't get that done, we'll burn twice the coal we ought to when we get outside—"

"All right, chief," interrupted Pettengill. He wasn't going to have the ship's sea orders discussed in front of this unknown stranger. But the matter was serious: excessive fuel consumption in a blockading steamer could mean she'd spend half her time running back to Hampton Roads for coal. "Go over to the Yard engineer's office," he told the chief, "and make it clear to him that if his people aren't here within a half-hour, Captain Banks'll be calling on the commandant to find out why."

"Fine," said the chief bitterly. "All I've got to do is run goddam errands. Oh, well, I'll try. It'll give me a chance to remind the old buzzard about those three coal heavers I'm short of. I notice they didn't turn up in this draft that just came aboard. I've got to have three more bodies down below there if you don't want me yelling for deck hands to pass coal every time you want some speed out of this hooker."

He went off, still grumbling, after the fashion of chief engineers the world over. Pettengill swung back to his visitor.

"Sorry, Major Allen, but you can see I haven't the time—"

"You have the time to glance at this, I think," said Allen, unfolding a piece of paper from his well-worn wallet.

The paper was a Navy Department letterhead. It bore two lines in spidery handwriting:

> The bearer is Major E. J. Allen, chief of the Federal Secret Service. He will be afforded all proper facilities in the discharge of his duty. Gideon Welles.

"Come up on the bridge, then," said Pettengill. "Nobody there just now."

He led the way up the ladder, his mind a whirl of sudden anxiety. What did the Federal Secret Service have to do with him, or with the *Valiant*?

"Well, Major Allen?"

The gimlet eyes surveyed Pettengill's six feet two plus of lanky body from the battered straw hat on his head down to the outsized feet.

"Mr. Pettengill," he said, "I understand you've been serving in the Potomac Flotilla the best part of three months."

"That's right."

"Then you must be aware that boats are continually passing back and forth across the river between the Maryland and Virginia shores, carrying supplies and information to the Rebels?"

Pettengill felt the hot tide of anger begin to rise at the back of his neck, but he kept his voice steady:

"I suppose boats do pass. We stop 'em when we catch 'em, and we've sent in every boat we've nabbed on or approaching the Virginia shore, according to orders. I may add that your Provost Marshal here has seen fit to turn loose most of the persons we have arrested in the performance of this duty. But how d'you expect the Flotilla to stop all traffic by day and by night along a hundred and twenty-five miles of river channel with nothing more than this ship, half-a-dozen old river steamers, which spend half their time having their engines patched up, and the *Pawnee* sloop-of-war, which the nervous Nellies uptown have kept at anchor off the Arsenal these past ten days with her guns trained on the Long Bridge, to stop the Rebels from crossing, since the Army doesn't seem able to do it?"

"I am not unaware of the difficulties," Major Allen said in his matter-of-fact way. "But we have reason to believe that there is a regularly organized spy-ferry service operating across the Potomac below this city, conveying Rebel dispatches which are forwarded by mounted couriers to Fredericksburg and so on to the headquarters of the Rebel army at Manassas, or to Richmond by the cars. We know that reports of everything that's said or that happens in Washington reaches the Rebels daily. Daily, Mr. Pettengill. Regular as clockwork. That means organization. It means relays of horsemen, standing by round the clock at established points. It means a regular rendezvous and headquarters on the Virginia side, perhaps several such stations." Allen was driving home each point by prodding Pettengill's chest with a monitory finger. "So, Mr. Pettengill," he summed up, "maybe it isn't too unreasonable for us to expect the Navy's patrols to detect and put a stop to so elaborately organized a system of ferriage."

"Elaborate pipe dream!" Pettengill exclaimed. "You haven't the wit to catch the spies who're sending the information, so you're trying to blame the Navy for your own incompetence. It's an old Army custom."

He was taking a high line, it was a cover for a very real and mounting worry. This fellow was leading up to something.

"Indeed," murmured Allen, still unperturbed. He took out a little notebook, thumbed through it, ran his finger down a page, grunted, focused his gimlet eyes on Pettengill's face again.

"The commanding officer of this ship, I believe," he said, "is Lieutenant Pendleton Banks?"

"Right."

"Born in Virginia?"

"I wasn't there at the time. Look in the Navy Register," Pettengill said savagely.

"And though his ship is being prepared for sea, Lieutenant Banks is not aboard? Just where is he now, Mr. Pettengill?"

"He's at the City Hall getting a marriage license, if that's any of your business."

Allen consulted his notebook again.

"Quite so," he agreed. "To marry a Miss Virgilia Seabright, of Portsmouth, Virginia. Correct?"

Pettengill couldn't trust himself to speak. He just nodded. The stir and bustle along the *Valiant*'s deck, fore and aft, seemed very far away. Crossmore's malice was in this business somewhere.

"With whom I understand you are acquainted?"

Pettengill nodded again.

Allen went on rustling through his notebook.

"Miss Seabright arrived in Washington this morning, I believe? By way of a flag-of-truce boat to Hampton Roads and the Baltimore steamer? Accompanied by her sister, Miss Terentia Seabright?"

Terry Seabright here in Washington! Virgilia must be out of her mind to bring Terry along. . . .

Allen closed his notebook with a snap, returned it to his pocket.

"Now, Mr. Pettengill," he said coolly, "let us understand each other. You're a Northern man, an officer of unquestioned loyalty—wait, let me go on. Your record is known to me. You served two years in the African Squadron, where you captured and brought to justice the notorious slave runner Edward Harris."

"I carried out a plan to that end devised by Lieutenant Pendleton Banks. He was executive officer of the ship in which I was serving."

"Indeed," said Allen. He went right on, ignoring the interruption. "You served with distinction during the affair at the Norfolk Navy Yard. You are highly spoken of by Captain Du Pont and Captain Rowan. You will go far during this war, with such a beginning, provided you are not lured into error."

He paused. Pettengill said nothing.

"Now, young sir," Allen continued, "you and I, as loyal citizens of the United States, must of course rejoice when we find a Southern-born officer choosing loyalty to his flag above the claims of home and friends. But those are strong ties, Mr. Pettengill. They are not easily broken. Now consider the present situation. Whatever you may think of it, we are convinced this spy-ferry service I spoke of is in regular operation. We know, for example, that a spy carrying the news of McDowell's advance on Centreville—news that enabled the Rebel generals to inflict the terrible and bloody defeat on our army at Bull Run—was ferried across the Potomac River three nights before the battle, and at a place not far from where this very steamer *Valiant* was supposed to be patrolling. Commanded, Mr. Pettengill, by an officer of Southern birth."

"Get off this ship!" Pettengill spoke through his teeth; even as his rage took control, he kept his voice down. But the major jerked back from Pettengill's blazing eyes as though expecting blow to follow utterance.

"Mr. Pettengill, you're making a mistake."

"I may be, but you'll not stand here on Captain Banks' own bridge and hint around that he's a traitor. Not in my hearing, you won't. Get off this ship before I throw you off. Move."

He was moving himself, crowding Major Allen toward the bridge ladder.

"Just one moment, Mr. Pettengill!"

"Not one second." Pettengill reached for the major's collar. The major dodged and went down the ladder, Pettengill at his heels.

"The gangway's there. Ashore with you!"

"I'll have to report your attitude to the Navy Department," announced Allen. Swift inspiration knifed through Pettengill's red fury with cooler counsel.

"As you like, Major Allen," he said, aware that several of the crew were within hearing. "But for your information, the senior officer present of the Potomac Flotilla is Captain Rowan of the *Pawnee*, at anchor off the Arsenal. I cannot receive your communication. I suggest that you go aboard *Pawnee* and present the matter to Captain Rowan. That would be the proper procedure. Good morning, Major Allen."

Pettengill had crowded the little man to the gangway by this time, leaving him no room to do anything but go down the brow to the wharf; he left with quiet composure, walking across the Yard without a single backward glance.

"I hope he tries to tell his tale to Rowan," muttered Pettengill. Red-haired, Irish-born Commander Stephen Rowan of the *Pawnee* would stand beside Pendleton Banks tomorrow and hand him the ring to put on Virgilia Seabright's finger. He would be quite capable of tossing the head of the Federal Secret Service over the *Pawnee*'s side at any suggestion that his friend might be a traitor.

But deep in Pettengill's anxious heart, a voice cried danger—this is not the end: fear rules in Washington; fear is enthroned in higher places than you or Banks or Stephen Rowan can reach, fear that strikes blindly, fear that seeks a scapegoat for defeat and incompetence. . . .

A carriage rattled into view from around the same corner where Allen had just disappeared and came briskly along the roadway toward the dock. It drew up near the foot of the brow, the door opened, and Lieutenant Pendleton Banks jumped out, very trim and neat in blue "summer frock coat" and white pantaloons. Cap under arm, he held out his hand. Pale-blue dimity billowed from the carriage door, a small foot in a pale-blue slipper groped for the step, a slender hand came out to meet Banks', and Miss Virgilia Seabright, bending her head to avoid the door's edge, emerged with careful dignity and immediately fell to fussing with her ash-blond hair. Banks was reaching into the carriage again.

A dainty little figure swung out of the carriage in a swirl of yellow-flowered white petticoats. Miss Terentia Seabright shook loose her honey-blond curls as she tossed her hat back into the hack.

Banks, taking a feminine elbow in each hand, steered the girls toward the *Valiant*'s gangway.

"Attention on the spar deck!" squalled young Master's Mate Casson, who had the forenoon watch. Everybody topside stopped working and gawked at the two lovely visions floating along beside the captain.

"Belay that, Mr. Casson!" roared Pettengill, striding toward the entry port. "Carry on, all working parties."

He'd be damned if he was going to have his ship's work interfered with, even if his skipper was ass enough to come lugging women aboard when the ship was messed up getting ready for sea. . . .

In the annoyance of having his beautiful ship displayed to fussy female eyes, Pettengill forgot Major E. J. Allen for a moment.

He stood stiffly erect beside Casson as the girls came up the slippery plank, picking their way over the cleats: Virgilia smiling, happiness aglow in her gray eyes, Terry with a look of faint disdain on her pert little face.

Behind them came Banks, his usually serene countenance one silly grin between its neat sideburns. And yet, were his eyes shadowed by a hint of anxiety?

Bitterly aware of the state of his once-white pants and shirt, Pettengill lifted his old straw hat and said:

"Welcome aboard, Miss Seabright, Miss Terry. Morning, sir."

"Before you start calling me Mrs. Banks, you'd better get used to calling me Virgie," Virgilia informed him, giving him both her hands. "Cal, I think it's a sin and a shame they won't let you come to see me married tomorrow. I wanted to go right over to the Navy Department and give that old Mr. Welles a piece of my mind, but Penny wouldn't let me, so I made him bring me right down here to see you."

For grave Virgilia, this was positively babbling.

"Don't blame the poor Secretary," Pettengill told her. "It's an old regulation, made long before his day, that won't allow the captain and the executive officer to be out of the ship at the same time. But it's kind of you to come, Virgie."

"What would you expect of the Yankee Navy?" jeered Terry, her freckled nose uptilting a trifle more.

"Hush your mouth, Terry Seabright," Virgie bade her.

If Terry had been talking in this strain since she had been in Washington, she wasn't doing Banks any good in his present circumstances. She wasn't doing Pettengill any good either, for she walked over to him, took hold of the flaps of his shirt pockets with her small hands, and stood on tiptoe to be kissed as though that were the natural procedure. Her gold-flecked brown eyes were dancing with amusement.

Pettengill, aware that his face was aflame, bent down to give her a quick peck on the cheek, but somehow her lips met his and clung for one electric instant. Through the quick hammering of his heart he heard Casson snicker, and mentally marked him down for the next dirty job that came along.

"I see the shear-barge is alongside," Banks remarked.

"Yes, sir," said Pettengill quickly. "It's our new Parrott rifle, and if the ladies'll excuse me I've got to see it hoisted in and mounted."

"I'll see to it myself," retorted Banks. "The girls came down here to see you, Pettengill, so you show 'em around the ship."

"A pleasure, indeed," lied Pettengill. Terry grinned at him.

"What a dirty ship," she observed with calculated innocence, looking along the littered deck. "But I s'pose with the refining influence of the Southern officers gone, you Yankees just revert to your usual habits."

Pettengill choked back a retort. The quicker he did this showing around, the quicker he could get back on the job.

He led the way aft, talking fast:

"We'll look at the after part of the ship first. Powder's coming aboard for'd, too many safety regulations to worry about. Here's the galley, fire's doused, of course, with the powder flag up. These spaces along the rail are the nettings where the crew stow their hammocks. Here's the wheel and the binnacle that holds the compass for the helmsman to steer by. I hope someday shipbuilders will get the idea that a steamer should have a steering position for'd. Of course we have sails too. This little house holds the gear for hoisting up the propeller to avoid drag in the water when the ship's under sail."

Terry yawned delicately behind one small hand.

"Fascinating," she said. "To a couple of girls brought up within spitting distance of a Navy Yard, positively enthralling. Isn't it, Virgie?"

"What you need," said Virgie sharply, "is a good spanking."

She turned to Pettengill.

"Couldn't we see where Penny lives?"

"Yes, indeed," said Pettengill. "Cabin's under the poop deck, right through this door."

There was no Marine orderly on duty, all hands were turning to on ship's work this morning. Pettengill pushed the door open. The girls cooed and murmured over the shining brass and polished mahogany: good cabin furniture wasn't too hard to come by as yet, quite a lot of it was in store from sailing ships laid up in ordinary. They peered into Banks' tiny stateroom and tinier bath, partitioned off the main cabin; they fiddled in the pantry, Virgie obviously making mental notes of the items of cabin stores she meant to add.

"Now," demanded Terry, "let's see where *you* live."

"Not quite so grandly, I can tell you," said Pettengill. "Back out on deck and down this ladder. Watch your step." Terry chuckled. "All right, sailor-girl, break your neck then."

Valiant's wardroom was right aft on the berth deck, with only a few small air-ports and no stern windows. The ports usually had to be kept closed at sea, but even now, with all of them open and the sun shining outside, the wardroom was gloomy enough. Two brass lamps swung in gimbals above the long table; a couple of transoms with white-covered cushions and a row of wooden chairs completed the spartan furnishings. Forward of the wardroom country, where the ladder was located, was the passage which gave access to the officers' rooms.

"Here's my room," said Pettengill, opening the door of the after room on the starboard side, and hoping the girls would notice the little brass plate that read FIRST LIEUT. Of course Pettengill wasn't a lieutenant—yet, but he was holding down a lieutenant's billet, just as Banks was holding down a commander's: only five days ago Congress had passed a bill providing for the appointment of acting lieutenants to serve "until the suppression of the present insurrection."

"Come right in," he invited.

"Oh, how dark and dismal," cried Terry. "Why, Cal, that bunk's not nearly long enough for you. And you can't even stand up straight."

True enough: the berth deck had only five feet eight inches of headroom, while there was six feet two of Pettengill. As for the bunk, he was bitterly aware that it was three inches too short; he had meant to have Chips do something about that one day, but he hadn't gotten around to it. There was just space enough in the room for the bunk, with three drawers under it, a desk, a chair, a cupboard, and a washbasin. The wall decorations were Pettengill's sword and revolver and a cracked mirror.

"I think it's very nice," said Virgie.

"You're very polite, Virgie," Pettengill said. "I know it's a stuffy hole. But you should have seen the steerage in the old *Sheboygan*, where I lived for two years off the coast of Africa. We slung hammocks there, and we had to keep our shoes triced up to the hammock hooks at night so the cockroaches wouldn't carry 'em off and eat 'em."

"Ugh!" Terry exclaimed. "Let's go up where there's some air."

"Why don't you girls stay in the skipper's cabin and take it easy while I go see how he's getting on?" Pettengill suggested. He was burning to get Banks off to one side and tell him about Allen's visit.

Rather to his surprise, Terry promptly said:

"Oh, lovely. Let's, Virgie."

"I'll send the steward along with something cold to drink," Pettengill promised as he shooed the girls through the cabin door again, and then galloped forward as fast as his long legs would carry him.

The Parrott rifle swung against the sky as the great shears lowered it slowly toward its mount on the *Valiant*'s forecastle. Gear groaned and creaked under the weight of fifty-four hundred pounds of iron. Banks stood by the pivot mount giving his orders quietly, as he always did, and as always men jumped when he spoke.

This was no moment to call him aside for conversation. Anyway, here came the gunner.

"Powder's all aboard and stowed, sir."

So Pettengill had to go below, inspect the magazine, and check the powder-list received from the Yard. By the time he had done this, locked the magazine doors, and got back on deck, the new rifle nestled comfortably on its trunnion plates and the gunner's gang were screwing down the cap-square bolts. Hodgson, leaning over the rail, was making known to the crew of the shear-barge his opinion that they were far better suited for agricultural pursuits than for handling yard craft alongside naval vessels. Banks was standing with one of the Yard ordnance officers running over a list of ammunition for the Parrott: "Only two hundred shell and two hundred shrapnel? Damn it, man, there's a war going on—" "We'll get more to you within a month or so, Captain." "I've heard that yarn before! Now see here—"

Pettengill remembered his promise about cold drinks, had the word passed for the cabin steward. He hoped there was some ice aboard somewhere. None in the wardroom this past week. Now the ordnance officer was taking himself off.

"Captain," said Pettengill, "I ought to tell you—"

"Messenger from the commandant's office at the gangway, sir," interrupted Master's Mate Casson. "Says he has to have your personal receipt for his message."

He watched Banks scrawl his signature in a book, hand it back to the smart Marine sergeant, and rip open the yellow envelope.

"Damnation!" barked Banks as he ran his eye down the sheet. "Look at this, Pettengill."

Pettengill didn't want to look at it. He was afraid of what he was going to see. But he looked—and laughed with relief.

The message read:

> Lieutenant P. Banks, Com'd'g U.S.S. *Valiant:* Telegraphic order from Secretary Navy directs you proceed immediately with vessel under your command down Potomac River to meet U.S.S. *Union,* wearing flag of Flag Officer Silas H. Stringham, Commander in Chief, Atlantic Blockading Squadron, and escort that vessel past the reported Rebel batteries at Mathias Point en route to this Navy Yard. *Union* is expected to depart Hampton Roads 1:00 P.M., should be off St. George Island approx. 10 P.M., where she will if necessary await your arrival. Your recognition signal two red lanterns at foretruck. *Union* will display flag light. Yr. obt. svt., J. A. Dahlgren, Commdt.

Banks scowled.

"What's so funny?" he demanded. "When the devil do they think I'm going to finish getting ready for sea? Blast that telegraph line they've put in between the Department and the Yard! All it's good for is to transmit Uncle Gideon's fancies and make life hell for sailors. Oh, very well, if we get underway by four bells we can go down with the tide: that should bring us off St. George's a little ahead of time. Can you have her ready by then?"

"Yes, sir. If the engine room can make it. I'll go stir up the chief right away. He'll have a conniption fit."

"Let him. Jump at it, Pettengill, and— Blast! I forgot the girls. Where are they?"

"In the cabin, sir."

"I'll go chase 'em ashore. They're staying with the Dahlgrens tonight, so they won't have far to go. Carry on."

"Aye aye, sir," said Pettengill.

Chapter Twelve

The chief engineer had brought forth miracles of improvisation: the Yard people had turned up with those cylinder casings; and the chief's disposition was sweetened by the arrival of two of his needed coal heavers. Nothing much to look at, he grumbled, but anyway bodies. The *Valiant* was making something like thirteen knots downstream, which should bring her to the rendezvous off St. George Island nearly an hour ahead of time. The mess on deck was cleared up, the hands had had their supper, and Pettengill was improving the remaining hour or so of daylight by drilling the crew of the new 60-pounder Parrott. All this, added to the excitement of a possible chance to try it out on Secesh batteries and interesting speculation about what brought the flag officer so suddenly to Washington, should have given Pettengill a comfortable inner warmth of satisfaction.

Instead, he was acutely miserable. He applied himself to the details of gunnery instruction with intense attention to keep from brooding over what Banks had said when Pettengill at last got a chance to tell him about Allen's visit. In the back of his mind, the bitter memory still festered. ("Damn your impulses, Pettengill! Don't you know these detectives are as vain as play-actors? Now he'll never stop trying to prove how right he was. The man's dangerous—a regular bloodhound. And he has the ear of the President himself. To say nothing of Crossmore. Couldn't you have used your head and given him the kid-glove treatment just for once instead of kicking him down the gangplank?") That had hurt. Probably because there was too much truth in it. So Pettengill kept himself busy and out of Banks' way.

"Never forget, Jackson," he was saying to the half-naked quarter gunner—even with the approach of evening it was still steaming hot on the Potomac—"never forget that with this gun, you've got both shell and shrapnel to think about. Shell are painted red, shrapnel

[147]

are painted white, so there's no excuse for mistakes. Shell has a bursting charge, to destroy material targets like walls or earthworks. Shrapnel's full of lead bullets to destroy Johnny Rebs, if you're lucky enough to catch 'em in the open. With shrapnel, you always use a time fuze."

"Sort of like long-range canister, sir?" ventured Quarter Gunner Jackson.

"That's it exactly," agreed Pettengill. "Canister's no good much over four hundred yards, as you know: the balls start spreading as they leave the muzzle of the gun. But with shrapnel you can throw your bunch of bullets as far as you can throw a shell and then let 'em fan out. Very effective against men in the open. *If* you set your fuze right. Now—"

"Cap'n's coming on the fo'c's'le, sir," warned Jackson quickly.

"Carry on with loading drill," Pettengill ordered, "and mind you impress on your rammermen that the projectile must be pushed clear home. Otherwise we'll be having a burst gun and half-a-dozen dead men. Evening, sir."

"Evening, Pettengill. Hard at work, I see."

There was still a shadow in the dark eyes, a tautness about the corners of the mouth under the clipped mustache.

"Yes, sir," said Pettengill, trying to be very matter-of-fact. "It'll still be light when we come off Mathias Point, and if there are Secesh batteries, which I doubt, they just might take a crack at us. Since we're authorized to return fire, and have a gun that'll reach 'em, I thought we ought to be ready to try it out."

"Quite right," nodded Banks, and walked over to the starboard rail, out of hearing of the gun crew as they jumped about under the lash of Jackson's tongue. Pettengill followed reluctantly, knowing Banks wanted to talk.

"Sorry I popped off at you, Pettengill," Banks said. "Fact is, I'm worried as hell. I won't know an easy moment until I'm well away from Washington and out to sea."

Better not let Virgie hear you say so, thought Pettengill. Aloud he murmured: "I'll be glad of that myself, sir."

"I called in at the Department this morning," Banks went on, "to pay my respects to Captain Du Pont, who's making up plans for naval operations. The place was full of civilians, some of 'em Allen's gumshoes, I'm sure. A couple of these seedy characters looked me over as though I might have a bomb in my pocket. Du Pont says whispers are going around about every Southern officer who's stood by the flag: Percy Drayton, Steedman, Missroon, S. P. Lee, Jenkins, Captain Farragut, and a dozen more, as fine and loyal a lot of men as heart could wish. Du Pont's even had a few nasty remarks tossed his own way because, forsooth, he comes from Delaware, a slave State. He told Welles to his face, for God's sake, bury the slavery question and let's all work and fight together to save the Union. Uncle Gideon didn't like it much. Not the right flavor for the times." Banks hammered an angry fist on the rail. "I tell you, Pettengill, it's not enough these days just to be loyal to your country and do your duty. You have to be loyal according to the abolition pattern. You don't know how lucky you are to've been born in Connecticut.

"And," Banks went on, "here I am not only Virginia-born but marrying a Virginia-born girl the day before I go to sea. And then there's Terry—"

"Sail ho!" yelled the bow lookout suddenly.

"Where away?" came Acting Master Hurlbut's answering hail from the bridge.

"Broad on the starb'd bow, sir! Sloop. Close inshore just under that house."

On the *starboard* bow—that was the Virginia side!

Pettengill's glasses were at his eyes. Yes, there she was, almost invisible in the shadow of the high bank, her gray mainsail just disappearing. Must have let it go on the run as soon as the *Valiant* showed up around the bend of the river, but not quite quick enough.

"Stop the engine, Mr. Hurlbut!" Banks was shouting. "Half astern! Go get her, Pettengill!"

"Away duty boat!" roared Pettengill, and went racing aft.

The standing orders of the Potomac Flotilla required that whatever the mission of any of its vessels might be, the capture or destruction of any craft attempting to reach or communicate with the Virginia shore took precedence over everything else.

The crew of the duty boat—which was the gig, as being the best compromise between the cutters, which drew too much water for these shallows and sand bars, and the dinghy, which didn't hold enough men—had her already swung out by the time Pettengill reached her. The afterguard was standing by the falls.

"Lower away together!" Pettengill flung his lanky body over the rail into the gig's stern sheets. Down she went. The *Valiant* had almost lost way now, her screw boiling in reverse under her stern. "Let go aft! Let go for'd! Sheer out! Give way!"

Eight oar blades bit the water, and the gig leaped over the smooth surface of the Potomac toward the shore. Not three minutes had passed since the lookout's hail. Behind him, Pettengill could hear the roar of the spring-rattle calling the crew to quarters: it was standard procedure with Banks that a boat sent ashore on the enemy side of the river in daylight must always be covered by the ship's guns. Those shadowed slopes, thick with pines, might shelter a regiment of riflemen or a battery of hidden fieldpieces. Pettengill fished a revolver from the boat-locker and buckled it on; he scarcely needed to take note that his crew had pistols and cutlasses belted at their waists, the duty-boat's crew went armed throughout their watch on deck.

He gave his attention to the shore toward which the gig was flying as fast as stout ash and stout muscles could drive her.

The sloop seemed to be alongside a small wharf, low down at the water's edge; her hull was half-hidden by rushes. If the quick-eyed lookout hadn't spotted that collapsing mainsail, her spars would barely have been made out against the dark background of pine trees.

Pettengill thought he had seen a couple of figures dart into the shelter of the pines when he had first focused his glasses on the sloop. Now he could see no one moving, either on the sloop or the wharf or the more-or-less open slope that rose from the wharf to the house. The house itself was a two-story frame building, with a porch along the side facing the river and outbuildings behind it. The forest closed in on it: beyond the outbuildings, the pine-clad hillside rose steeply to the skyline; there Pettengill saw a curious little notch which might mark a place where a road had been cleared through the woods. Yes, as he lifted his glasses to it, he saw a mounted man appear in the notch, pause for an instant, and then vanish down the farther slope.

The bows of the gig smashed through the rushes. Three more strokes would bring her up to the sloop.

"Lay her alongside, cox'n. Jurgens, Knapp, Foley, follow me. The rest of you stand by the boat. You, cox'n, keep your wits about you. Trail bow! Way enough!"

Pettengill leaped to the sloop's deck as the boat touched her side, his three seamen close behind him. Not a soul in sight on that deck, scattered with the litter of hasty flight, nor in the little cabin aft. "Nobody in the fo'c's'le, sir," called Foley.

"Come on, then!"

Pettengill trotted up the slope toward the house, cocked revolver in his hand. Jurgens was close behind him; Knapp and Foley spread out on either side to go around the house. In the Potomac Flotilla, searching suspected houses had become a routine job.

The door was open, the house silent, as Pettengill went up the steps to the porch. It was a simple house: a central hall straight through, with a room at each corner, and a stairway leading to the upper floor where the pattern was repeated. There was no one in any of the rooms; five minutes' quick search established that fact.

In the lean-to kitchen at the back of the house, an iron pot bubbled quietly on a huge range—hominy grits, by the smell of it, enough to feed a dozen people. Sides of bacon swung from the kitchen roof beams; a barrel of flour and some sacks of corn meal were stacked against the wall.

Beyond the kitchen were low buildings that looked like stables. Pettengill pushed open the door of the nearest. A row of empty stalls, and the smell of fresh manure. The next building was a bunkhouse: four bunks on each side, with tumbled blankets in some of them. The place smelled of tobacco and sweaty bodies. Tin plates, odds and ends of saddlery, a few articles of clothing were scattered about, including a gray shell jacket with yellow facings, such as Confederate cavalry were beginning to wear. A saber stood inconspicuously in one dark corner. Pettengill picked up a crumpled newspaper from under one of the bunks. It was the Richmond *Enquirer* of July 27, two days ago, its headlines still full of brag and bombast about Bull Run and the "coming fall of the abolition Capital."

Words that Major Allen had spoken flashed into Pettengill's mind as he stood there: "organized spy-ferry service . . . relays of horsemen, standing by round the clock . . . a regular rendezvous on the Virginia side . . . perhaps several such stations . . . mounted couriers to Fredericksburg and so . . . to Manassas or to Richmond by the cars . . ."

He had no doubt at all about what he had found. But what was he going to do about it? Abruptly he took his decision.

He tucked the newspaper inside his jacket. It might contain useful military information. Everything else he left undisturbed.

He walked out of the bunkhouse and called loudly to his men:

"Back to the ship, lads. Nobody here, and we mustn't keep the captain waiting. We've got the sloop, anyhow, and that's the main thing."

The horsemen were well away, but Pettengill hoped that some of the sloop's crew might still be hanging around within earshot.

He strode briskly down the slope to the wharf.

"Six hands at the oars; cox'n, take two men and bring off that sloop. The ship'll take her in tow. Shove off. Give way."

Ten minutes later, with *Valiant* underway down the brown flood of the Potomac again, the sun sinking behind those Virginia hills, and the captured sloop bobbing along astern at the end of a towline, Pettengill paced the quarter deck with Banks explaining what he had done and why.

"Call it another of my damned impulses if you like, sir. I'd have been justified, with all that evidence, in burning the whole shebang to the ground. The choice was either to do that, or to leave the empty nest untouched in the hope the birds may come back to it. The best answer you could throw in Allen's teeth would be a handful of captured Secesh spies and couriers."

"H'm," muttered Banks. "Maybe. But won't he say now that I found a spy station and left it untouched?"

"He might, but then if I'd burned it, he could say I'd done so, at your order, to destroy evidence that might've pointed to you, or maybe just to throw dust in his eyes. Anyway, remember he'll know nothing about this until you turn in your report on your return to the Yard tomorrow: and by that time we'll have had a chance to take another look at the place on our way back upriver. They won't do much spy-ferrying tonight. We've got their sloop, and it'll take time to get another craft."

Banks put a hand on Pettengill's shoulder.

"You're doing the best a friend could, old man," he said warmly. "I'll play the string out with you."

Any open expression of feeling always embarrassed Pettengill. He was glad that the quartermaster struck seven bells just at that moment, the silvery strokes echoing from the high banks of the Potomac on either hand.

"You'd better get some rest, sir," he suggested. "You'll have to be back on deck when we meet the flag. I'll just go up on the bridge and see us safely past Mathias Point."

"Make it so," said Banks. "And I'll thank you not to hang the old girl up on any sand bars, Pettengill. Just remember I've a trifling appointment to hear a marriage service read at the Navy Yard tomorrow afternoon at three o'clock, followed by that confounded reception the commandant insisted on."

"Thus cutting off one hour of a twelve-hour honeymoon," murmured Pettengill, matching his skipper's mood. "Very inconsiderate of the old boy."

"Damnably," agreed Banks. "Call me if anything happens, and anyway as soon as you make out St. George Island."

"Aye aye, sir," said Pettengill and walked forward in the twilight to the bridge ladder. Hurlbut was still on watch, a taciturn State-o'-Mainer fresh from the merchant service, a good seaman but knowing nothing of gunnery or naval routine like most of the new wartime appointees. Pettengill knew well how thankful he was for his two years as master's mate in the *Sheboygan:* those two years had given him a start as a naval officer at a moment when even partly trained naval officers were beyond price.

"Good evening, sir," said Hurlbut.

"Evening, Mr. Hurlbut."

Hurlbut was at least thirty-five years old, twelve years Pettengill's senior. But he stood here saying "Good evening, sir," because of just that little difference in Navy experience. Pettengill stood quietly at the end of the bridge and savored this morsel. He debated the advisability of going to quarters, passing Mathias Point, decided against it. He could count on his men to be at their guns within two minutes after the rattle was sprung, and only the rifle gun would be of use anyway. He had already seen to it that six rounds of shell were handy on deck for the Parrott: at this speed and in the fading light he would have no time to use more than that.

He leaned against the bridge-rail and watched the line of light fade along the crest of the Virginia bluffs. From time to time Hurlbut spoke to the helmsman below the bridge on the spar deck. Pettengill's own knowledge of the channel told him that the watch officer knew exactly what he was doing. It might be different when young Master's Mate Casson came up to take the eight-to-twelve watch. Below Mathias Point there were only two temporary range lights in place. Comfortable in Hurlbut's competence, Pettengill began thinking again of the spy-station, trying to devise a scheme for surprising the place in the morning. It would be just about slack water at St. George Island. They would come back upriver with the flood, so they should approach the spy-house along toward daybreak.

Casson came up the ladder; there was the stir on deck that heralded the changing of the watch. Some of the black gang were coming on deck already; they stood their watches by the engine-room clock, paying small heed to the ship's bell. The light of a shaded lantern fell across one weary coal-blackened face, and glinted on a pair of gimlet eyes that Pettengill recognized even though they peered out from rings of soot. The man lurched forward, staggering with fatigue.

Pettengill swore savagely under his breath.

He remembered the coal heavers the chief had been fretting about, and he remembered that Allen had been standing by and heard that fretting. He had come to spy on Banks in person. "I ought to throw him overboard," Pettengill muttered. Then he had a better idea.

Eight bells had struck, Casson had taken over, Hurlbut was just going down the ladder.

"Would you mind asking the chief engineer to come up on the bridge, if he hasn't turned in, Mr. Hurlbut?"

"Aye aye, sir."

Presently the chief appeared, ready with grumbles.

Pettengill cut them short.

"Chief, is there any coal in those special side bunkers we had fitted, to give some protection to the steam drum and the top of the boiler from shellfire?"

"No, of course not," the chief snapped. "We were supposed to coal ship this afternoon and I was going to fill 'em then, but off we go on this wild-goose chase—"

"Very well," said Pettengill. "That's Mathias Point looming up ahead. There may be Secesh guns there. We have to pass 'em now, and again in the morning. Turn to your off-duty men and pass some coal into those two bunkers."

"That's a hell of a job in this heat," the chief protested. "It's a hundred and five on the engine-room thermometer right this minute."

"Too bad. But you've got to get those new hands of yours toughened up sometime. Get 'em at it."

"You're a hard man for a youngster," the chief mumbled, and went to do as he was told. Pettengill grinned into the gathering darkness above Mathias Point. Mr. Major E. J. Allen would learn what it meant to ship as a coal heaver in the Navy. . . .

Flag Officer Silas H. Stringham—"Stringham in name and Stringham in person, he's as stringy as a string bean" was what the lower-deck said of him—sank into a chair in the *Valiant*'s cabin and smiled bleakly at Banks and Pettengill. Commander Case, his fleet captain, hovered in the background.

The beat of the propeller testified to the fact that *Valiant* was underway, upriver this time, headed back for Washington.

"No use risking the poor old *Union* passing batteries," Stringham said, "when I can leave her safe out here and take passage with you. Besides, I can make good use of the time going over the work I've cut out for you, Captain Banks. I abhor wasting time. Better have your first lieutenant stay with us: he ought to hear this. You have the charts, Case?"

"Right here, sir."

The fleet captain started to unroll a huge cylinder of charts on Banks' table.

"Not too much room," grumbled Stringham.

"Perhaps the wardroom table might be better, sir," suggested Banks. "It's much larger. Hot down there, though."

"After fifty-two years in the Navy," said the flag officer, "I can endure heat or cold without distress."

There was nothing to be said to that, and the four men went down the ladder to the stuffy wardroom, where Case spread out the charts and weighted down the corners with coffee cups.

The flag officer, disdaining a proffered chair, took his stand at the middle of the table, his fierce old eyes glinting in the lamplight. Whatever else might be said about Silas Stringham, he was a fighter. Pettengill could feel that just by looking at him. This was a man who would do to follow into battle. However, Pettengill could have cheerfully wrung his skinny neck. With him aboard, it would be almost impossible to do anything about the spy-nest that morning; he was just the sort that would come popping on deck the minute the engine stopped, asking what the hell the delay was and overruling any "waste of time."

"Gentlemen," said the flag officer, "I invite your attention to this point." The chart on top of the pile was the Atlantic Coast from Cape Henry to Cape Fear, part of Virginia and most of the North Carolina shore line. The flag officer's pencil point rested on Hatteras Inlet.

"There are Confederate fortifications here. It is the view of Captain Du Pont and his associates who are making our operational plans that earth or sand forts can be overwhelmed by the rapid fire of the shell-guns with which our naval vessels are now armed. To my mind, this remains to be proved. It has long been an accepted axiom of sea warfare that the man who risks ships against forts is a fool, as I believe Lord Nelson once said. However, I admit there are new elements to be considered: improved sights and elevating gear, providing a higher rate of aimed fire than Nelson ever knew; the destructive qualities of explosive shells detonated by the fuzes now available; and the fact that steam warships can keep in motion, choosing their own approach and maneuvering as may be most advantageous to them, independent of the wind. I am quite willing to give the proposal a thorough trial. It is to concert the final arrangements with Captain Du Pont that I am now on my way to Washington."

To sit in on the battle plans of the Commander in Chief of the Atlantic Blockading Squadron was a wonderful experience for Pettengill. His military imagination bestirred itself. If these forts at Hatteras Inlet could be knocked out, no Southern seaport could be called secure, except perhaps Charleston with its great masonry forts, and even there—

But the flag officer, having paused for effect, was talking again:

"I have the gun power. *Wabash, Minnesota, Susquehanna* have the bulk of it, and I'm getting *Pawnee* with her heavy nine-inch broadside battery and light draft for inshore work. But I lack detailed information of the area, and especially of the progress of the enemy fortifications. I lack that information because, up to this point, the Department has not been able to make available for my use a fast and well-armed steamer for a reconnaissance of the selected position and surrounding waters." He waved a finger, and Case made haste to substitute a larger-scale chart of the Hatteras area. "This, gentlemen," said the flag officer, glancing from Banks to Pettengill, "is where you come into my plans. I have succeeded in prying your steamer away from the Potomac Flotilla, on which duty her seakeeping qualities and speed are wholly wasted, and I shall require you to make a thorough reconnaissance of the enemy positions and the sea-approaches to them in such manner—in such manner, mind you—as shall not excite undue suspicion of my intentions."

His pencil began moving about the chart:

"I desire to know the depth of water in these inlets—" the pencil moved from Hatteras Inlet north to Oregon Inlet, south to Ocracoke Inlet—"whether either is fortified, and to what extent, whether the lighthouses along the coast are in operation; reports vary on this point, but my particular interest is in the state of construction and armament of the forts *here*." The pencil stabbed at Hatteras Inlet again. "There are," he added, "enemy armed vessels in the vicinity, based in inland waters, coming out when weather permits to prey on passing merchant ships. Your steamer is the first I have had which carries little enough draft to penetrate the inlets and yet is of sufficient force to cope with chance enemy craft, or even to exchange a few shots with the forts without undue risk. Indeed if you could contrive to convey the impression that your purpose in those waters was the pursuit and elimination of these Rebel commerce-raiders, you would meet my desires precisely. It is of the first importance, gentlemen—of the very first importance—that no hint of my actual intentions should reach the enemy, so that my blow may fall on him like a bolt from the blue. I need not, I am sure, emphasize to you the primary importance of surprise in warfare."

The bleak smile flitted across his weather-beaten face again: a face that was almost unique in the Navy of '61 by reason of being clean-shaven.

"The unhappy experiences of the Army in recent days," he added, "would not incline me to view with leniency any laxity within my command in regard to keeping military information secure."

There's a lad down in our stokehole shoveling coal, who'd have chills and fever if he heard the flag officer talking like this to Penny Banks. It's a good thing I fixed Gumshoe Allen so's he couldn't get at the flag officer with his pretty tale. . . .

"Now, Captain Banks," the flag officer said, "it's usual at this point to ask the officers concerned if there are any questions. But the hour grows late, and having stood a few watches myself here and there, I am going to make no further demands on your time tonight. I desire you to keep these charts, to study them and think about what I've told you, to discuss the various problems involved with your executive officer if and as you see fit. Day after tomorrow I'll take passage back to Hampton Roads with you, and you can then ask such questions as occur to you. You will leave Hampton Roads the following day and proceed to carry out your reconnaissance. Thank you, gentlemen, and good night."

"May I accompany you to my cabin, sir?" asked Banks. "You'll have my stateroom, of course, and I'm sure we can make the fleet captain comfortable on the sofa. I'll be on deck for the rest of the night. I want to do some thinking, and I think best in the open air."

"I'll stay on deck, sir," offered Pettengill. He had never been more wide-awake in his life, and he wanted to do some thinking, too.

"You'll not," replied Banks. "You'll turn in and get some rest. I had mine on the way down."

The flag officer and Case were already going up the ladder. Banks rolled up the charts, stuck them under his arm, grinned at Pettengill to take the sting out of his curt order, and followed. Pettengill stood there a moment listening to the steady thump-thump of the propeller under his feet. The clock on the bulkhead told him it was ten minutes past one.

Master's Mate King would have the mid-watch—no more experienced than Casson, but with Banks on deck that didn't matter. They'd got off from St. George Island a little after eleven. Say, four hours up to Mathias Point from here; once safely past, he'd see what could be done about the spy-nest. Allen down in the stokehole was a time bomb, ticking away: somehow he had to be doused before he went off and blew up all Banks' hopes and future. This wonderful mission was Banks' great chance to make a name in the Union Navy that nothing could thereafter call into question. And, to be honest with himself, success in that mission would almost certainly make Acting Master Pettengill into Acting Lieutenant Pettengill at the same time it made Banks a commander. But it might all blow sky-high if Allen got to the flag officer with his imaginings. Maybe inspiration would come in the morning. . . .

Pettengill set his ever-reliable mental alarm clock for 4:30 A.M. and walked forward into the wardroom country, his ear picking out the raucous snores of the chief engineer across the way and the high-pitched wheeze-and-whine of the paymaster. Most of the doors were hooked back for air, but Pettengill's door was closed as he had left it that forenoon. He opened it, stepped over the brass-bound coaming and closed the door behind him, struck a match and applied it to the wick of the lamp over his desk. The flame took hold.

"A fine time to be coming to bed, Caleb Pettengill," said a reproachful voice.

Terry Seabright sat on his berth, knees drawn up under her chin.

"What the blazing hell—"

"Am I doing here? Why, I just came along for the boatride."

"But—but how—you mean you've been here ever since we left the Yard?"

"Uh-huh. I bolted the door and stayed mum. Somebody tried it a couple of times, the steward, I s'pose, but when he found it bolted he went away. I reckon you're a man that nobody wants to disturb without good reason, Cal. Only now I'm awful hungry."

"You can stay hungry!" Terry must have been here the whole time the flag officer had been talking in the wardroom! If she had eased the door open a crack, she could have heard every word that had been spoken.

His horror must have shown on his face, for Terry nodded and said:

"You're right, Cal. I listened with the greatest interest to what Flag Officer Stringham had to say. And just what—" she bounced suddenly to her feet and faced him defiantly—"just what do you think you're going to do about it, now that you know I was listening?"

"I'm going to march you straight up to Captain Banks and let him deal with you!" Pettengill informed her. "I hope he puts you in irons. Come on."

He reached for her, but she drew back, eyes snapping.

"If you do," she warned, "I'll tell Flag Officer Stringham that I spent the afternoon and most of the night in your cabin—at your request and with my dear brother-in-law-to-be's full knowledge and permission. The two of you'll deny it, of course. Who do you think will believe you?"

The venomous way she spat out that phrase "my dear brother-in-law-to-be" hit Pettengill like a smack on the jaw. But a sailor's instinct for rocks and shoals kept Pettengill's mind steady. At all costs he mustn't let Terry realize the real strength of her position. He eyed her with what he hoped was an expression of faint amusement.

"You little devil!" he said. "A fine scandal that'd make! Of course it's an old Navy custom to let the crew bring their women aboard in port, but it's not quite the thing for officers—"

Her little fist crashed against his mouth.

"You—you filthy—Yankee!"

She was sobbing with rage: he grabbed her wrists, pushed her back on the berth. It was lucky that Hurlbut in the next room was a heavy sleeper who had to be dragged out of bed by the bridge messenger when he was called to relieve the watch.

"Take it easy, Terry," he advised. "It was your own idea. I was just showing you where it would lead you."

Tears of fury and frustration were flowing down her cheeks. He had put over his point: a woman had far more to fear from the voice of scandal than a man. No one was likely to believe that Pendleton Banks had connived at the dishonoring of his sister-in-law, but almost everyone would be only too ready to believe that she had been up to tricks with Pettengill.

"Besides," Pettengill voiced his thoughts, "besides, Terry, you'd break your sister's heart. And what's she done that you should do that to her?"

"She's marrying a traitor, bringing shame on the name of Seabright."

Pettengill stared down at the angry little face.

"She'll be frantic with worrying about you right now," he reminded Terry. "She's probably got the whole Navy Yard stirred up, looking for you. This is a mess, Terry. If I don't take you to the captain, what do you expect me to do with you?"

Terry pulled one hand loose and brushed the tears from her eyes.

"Get me something to eat, first," she begged. "I'm really hungry, Cal. I haven't had a bite since breakfast."

"But—"

"Don't worry about Virgie. I fixed all that. D'you think I'm a ninny? I told her I was going uptown to see a couple of Norfolk girls who are staying at Brown's Hotel, she knows them. I said I might even stay all night with them, that the air of a Yankee Navy Yard choked me. Virgie won't be fretting yet. Now will you get me something to eat before I starve to death right here in your room?"

"Not," said Pettengill firmly, "until you tell me how you contrived to stow away here."

The smile returned to Terry's tear-stained face.

"Oh," she said, "that was easy! Virgie wanted to stay and have dinner with her dear lover in his cabin, so I just stuck up my nose and said no thank you, I'd be going ashore; the way I said it made 'em both so mad at me they told me to go ahead, and that gave me the chance to be so mad at *them* that I wouldn't let Pendleton Banks escort me to the gangway. So I just slammed the cabin door behind me good and hard and ran down the ladder and in here. Nobody saw me at all. But I'm hungry. Please, Cal?"

"One more question first: Why did you do it?"

"Why, Cal! For the South, of course! That's why I came to Washington with Virgie. You don't think I'd ever, ever have come just to stand up with her while she married a traitor to the South, do you? But to be inside a Navy Yard, to have a chance to meet silly men who always think a girl's too stupid to understand their big talk! I just couldn't refuse such a chance. And then when I heard Captain Banks tell Virgie the ship was going down the river to escort Flag Officer Stringham to Washington, I knew it meant something big. I thought maybe if I went along I might find out what. Of course I didn't count on any such luck as I had, but I figured one way or another I could make enough trouble and worry you men so that you'd let something slip. Anyway it was my duty to my country to take the chance. You see that, don't you, Cal? You'd've done the same for the North?"

For once, Terry was being sincere.

"I don't know," Pettengill said. "Promise me you'll stay here while I go rummage in the pantry?"

"Of course, Cal. Where else would I go?"

"The good Lord only knows."

He went out, softly closing the door behind him, hoping the steward hadn't locked the pantry. He had, though, and Pettengill was forced to fall back on the usual recourse of the night-prowling officer: push up the slide of the serving window and grope around in the dark for whatever might be within reach. He found a dish of cold beans, a half-loaf of bread, and a couple of apples. The wine-mess locker, to which he carried a key, yielded a bottle of claret. He lugged this loot back to his room. Terry was delighted.

"Why, it's a regular picnic! But you didn't bring any silver or napkins, just like a man!"

"Can't get at 'em. Locked up. There's a spoon in that dish of beans."

"I'm too hungry to care!" Terry started wolfing beans, carefree as a little seagull gobbling herring. Pettengill watched her. Now that he knew she had deliberately stowed away in the hope of obtaining military information, he realized that the same idea would instantly occur to Allen, for of course, once the wedding was over, Terry would be going back to Portsmouth by the flag-of-truce boats which still operated with fair regularity. And Banks was responsible, or would be held so. He was the captain of this ship. It was he who had suggested the wardroom as the most convenient spot to spread out those charts: Allen would say he had done so deliberately, to bring the discussion where Terry could overhear it. The whole thing was made to order for Crossmore. Welles wouldn't dare take a lenient view, even if he wanted to.

But it was Pettengill's duty, regardless of the consequences, to arrest Terry and take her to the captain. Now that she knew the flag officer's plans, she was far too dangerous to be allowed at large. She could not be permitted to take that information south with her.

Something was nagging at Pettengill's mind, something about the charts. Terry's spoon scraped up the last of the beans. She poured claret into Pettengill's water glass, held it up to him:

"A glass of wine with me, Mr. Pettengill? A loving cup?"

"I hope," said Pettengill, "it chokes you."

Tears of hurt reproach rather than anger welled up in her eyes.

"Why, Cal! You can't feel like that, just because—because we're enemies—only we aren't really, and anyway I don't know where—"

Her hand flew to her mouth. Emotion had betrayed her. That was it! *The flag officer had not mentioned a single geographical name during his talk.* He had just pointed at places on the charts as he went along. As far as Terry could know, his objective might be anywhere along the coast from North Carolina to Florida. That whole coast was one maze of inlets and inland waters, and from such reports as Pettengill had seen, he knew there were Confederate forts being built at a number of these inlets, and armed with guns taken at Norfolk. All Terry really knew was that the flag officer intended to make a descent on one such point and was ordering a reconnaissance in preparation. She didn't know which one. What she had heard wouldn't help the Rebels. Pettengill and Banks had gone through that Richmond paper. It was full of rumors about a naval descent on the coast. Wilmington, Charleston, Savannah, Fernandina were all mentioned, together with frantic boasts about what would happen to the "abolition kangaroos" if they dared try such a thing. Names of the ships in the Atlantic Blockading Squadron were also known and printed, with fair accuracy. The vital element of information was *where* the blow was going to fall.

He was under no immediate compulsion to see her safe in custody. He might be able to sneak her ashore in the morning without anyone, even Banks, knowing of her presence—if she would co-operate.

If she would co-operate. But that was a big *if*.

Pretending not to have noticed her slip, Pettengill bent down and kissed the tear-filled eyes.

"Don't cry, honey," he said. "Of course we're not enemies. Ever."

She smiled through her tears.

Why, she really likes me. . . .

Pride made him heedless of recent painful experience.

"Then—then you'll drink our loving cup with me?" she wheedled.

"Surely." He gulped down a hearty swallow; it wasn't very good claret, and claret wasn't Pettengill's tipple anyway. Barbados rum was his idea of a man's drink, but he smacked his lips and pretended to enjoy the sour stuff. "Here, Terry, your turn."

She sipped daintily, eying him over the thick rim of the Navy-issue tumbler.

"We could have fun, you and I, if it wasn't for this war," she said, handing the glass back.

Pettengill sat down on the berth.

"I thought you hated all Yankees, Terry?"

"I don't hate you," she said. "You're just doing your duty, same as I am. It's turncoats like Pendleton Banks I hate."

She got up from his desk-chair where she had sat to eat her supper and climbed up beside him on the berth. He put an arm about her.

"Maybe," she murmured, "maybe I'm just being a little fool. Only I can't help how I feel, can I? I could've killed you when I saw you going ashore in that boat to capture that poor little sloop. I watched you right through that porthole. People make their living with boats like that. Fishermen and traders and so on. Couldn't you let them keep it?"

"Duty, honey, like you said," Pettengill told her. "Orders are to pick up boats found on the Virginia side."

He felt her body stiffen in the curve of his arm.

"Orders! Yankee orders! Ruining the lives of peaceful people that never did you any harm! Fine orders!"

"There was evidence that Confederate soldiers had been in that house where the sloop landed!"

"Oh," she said and relaxed a little.

"I'm sleepy," she murmured. "I wish—"

"You wish what?" Something in her voice sent the hot blood to his temples.

"I wish we could just—just forget the war—and—" She reached up both arms, twined them around his neck, pressed her mouth to his.

Then she pulled back, pushing him away with both hands.

"No! No—no, Caleb. I'm not such an idiot as you think. I know I've failed. I know what you're thinking: I gave myself away when I said I didn't know where, and you didn't miss that. So you've figured out by this time that you can keep me here till morning and smuggle me ashore tomorrow, with no trouble for your darling captain." Her eyes flashed. "That," she said through her teeth, "won't work. I can't sit here and—"

"What difference does it make? If you knew the whole story, d'you think I'd let you off the ship with it?"

He grabbed her to him and kissed her again, roughly this time. She didn't fight, but there was no response in her stiff lips.

"If I knew," she muttered, "you couldn't hold on to me once we get to Washington. Not without arresting me—and saying to the world that Pendleton Banks is marrying the sister of a Southern spy."

If she knew, she was saying, she'd relax until she got to Washington.

Exactly as though she understood what was in his mind, Terry lifted a hand and let her fingers dribble across his rough cheek.

"Ah, Cal," she whispered.

"Terry, Terry!" He seemed a man torn by temptation. "If I tell you—"

She twisted herself around on the berth and lay back across his knees. Her lips were half-parted, her eyes hot with promise.

"Port Royal," lied Pettengill. "Port Royal, in South Carolina."

He snatched her up to him, her lips opened to receive his kiss— Knuckles rat-tatted on the door.

"Mr. Pettengill! Cap'n wants you on deck right away!"

Eight bells rang sharply as Pettengill clattered up the ladder to the quarter deck. Dawn light was faint on the crests of the Maryland hills.

"Sorry to cut your slumbers short, Pettengill," said Banks, looming up out of the shadows. "But the flag officer's early astir and has just sent for me. We're coming up to Mathias Point, and I thought you'd better be on deck. Hurlbut's just taken the watch. A good man, but no gunnery expert. Wouldn't do not to make proper reply if those batteries open up on us, not with the flag officer aboard."

He vanished down the companion without more words. Pettengill walked slowly forward toward the bridge.

Shame had him by the throat: to lie to Terry for no better purpose than to—

But she was trying to play you for a sucker too, Pettengill. You don't even know whether she would have really— Anyway, now she thinks she has the secret. She'll stay quietly in your room, confident she'll be going South in a couple of days: plenty of time to carry the news. She'll pass on false information which will keep the Johnnies busy in the wrong place. And you have nothing to reproach yourself with when you meet Virgie again. . . .

Pettengill went up the bridge ladder, feeling better at every step. He even began to be sorry for Terry.

"Good morning, sir," said Acting Master Hurlbut.

"Morning, Mr. Hurlbut. How far d'you make it to Mathias Point?"

"Matter of ten minutes or so, I'd say, sir. We've been making good about twelve knots, average."

"Too dark for any shooting then." Pettengill turned his mind to the problem of the spy-station. Mathias Point loomed against the sky, loomed and slid past, dark and silent.

Should he put up to Banks—and the flag officer—a proposal to make a raid on the spy-house? . . .

An armed boat, lowered downriver a way, out of sight, *Valiant* going on past, seemingly unconcerned, then the boat's crew closing in, slipping along the shore, a quick dash, the place surrounded. . . .

It just might work. Two or three prisoners as tangible evidence, then burn the place. Allen was right here to see it all done. All would depend on surprise, of course. They might use the sloop—she was still towing astern, he could just see her topmast swaying against the gray sky—but there'd be no better chance of surprise with her than with a boat, though she'd carry more men. The growing light was the worst handicap. He was wasting time, and he had little to waste. . . .

Pettengill went down the bridge ladder and started aft.

If Banks supported him strongly, the flag officer might not be obstructive. . . .

Someone was coming forward along the starboard gangway past the engine-room hatch. In the gray dawn, Pettengill recognized Commander Case, Stringham's fleet captain, or chief of staff.

"Morning, sir," he said. "I hope the flag officer's not too busily engaged?"

"He's busy as all hell, and this is no time to barge in on him," grumbled Case. "Better put it off, is my advice. He woke up in one of his 'Now let's get down to brass tacks' humors, and he's hammering away at details with poor Banks." He yawned. "Never apply for a staff job, Mr. Pettengill," he counseled, "if you want to get more than two hours' sleep out of twenty-four. While matters are in the planning stage, anyway. I'll be damned glad when this Hatteras affair's behind us and we can get on to the main business at Port Royal."

"Port Royal, sir?" Pettengill gasped. "Did you say Port Royal?"

"That's what I said. Oh, I forgot you haven't been told that part yet. Your skipper's hearing all about it now, he'll tell you later on. It's the Old Man's policy that the second-in-command of any operation must always know the orders and plans. Gist of it is," the fleet captain went on, cheerfully, "Hatteras is just a try-out to prove whether ship's guns can really knock out shore batteries. If Du Pont's idea works there, it'll work at Port Royal, and that's the real objective. The harbor of Port Royal will make an ideal base of operations for the blockade. But you'll hear it all in detail from your skipper. Think I'll just go on the bridge for a breath of air."

Pettengill was sick with horror. He had picked the name of Port

Royal out of thin air, as a place where there were plenty of inlets and connecting waters that would answer the flag officer's description. But now—

He must report Terry's presence to the skipper instantly, and have her put under guard. He must report just why she was dangerous, just how he'd come to say that fatal name, Port Royal, to her. . . .

Pettengill squared his shoulders and started for the cabin ladder.

A yell from the bridge lookout brought him up short.

"Sloop's adrift, sir!"

He leaped to the rail, leaned outboard. There was light enough now to show him the sloop bobbing in the *Valiant*'s wake, drifting rapidly astern, and a tiny figure heaving away on the jib halliards, a figure about which something white fluttered. Terry!

The jib was rising slowly as she tugged at the heavy canvas. Now its upper part caught the wind, and the sloop began moving inshore.

"Full astern, Mr. Hurlbut!" yelled Pettengill. "Away duty boat!"

Just ahead, on the Virginia shore, he could see one gable-end of the spy-station.

Banks came charging up the cabin ladder, alerted by the hammering of the backing screw under *Valiant*'s stern.

"What the hell, Pettengill!"

Pettengill grabbed his skipper rudely by the arm, talking fast: he could hear somebody else coming up the cabin ladder, the flag officer, doubtless.

"Terry, sir—in the sloop—making for that spy-station. She was concealed below, heard everything the flag officer said last night."

"My God!" gasped Banks.

Someone brushed past them and went over the rail, hitting the water in a clean dive and striking out for the sloop with a long overhand stroke. Pettengill thought he had caught a flicker of gimlet eyes as the fellow dived.

The flag officer came up sputtering questions.

The *Valiant* had almost lost way by this time.

"Get after that sloop, Mr. Pettengill." The ring of command was in Banks' voice.

"Aye aye, sir. And if they get away—" he pointed to the gap in the dark pines, now clearly visible against the skyline—"shrapnel, sir—shrapnel on the road leading up to that notch. I'll fire three pistol shots as signal."

"I understand," Banks said, his mouth set in a hard, grim line. "Get going. Excuse me, sir. I had—"

[166]

But Pettengill heard no more of Banks' excuses to the flag officer. He was running for the duty boat, running to get ahead of any countermanding order from Stringham. The gig was already in the water. Pettengill slid down the fall, yelling "Let go! Give way!" Hurlbut, the good seaman, had used the helm to bring *Valiant*'s stern round as she backed—that saved precious minutes now.

"Break her up, lads!" implored Pettengill.

He could see Allen plowing through the water, halfway to the slowly moving sloop. Terry's soft muscles didn't have the strength to hoist the jib all the way, and the wind was fluky. But there was an eddy here with an inshore set that was helping her a little.

"Lift her, lads, lift her!"

How neatly she had wormed out of him the fact that this house might be a place where she could find help; that had been in her mind as she had gone on to extract from him the crucial item of information she needed. Even while she'd lifted her lips for his kiss, her scheming little mind had been figuring how she could get rid of him, sneak on deck, slide down the sloop's towline, cast off and make for shore. . . .

But now Terry was in trouble.

Allen had reached the sloop's stern; Terry had given up hauling on the jib halliards and was at the tiller. Allen grabbed at the rudderpost and started to pull himself up. Terry leaped to her feet, whirled round, and saw him. His hands were on the taffrail as he heaved himself out of the water. The sloop yawed. Terry snatched the tiller from the rudder-head and swung it with both hands.

It was a good lusty swipe. Allen went off the taffrail and into the river with a mighty splash. He came up twenty feet away and started swimming again, apparently not hurt.

The sloop was losing way amid the rushes along the shore.

"Lift her, bullies!" The gig's bow was only yards from the sloop's quarter.

A rifle cracked on the shore, and a bullet whined over Pettengill's head. Another. He could see gray figures moving among the pines. They were trying to delay him, cover Terry's landing. The fact that she had their sloop and was being chased by a Yankee boat would be credentials enough for Southern troopers.

The gig was right on her.

Terry flung the boat one frantic glance and ran forward toward the sloop's bows, screaming at the top of her voice:

"Port Royal! The Yankee fleet attacks Port Royal! Ride! Ride with the word! Port Royal!"

The men in gray—there were three of them—hesitated not one second. They turned and dashed for the stables behind the house.

The gig crashed alongside the sloop. Terry was ripping off her dress. She waved one bare mocking arm at Pettengill and dived overboard, half-swimming, half-wading through mud and rushes toward the shore.

"Up to the wharf!" roared Pettengill. "Never mind the girl—or that other fool in the water." Allen had found a mudbank and was wading ashore, waist deep.

Coolly now, Pettengill was calculating time and distance and slope; if they were already saddled up, it would make a difference.

His feet hit the wharf just as Terry's slender figure disappeared behind the house. Horses' hoofs beat a diminishing crescendo on hard earth; they were away, fast. Pettengill ran as he had never run before, got to the end of the house just in time to see the last horseman vanish among the pines.

Terry, panting, defiant, leaned against the corner of the kitchen and laughed. Her wet undergarments clung to her body, molding every curve. Her shoes were gone, her honey-blond hair hung in strings about her face. But she could laugh.

"You've caught me," she panted. "But they got away."

"Not yet," said Pettengill.

He lifted the revolver he had taken from the boat locker, the same one he'd used the night before. Three sharp pistol shots echoed across the water to the waiting *Valiant*.

Allen came puffing around the end of the house, a little derringer in his hand:

"What's that shooting?" he demanded. "Where did those Rebels get to?"

He was a mess. Coal dust was so ground into his face and neck and hands that even a bath in the river hadn't washed it away. Blood oozed from a nasty lump on one side of his head. But determination glittered in his gimlet eyes. They fixed themselves on Terry.

"Miss Terentia Seabright—"

The wicked double-crack of a rifled gun cut short whatever Major Allen was about to say. Something howled viciously overhead; well up the hillside there came a sharp report as flame lived briefly at the heart of a puffball of white smoke.

Terry stared at Pettengill, horror chasing triumph from her eyes.

"You won't do much with shellfire in those woods, mister," Allen said. "Anyway it burst short."

"Not shell," said Pettengill, "shrapnel. For your information, Allen, there are four hundred thirty-five lead balls in each of those projectiles. The spread is about ten per cent of the distance from the point of burst to the point of impact. And the slope of the hill is about right for grazing fire from down on the river. I don't think you need to worry about those couriers getting away—"

"Murderer!" gasped Terry.

"—if we don't have trouble with the fuzes," concluded Pettengill. Cr-rack! Bang!

Another puffball, farther up the hill. Somewhere up there a horse screamed.

About ninety seconds between shots. Rifled guns weren't too easy to load, especially with a half-trained crew; their rate of fire left much to be desired. Still, there would be time for four road-sweeping shots before the first horseman could possibly reach the crest. That should be enough.

"We might," Pettengill suggested, "go on up there now and just make sure. Cox'n, stay here with this lady. Wrap her in a blanket and see that she's here when I get back."

The road was little better than a bridle path, with the pines close-banked on either side. It demanded good gunnery to sweep the straight stretches, insofar as these could be made out from the ship. Banks must be laying that gun himself; there was no one else aboard *Valiant* who could do it as well.

The slope was steep.

Another shell burst above and beyond them as they plodded upward. Then the path turned, and there lay a gray figure sprawled beside it; one glance told Pettengill the man was dead. Dead and mangled, at least three balls must have ripped into him. His horse was nowhere in sight. A hundred paces farther along, they came upon a dead horse with its wounded rider's leg pinned under it. The man's eyes were glazed with agony, and he had ceased to struggle, just lay there.

"Get him out from under, a couple of you," Pettengill called to the seamen who were following them. "Give him first aid."

Another shell. Here the tree trunks were ripped and gashed by bullets; fresh-severed branches littered the path.

They found the last gray-jacketed rider about fifty yards below the crest, dead trooper and dead horse lying close beside each other.

From the top of the hill the road stretched away down into the farther valley through more open country, empty of other riders.

"That's the lot," said Pettengill to Allen.

"Scientific shooting, I'd say," Allen said. "Wonder who was aiming that gun?"

"Captain Banks. No other officer aboard with gunnery experience." The eyes of the two men met.

"It runs in my mind, Mr. Pettengill," said Allen slowly, almost reluctantly, "that I could be wrong about that skipper of yours."

"There's no more loyal officer wearing the uniform!" Pettengill replied. Then he added: "You know that young lady down there's the sister of the girl Captain Banks is going to be marrying this afternoon? She was out of sight from the ship when the firing began; for all he knew, she might have been riding up that road with the others. Maybe you can imagine what that thought meant to Captain Banks. But he aimed his shrapnel true just the same, because that was his duty."

"By God!" exclaimed Allen. "I hadn't thought of that. But you're right. I reckon I'll be making Captain Banks a mighty humble apology. And you too, Mr. Pettengill."

He held out his hand. Pettengill gripped it hard. Together they started walking back down the hillside.

"I was watching you when you came off from here last night," Allen went on. "I took note of the place and recognized it again this morning when I came on deck. They had me up all night, passing coal. Then I saw Miss Seabright in the sloop, and I heard you tell Captain Banks she had information, so I took off after her. She's a very determined girl. What was she doing on the ship, anyhow?"

"She stowed herself away," Pettengill told him, "during all the confusion when we were getting ready for sea. I found out about it this morning, but before I could get Captain Banks away from the flag officer to report the matter, she'd given me the slip and was off in the sloop."

Allen shrugged.

"Doesn't matter now," he said. "I'm quite satisfied that neither you nor Captain Banks had any prior knowledge of what she was up to. Of course we'll have to make sure the young lady doesn't communicate with any of her Rebel friends for a while—till her news is stale anyway."

"You mean—"

"I mean we'll have to put her where the dogs won't bite her for a couple of months," Allen said. "Then we'll send her South, when it's too late for her to do any harm. She must've done a mighty sharp job of listening last night, the little devil."

"H'm," said Pettengill. Allen apparently wasn't going to start nosing into details. He probably didn't know too much about the Navy's plans anyway, and he certainly wouldn't start asking questions of the flag officer.

Allen chuckled.

"You'll forgive me, I hope," he said, "for suggesting to you, on the basis of considerable experience, that Secesh dames can turn out to be explosive playmates, Mr. Pettengill."

Pettengill felt his face getting hot. Then he grinned. As Allen had just said, that didn't matter too much now.

The shadow that had lain so dark across the path of the future, of his future and Banks', had lifted. He quickened his step, striding down the bullet-spattered path through the first rays of the sun that peeped above the hills of Maryland.

Terry might be in need of comforting. . . .

Chapter Thirteen

The U.S.S. *Valiant* rode easily to her anchor off Charleston Bar, the swells rolling under her.

Pettengill, trotting up the poop ladder, drew a deep breath of salt air into his lungs: the tang of the sea was delicious after the coal gas and steam of the engine room.

He paused an instant at the head of the ladder for a quick look around. It was late afternoon. The *Valiant*'s crew had been piped to supper at four o'clock: now they loafed on deck, enjoying what remained of the evening sun. Pettengill thought sadly of white-haired Quartermaster Aycock, lying under a stone marker in a Washington cemetery. He wondered how long it would be before he'd be mourning other shipmates, or be under a stone marker himself.

For the war was on now. The roar of the guns at Hatteras Inlet had been Pettengill's baptism of fire. He had learned there, among other things, how desperately the men of the South would fight, even against overwhelming odds. There would be no quick and easy end to this business.

Much of it would be this weary, unsatisfying blockade duty. If you could call this a blockade. The majestic spars and hull of the big frigate *Wabash*, one of *Merrimack*'s sisters, lay a quarter-mile away; up the coast was the sloop-of-war *Vandalia*, watching Maffitt's Channel. These two, and *Valiant*, were all the ships available to watch the most important Atlantic harbor of "the States now in rebellion against the central government" five long months after Mr. Lincoln's blockade proclamation had been issued. It wasn't good enough, as the captains of the British warships that nosed regularly up and down the Southern coast were reporting to their Government.

Pettengill grunted and walked briskly aft.

Banks, sprawling in a canvas chair near the taffrail, looked up and chuckled.

"Evening, Pettengill," he remarked. "I see you've been grubbing around with the black gang again."

"Damn that issue soap. I thought I'd washed down alow and aloft."

"You missed a half pound or so of coal dust in your port ear. Don't see how you can blame the soap for that, considering the size of the job. But I'm glad you've come up for air, Pettengill. I've been wanting a word with you, and there's been no chance since we shoved off from Hampton Roads day before yesterday, what with that spell of weather we ran into off Hatteras. Steward! Rouse up a spare deck chair for Mr. Pettengill, and you might bring along some coffee and my leather dispatch case."

"Aye aye, sir," wafted up the cabin companion.

"Speaking of coal, sir," said Pettengill, "we used too much coming down. That's what I've been talking to the chief and Pete Hewitt about. Pete thinks he can get a more economical adjustment of the cutoff valves and save maybe another five per cent or so on coal. The chief's doubtful but willing to try. I kind of think Pete might be right. With your permission, sir—"

"I hope this isn't anything drastic Hewitt has in mind," said Banks. His voice droned in recitation: "Alterations in steam machinery other than necessary repairs shall be made only on written authority of the Navy Department."

"I know, sir," said Pettengill. "But—"

"And I know Pete Hewitt," interrupted Banks. "So do you. We were both shipmates with that red-haired tinkerer long enough in *Sheboygan*. He'd've rebuilt her whole steam plant if he'd been allowed. And he was only the junior watch-standing engineer then. Now he's got that little gold shoulder strap of a first assistant on his jacket, he's acquired more expansive ideas along with it."

"I'm glad you used that word, Captain. This is a question of using steam expansively. That's what cutoff valves are for. By cutting off the steam at just the right moment, in connection with the stroke of the piston, and letting expansion do the rest, you make the most efficient use of all the natural forces."

"Stow it, Pettengill," Banks interrupted again. "You know damned well you can talk rings around me when it comes to steam engines: a matter I mean to correct as soon as I have time. I'm coming to realize that no man's fit to command a steam warship who doesn't understand his own motive power. If this is just a matter of adjusting valves and that sort of thing, tell the chief and Hewitt they can go ahead, but no rebuilding jobs, mind you. Short of that, I'm glad enough of anything that'll save coal. An extra day's coal for a blockading cruiser can make the difference between nabbing a fat prize and losing her."

Pettengill laughed.

"If anybody gets any fat prizes on this Charleston blockade, it'll be us," he predicted. "Look at 'em." He waved a scornful hand. "There's the old *Wabash:* engines built as an auxiliary to sail, one horsepower for every four tons' displacement. She can do all of nine knots under steam alone. And up the coast there, we have the *Vandalia.* The *Vandalia,* forsooth. A sailing sloop-of-war on a blockade in this year of steam, 1861, when any blockade runner in his senses is going to use a fast steamer and try to run in or out at night. No wonder old Captain Mercer gave you such a cordial reception when you reported yourself aboard *Wabash* this morning. At least he has one ship that can chase, now we're here."

"He said something like that himself," Banks remarked. "He's worried, of course. Mercer's senior officer on the blockade off Charleston: the cradle of the rebellion, as they say up North. There's no place northern public opinion is so sensitive about. Navy Department's all clogged up with complaints already about ships going in and out. Welles and Fox throw harpoons into Stringham, and Stringham pulls 'em out of his quivering flesh and passes 'em along. There's no use pretending Mercer has an effective blockading force: it'd take at least six fast steamers to close this place up tight, round the clock and in all weathers. But he's responsible just the same, poor old boy."

Pettengill nodded. He looked up the mouth of Charleston Harbor, past the grim water-girt walls of Fort Sumter to the shining spot where the gold ball on the spire of Saint Michael's Church glittered above the haze, more than four miles away. For many years that ball had been the homing symbol for Charleston-bound ships: at night it was now replaced by a bright range-light which, lined up with another on Sumter, guided the blockade runners slipping in from sea. And they did slip in. It was virtually impossible to stop them, and it would continue to be impossible until more ships of the proper types were available for blockading duty and until the base at Port Royal was in Union hands so there would be a coaling station nearer than Hampton Roads, 420 miles to the northward.

"Maybe when we get these new gunboats and steam sloops-of-war they're building—" he began.

"Here's the steward. Sit down and rest that over-sized frame of yours. Leave the coffeepot here, Scipio."

Pettengill sat down, sipped coffee, and watched Banks fish a key out of his pocket and unlock the dispatch case. He could tell from the skipper's expression that something interesting was coming out of that case.

Something important too, from the way Banks sat up and looked carefully around. They were alone on the poop deck. Master's Mate King, who had the first dogwatch, was pacing the narrow bridge up forward of the funnel with his quartermaster, telescopes under arm. He was far out of earshot. No one else was likely to invade the captain's privacy.

Banks leaned back, took out a folded letter, and closed the case. He tapped the letter gently against the palm of his left hand.

"You may have heard that in his official report of the capture of the Hatteras Inlet forts, Flag Officer Stringham didn't overexert himself to make favorable mention of the captains of his ships and the other officers under his command."

Pettengill nodded. The whole Atlantic Blockading Squadron was buzzing with resentment.

"Well," Banks went on, "it appears that he opened up a little in his private correspondence with the Department. At any rate, he gave us some credit for our reconnaissance reports as well as for what small share we had in the bombardment itself."

Pettengill sat up straight, slopping coffee on his clean white pants. "The hell he did!"

"Read for yourself." Banks passed him the letter. "That's from Du Pont."

Navy Department, September 6, 1861

My dear Banks:

You'll be glad to hear, I'm sure, that the Flag Officer has written Mr. Welles in the warmest terms of the great value he attaches to the reconnoitering work in the North Carolina inlets done by your *Valiant*. He goes so far as to say you contributed in large measure to his success on August 28-29 at Hatteras. Also that *Valiant* was "capably and effectively handled" during the bombardment itself, especially by "going close inshore under the fire of the enemy batteries to cover the *Monticello* when the latter ship went aground." For Stringy, this is practically lyrical, as you'll be aware. Mr. Welles is impressed, having sized up the F. O. with his usual shrewdness.

So the net result is, I can tell you privately, that you'll make your number as Commander when the retiring law (just passed) has cleaned out the old fogeys from the Register, with no more nonsense about where you were born, and you're safe to get one of the new sloops-of-war. You should have your orders within a month, or less.

Pettengill looked up at Banks.

"Commander—and a steam sloop-of-war! That's great news!" he cried.

"Go on," invited Banks. "Read the rest of it."

Pettengill turned to the next sheet:

The Flag Officer also was thoughtful enough to include a few kind words about your executive officer, our young friend Pettengill. Something about his "ably seconding" your efforts, and going in with your boats to provision the troops ashore that first rough night at Hatteras Inlet.

In consequence, Pettengill's to be appointed Acting Lieutenant within the next few days.

Du Pont's forceful script blurred before Pettengill's eyes; he could hardly read on:

There's a peculiar distinction connected with that. You'll have noted that a few merchant marine officers of experience are being appointed Acting *Volunteer* Lieutenants. The use of the word "Volunteer" is intended to make clear that they are temporary officers, not in the line of promotion.

But there are also several officers who were formerly lieutenants in the Navy and resigned, well before the war, who have offered their services in the present conflict: Colhoun, Mygatt, Watmough, Baldwin. These gentlemen have been given appointments as Acting Lieutenants for the time being. A special bill is being prepared for presentation to the next Congress to put them back on the promotion list. I have an idea that Welles means to include Pettengill's name in that bill, which is why he's going to make him Acting Lieutenant now to emphasize that he doesn't regard him as a volunteer officer but as regular Navy.

Meanwhile, as Acting Lieutenant, I'd say there's every likelihood that Pettengill will be appointed to command one of the new gunboats. Mr. Welles has a rigid sense of justice: I think his conscience has been bothering him about depriving Pettengill of the command of the *Brother Jonathan* to please Senator Crossmore, even though you came along with a better billet in the nick of time. Crossmore's failing to get on the Naval Committee makes it easier for Uncle Gideon to make amends, of course.

Give my warm regards to Pettengill and tell him for heaven's sake to keep out of trouble these next few weeks until he has his commission in his pocket. I look forward with great pleasure to seeing his name in next year's Register.

My hearty congratulations on your own prospects, which have been nobly earned. As for myself, my task here is nearly finished. I'll be sniffing salt air shortly. I expect to have work for both you and Pettengill which may turn out more to your taste even than the fine job you both did for Stringham.

Ever yours,
Frank Du Pont

He was going to have his name in the Navy Register as Lieutenant, U.S.N.—regular Navy, in the line of promotion! . . .

Through the mist of his happy excitement, Pettengill saw Banks' eyes.

"You had a hand in this, God bless you!" he burst out.

Banks shook his head.

"Not much of a hand. I did write Du Pont a note. Apparently he's taken a shine to you, Pettengill. He's the man to thank. You couldn't have better luck in the Navy than to have Frank Du Pont take you under his wing."

"He's a great man; you can tell it the minute you see him."

"A great man, and a proud one," said Banks. "If nobody'd ever used the expression *noblesse oblige* before, it would have had to be invented to describe Du Pont. Give him loyalty, as he understands loyalty, and he'll give you loyalty in return right down to the time the last cat's keel-hauled, and regardless of what it costs him. But don't ever allow him to get the idea that you've let him down. His pride in himself is immeasurable: it's something you and I couldn't conceive of. In fact, he couldn't put it in words himself. He just feels it."

"You mean nobody can disagree with him, even though convinced they're right?"

"It's not that," Banks answered. "You can disagree with him, and forcefully if you feel it necessary. He'll listen, and he won't hold it against you. You can prove him wrong, and he'll acknowledge error with grace and generosity. But Du Pont's like the sun: there can only be one celestial body in his firmament. Disagreement and argument can take place only within the limits of his own solar system. Beyond those limits, it's disloyalty. If you bask in the warmth of the Du Pont sun, you can't seek a rival sun—and ever hope to return."

"You mean he has a streak of jealousy?"

"Not quite the word. Just pride, the kind of pride that might lead him some day to attempt the impossible because he couldn't bring himself to say 'This thing can't be done—not even by Samuel Francis Du Pont.' It's a fault, I suppose, but it's a fault of greatness."

"What does he mean here, about keeping out of trouble these next few weeks?" Pettengill asked.

"He may have a funny idea that trouble sort of follows you around," said Banks. "Of course I can't imagine what would put such a thought in his head, but— Anyway, you see all this acting lieutenant business and appointing you to a gunboat is administrative action. The only way you can get on the promotion list and drop the 'acting' is by an Act of Congress. Colhoun, Watmough, and the rest were lieutenants for years: but they resigned, and it takes an Act of Congress to get them back, too. Your case is unique. You're the only officer with sea service in a lieutenant's billet who hasn't held the rank of at least master in the line of promotion. So Uncle Gideon figures he ought to slip your name in with the rest, and making you acting lieutenant is the proper preliminary step: it gives you the same title as the others hold, makes it less likely that some fool on the Naval Committee will ask too many questions. At least, that's how I read it. As for keeping out of trouble, Du Pont's thinking it wouldn't help your prospects if the name of Pettengill were to become unduly prominent in some unfortunate way right now. This is the tenth of September, and in December, Congress will be meeting again."

"You've never seen such a duty-struck exec as you're going to have from now on," Pettengill cried.

"There's another thing, too," Banks said. "Lieutenants who can be trusted with command, or as executive officers of large ships, are in damned short supply. You remember that Department order last week, detaching eighteen lieutenants from various ships of this squadron to be assigned to command gunboats? Count 'em up. There are twenty-three of the ninety-day gunboats being rushed to completion, plus twelve double-enders, plus at least twenty fair-sized steamers like this one that have been brought into service and rate at least a lieutenant in command. Then there are fourteen new screw sloops that ought to have a commander and at least two, if not three, lieutenants apiece. The eighteen lieutenants they got by that order aren't a drop in the bucket. They'll be commissioning kids right out of the Academy without serving a day as master. So why shouldn't you have your due?"

"I still can't believe it. But I can tell from what you say that you've been pulling for me, and I haven't—I—I just can't find the right words to tell you how grateful I am."

"I wouldn't be doing my duty if I didn't put in a word for an officer who can serve the country as I know you can."

Pettengill, gulping with emotion, sought a change of subject.

"Well, thank the Lord for small favors, too. I'm glad I'm safe at sea, with no females around. Every time I've been in hot water since I got back from Africa, there's been a woman mixed in it someplace."

Banks looked grave.

"I've told you the good news first," he said. "I have another letter in that dispatch case. Too dark to read it now, but I know it by heart. It's from Virgie. You and I needn't beat around the bush with each other, Pettengill. You have a soft spot in your heart for that little hellcat sister-in-law of mine, haven't you?"

"I—I suppose I do. Anyway, I seem to think about her a lot. Which is more'n she does of me."

"Virgie says Terry's in love with you," Banks said. "No, don't get excited. Virgie also says Terry's made up her mind: as soon as they send her South she's going to marry my brother Farnifold."

"What!"

"That's it, and God forgive me for being the one who had to tell you. You know where Terry is, of course: locked up in a house on F Street with a few other Secesh ladies who're under suspicion. Virgie's been to see Terry three-four times. Terry's all wound up with conflicting emotions; she seems to have the idea that her loyalty to this damned rebellion ought to find expression in giving herself to some hero who's fighting for her cause. Of course she's known Farny all her life; he's been tagging after her since she was old enough to walk, and she's always treated him like a pet puppy. But now he's a hero."

"Her hero!"

"Exactly. I'm sorry, Pettengill. If I had that brother of mine here, I'd kick his stern sheets up to the maintop and down again. I'd teach him to steal your girl after you saved his life."

Pettengill stared at his skipper through the gathering shadows. "You know about *that?*" he demanded.

"A lot of people know it," said Banks gently. "Alex Murray's one of my oldest friends, he told me the whole story. I think he told Du Pont, too. And Rowan. It's a tale that'll do you no harm with men of that stripe, Pettengill. Nor with me," he added still more softly.

"But Terry—if she's in love with me, how can she be engaged to Farnifold?"

"She's not like her sister," said Banks. "Virgie, God love her, is capable of saying 'Whither thou goest, I will go.' That's not easy, pulling up roots."

"Not easy for you, either, sir."

"No, but with me it's a matter of duty, and an oath I took. Of course you know that when this war's won, it won't be the end. For us. Neither Virgie nor I can ever go back to Portsmouth again. Terry can't face that: she wouldn't want to face it, her loyalties run in different channels. Maybe if she'd been engaged to you before the war, she might—but what does that signify now?"

"Nothing. She's made her choice. I suppose she's written to your brother and got it all fixed up?"

"She's not allowed to write South. But all she has to do is snap her fingers when she gets there, and Farny'll come arunning with his silly tongue hanging out. He's still at the Norfolk Navy Yard, I hear: they've made him master in what they're pleased to call the provisional Confederate Navy."

"I guess," said Pettengill, "I'll never understand much about women."

"No man does. You have to take 'em as they come, and hope you'll finally find a good one that understands *you* and loves you in spite of it. Then, my lad, you've got a treasure."

"Here's one lad," said Pettengill, "who's going to waste no more time treasure-hunting! If they give me a gunboat, she'll be bride enough for Caleb Pettengill. And trouble enough. To hell with women. Let 'em make trouble for somebody else."

Banks said nothing.

Pettengill sat there glowering into the gloom. He was going to be Lieutenant Pettengill, U.S.N., and command a gunboat. That was a prospect he wouldn't risk for all the females from here to California.

"Let her go South and stay there."

"Sensible attitude," said Banks.

"I suppose she'll be going right after—" he dropped his voice— "Port Royal?"

"I'd imagine so," said Banks. "That won't be long now, from what I read between the lines of Du Pont's letter. He's to have a flag and be in command. I expect that's where he means you and me to do that work he writes of. So— What's that?"

Bright light flared high in the heavens, white light and crimson light.

"Two rockets from *Wabash,* sir, white and red!" hailed Master's Mate King from the bridge, his voice hollowed by the speaking trumpet.

"Squadron signal. Captain Mercer sent the list over this morning," said Pettengill. "Commanding officer of *Valiant* report aboard immediately."

Banks rose to his feet.

"Tell King to call my gig alongside, will you, Pettengill? Wonder what's fretting the old boy now?"

"Trouble," prophesied Pettengill, as he started forward.

Chapter Fourteen

The two ships, pursuer and pursued, were alone on the sparkling sea. Alone save for one ominous smoke-plume on the northern horizon, and the lonely palm-crowned islet toward which the smaller ship had turned her desperate prow, seeking sanctuary.

Pettengill, standing spraddle-legged on the U.S.S. *Valiant*'s bridge, peered through his glasses at the chase with fierce and hungry eyes. Beneath his feet, the planking pulsated to the beat of the *Valiant*'s hammering engine; the smoke of her last gunfire was pungent in his nostrils. At two miles, a hit would be pure luck: but the *Valiant* was closing the range steadily, if slowly, and there were two good hours of daylight left.

The Confederate privateer *Magnolia* would never see Charleston Harbor again.

Unless—

Damn that island! We had the luck, the incredible luck, to sight this Johnny Reb in the open Atlantic, and we'll be within point-blank range of her in an hour. Why does this miserable little patch of white sand and green foliage have to pop up out of the ocean right under her bows? Deadlight Cay, the chart calls it. Anyway, it's a British island, one of hundreds of cays that make up the Bahama Archipelago, a colony of the British Crown. In law, that fellow's safe now: he's well within the three-mile limit. He's covered by Queen Victoria's Neutrality Proclamation of—when was it?—last May sometime, May 13, 1861. Only he's not covered by any British guns. Not a sign of life of any kind on the island, except that ruined lighthouse. Smoke up north's probably the British corvette we spoke off Cat Island last night, coming to see what all the shooting's about, but she can't get here in time to save the *Magnolia*. So now poor Banks can worry about whether he'd rather be broken to cool off the outraged British or for failing to carry out Captain Mercer's orders to "capture or destroy the privateer steamer *Magnolia* at all hazards." . . .

"Prime!" The breeze whipped the boyish treble of Master's Mate Casson back from his station on the fo'c's'le. He was ready to try another shot with the 60-pounder Parrott rifle. Pettengill glanced at Banks, standing beside him on the narrow bridge. Banks' face was impassive as always in its frame of neatly trimmed dark sideburns. He showed not the smallest sign of even thinking about such an order as "Cease firing."

"Stand by!" squalled Casson.

Pettengill could see the bronzed torsos of the gun crew as they leaped clear of the recoil. Casson was bending forward, taking one last squint through the eyepiece of the bar sight. This would be the tenth shot since coming within distant range. No hits, but a couple had fallen close aboard the *Magnolia*.

For the past hour, Pettengill had been itching to be up forward laying that gun himself. But he had resisted the impulse. During the bombardment of the Confederate forts at Hatteras Inlet, young Casson, in charge of the broadside battery of eight-inch shell-guns, had shown signs of becoming a competent gunnery officer, with a little more experience and training. One day, almost any day, the continued existence of the *Valiant* and every man aboard her might depend on having a reliable officer handling her guns, while Pettengill's full attention would be absorbed by the executive officer's proper duty: handling the ship.

Pettengill's responsibility to his captain was to develop the talents of the human raw material under his charge and not to do other men's jobs for them just because he could do them better. There was a selfish thought there, too. Pettengill had already made up his mind to try to get Casson as his own executive when they gave him that new gunboat: whereupon Casson would have the job of whipping human raw material into shape, and Pettengill's reputation would in part be dependent on how well Casson did it.

So he stayed on the bridge where he belonged and let Casson carry on.

The sharp double-crack of the rifled cannon smote on Pettengill's eardrums. His glasses were at his eyes again as the smoke swirled past his head. Time of flight for the Parrott shell at this range was maybe twelve seconds; a phantom pendulum ticked them off: seven—eight—nine— Pettengill's eyes never left the low-lying, rust-mottled steamer with her white wake trailing astern, half-veiled in the cloud of coal smoke pouring from her funnel. Ten—eleven—

Gray smoke erupted suddenly from the deck of the *Magnolia,* well abaft the funnel. She yawed like a stricken sea animal, then came back on her course, the gray smoke trickling out of her and changing slowly to a darker shade as it gained in volume. On the *Valiant*'s fo'c's'le the gun crew danced and yelled in savage glee.

"We hit her that time, sir," said Pettengill, tuning all excitement out of his voice in imitation of his skipper's on-duty manner.

"So I note," replied Banks drily. "Burst in her afterhold, I'd say, amongst whatever cargo she may have there. Too bad it wasn't far enough for'd to get her boiler. She's still going. D'you see any opening in that reef, Mr. Pettengill?"

Pettengill snapped up his glasses. He had taken subconscious note of the white line of offshore breakers around the cay—all these islands had coral reefs—but he hadn't been thinking about it as carefully as he ought.

At this rate he'd never be fit for command. . . .

"No, sir," he confessed. "I don't see a passage anywhere."

"Neither do I," said Banks, "and if there isn't one, our friend will be piled up in just about five minutes unless he changes course or heaves to. Have a quarter boat swing out, Mr. Pettengill, if you please. If he strikes, I'll want you to go in to pick up any prisoners you can get and to make positive identification of the wreck." He grinned. "Reminds me of the time we sent you up that stinking African river after Harris the slave runner. What I want is the same thing Captain Nicholl wanted then: tangible evidence that'll look convincing when it's written down in cold black and white."

"Aye aye, sir," said Pettengill. "Messenger! Pass the word for the bo's'n's mate of the watch."

He knew what was in Banks' mind. Northward, that smoke trail was a little more distinct.

Banks wanted to get his evidence and his prisoners and be well away from Deadlight Cay before any British man-o'-war arrived on the scene. There was all the difference in the world, when it came to fighting off the British with one hand and the State Department with the other, between vague charges based on enemy complaints and definite charges based on the testimony of British official eyewitnesses with facts to swear to. That was how tough old Secretary of the Navy Gideon Welles would figure it.

Any day now, the British might declare that they didn't recognize

Mr. Lincoln's shoestring blockade which was cutting off their profitable cotton trade. Secretary Seward, of the State Department, wouldn't like a Yankee cruiser captain violating British waters at such a time: but Pettengill had a sneaking idea that Secretary Welles, of the Navy Department, wouldn't care too much about Her Britannic Majesty's outraged feelings provided she couldn't prove her case. Besides, this *Magnolia* was something special.

Why didn't the fool heave to! Good God, she was right on the reef! . . .

The bows of the little steamer fairly leaped out of the water, then settled back as she came to a dead stop. A rending and crashing of timbers echoed across the sunlit ocean. A following sea broke heavily against the steamer's stern, thrusting her forward a few feet. The next smashed into her without budging her at all. A geyser of steam rose suddenly out of the smoke that swirled around her.

"He's hung her up, sir," said Pettengill unnecessarily.

"And she's afire," said Banks. Thickening black smoke clouds were now belching from the stricken steamer. "Half speed, quartermaster. I don't want to be on the reef with her. Starboard two points. I'll go in as close as I can, Pettengill. Then you carry on, and mind you keep an eye peeled for the recall flag. Nobody's to go ashore unless you find it absolutely necessary in executing your orders. If that's a Limey coming down on us, I may not have time to wait for stragglers."

"Aye aye, sir," said Pettengill, and went clattering down the bridge ladder.

They were lowering a boat from the bow of the beached steamer before Pettengill's cutter was halfway to her. Through the eddying smoke, Pettengill could see the boat pulling shoreward, across the smooth water inside the reef. It appeared to be full of people, but if they all took to the bush, he'd have a tough time getting the prisoners Banks wanted.

He could read the name on the privateer's stern now: MAGNOLIA—CHARLESTON.

Not that there had been any doubt about her identity. The Union spy in Charleston who had sent out the warning to the blockading squadron had even included a sketch of the privateer. He was a thorough man. The plan, he reported, was for the *Magnolia* to proceed to the Mayaguana Passage, in the southern part of the Bahamas, there to intercept one of the Panama mail steamers which habitually used that route.

It was the receipt of that warning, sent off in a fishing boat from one of the inlets south of Charleston, which had caused Captain Mercer to summon Banks aboard the *Wabash*, with orders to get underway and maintain extra vigilance. And when, despite all the extra vigilance, *Magnolia* broke out through the blockade that same night and got away, Mercer's orders had sent the *Valiant* racing southward toward the Mayaguana Passage in pursuit.

Mercer was frantic for fear the privateer would catch one of the big packets and he would be blamed for letting her get to sea. Of course the old boy could hardly be expected to maintain a tight blockade outside Charleston Bar with only the slow old *Wabash*, the *Valiant*, and a sailing sloop-of-war. But he knew, and Banks and Pettengill knew, that when bad news broke, civilian politicians were only too ready to look for someone in uniform to blame. Pettengill had served in those Panama steamers before he had entered the Navy: he could imagine the howl for blood that would go up from nabobs like Allan MacLane and Bill Aspinwall if one of their great ships was grabbed by a Rebel sea-raider.

But now the bold little *Magnolia* was done for. She sagged over the reef with a broken back, and the oily smoke rose ever thicker from her midships section. She wasn't much to look at, just two pole masts and a rusty funnel sticking up from a flush deck: nothing else, not even a pilothouse, though there did seem to be some kind of gun for'd under a canvas cover. It looked like an old 32-pounder. No wonder her skipper hadn't tried to fight: one gun against the *Valiant*'s Parrott rifle and the six 8-inch shell-guns she carried in broadside!

The privateer's stern was sagging lower. As the long swells slammed into her, her taffrail was at times only a couple of yards above the water.

"Think you can bring the boat in close enough so I can make a jump for that rail, Mr. King?" Pettengill demanded.

There might be someone left aboard, or he might lay hands on some of the ship's papers.

Master's Mate King, the boat officer, gave Pettengill a startled glance.

"Reckon I can, sir. I'd suggest easing down stern first. Kraus! Pass that steering oar aft here! Steady all till I unship the rudder."

Pettengill kicked off his shoes and crouched, keeping out of King's way until the last minute but ready to jump at the moment of opportunity. The cutter's head came around.

A running figure burst suddenly out of the smoke that hid the *Magnolia*'s midships section, racing for the taffrail.

"My God, a woman!" cried King.

A woman it was—a woman in a brown dress, billowing skirts held high in both hands to free her slender legs for running, brown hair streaming from under her hat.

"Come back here, damn you!" roared a man's voice. A soot-blackened, muscled rascal, bare to the waist, caught up with the woman in two mighty leaps, grabbed her shoulder, and flung her away from the rail. His hand closed on her arm. He dragged her, fighting like a trapped wild thing, back up the sloping deck and into the smoke again.

"Put me aboard there, Mr. King! Lively!" barked Pettengill.

He unfolded his tough lanky frame from the stern sheets of the cutter as the oarsmen eased the boat in, stern first, under King's careful eye.

Balancing himself, ready, Pettengill remembered something.

"If the ship hoists the cornet, Mr. King, don't wait for me if you don't see me. Return to the ship the moment you see the signal."

"Aye aye, sir," said King. "But—"

"No buts. That's an order."

The sea lifted the cutter's stern as he spoke. He leaped, felt his hands close over the rail.

"Give way!" yelled King. "Pull, damn you!"

The cutter was already yards away as Pettengill swung himself up and over the rail. He gave her no backward glance.

He dashed along the privateer's deck, straight into the smoke. The bite of burning turpentine filled his nostrils. He could smell steam, too, and coal gas. He tried to hold his breath as he ran. Somewhere ahead he heard the woman scream. The deck was fire-hot under his feet, this hooker wouldn't last much longer, with turpentine burning in her 'tween decks.

He was out of the smoke again. The for'd part of the ship was clear of it. What fitful breeze there was blew offshore, pushing the smoke away, and in the privateer's bows the sooty man was in the act of throwing the woman in the brown dress over the side, or jumping over with her. He was lifting her, struggling and kicking, off the deck.

"Belay that!" roared Pettengill as he charged.

[187]

The man dropped the woman and whirled, whipping a knife from his belt. There was no time for Pettengill to get his revolver out—he should have done that already. His left hand closed on the thrusting wrist as the knife flickered at his belly: the soot was greasy, his hold slipped, but he had diverted the blade long enough for his right fist to finish its swing. The man jerked his head back and Pettengill's knuckles smashed against his throat instead of his jaw. He staggered, gasping, his soot-smeared face twisted with pain and rage, and the edge of Pettengill's left hand chopped down on his arm as he made a desperate pass with the knife. The knife clattered to the deck. Two flat reptilian eyes glared at Pettengill out of their rings of soot.

"Harris!" Astonishment jerked the word from Pettengill's throat. Edward Harris, slaver captain, the man Pettengill had captured in Africa in March and delivered up to Federal justice.

Pettengill's fingers were just closing on his revolver butt when the deck buckled suddenly beneath him. With a roar like an erupting volcano, the fire inside the little steamer broke its bonds and leaped skyward in thunderous fury. Its hot breath was the touch of death. Pettengill's shirt was smoldering; his straw hat caught fire. In the back of his seaman's mind, he understood what had happened. The fire had been in the afterhold, the after engine-room bulkhead had given way, the engine space and the open fiddley had made a draft chimney for the flames, and instantly the ship was burning fore and aft, her frames, timbers, decks igniting like matchwood.

Scorched, dazed, choking, Pettengill staggered toward the rail. Hungry tongues of fire were thrusting through every crack in the deck planking. It was hopeless to think of getting back to the stern where his boat waited. Over the bow into the water inside the reef was the one chance.

Harris must have taken that chance already—he was gone. The woman lay on the deck, groaning.

Was the water inside the reef deep enough to dive into without breaking his neck? He'd be burned to a crisp in a couple of minutes if he stayed where he was. And the privateer's magazine must be right under his feet. . . .

He grabbed at the woman, dragged her upright. She broke from his grasp suddenly, caught her dress at the neck with both hands and ripped it off, kicking the clinging skirts aside. Slim and graceful in corset and petticoat, she went over the bows in a perfect dive.

Pettengill followed.

He hit the water with an awkward splash, went deep, arms and legs flailing as he fought to get back to the surface. His head came up into the smoke-filtered sunlight. His heavy cap-and-ball revolver dragged at his waist; he loosened the belt buckle and let it go. Just ahead of him, he saw the woman swimming easily, steadily, for shore with a neat crawl stroke, her bare arms flashing. Farther ahead, much closer to the beach, Harris was swimming.

The water was clearing Pettengill's brain.

He might try to swim around the burning ship and hope the boat could pick him up, but there was enough sea beating on that reef to make it doubtful whether he could get through without serious injury from the jagged coral heads. Given time, King might find a hole where he could take the boat inside. The place for Pettengill was on the beach where King could see him. And there was still the chance he might lay hands on Harris and have at least one prisoner for Banks. . . .

He tried to swim faster toward the shore. He saw Harris hit the beach and go running across the strip of sand to vanish in the green mass of junglelike growth that underlay the towering palms.

The muffled roar of an explosion rolled across the lagoon: a moment later debris came splashing around the swimmers. The flames had found the *Magnolia's* magazine at last. The woman was still swimming, unhurt.

Ten more strokes, and Pettengill's kicking feet hit sand. He stood up. The woman was wading ashore just in front of him. She had gotten rid of her petticoat in the water: now she was clad only in a pink corset over a white undergarment, a chemise and pantaloons in one, that clung wetly to her breasts and her slender thighs.

Pettengill swung anxious eyes seaward.

"Goddam the luck!"

The light offshore air that had kept the smoke moving had dropped to a dead calm. A vast cloud of black oily smoke spread out from the burning ship; some of it climbed skyward, impelled by the draft of the combustion, but much of it was rolling out heavily over the surface of the sea and along the reef, making an impenetrable screen through which Pettengill could see nothing at all—neither boat, nor ship, nor signals.

The bow of the *Magnolia* was sagging inside the reef: her funnel had collapsed when her magazine let go, and so had both masts. But there was enough left of her to go on burning for quite a while. To go on producing this accursed, thick, rolling smokescreen.

Master's Mate King was a good seaman, but he was not possessed of a resourceful or an imaginative mind. He would be quite likely to have given Pettengill up for lost after the magazine blew up. Banks, out on the ship, could have no idea what might be happening to Pettengill, though he must have seen Pettengill board the *Magnolia*. And Banks had his ship and his duty to take priority in his decisions.

Pettengill had to get himself out of this situation alone. And do it before Harris made contact with the other Johnnies who had already come ashore; they probably had guns with them.

If he could get their boat! . . .

There it was, about two hundred yards along the beach near the gaunt timber framework of the abandoned lighthouse.

"Come on, we'll make for that boat," Pettengill said to the woman.

"Wait!" she begged in a choking voice. Her hand clutched at his arm. "Get this thing—off me; elastic's shrinking—can't breathe—"

She was plucking at the metal fastenings of her corset with futile, frantic fingers. It was so tight on her body that she couldn't free the fasteners. Pettengill fumbled in his wet pocket, found his knife, pried the blade open.

"Stand still," he ordered. He ran his knife's point down the edge of the laced corset-opening in back, cutting the laces at the eyes. The corset came away in his hand; the woman drew in a long shuddering breath and said, "Thank you." Then she suddenly blushed scarlet.

"I—I'm—not dressed!" she stammered.

Pettengill let his drill trousers drop around his ankles, kicked his feet out of the sopping mess.

"Get into those and follow me," he commanded, and ran, clad only in shirt, drawers, and one sock—he had lost the other swimming ashore—along the beach toward the boat.

The Johnnies had run her pretty well up on the sand, probably to keep her from being floated off by the next tide. As Pettengill came nearer, he realized that she wasn't going to be any help to him. She was a small cutter, the 22-foot type known in the U.S. Navy as a brig's cutter; she would weigh well over half a ton, bare hull. Judging from the deep footprints in the sand it had taken fifteen or twenty men to run her up to the spot where she lay. For all his strength, Pettengill wouldn't be able to budge her an inch by himself.

He looked angrily at the rolling smoke.

If he could only get above it . . .

Up there on the top platform of the lighthouse where the light had once been placed, he might be able to see above the smoke, even signal to King or to the ship. There would be a chance they could get him off. He was still holding the pink corset in his hand. It was stiff, so it would make a much better signal flag than his wet shirt.

The ladder to the first platform looked rotten and half its steps were missing. Pettengill took the edge of the corset in his teeth and swarmed up the palm-log corner upright. The ladder to the upper platform was in fair condition. Up he went; one rung broke under his weight and the whole structure groaned and swayed as he grabbed at the edge of the platform and lifted himself through the trap door. He peered eagerly seaward.

The boat was still hidden from him, down behind the smoke, but he could see the topmasts and the upper end of the funnel of the *Valiant*. There'd be a lookout aloft, and certainly the man would have his eyes fixed on the beach.

On the rim of the sea, northward, the smoke-plume he had seen earlier was now a steamer, hull up, which meant she was coming full speed, maybe eight or nine knots. She looked like the barkentine-rigged British corvette, H.B.M.S. *Heron*. The smoke of the burning *Magnolia* had drawn her down. Banks wouldn't dare stay much longer.

Pettengill continued to wave the spread-out corset above his head with both hands in the hope that the lookout would spot it, but he could see no sign that his signal was observed.

Now a flag was rising to the *Valiant*'s foretruck. It was limp in the dead air, and he could barely make it out; seemed to be brightly colored. Now—now a vagrant breath of breeze lifted it for an instant: red and white quarterings. The cornet. "All boats return immediately."

The smoke lay thick and impenetrable along the face of the reef and spread in oily convolutions over the sea. Somewhere under that smoke Pettengill's only hope of getting off this island was probably pulling back to the ship. Banks could spare no more time for further search when King reported Pettengill missing: he could not risk positive identification of his ship by the oncoming Limey corvette. If he did, he might be risking his country's safety. Trouble with Britain now, with the Union torn apart by civil strife, might prove the final disaster. It was one thing to destroy a Southern privateer on a deserted British beach. It was quite another to get caught in the act.

A gun sounded to seaward. Banks was calling sharp attention to his recall signal. Smoke was swirling up from the *Valiant*'s funnel.

Pettengill went slowly down the broken ladder, the useless corset still in his hand. He dropped from the edge of the lower platform to the sand where the woman waited.

"Would you mind," she asked in a voice as cool as if she'd been in a drawing room, "telling me exactly who you are and what you're doing here?"

Pettengill looked at her, really seeing her for the first time.

Large dark-blue eyes met his steadily. She had twisted her brown hair together somehow and tied it with a strip of rag, probably torn from her underwear. Pettengill's bandanna was tucked neatly inside her chemise top, covering her breasts. Pettengill's pants were drawn up and tied close under her breasts; the legs were rolled, flopping about her ankles. She was just a girl, no older than Pettengill; yet she wore her weird costume with dignity. Her accent was pure New England, like Pettengill's own speech, but she had been aboard a Southern privateer. She was certainly not the type to associate with Harris, still she had sailed with him.

"My name," she said, "is Prudence Pryor. *Miss* Prudence Pryor." She waited for Pettengill to introduce himself.

"I suppose you might say I'm a marooned traveler, as you are," he said, choosing his words carefully.

"Nonsense!" she retorted. "You came from the Union warship that's been chasing the poor little *Magnolia* all day. You boarded the *Magnolia* at considerable risk of your life. Why? You know Captain Harris. You're tied up with his schemes in some way."

"Not in any friendly way, would you think?"

"Thieves have fallen out before," she snapped. "If you're quite finished with my corset, may I— Oh!"

Pettengill saw the quick alarm in her eyes. He whirled—and went down under a sudden rush of sweating, snarling bodies: bodies that had charged so swiftly from the edge of the jungle that they were on him without warning. He slammed a fist into a bearded mouth, brought up a bony knee and heard somebody yelp; got an elbow under himself and almost gained his feet with half a dozen of them clinging to him. Then somebody clipped his skull from behind. Reeling, he tore one arm free and felt his knuckles crack against bone, but he wasn't co-ordinating now, he was sick and dizzy. The swarthy face of Edward Harris was there, in front of him. He dived at Harris, head first, crashed into the man and went down. Harris rolled from under him and then they had him, pinned fast, two or three of them to each arm and leg. They pulled his arms down to his sides, and he felt the harsh bite of rope around his body.

"Tie his ankles," snarled Harris in a breathless, gasping voice. "Drag him back in the brush out of the way. Then turn to with those rollers. I want that boat out of sight and the sand smooth before those Limeys get close enough to see things. Smoke's clearing, and it'll be daylight for another hour yet."

Three or four of the men dragged Pettengill across the sand and into the cool shade of the jungle.

"Goddam mosquitoes," said one of his captors, slapping angrily.

"They'll eat him alive," said another, a big fellow with a red beard. "Here, we'll put this thingamabob over his face. Keep the worst of 'em off."

Pettengill lay quite still for a little while, ignoring the clouds of mosquitoes as best he could. The pink corset lay across his face, but it wasn't much of a shield. Luckily, his salt-cured hide was fairly tough. His head throbbed: he couldn't put two thoughts together. He could hear the men working with the boat, could hear Harris giving orders. "All together, hearties! Heave!"

Why did Harris want that boat out of sight of the British?

Pettengill couldn't make his aching brain think. He kept shaking his head, trying to drive off the mosquitoes that were now busy around his face. He only succeeded in pushing the corset away, so he made himself sit up and gave his attention to getting one arm loose. His lanky frame was limberer than it looked, and the rope around his body had been hastily fastened. He got the rope worked down below his left elbow and hauled his arm out. Now he could cope with the mosquitoes. He leaned against the bole of a palm tree, still weak and dizzy, and slapped at them with the corset; it took continuous exertion to keep them from his bare legs as well as his head and neck. His eyes were swelling from innumerable bites.

He slapped at the mosquitoes on his legs and then quickly swiped at those on his face. The corset was almost dry now. So dry it crackled. Why would it crackle? He looked at it, turning it over, examining it inside and out: a piece of fabric was stitched to the inside. It looked like waterproof material. That was the part that crackled. He got hold of one corner with his teeth and pulled. It came loose, ripping the corset all the way down between two of the whalebone stays. Pettengill used his teeth again to tear open the little pocket of waterproof material that he now held in his hand. There was a rectangle of parchment inside. Enough fading sunlight trickled into the jungle for Pettengill to make out a jumble of letters and figures. Pettengill had seen enough code messages by this time to know what he was looking at.

No wonder she wanted her corset back. But why hadn't she come after it? . . .

Pettengill became obsessed with the question of where to hide the code message. He swiped at the mosquitoes and tried to think. His shirt pocket was torn away. He had no shoes. But he still had one sock. It took considerable contortion to get the scrap of parchment into the sock and down under his foot, but he managed it. He might have spent the time better in trying to untie the rope on his ankles and get his other arm free. But he could think of nothing but hiding that miserable piece of parchment.

He could hear the men crashing around in the brush, hear Harris' voice occasionally, giving orders.

Harris must've been the *Magnolia*'s skipper. Why did he drive her on that reef? . . .

Pettengill's head throbbed unbearably with the effort to worry this out. He slapped mosquitoes and thought about Miss Prudence Pryor.

If that was her name. Another Secesh dame! . . .

Somebody was coming now. A shadow moved, took form.

"Well, friend Pettengill," said the smooth voice of Captain Edward Harris, "I suppose you've been expecting me?"

Pettengill said nothing.

"Five thousand sea miles and a couple of oceans ago," murmured Harris, "you took me prisoner and I promised you that I'd keep you in mind. Now you're *my* prisoner."

The fading light gleamed on his white teeth as he took a clasp knife from his pocket and snapped open the blade.

Pettengill had only one chance. Harris hadn't noticed, apparently, that Pettengill had an arm free. And to use a knife, he would have to come within reach—

Pettengill braced himself to fight for his life—with one arm.

"The Fates," went on Harris, "being women, play curious tricks. Having delivered you into my hands, they place me under the imperative necessity of keeping you alive—for the present. For another day or two at any rate. By that time I'll know whether my hopes— but all that can hardly matter to you. Later, I shall enjoy our reckoning at greater leisure. It is but put off in any event."

He thumbed the edge of his blade.

"You came near to getting me hanged, you know, Pettengill," he observed, slapping at the mosquitoes. "I was admitted to bail by the Philadelphia court, but orders came from Washington to revoke the bail-bond, since slave running was now to be dealt with as a capital offense. Luckily, I was forewarned and went South a jump or so ahead of the marshal."

"So that's why you ran on the reef rather than surrender! You had a rope waiting for you if you were taken."

"Precisely," agreed Harris. "A rope that you had woven. I'll keep that in mind when the time comes to settle accounts. But meanwhile—"

"Cap'n Harris!" a voice called, not far away, accompanied by crashing noises of someone's coming through the bush. "Cap'n Harris!"

"This way, Grogan!" called Harris.

There was just light enough for Pettengill to recognize the big man with the red beard who had laid the corset over his face. Two or three others came out of the brush at his heels.

"The Limey man-o'-war's hauled off, sir," Red Beard reported. "Vic's up on the lighthouse platform, says she's bearin' away southerly, likely tryin' to catch up with that goddam Yankee cruiser."

"Southerly," murmured Harris. "I don't know that I care for that. But still, they'll be playing hide-and-seek among the islands. We'll have our chance. I think we can start working the boat around to the south side of this cay now, where we found the opening in the reef while we were cutting the rollers. Take charge of this man, Grogan, and we'll bring him along. Cut his ankles loose so he can walk. But be careful, he's tough and tricky. Tie his wrists behind him before you free his feet. I note he's worked one arm loose from those lubberly lashings you put on him."

Pettengill submitted to having his wrists tied without any attempt at resistance. Aboard the boat, he'd be at home. His chance would come. He stood up when Harris cut the lashings on his ankles. His feet were numb; he stamped them, leaning against a tree. The light was almost gone.

"Let's get out on the beach where we can see something," Harris ordered. "What's this? Oh, Miss Pryor's precious corset. I'll bring it to her. March."

Chapter Fifteen

The first rays of the morning sun, slanting over the cutter's gunwale against his swollen face, woke Pettengill from uneasy slumber. Instantly he knew something was wrong. He lay quite still, trying to figure what it was. The cutter's motion was sluggish under the pressure of lugsail and jib; that was to be expected, overloaded as she was with twenty people, including Pettengill and the girl. Sixteen bodies was the load limit for her type. She was running free now, on even keel, the wind almost astern. Then the wind had changed a little during the night? But wait, Harris had changed course. Earlier, he had been steering almost due east, as the stars had told Pettengill. Now the rising sun slanted across the port gunwale. That was what was different. Pettengill estimated the course as SSW. He wondered how far Harris had run to the eastward before changing course. It couldn't have been very far; he had been lying as close to the wind as he could. Well, say twenty—twenty-five miles. Then change to SSW. Pettengill reconstructed the chart in his mind. Roughly, that course would bring the boat right into the upper end of the Mayaguana Passage.

The Mayaguana Passage was the place where, according to the spy's message—in which Captain Mercer had fully believed—the *Magnolia* intended to lie in wait for one of the Panama mail steamers. So Harris had made his easting to let the *Valiant* and the Englishman get well out of the way, and now he was making for the Mayaguana Passage as though he still had a privateer steamer and a 32-pounder gun with which he could hope to bring to and capture a big Panama liner.

His men had small arms: a pistol in every belt, a few cutlasses, half-a-dozen muskets. But the days of the bold buccaneers were over long ago, when a few desperate men might hope to lay a shallop alongside a tall galleon out of Panama and take her by boarding. The age of steam had written finis to all that. No mail-packet captain in his senses would allow armed men to come aboard his ship: nor did he need to. All he had to do was to keep on going if he didn't like the looks of what he saw floating around. Only cannon could make him stop.

Pettengill looked at the ex-slaver from the corners of his eyes. Harris sat there easily with one arm draped over the tiller. There was an air of determination about the man which was matched by the queer suppressed excitement that Pettengill could sense among the crew.

They were a rough-looking lot, the crew of the *Magnolia*. More or less what you'd expect in privateersmen, and yet just an edge different. Grogan seemed to be a mate of sorts, and there was a skinny fellow with a harelip who might be an engineer. Most of the others were more like water-front ruffians than decent mariners, though they jumped to their duties smartly enough whenever Harris gave an order. From a stray remark here and there it was apparent that some of these men had sailed with Harris on slaving voyages. Certainly he had them under firm control. . . .

Sometime during the night, or before leaving the island, Harris had washed off the soot and had put on a fairly clean blue shirt. Prudence Pryor was sitting beside him, her hair blowing about her face. Up to the time he had fallen asleep, Pettengill hadn't heard her exchange a word with Harris, and she wasn't talking now. She looked worried.

She had a kind heart, though, thought Pettengill gratefully. All through the night, whenever the water-pannikin had come around, she had used part of her own allowance of fresh water to bathe Pettengill's swollen eyes. That he could see at all this morning he probably owed to her. And it was she who had insisted that they re-tie his hands in front of him, so he could lie flat. Pettengill moved his head so he could look up at her, but her eyes were fixed on some far horizon.

The movement reminded Pettengill that he was still acutely uncomfortable. His feet were numb again, and the bottom boards of the cutter were hard on his back. He ached all over, and where he didn't ache he burned or itched. His throat was a furnace, but he wasn't going to beg Harris for water.

"Grogan!" said Harris suddenly.

"Sir!" said Grogan from somewhere for'd.

"That land under our lee—what d'you make it? You know these islands."

"Samana Cay, I'd say, sir," Grogan replied.

"My thought," nodded Harris. "Then in another hour or so—"

He cut off what he was about to add, with a quick glance at Prudence Pryor. She did not even turn to look at him, or the distant island.

Pettengill could have filled in the unspoken words: In another hour or so, we'll be right in the mouth of the Mayaguana Passage, if this wind holds. Trying again to remember the chart, Pettengill recalled that there were a couple of tiny cays off to one side of the passage where Harris could lie in wait, if that was what he meant to do.

Pettengill began to build a small hope in his mind. Banks would certainly have given the *Heron* the slip by this time, he had the speed of her by four or five knots. Then he might go back to Deadlight Cay to pick up the crew of the *Magnolia*, if they were still there, and try to find out what had become of Pettengill. But first he just might take a quick look into the Mayaguana Passage to see if anything was in sight. He knew—because Pettengill, out of old-time knowledge, had told him—that the mail steamers generally left Aspinwall for New York on the tenth of each month. This was the thirteenth. And from Aspinwall to the Mayaguana Passage via Cape Maysi was just about a three-day run. For all Banks knew, there might be other Rebel privateers at sea with Harris' idea in mind. Yes, Banks almost certainly would have a look at the Mayaguana Passage before heading back for Deadlight Cay. If he did, this little boat, so full of men that her gunwales were almost awash, was certain to engage his interest.

When was that water ration coming? Pettengill licked his dry lips, hoping the Pryor woman might notice. But she wasn't looking at him. He closed his eyes and tried not to think about his burning throat.

He dozed a little, but roused suddenly as he heard Harris snap out:

"What's that?"

"I think I see smoke, cap'n. On the port bow, way down on the horizon."

Pettengill saw Harris grab for an old-fashioned brass telescope and clap it to his eye. He looked for a long minute, adjusting the tubes.

"By God, you're right. Smack in the channel, too."

The boat heeled a trifle as he shifted the tiller.

"Here, Grogan. Take the helm. Run right down to her. I want to take a look around and make sure we've no unwanted company."

He made his way for'd over the thwarts and braced himself against the stubby mast, sweeping the horizon with his glass. When he came back he was grinning.

"I'm pretty sure that's our friend," he remarked, "and there's nothing else in sight. We're in luck, bullies."

An inarticulate growl of delight ran from thwart to thwart.

"You all know what you're to do and how you're to act," Harris said in a brittle voice. "The man who makes the wrong move I'll deal with personally. If any of you have a question to ask, now's the time."

No one spoke.

"Very well. Grogan, gag the prisoner. Might's well get that done while we've plenty of time."

Grogan knelt beside Pettengill, a tholepin and some rope yarns in his hand. Pettengill set his jaw. Harris took out his clasp knife: the blade glittered in the sunshine.

"Open your jaw or have it pried open," he said.

Pettengill opened his mouth. Grogan put the tholepin between his teeth, athwart his face, and lashed it fast with rope yarns knotted tightly behind his head.

"That," said Prudence Pryor in a cold voice, "is unnecessary and wicked brutality, Captain Harris."

Harris leaned close to her and began talking in a tone so low that Pettengill could not make out his words. But he saw the girl turn pale and shrink back, staring at Harris as though she could not believe her ears. Then Harris snapped his knife shut and put it in his pocket.

"We understand one another, I think," he remarked. "Where's that telescope?"

Pettengill lay there and cursed Harris in his heart. The tholepin was lashed so tightly that it pulled his mouth out of shape: the pain he suffered now was going to get worse every minute.

"That's our ship," cried Harris, snapping the telescope shut. "She's coming up fast. Another half-hour and she should be within hail. I'll do the talking, remember."

What did Harris mean to do with Pettengill, trussed and gagged? His head was aching again. A long time later he heard a distant hail, "Boat ahoy-y-y!" and became aware of the approaching throb of a steamer's screw.

Grogan was at the helm; Harris had gone for'd. He was yelling something, it sounded like "Castaways! Shipwrecked seamen in distress!"

With guns, thought Pettengill sardonically. Do you take that skipper for a fool?

But the beat of the propeller slowed.

"What ship?" demanded the hailing officer, with the booming effect inseparable from the use of a speaking trumpet.

"Confederate privateer *Magnolia!* Wrecked on Deadlight Cay!" answered Harris promptly and truthfully.

A deeper voice hailed:

"You have arms in that boat, you Rebel rats!"

Harris spun around, snatched up a boat-stretcher.

"I told you to throw those guns overboard!" he yelled at the top of his voice. "Do it at once, as you promised me! Every gun! Every pistol!"

He came charging over the thwarts, laying about him with the boat-stretcher on the backs and shoulders of his crew.

"Over with them!" he howled, apparently transported by fury.

And before Pettengill's unbelieving eyes, they obeyed. Splash—splash—splash, into the sea went pistols, muskets, dirks, and cutlasses until not a single lethal weapon, except what Harris might have hidden on his person, was left in the boat.

Panting from his theatrical exertions, Harris cried:

"These are honest men, captain, repentant men. I answer for them. We need help. And as you see, we have a woman aboard."

"Come alongside," said the deep voice. "No nonsense, mind."

"The boat-handling's your job, Grogan," muttered Harris.

The boat heeled as Grogan put the helm over, and the upper masts of a full-rigged ship came into Pettengill's range of vision; then the topmasts; the funnel, trailing thin anthracite smoke; the house flag high at the foretruck; the ensign at the spanker-gaff; all *ataunto.* No sails set: she was using steam alone.

She was the *Orient Queen,* of the Panama line. Pettengill knew her well, though he'd never served in her. Now he could see the upper tier of cabins, amidships, and passengers crowding to the rail, waving excitedly. Her skipper's name was Castleton, a tough old sea-dog of the hearty type. Pettengill had met him but not sailed with him. He heard the stop-bell in the liner's engine room, then three bells for "slow astern." The screw thrashed in the water, the great ship lost way.

The sea was easy, almost glassy. Grogan brought the boat right up under the towering side of the liner, where falls had already been sent down to hook her on. Captain Castleton knew his business: no use taking the trouble to launch a boat of his own, since this was clearly a ship's cutter fitted with ringbolts fore and aft so she could be hoisted in. And he had a steam winch to do the job.

There was a row of curious faces at the rail. Pettengill recognized the beet-red face of Captain Castleton. Would Castleton recognize him? Probably not, especially with his face swollen by mosquito bites and distorted by the gag, but there'd certainly be one or two of the mates or engineers who'd sailed with Pettengill at one time or another and knew him well. On board a Panama liner, Caleb Pettengill would have no trouble establishing a maritime identity that would give him credence with sailors against any lie Harris could tell. Pettengill began to anticipate with mounting glee the moment when they'd take the gag out and he could start talking.

"Hook on," bawled someone. "Stand by there, some of you lubbers. Fend her off! Ready! Hoist away!"

They were putting rope fenders over the rail as the boat rose from the water, the winch chugging briskly. Fore and aft, a couple of sturdy rascals with oars kept the swinging boat clear of the ship's side. There wasn't much motion anyway.

Up she went until she was almost level with the main-deck rail.

"'Vast heaving," roared Castleton. "Now then, come aboard one at a time. Search each man for arms, Mr. Fifield, as he comes over the rail."

Captain Castleton was taking no chances with people from a Southern privateer.

With unctuous politeness in his voice, Harris asked:

"May I bring my sister aboard first, sir? She is suffering much from privation and exposure."

"Certainly. Ladies first, always. Rule of the sea." That was for the benefit of the passengers, goggling down from the hurricane deck. "Are you in charge of this boat, mister?" he went on to Harris.

Harris was making a fuss of helping Prudence Pryor get to her feet.

"In a manner of speaking, sir," he answered. "That is, under the hand of Providence. But I am not a mariner, save on the boundless ocean of God's mercy. My name is Elihu Thompson. I am an unworthy servant of the Lord, seeking, with my sister Prudence, to bring His word to the people of these islands. The fishing boat in which I had taken passage was cast away on Deadlight Cay, and her owner drowned. My sister and I had been on that deserted island for a week when the Rebel privateer *Magnolia* was driven ashore on the reef by the guns of one of our gallant cruisers—"

He was interrupted by a ragged cheer from the gawking passengers. By this time he had bustled Prudence over the rail, and had followed her himself.

"—and since then we have been engaged in trying to persuade these unhappy sailors of the error of their ways. In which, the Lord helping us, I think we have had some success."

"Hah!" snorted Castleton, peering into the boat. "Who's the lubber you've got there lashed and gagged?"

Pettengill wriggled and tried to say who he was, but all he could get out past that tholepin was a sort of hoarse croak.

"That person, sir," said Harris smoothly, "is, I fear, a scoundrel beyond the reach of redemption. He is the *Magnolia*'s captain, a wretch named Edward Harris who, I understand, is not only a pirate in his present occupation but has a long record as a captain of slave ships. For which crime I consider that no repentance can earn him forgiveness, human or divine."

"Edward Harris!" thundered Castleton. "Why, the scoundrel's notorious from Cuba to the Congo. I heard the Navy nabbed him off the coast of Africa this spring. He seems to have slipped through their fingers, if this is the same man."

"Here are the papers I took from his person, after I had induced his crew to turn against him and make him prisoner," Harris announced. Pettengill couldn't see just what was happening, but he heard the rustle of paper and heard Castleton's jerky remarks.

"Letters of marque and reprisal . . . Jefferson Davis, President of the Confederate States of America . . . to Edward Harris, Esquire, master mariner . . . on the high seas against the United States of America, their ships, vessels, goods and effects and those of their citizens . . . steamer *Magnolia,* of Charleston. Bah! Damn outright black piracy, that's what I call it. You've earned the gratitude of every decent sailor, Mr. Thompson, by ridding the seas of such a villain. Mr. Fifield! Have the master-at-arms double-iron that pirate and throw him in the brig. Put a guard at the brig door. I'll come see him hanged when the courts are through with him."

They tumbled Pettengill on deck and brawny hands half-dragged, half-pushed him down two ladders to the orlop deck and forward to the brig. There they cut away the gag. Pettengill had furious speech boiling up inside him, but he found he couldn't talk: his throat was too dry, his lips and tongue too swollen. They ironed him, wrists and ankles, and shoved him into a dark little iron box about six feet by four, with a pannikin of water and some hard bread. The door slammed shut; he heard a bar fall into place, a lock click.

Pettengill sat down on the deck and addressed himself, with grim self-discipline, to the task of recovering his lost voice, aided by careful swallows of water.

Half an hour or so of sipping water and washing his mouth with it somewhat reduced the swelling. Pettengill addressed a few well-chosen words to the darkness on the subject of Captain Edward Harris, and found them quite understandable.

He got carefully to his feet, remembering the six-foot headroom characteristic of ships of this class, and put both hands on the iron door, feeling for the air holes that were the only ventilation of the cell. The brig door gave on the orlop deck, just under the for'd hatch. Pettengill could see the gleam of sunlight, which meant that up on the main deck, the hatch was open; that accounted for the occasional whiff of fresh salt air that penetrated to the orlop. In bad weather, with the hatch battened down, the atmosphere in the brig would be unbearable.

Along with the fresh air came also a whiff of pipe smoke.

A guard was on duty, by Castleton's order. The man was probably leaning against the bulkhead near the door.

"Ahoy, there, sailor!" hailed Pettengill, mouth to air hole.

"Huh?" The sound was no more than a grunt.

"Sailor! I want to see the captain."

"Shaddup, y' pirate bastard," said the guard.

"I'm no pirate. Get the captain down here and I'll prove it," persisted Pettengill.

"Y' take me fer a greenhorn? Shaddup."

Further persuasion would only make this man more stubborn. His relief might be a different type. Pettengill sat down again, irons clanking dismally, and tried to calculate when the relief would be due. At eight bells, he supposed, when all sea watches were relieved. He thought eight bells of the morning watch had already struck, though he wasn't sure. Then this fellow would be on post till noon, at least three hours away, maybe more. Pettengill was churning with anxiety. Harris hadn't worked out this little comedy of his without a definite plan and purpose.

[203]

Pettengill was disappointed in Prudence Pryor. Somehow during the night he had begun to get the idea that she might be taking a shine to him. Perhaps it was the gentle touch of her fingers as she bathed his swollen eyes. Certainly she hadn't talked to him. Still, somehow—

Forget it, he told himself. You've got other things to think about that are a damn sight more important.

There had to be a mate or an engineer aboard who would know him. Fifield was a callow youth whom Pettengill had never seen before. But the chief mate or the second, or the chief engineer, or the purser, one of them must have been shipmates with Pettengill, east coast run or west. Even if Castleton didn't remember him, there would be someone who knew him well, who'd vouch for him.

The problem of establishing contact, however, as the day wore on, began to assume the proportions of impossibility. The relief guard who came on at noon was a nervous Jamaican Negro who wouldn't even answer Pettengill's pleas. At 4 P.M., he heard the jangle of keys: the brig door was flung open by the master-at-arms, a burly fellow with a fixed scowl, attended by a colored mess cook carrying a pannikin of water and a wooden trencher of ship's bread.

"Five minutes to go to the head, pirate," the jimmy-legs said. "Stir yer bones."

"I've got to see the captain right away, master-at-arms," said Pettengill as impressively as he could. "There's been a mistake: I'm a United States naval officer. Captain Castleton must know—"

"Stow yer gab," said the master-at-arms. "If ya' wanna go to the head, get movin'. Once I shut this door it stays shut till eight bells in the mornin' watch."

The head was a place Pettengill certainly needed to go. So he obeyed the order, shuffling along a narrow passage with the irons clanking about his feet.

"United States naval officer, he says! 'Ja hear that, Carlson? Ain't that a yarn fer the Marines?"

The new guard on duty haw-hawed dutifully. So did the mess-cook.

Pettengill, emerging from the head, tried another tack.

"All right, tell the chief mate—what's his name again?"

"Davy Jones!" replied the master-at-arms, enchanted by this time with his own wit. "Haw-haw-haw! Git in yer stateroom, mister naval officer!"

[204]

He gave Pettengill a brutal push. Pettengill's feet, encumbered by the irons, stumbled against the coaming; he saved himself from plunging headlong into the cell only by a quick grab with both hands at the upper edge of the door.

The master-at-arms roared with happy laughter.

"In yer go!" he crowed. "Sleep soft, admiral!"

He slammed the door shut.

"Tell the chief mate Caleb Pettengill wants to see him!" yelled Pettengill. He had no idea who the chief mate was. But it was the best idea he could think of.

His only answer was renewed shouts of laughter that faded into silence as the master-at-arms went up the ladder.

His hope was in the love of sailors for talk and gossip. The master-at-arms would certainly hold forth in the petty officers' mess about how he'd put that Rebel pirate in his place. The messman would talk, too. So would the guard when he went off duty. Sooner or later, the talk would come to the ears of an officer—might even, with great good fortune, come to the ears of an officer with an inquiring and alert mind.

Meanwhile, Harris was maturing his scheme.

Harris was aboard the *Orient Queen* with sixteen of his own men. A gang of castaways would be berthed for'd with the steerage passengers. Harris would be given a spare stateroom, if there were any. So would his "sister." But in the role of a missionary, Harris would be able to say he had to visit his men to look after their spiritual welfare.

But where could they get arms to replace those they'd thrown away? Somewhere in the back of Pettengill's mind there was a vague memory that he had seen a Navy Department memorandum about furnishing small arms to the Panama liners for self-defense in case of need. He was still trying to recall the details when he dozed off.

He woke to instant awareness of someone's tapping gently on the iron door. He was on his feet as swiftly as the irons would let him.

"Who's there?" he demanded, keeping his voice low.

"Prudence Pryor," came the whispered answer. "Tell me who you are—quickly. I must know."

"Caleb Pettengill," said Pettengill distinctly. "Acting master, United States Navy. Executive officer, U.S. steamer *Valiant*."

"You're telling me the truth?" Her whisper was desperate with urgency. "I'm risking my life coming here. If Harris finds me— All right, I believe you. But how—"

"The guard?"

"Asleep. But he may waken."

"Get to the captain," Pettengill bade her. "At once. Tell him my name and rank, and where you first met me."

"He won't believe it," gasped the girl. "Harris has taken care of that. Says I'm out of my mind—exposure and privation. Keeps me locked in my stateroom: I broke out, but he'll kill me now if he—"

"Wait. Have you heard the names of any of the ship's officers?"

"Only one or two; a Mr. Wainwright is chief mate—"

"Get to him. Quick! Tell him Caleb Pettengill who was shipmates with him in the old *Champion,* is down here in irons. Don't argue. Get going."

"I'll try." She was gone: Pettengill could hear the soft patter of her feet on the ladder.

There could scarcely be two Wainwrights holding mate's billets in this line of hookers. Charlie Wainwright had been second mate of the *Champion* on the Frisco-Panama run when Pettengill had first shipped in her as a gawky kid A.B. almost eight years ago. Charlie had helped Pettengill bone up his navigation, helped him get the fourth mate's billet aboard *Champion* after he'd passed for his ticket. They had been shipmates two more years after that, had stood back to back in many a water-front brawl: together they'd cleared the deck that bloody night when Walker's guerrillas had tried to take the ship over.

Pettengill waited in a fury of impatience.

At last feet clattered along the deck above; lantern light gleamed at the hatchway, gleamed an instant later on brass buttons as a white-clad figure came down the ladder on the run.

"Cal! Cal Pettengill! You in there?" roared Charlie Wainwright's voice.

"Ahoy, Charlie!" shouted Pettengill, mouth against the air holes. He heard a thump and a yelp, and Wainwright's voice again:

"Up, you lazy lubber! Sleeping on watch! I'll log you for that! Hold this lantern. Get that brig open and look alive doing it, master-at-arms!"

Keys jingled, the door swung back.

Pettengill stumbled out into the lantern light, and Wainwright flung a steadying arm around his shoulders, peering eagerly into his face.

"By God, Cal, it's you sure enough!" he cried heartily. "But what—never mind, first thing's to get those irons off. Jump to it, Legs."

"But, sir—the captain's orders—" began the master-at-arms.

"I'll answer to the captain!" barked Wainwright. "Do as you're told! Cal, how the devil—heard you were in the Navy."

He was pumping Pettengill's manacled hands as the jimmy-legs knelt to unlock the leg irons.

"So I am," cut in Pettengill on Wainwright's incoherent excitement. "I was in a steamer that chased the *Magnolia* ashore on Deadlight Cay, burned her on the reef. The skipper sent me in with a boat's crew. I got stranded and Harris captured me."

"Harris? But that's the name—"

"That's the name of the bastard who's passing himself off as a missionary. That's why he brought me aboard here with a gag between my teeth. As a decoy duck to hornswoggle your Old Man. He's Harris—skipper of that privateer."

"Good God! Then what's he up to?"

"What he's up to," said the chilly voice of Prudence Pryor, "is capturing this ship."

She stood at the foot of the ladder, the lantern light gleaming on her neatly arranged brown hair and on some sort of bluish dress she had apparently borrowed. Her eyes were glittering.

"I'd suggest," she went on, "that you gentlemen defer the questions and get moving; you have no time to waste. Harris is making his move. He has his own men plus his friends that shipped steerage from Aspinwall—"

"But no arms," interrupted Pettengill. "Unless—"

Wainwright caught up the unspoken question.

"Fifty Sharp's rifles, Cal. Took 'em aboard at New York last voyage."

"Where're they stowed?" Pettengill's ankles were free now: he was holding out his wrists to the master-at-arms.

"Locked racks—passage just for'd of the skipper's cabin. The Old Man keeps the keys on his cabin key board, along with the keys to the treasure room. We're carrying a million dollars in California gold this trip."

"So that's what Harris is after!"

"Of course," said Prudence Pryor.

"Jesus!" gasped the master-at-arms as one wrist iron came open under his fumbling fingers. "Mr. Wainwright, what—"

"The arms-rack keys, they're the keys to the ship!" snapped Pettengill. "I'll block that move. Back me up quick's you can, Charlie."

He was halfway up the ladder as he said the last word. An instant later he was up the next one and racing aft along the main deck under the tropic stars. To his right, as he ran, were the lighted windows of the main saloon. It was almost deserted now, save for a few weary stewards putting things to rights and one night-owl poker party in shirtsleeves, half-hidden in a cloud of cigar smoke. The rows of steamer chairs along the deck were empty. From all the signs, it was well after midnight, no hint of dawn in the east yet.

Ahead was the empty expanse of the afterdeck. Pettengill slid to a stop, trying to figure the layout of the ship. The *Orient Queen* didn't have a poop, like *Champion:* she was flush-decked aft. This hatchway to the right, at the foot of the mizzenmast, must give access to the cabin country. Pettengill swung toward it. At the foot of the ladder he could see a bulkhead, a polished door—and the faint gleam of a dimmed lamp on rifle barrels in serried rows.

He started down, but as his bare foot hit the first step of the ladder he saw that door—it had to be the door to the captain's cabin—open slowly.

Captain Edward Harris stepped noiselessly out into the passage. In one hand he held a bunch of faintly jingling keys; in the other, a knife with a dark stain on the blade.

Somewhere for'd, a bo's'n's pipe squealed and a hoarse voice roared:

"All hands—all-l-l hands on deck!"

Harris started, shot a quick glance upward, then called a sharp command:

"Lively, bullies! Come and get 'em!"

Out of the shadows of the passage beneath the ladder they came swarming, jostling each other, jamming the passage as they reached eagerly for weapons. Pettengill dropped to his knees, tore with frantic fingers at the brass pins which held the upper end of the ladder. One came free. He held up the ladder with one hand, worked at the other pin: it was out, and the heavy brassbound mahogany ladder ripped free from his grasp and crashed down on the heads of the men in the passage. And as Pettengill leaped into the howling vortex, he roared at the top of his voice:

"Shoot 'em down, men! Mr. Wainwright! Cut 'em off at the midships gangway!"

He was in the middle of a shouting, squalling, ill-smelling mass of bodies, laying about him with the heavy iron handcuff and the short length of chain which was still attached to his right wrist, a fearful weapon at close quarters: it smashed into faces and against heads and shoulders and upflung arms. The mass of men was yielding, breaking back for'd along the passage as panic sucked away their courage.

Sharp pain ripped at Pettengill's shoulder, furious hands clawed at him. Harris was on his back, stabbing, and he was screaming: "Come back here, you cowards! It's only one man!"

He had one arm locked around Pettengill's neck now, dragging him back and down: Pettengill tore free of that clutch, slamming an elbow back; he heard Harris grunt, felt the knife point again, but he was swinging away from it, it didn't go deep. For an instant he saw Harris' head silhouetted against the light of the bulkhead lamp. He swung his manacle at it, the iron thudded on bone. Harris went to his knees. Pettengill wrenched the arms-rack keys from Harris' fingers. As he did so, a voice at the hatchway above his head roared through the groans and curses of the injured men who still writhed beneath the ladder.

"Cal! You there, Cal?"

Wainwright's voice.

"Come on, Charlie!" Pettengill called, kicking at Harris. The red-bearded Grogan was coming toward him, a couple of others too.

"Follow me, hearties!" shouted Wainwright, and came dropping through the hatch; his white-clad legs hit Grogan, knocked him sprawling. Wainwright was down too, but he was up on one knee instantly, and the revolver in his hand banged like a 12-pounder in the narrow passageway.

A seaman in a striped jersey dropped through the hatch, cutlass in hand. Back in the darkness a voice shrieked:

"Run for your lives! It's a trap!"

Harris hacked at Pettengill's bare shins with his knife, wriggled away like a snake and dived through the half-open door into the cabin. Pettengill flung the keys at Wainwright and plunged after Harris. The lamp was dimmed here too. Harris was up on the cabin table leaping for the skylight, and Pettengill's fingertips just grazed the soles of Harris' shoes as they went up and out of sight.

The cabin door was jammed with shouting seamen. He'd never get through there. Then he saw a gleam of white—

"See to the skipper, Charlie! He's hurt!" yelled Pettengill from the table top and leaped for the skylight coaming. His fingers closed over it, and he heaved his lanky body up and over the coaming to the starlit deck. The faint glow of coming dawn gleamed on slashing steel. Pettengill dodged, struck with his iron flail—struck and missed, but Harris had dodged too, the deflected blade ripped through Pettengill's flapping shirt. Pettengill brought up a knee before Harris could recover his balance. He screamed like a woman as it smashed into his face, then turned and ran toward the glowing rectangles that were the after windows of the main saloon, skirting round the crowding seamen who were still blindly trying to jam their way down the hatch.

There was a crash of breaking glass as Harris dived straight through the first window he reached. Pettengill saw him go to his knees, blood running down his face. Pettengill knocked jagged bits of glass from the windowframe with a sweep of his wrist iron and vaulted through. Harris came up, snarling through his bloody mask, and crouched, ready to spring, hurt but still deadly, knife in hand.

Pettengill snatched up a chair, charged with its four legs advanced like bayonets. Harris tried to sidestep, stumbled, and rolled away from Pettengill's lunging weapon. The end of one chair-leg hit his arm. He dropped the knife, scrabbled for it, then bounced to his feet, spitting blood. Pettengill dropped the chair and closed in. His left fist took Harris fair on the point of the jaw. Harris went backward over a yellow satin settee and lay quite still on the rich carpet beyond, a dark stain spreading around his head.

A woman screamed. A man cried out: "You bloody murderer!" For'd, where the passageways from the main-deck staterooms opened into the saloon, half-dressed passengers were hovering, staring with horror.

"Get out of my way, you idiots!" called a high clear voice, and Prudence Pryor burst through the jam. Hair disordered, blue dress fluttering, she ran across the saloon to Pettengill. Just as she reached him, young Fifield, revolver in hand, flung himself through the door that gave on the port gangway.

"Mr. Pettengill!" he cried. "Mr. Wainwright sent me to help you."

"It's all right," said Pettengill, jerking a thumb toward Harris. "Have a couple of these stewards take him to the doctor. I'd like to save him for the hangman."

"He'll have to wait," said Fifield. "Doc's with the skipper. The Old Man's in a bad way, I'm afraid. Mr. Wainwright's rounding up the rest of the pirates."

Pettengill, exhausted, flung himself on the yellow settee. Prudence Pryor touched his shoulder.

"You'd do well to see the doctor yourself, my friend," she said tartly. "Look at you, bleeding all over that beautiful couch."

Pettengill's shirt hung in ribbons from one shoulder; that was all he had on except the single sock and what was left of his drawers. Chest, arms and legs were one smear of blood, some of it his, some of it Harris'. His shoulder throbbed where Harris' knife had ripped it; he stung in a couple of other places; the gash across his right shin was still bleeding.

Prudence tugged at his arm.

"Come along. You've got to take care of yourself," she commanded.

Fifield was barking orders at two stewards who were trying to pick the limp Harris off the deck.

"Stand by with your gun, Mr. Fifield," snapped Pettengill. "That man's dangerous while there's breath in him. All right, Miss Pryor. I'll make my way below. Doc's in the cabin. When he has time, he'll fix me up."

He was on his feet, swaying. He staggered toward the gangway door; lifting his feet over the coaming was an effort—two separate efforts. He lurched across the strip of open deck and leaned on the rail; the dawn wind blew fresh across his knife-torn, weary body. The sky had shifted from black to gray.

"Below with you," urged Prudence.

"Wait—in a minute—"

Suddenly his mind was crystal clear. He turned his head, met Prudence's eyes fairly.

"I haven't thanked you for what you did for me earlier this morning, Miss Pryor," he said. "I'll never forget it—not as long as I live. You risked your life to save me."

The girl gasped.

Gently he added, high-borne on the crest of romance:

"That memory'll be with me in the dark watches of the night, in storm and in battle—always. Always, Miss Pryor."

"Must I remain—just a memory, Mr. Pettengill?"

She sounded almost as though she might be closer to laughter than tears.

"The war divides us, Miss Pryor," he announced. "But you're not to worry. Your secret's safe with me. How could you suppose otherwise?"

"Look!" she cried suddenly. Pettengill's eyes followed her pointing finger. The light was much stronger; he could see land over there on the port beam—Crooked Island. And round the northern point of the island, the signal "Heave to immediately, I wish to communicate" fluttering from her fore-topgallant yardarm, came the U.S.S. *Valiant*.

"Made a lot of difference if she'd shown up an hour ago," grumbled Pettengill.

"You get below to the doctor," ordered Prudence Pryor sternly.

Chapter Sixteen

The sun was streaming brightly through the porthole of Charlie Wainwright's stateroom. The *Orient Queen* plowed through the swells that rolled in from the Atlantic, her engine turning over dead slow. Pettengill, stiff with bandages, lay back in Wainwright's hammock-chair; soap and water, a razor and a suit of Wainwright's clean whites had made him feel like new. In a few minutes they would come to tell him the *Valiant*'s boat was alongside to take him back where he belonged. Everything else was taken care of. Harris was patched up and in irons. His men were under guard down on the orlop; Casson and twenty hands from the *Valiant* had been put aboard to look after them. And the *Valiant* was going to see the *Orient Queen* safely into New York.

Captain Castleton, the doctor said, would probably pull through: Harris had stabbed him as he lay asleep in his berth, but the knife had missed the heart. That might or might not mean anything to Harris, who would most likely hang. And there would be no nasty kickbacks from the British now for the affair at Deadlight Cay; the Navy Department had too good an answer in the catalog of Harris' crimes.

Pettengill had had time to realize that saving a ship carrying a million dollars in California gold to enrich Mr. Lincoln's treasury had ensured his lieutenant's commission and the gunboat command.

He hadn't thought about it much while he'd been in the thick of the mess, yet he'd come close to losing all his bright prospects: missing his ship, getting himself captured, allowing himself to be used as a decoy by Harris. If it hadn't been for Charlie Wainwright—and Prudence Pryor. . . .

"You're looking better, I must say, Mr. Pettengill," said Prudence Pryor's cool voice from the doorway. She was still wearing the bluish dress, but her hair was neatly arranged again; her eyes sparkled. She stepped through the door and closed it behind her as Pettengill swung to his feet.

Tenderly Pettengill enfolded her in his big arms, her chin came up, he pressed his lips to hers. For an instant her mouth seemed to return his kiss.

Then—he didn't know quite how it happened—she was free of his embrace and standing back from him, a queer little smile quivering at the corners of the mouth he had just been kissing.

"Your capacity for misinterpretation, Mr. Pettengill," she murmured, "should be proverbial in naval circles. I did not close the door to permit romantic farewells, but to prevent being overheard in what I came to tell you."

His face was suddenly hot with embarrassment, he knew his ears were getting red.

"You are apparently under the impression, Mr. Pettengill, that my efforts to secure your release from the brig were occasioned by personal feeling." The dark-blue eyes still sparkled; to his horror Pettengill realized that they were dancing not with passion but with amusement. "I'll have to set that straight," she went on. "I was just doing my duty, under rather difficult circumstances. I gather from your reference to keeping my secret that it was you, and not Harris as I'd supposed, who ripped open my poor bedraggled corset and took that scrap of parchment from it. I presume you have it about you somewhere at this moment?"

"I—yes—but I won't turn it over to my—"

"You are quite at liberty to deliver it to your captain. You might even suggest that he translate it by means of his code book. If he does so, Mr. Pettengill, he will discover that it will identify me, not as a Southern spy, as you obviously imagine, but as an agent of the United States Treasury Department."

She kept right on talking, every word adding to Pettengill's agony. She had volunteered to go to Charleston to investigate reports that Northern traders were trying to cut in on blockade-running profits, dealing in turpentine and other naval stores. She had passed as an agent for such a firm, and had actually made a decoy purchase of turpentine—the same that had been aboard *Magnolia*—through the connections she had established. She had known all about the *Magnolia*'s real mission: to intercept the gold shipment. It had been the talk of Charleston. The scheme had originated with Rebel sympathizers in San Francisco, some of whom had shipped aboard the West Coast steamer that took the gold down to Panama, meaning to cross the Isthmus and ship steerage in the *Orient Queen*. But they needed arms and a leader who could navigate the big ship. These the *Magnolia* would supply.

"It was the telegraph that did it; there's only a two-day pony-express gap between the ends of the lines now. The conspirators in San Francisco got their messages through in plenty of time for their friends in Charleston to make the necessary arrangements to intercept the *Orient Queen*," she explained.

"You mean the telegraph's working freely to Charleston—in wartime?" Pettengill said, incredulously.

"No, silly. To Philadelphia—to Harris. The Frisco people knew him. That's why he went to Charleston when he jumped his bail. I didn't know all these details when I sent out a warning to the blockading squadron about the *Magnolia*. I hope, by the way, those two brave colored fishermen were suitably rewarded."

"I don't know."

"So," went on Prudence in her matter-of-fact way, "when I heard what was really going on, I shipped as a passenger for Nassau in the *Magnolia*. To look after my turpentine. Harris didn't like that, but he didn't want to kick up a fuss. There was too much talk already; it's incredible how quickly everything gets known in a place like Charleston. What I had hoped, of course, was to be on hand if the *Magnolia* was stopped; otherwise to reach Nassau and give my information to our consul there, who might be able to communicate with a naval vessel. But once we were clear of your not-too-vigilant blockaders, Harris told me he'd changed his mind: he was going to run straight for the Mayaguana Passage without touching at Nassau."

Prudence had been suspicious of Pettengill because he obviously knew Harris. Harris hadn't enlightened her as to who Pettengill really was, even when he had determined to use the cutter to make one last desperate try for the *Orient Queen*.

"And you, Mr. Pettengill, being suspicious of me, were equally uncommunicative," she pointed out. "So I wasn't certain: and when we were approaching the *Orient Queen* and Harris told me that he had a rope already around his neck, that he would kill me instantly, come what might, if I contradicted any of his statements, I decided to wait on events. After we were aboard, he further handicapped me by thoughtfully explaining to the captain that his poor sister's mind was affected by privation and exposure—hallucinations and all that. He wound up by locking me in my stateroom. Fortunately I still had your trousers, and your knife—with which you operated on my corset, you'll remember—was still in the pocket. That's a good seamanlike knife, Mr. Pettengill, but I'm afraid I broke the blade forcing back the lock of my stateroom door. By that time I'd had a chance to think, and I'd come to the conclusion that you must be a United States officer. If so, you and I together might be able to make the captain believe our story. But I had to be sure. That, Mr. Pettengill, is why you found me at your door in the small hours of this morning."

Prudence was having a wonderful time.

"The call of duty brought me there, Mr. Pettengill, not the call of romance," she murmured. "I can imagine, of course, that your previous experience with my sex may well have given you the impression that your—ah—charms are irresistible. In my case, alas, they did not—"

The door opened suddenly. Charlie Wainwright's ruddy face beamed at them.

"Have to cut the farewells short, I'm afraid, Cal, old man. Your boat's alongside."

"We'll see each other in New York, of course, Mr. Pettengill," said Prudence Pryor. Wainwright's grin broadened as he favored Pettengill with a knowing wink. Pettengill gave her outstretched hand a feeble shake and headed for the passage, muttering something about good-by and good luck.

Outside, where the bright sunlight sparkled on the sea, a cheer arose as Pettengill came up the companionway. The rail of the hurricane deck was jammed with passengers, waving and yelling as they craned their necks to see the hero leave the ship. All the *Orient Queen*'s officers were at the gangway to bid Pettengill farewell; two or three of them, besides Charlie, he had sailed with in the old days.

The *Valiant* was lying to a cable's length off, smoke trickling from her funnel, and Banks' white-clad figure on the bridge.

"Good-by, Charlie. God bless you. I hope the skipper's going to be all right, but I hope you'll get the command, too." Pettengill pumped Wainwright's hand once more and went over the side and down the ladder where Master's Mate King waited with the same cutter from which Pettengill had gone aboard *Magnolia*.

He was safe—safe from women again, and from women's laughter. Pettengill dropped into the cutter's stern sheets.

"Happy to see you, sir," said King.

"Shove off, Mr. King. Return to the ship."

High above his head, on the *Orient Queen*'s decks, the passengers were still cheering. Three blasts on the whistle marked Charlie Wainwright's parting salute.

Pettengill turned to wave acknowledgment.

Then as the last whistle-blast died away, a voice rang out—Prudence Pryor's voice, high and clear, every syllable horribly distinct:

"Ahoy-y-y, Mr. Pettengill! Don't forget! When we get to New York you're going to buy me a new corset!"

Chapter Seventeen

Pettengill had fallen in love at his first sight of her. She had gone to his head like strong drink; he had lavished his time, his strength, his money, and his heart's devotion upon her, knowing all the time that the day of reckoning must come, but no more able to check his course than as if he had been driving before the violence of a hurricane.

"Handsomely with that iron plate!" he called. "You want it to go right on through her bottom?"

The master blacksmith flung him an ill-tempered glance. Sweat channeled the grime on his fat cheeks, deep lines creased his bulging forehead.

"That's the last one, Cap'n Pettengill," he grumbled. "And it's glad I'll be to see it bolted fast to yer bulkhead. Ye're no easy man to be dealin' with. Fer the love of heaven, git that bulkhead painted over in a hurry so's them iron plates won't be so conspickus like. If the naval constructor ever finds out about 'em, 'tis Henry Casey who'll be runnin' fer the Allegheny Mountains, so it will."

"He won't find out from me, Mr. Casey," Pettengill said. He looked hard at Casey and jingled the gold coins in his trousers pocket. Master Blacksmith Casey scowled.

"The things," he bewailed, "that a pore man'll do fer money."

Gear groaned as the two-inch wrought-iron plate was lowered carefully down the after hatch of the U.S.S. *Lycoming*. Pettengill's *Lycoming*. Pettengill's love.

One day that plate might protect her vitals from deadly injury: it or one of its mates in the solid two inches of iron armor that had been bolted to her thwart-ship bulkheads, forward of the boilers and aft of the engine room, to guard the machinery space from raking fire.

That was far from all. The wiseacres in the Bureau of Construction, Equipment, and Repair who had designed *Lycoming* and her sister double-enders would have found quite a few surprises if any of them had chanced to come aboard her now.

Pettengill looked soberly at the iron coaming around the engine-room hatch—the top sloping inboard: this was to defend the machinery against plunging fire. He knew without looking that the paddle-guards were of inch-thick iron plate and came well below the wheel centers. The two round pilothouses, one at each end of the hurricane deck, were plated with brass. Iron would affect the compasses, and Pettengill, though he had encountered compensating magnets in the merchant service, had no time to work up the theory and have them properly installed. Brass plates would stop a rifle ball, and that was all he needed to protect his helmsman from poor Aycock's fate. He had followed Banks' idea (as applied in *Valiant*) by providing side-bunkers to shield the sides of the machinery space with a three-foot thickness of coal—coal which was never to be used unless all other bunkers were empty. But they gave *Lycoming* another sixty tons of emergency coal capacity, which could mean three to four days' extra steaming at what Pete Hewitt called economical speeds.

None of these alterations had been authorized by the august graybeards of the Navy Department. They had originated in the fertile brains of Acting Lieutenant Pettengill and his eager helper, Acting Chief Engineer Pete Hewitt. They had been installed by the simple process of bribing the master workmen and quartermen of the Philadelphia Navy Yard to do the work and then "finding" the material to do it with.

Only two weeks ago, Pettengill had made the astonishing discovery of how co-operative a public employee can become when he hears the jingle of coins. That first occasion had been merely a matter of wire tiller ropes. The next step had been to increase the size of the pilothouses and install big ferryboat-type steering wheels for easy steering and quick turns in the narrow channels where the *Lycoming*, like all double-ender gunboats, was intended to do most of her fighting. Fortunately there were several ferryboats at the Yard in the course of being converted into gunboats. Then came the watertight compartments, with movable slides which allowed water to run free fore and aft when desired, but could quickly isolate underwater damage by gunfire or torpedo. A hundred dollars to the master carpenter had settled that problem. After that, Pettengill just went on and on pampering his darling.

As he stood by the hatch watching the plate being swayed in toward the vacant space on the bulkhead, Pete Hewitt came trotting down the ladder from the hurricane deck.

"I've got those blowers installed," he reported. "I'll guarantee to give you fifteen knots, if not sixteen, any time you need it. But don't ask for it unless you do: she'll eat two and a half tons an hour under forced draft with those things going full blast."

Pettengill looked soberly at Pete's cheerful freckled face.

"You're a wizard, Pete," he said. "How'd you ever get 'em over here and aboard without the Yard engineer catching up with you?"

The blowers had been designed for one of the new sloops-of-war, a ship of nearly twice the *Lycoming*'s displacement of 1,250 tons.

"Oh, they only weigh a ton and a half apiece," said Pete. "I just backed up a couple of drays, brought over the movable crane and h'isted 'em, and off we went. Of course it was kind of dark. One thing about 'em I didn't tell you before, the blower engines have twice the power of the ones we were supposed to get. I can run both the bilge and the feed pumps on 'em by fixing up a few connections, which means we can use both sets of pumps at once if we want to without turning over the main engine. How's that for fuel economy?"

"Wonderful!"

Pete looked around the busy deck, littered with odds and ends of gear and crowded with Yard workmen and the *Lycoming*'s own hands, all hard at work.

"Seems like you'll have your job cut out for you, getting ready to go into commission tomorrow," he remarked.

"We'll be ready," said Pettengill. He didn't enjoy being reminded of the ordeal before him. The commandant might really begin to take notice of his unauthorized alterations.

If Captain Du Pont had still been in command, Pettengill wouldn't have dared such wholesale Navy Yard thievery. But Du Pont was in New York, hoisting his flag in the steam frigate *Wabash* to take command of the brand new South Atlantic Blockading Squadron. He was Flag Officer Du Pont now, and he was also Pettengill's chief hope, for the first task assigned the new squadron was the capture of Port Royal, and Pettengill ardently expected to prove, in the heat of action, the worth in lives and fighting power of the changes he'd made in *Lycoming*. If he did, he had an idea that Du Pont would thereafter shield him from the fury of outraged bureaucracy. If only his sea orders would show up and make that hope a little more definite.

The new commandant at Philadelphia was Commodore Pendergrast, who was grumpy at being relegated to shore duty, but not ill-disposed toward Pettengill, and, fortunately, not gifted with an inquiring mind. Pettengill's main worry was the executive officer of the Yard, Commander Thomas Turner, a martinet with a sour temper and an eye for details.

So far, neither of these elderly mariners had set foot on *Lycoming*'s deck. The Philadelphia Navy Yard, like every other navy yard and civilian shipyard from Maine to the Potomac, was buried under a mountain of work, and its officers were tormented night and day with telegrams from Washington demanding miracles by tomorrow morning. The activity Pettengill had found there in April was nothing compared with the incredible confusion and turmoil of October. No less than four new steam sloops-of-war were under construction at the Yard itself, besides two double-ender gunboats, the *Miami* and Pettengill's beloved *Lycoming*. A dozen merchant vessels of various types were being fitted for naval service. And the Yard staff was responsible for supervising the construction of the huge armored frigate *New Ironsides*, which Cramp's Shipyard was just starting work on, and of four of the ninety-day gunboats being built by other Philadelphia contractors.

Pendergrast and Turner had only one lieutenant, one chief engineer, and one naval constructor to help them supervise all this. Pendergrast stayed in his office most of the time, swamped by papers: the others were far too busy with the big sloops-of-war and the outside jobs—especially *New Ironsides*—to pay attention to double-ender gunboats. Such trifles were left to the master workmen and their quartermen, and to harried officers ordered, like Pettengill, to "duty at the Philadelphia Navy Yard in connection with the fitting out of the U.S.S. *So-and-so*, and in command thereof when commissioned."

The Yard was heaped up and running over with a vast profusion of resources—stores, material, fittings, machinery. The naval storekeeper, a precise man accustomed to fretting over a missing copper bolt, was frantic. He couldn't even hire reliable help, with Army recruiters snatching all the men they could get and civilian shipyards offering double the Navy pay scale plus bonuses. All Pettengill and his accomplices had to do was to help themselves to whatever they fancied.

Pettengill's conscience did not trouble him.

He was doing this not for his own glory and profit, but for his ship and, beyond that, for the men who would serve in her and for the cause they would be serving.

The double-ender type was basically a sound conception. *Lycoming* and her sisters had been designed with the definite strategic and tactical purpose of controlling the maze of inlets, sounds, and rivers along the whole southern coast from North Carolina to Florida. These inland waters were now bases for privateers which raided northern commerce, and havens for blockade runners. They could become landing places for invading Union troops, arriving by surprise from the sea, and coaling stations could be established at some of them for the gunboats and for the seagoing ships which would still be needed to blockade the major harbors like Charleston from the outside. The gunboats, controlling the inland waters, would handle the rest of the blockade and help the Army where needed. This was, indeed, the only way that the blockade of the Confederacy's Atlantic coast could ever be made effective.

The double-enders were meant to operate equally well in either direction, thus avoiding any need for going about in narrow channels. That was why they were side-wheelers. A screw steamer going astern in such a channel, with treacherous currents and unknown shoals, was too hard to handle.

Lycoming and the others were sharp-ended at bow and stern. They were really two fore-bodies joined together, with a rudder and a steering wheel at each end, boilers and engine amidships, and open gun decks fore and aft. Between the paddle-wheel guards, and over the machinery space, a light hurricane deck or superstructure was built, which served as a bridge when underway and carried the two pilothouses. The *Lycoming* was schooner-rigged, but her sail power was merely auxiliary: fundamentally, she was a steamer.

Her heavy guns were a hundred-pounder Parrott rifle on a pivot mount for'd, and an 11-inch Dahlgren smooth-bore shell-gun on a pivot aft on the quarter-deck; all she had besides these were four howitzers, two 24-pounders and two 12-pounders. She was supposed to carry four 9-inch Dahlgrens in broadside, but they weren't to be supplied for the present, since there had been head-shaking in Washington over the proposed battery's being too heavy for her size. In fact, the after pivot gun was also supposed to be a nine-incher, but Pettengill had laid his hands on an 11-inch gun that was intended for one of the contract-built ninety-day gunboats. It was still lying on a barge moored astern of the *Lycoming,* covered with tarpaulins, waiting till the commissioning ceremony was over; on the quarter-deck it would be too "conspickus," as Casey would say.

"Y'know," Pettengill said now to Pete Hewitt, "it's a good thing in a way they held back on those four nine-inch Dahlgrens. You figger out yet how much extra weight in armor we've put on the old girl?"

"Fifty-two tons," said Hewitt.

"'Bout what I thought. Well, not having the Dahlgrens saves us sixteen tons of guns and, say, thirty-two tons of ammunition at two hundred rounds per gun, which is what our allowance table calls for. So it just about balances out, and we won't be having trouble about being too deep in the water. And I'd rather have some armor and some guns than no armor and more guns."

Lack of armor protection was the basic defect in *Lycoming*'s original design. Pettengill had been horrified when he first saw her. He had seen something of the results of that sort of stupidity in the Potomac Flotilla. A gunboat that was going to do her fighting in channels and rivers had to have her vitals protected, not so much against heavy guns as against musketry and field artillery. She wasn't intended to fight forts: her big sisters could do that. But from coastal jungles a hidden battery might cut loose on her as she came around a bend. That was the reason for the two-inch iron bulkheads forward and aft. They would stop a 32-pounder solid shot. For the rest, the chief need was to keep the shellfire of field-guns out of the engine and boiler rooms and to protect the helmsman against musketry. Granted that, *Lycoming* could take care of herself with her own firepower, but without this elementary protection, she would be fatally vulnerable, even to infantry.

"Fifty-two tons of armor," Hewitt said. "We've changed a wooden gunboat into an ironclad, that's what. Some day I'm going to work out what the dollar cost would be if all this was in the specifications. I'd guess we might's well have gold-plated her from bow to stern."

"Damn the cost," said Pettengill. "We've made her into the most efficient river gunboat in the world, and that's all I care about."

"You must've gone pretty near flat broke doing it," Hewitt suggested.

Pettengill laughed.

"Pretty near," he agreed. "But what's money for? Anyway, I got some prize money out of that *Ranee* business. And I had some back pay coming."

Besides, he reflected, he was now not only getting lieutenant's pay, $1,800, but the extra $450 allowed to "lieutenants commanding."

"You ought to hold out enough for one night on the town, when you get through that commissioning business tomorrow," persisted

Hewitt. "I'll swear you haven't been outside the gate since you reported at this yard. All you do is work all day and half the night, run over to the guardo and snatch forty winks, and right back again ahead of the sun. I don't think you even take time out to eat. What say you and me go out tomorrow night and find ourselves a couple of gals?"

"I can't leave my honey," said Pettengill, patting the *Lycoming*'s slender mainmast.

"There you go again," grumbled Hewitt. "All right, but I'll return to the subject. Unless you're still so churned up about that little Rebel gal you can't endure the thought of any common female."

"There's only one female critter I'm churned up about right now, and her name's *Lycoming*."

And that, Pettengill told himself as he swung down the ladder to see the last armor-plate bolted home, was gospel truth. He had neither time nor love to spare for any other girl right now. As for the future, he'd made suitable provision. He had written Terry a letter and sent it in Virgie's care. It was a very simple letter, though it had been hard to write. He had explained everything to her. She would be doing herself and him a great wrong if she married Farnifold Banks. He understood her feelings about the war and marrying a Yankee officer, even though he didn't sympathize with them. But she didn't need to marry anybody now. She could wait for him till the war was over. So why not do her best for the South, as he would for the North, and when the war ended, he would come and get her. Maybe people in the South would be bitter about getting licked, but it wouldn't be as if she was marrying an enemy while the fighting was still going on. And since Virgie was all the real kin she had—Penny Banks had told him that—and Virgie would have to live up North, why shouldn't Terry? She and Virgie would be company for each other while Banks and Pettengill were away at sea, as of course they both would be often enough, even in the peacetime Navy.

A good, sensible, straightforward letter. Maybe he should have told her how much he loved her, but it was silly to put things like that down on paper. There would be time enough to tell her when he saw her after the war. She would understand what he meant. It was just a week ago since he'd mailed the letter. He ought to be getting an answer any day now. . . .

They were tightening the last bolt. The gray solid look of the iron plating was a comforting sight. The painters would be there first thing in the morning, so if the commodore happened to come down the ladder, he wouldn't suspect the two inches of iron. Probably he wouldn't have time to make anything like a thorough inspection of the ship's innards.

It was more likely that the commandant, or Turner, might spot something topside that wasn't according to specifications, such as the paddle-wheel guards coming down so far below the shaft, or that queer in-sloping coaming around the engine-room hatch.

Pettengill was still worrying as he walked briskly along to the *Princeton* well after nightfall, his day's work finished. He had been assigned a little cubicle down on the berth deck, well for'd of the wardroom. By the time he opened the door, he had forgotten his worries and had his mind on mail. The wardroom steward distributed the mail to officers' rooms during the day.

There were two letters on his bunk. One was in a Navy envelope, the other was a heavy white rectangle addressed in a female hand.

He gazed fondly at the handwriting. He had never seen Terry's writing, except on the marriage register when she had stood up with Virgie and Penny Banks by special permission of Major Allen. This didn't look quite the same—it was too precise and firm—but he got a finger under the flap and ripped the envelope. A faint familiar perfume rose from the single folded sheet of note paper inside.

Dear Caleb:

I hope I may still call you that, despite misunderstandings for which I am sincerely regretful.

I am back again in my little house here in Philadelphia, and have just learned that you are once more at the Navy Yard.

Could we not let bygones be bygones?

That you may share that view is the sincere hope of

Your friend,
Emma Harrifield

P.S. I still have some of that old Madeira.

Physical excitement born of memory mingled with his disappointment. He ripped the note across and flung it on the washstand. Emma Harrifield would wait a long time to hear from her dear Caleb. He opened the Navy envelope.

This note was short too.

Navy Department, Washington City,
October 14, 1861

Sir:

When the U.S.S. *Lycoming* is commissioned and is in all essential respects ready for service, you will proceed with her to Hampton Roads, where you will report to Flag Officer S. F. Du Pont for duty with the South Atlantic Blockading Squadron under his command.

It is desirable that you should arrive at Hampton Roads as soon after the 18th inst. as the condition of your ship permits.

Very respectfully, your obedient servant,
Gideon Welles

Acting Lieut. C. Pettengill, U.S.N.,
  Commanding USS *Lycoming*,
    Through Commandant, Navy Yard, Phila.

His sea orders at last—and just what he wanted them to be, too. But this was the fifteenth! It was a full twenty-four-hour run to Hampton Roads at *Lycoming*'s estimated economical speed, about eleven knots. He couldn't possibly hope to get away by day after tomorrow. He would need at least another day beyond that, if not two. But, "as soon after the 18th" as possible gave him some leeway and by today's papers, Du Pont hadn't left New York yet. . . .

Pushing the Department order back into its envelope, he discovered another piece of paper.

Lieut. Pettengill:

In view of the enclosed orders, I am directing Comdr. Thomas Turner, executive officer of the Yard, to inspect the U.S.S. *Lycoming* as to her present state of readiness for sea immediately following her commissioning tomorrow afternoon.

Very respy.,
G. J. Pendergrast, Commdt.

Not so cheery.

Turner would be sure to ask questions about everything. He might even send over to the naval constructor's office for the official Department plans and specifications. These finicky old boys always had some fetish they attached primary importance to, but unhappily Pettengill had never so much as exchanged a word with Commander Turner.

He was too hungry to think clearly. He washed, changed to clean blue pantaloons and a blue jacket, on which the shoulder straps bore the lieutenant's silver foul anchor embroidered in the middle.

In the *Princeton*'s musty wardroom, a couple of officers were still at table. Pettengill scarcely glanced at them. He muttered "Evening, gentlemen," dropped into a chair and called to the mess boy.

"Bring me something to eat—anything. And strong coffee."

"That's a hell of a tipple for this late in the day, Pettengill," a familiar voice said. "How about a swig of that Demerara I promised you?"

Pettengill contrived to be cordial. The fat paymaster congratulated him on his promotion. They exchanged Navy scuttlebutt. Presently the other officer, a surgeon, got up and left. By that time Pettengill had absorbed some food and his second half-tumbler of Demerara.

"I suppose you're acquainted with Commander Turner?" he asked.

"Tom Turner? I sure am." The paymaster tipped the rum bottle. "Hell, I was purser of the *Congress* when he commanded her. That was in the Brazil Squadron, eight years back."

"He's inspecting my *Lycoming* tomorrow," Pettengill said, "and I've never met the man. What's he stickiest about aboard ship?"

"He's sticky about everything," the paymaster said. "Runs the tautest ship you ever saw. If Tom Turner's going to inspect you, you can just make up your mind you're going to get an inspection you'll remember, m'lad. Nothing's too small for him to notice, either."

Pettengill took another pull at his glass of rum.

"This won't help you," the paymaster went on, "but I guess Turner's main weakness is, he's devilishly ambitious. He'll make captain shortly, and he wants a big command; fact is, it's all over the Yard he's breaking his heart hoping to get the *New Ironsides*. From what I hear, he hasn't much chance. Too many captains well up the list want that iron monstrosity, and Turner has no Washington connections."

"Well," Pettengill said, "if that's his one weakness, you're right, it's no help to me."

"I said it was his *main* weakness." The paymaster's fat stomach bobbed at his own wit. "Rum's not the other one, nor cards. But the old boy does have an appreciative eye for a neat female figger—as who doesn't, hey, Pettengill?"

"That's no help either," Pettengill complained. "Guess I'll just have to take my medicine. It's only because my ship's new-built. She's going into commission for the first time tomorrow. There'll be fifty things wrong, and she sure won't be shipshape fore and aft with Yard workmen all over her."

"That's the way it goes these days," said the paymaster. "The minute a keel's laid, the Department wants to put a gun on it and send it to sea. One more for a nightcap?"

"Thanks, I've got some paper work to 'tend to," said Pettengill, getting to his feet. "Never any end to that. 'Night. See you again shortly, I hope."

"Good night, and good luck with my old skipper tomorrow," said the paymaster cordially.

Back in his stateroom, Pettengill went right at his "paper work."

Dear Mrs. Harrifield:

Thank you for your very welcome note, and the good news that you're back here in Philadelphia. Perhaps you haven't heard that my ship, the U.S.S. *Lycoming*, is to be put into commission at the Navy Yard tomorrow afternoon, Oct. 16th, at three o'clock. It would give me the greatest possible pleasure if you would honor me by being present at the commissioning ceremony. It is customary on such occasions for the new captain to offer refreshments in his cabin to the friends who have been kind enough to stand by him. While I can't guarantee you vintage Madeira, I'll do my best. Duty prevents my calling for you; may I hope to have the pleasure of meeting you at the Navy Yard gate on Front Street, say at a quarter past two? The bearer will wait for your answer.

Most sincerely yours,
Caleb Pettengill

He sealed and addressed the letter and went with it to the wardroom pantry, where the colored steward was still puttering.

"You'll be going out early in the morning on your market trip, won't you, steward?" he asked.

"Yes, sir."

Pettengill laid the letter on the pantry table, with two gold dollars on top of it.

"D'you suppose you could take time to deliver this letter for me—and wait for an answer?" he asked, and winked.

The steward grinned.

"Yes, *sir*," he said, whisking the dollars out of sight.

"Thanks. Send one of the boys over to the *Lycoming* with the answer if I'm not here," Pettengill directed, and went back to his room.

Without the bulk of the absent pivot gun, there was plenty of room on the *Lycoming*'s quarter-deck for the commissioning ceremony.

The sixty-odd men of the crew, about half what she rated, were drawn up along the port rail in their blue blouses with stars at the corners of the collars, neckerchiefs, white knife lanyards, and bell-bottom pants. For once every man had his hat set squarely on his head. They were mostly kids hoping the Navy would feed better than the Army. There were only a few old-timers, the product of Casson's diligent daily visits to the receiving ship.

The officers were better. There was Casson himself, lately promoted acting master; another acting master named Frye; two youngish master's mates; a bespectacled assistant paymaster; a baby-faced assistant surgeon; good old Pete Hewitt and four assistant engineers. Except for Casson and Hewitt, not one had had a day's naval service afloat. They were volunteers. Frye had been first officer in a steamer trading to South America; he was a thoroughly sound navigator and knew how to handle men. The engineers had been pronounced competent watch-standers by Hewitt; and the doctor came well recommended from the Pennsylvania Hospital. Pettengill had been lucky that Banks had approved the applications of Casson and Hewitt for transfer from *Valiant* to *Lycoming* before he had to relinquish command of his ship to a fresh-caught acting volunteer lieutenant. Now Banks was enjoying a few days' leave in Washington with Virgie before going to Boston to take over the new sloop-of-war *Tonkawa*.

Pettengill, listening to the harsh voice of red-faced Commander Turner reading the Navy Department's orders, wished Banks were here beside him. He was very conscious of Emma, standing there demurely in her blue watered-silk dress. Her hat was small, with light-blue and white flowers, and she wore a flimsy blue cloak trimmed to match. She looked as though she were on her way to church to sing in the choir. It was hard to imagine her yelling "Fire and sword for Rebels and murderers!" at the President of the United States, or dipping her handkerchief in the blood of a dead officer.

"Signed," read Turner, "Gideon Welles, Secretary of the Navy. Face aft! Sound off!"

The drums rolled. The commandant had not troubled himself to send the whole Navy Yard band just to commission a gunboat. A couple of Marine drummer boys were enough for that.

Pettengill, under the edge of his lifted cocked hat, watched the colors climbing to the peak of the spanker gaff, saw the commission pennant break at the main truck high above his head and flutter out gracefully against the overcast sky. Forward, the jack was being hoisted.

"Face inboard!" rasped Turner. He lifted his cocked hat to Commodore Pendergrast. "Sir," he said, biting off the words as though he hated each syllable, "I report the United States ship *Lycoming* in commission."

Old Eagle-beak hunched his drooping shoulders, lifted his head and looked severely at Pettengill.

"It is now my duty and—er—honor," he wheezed, "to deliver the U.S.S. *Lycoming* to the officer assigned by the Navy Department to command her, Acting Lieutenant Caleb Pettengill. Take over command, Mister—ah—Captain Pettengill."

"I accept command, sir," Pettengill said. Whipping his command orders from under his belt, he read them rapidly. "Mr. Casson, set the watch."

Young Casson was beaming. He didn't have a cocked hat—volunteer officers weren't required to buy them—but he lifted his cap smartly, his boyish voice had a snap of command in it:

"Take the deck, Mr. Frye. Start the ship's time and commence the log. Bo's'n's mate, call the starboard watch."

It had begun. From this day onward, as long as the *Lycoming* remained in commission, years, maybe, the long succession of watches that had just started at Pettengill's order would continue, day and night, in fair weather and foul, changing every four hours at the tap of the ship's bell. . . .

The pipe ceased shrilling: the hoarse call "All the starb'd watch" died away. Frye was at the gangway, binoculars around his neck; a quartermaster stood beside him, telescope in his armpit; a landsman wearing pistol and cutlass paced back and forth as sentry, since the *Lycoming* had no Marines.

"The watch is set, sir," reported Casson.

"Very well, Mr. Casson. Dismiss from quarters and carry on with ship's work. Commodore, I'd be honored if you and Captain Turner would join me and my officers in a glass of wine."

"Pleasure, Captain," croaked Pendergrast. Turner jerked his head in what was meant for a nod. He was looking at Emma Harrifield.

Pettengill was already bowing to her. "Mrs. Harrifield, may I have the honor of presenting Commodore Pendergrast, with whom I had the privilege of serving in the Home Squadron last spring? And this is Captain Turner, Mrs. Harrifield."

She graciously accepted the homage of the two grizzled old salts, and gave them each her hand. She had already met the *Lycoming*'s officers when Pettengill had first brought her on board. Turner's sunburned neck sparkled with perspiration above its edging of gold lace as he bowed over her hand.

"This way, Commodore, if you'll be so kind," said Pettengill. "I'm afraid you'll find things rather unfinished below, but we'll do our best."

He was aware that Turner, with heavy courtesy, was offering his arm to Emma Harrifield. She barely touched it with the tips of her fingers as they moved toward the companion ladder, the others trailing behind.

The *Lycoming*'s after berth deck was bare and clear; no partitions for the officers' quarters were up yet. Well aft, glassware glittered on a white-spread table; Pettengill's steward and three linen-jacketed mess boys were in attendance.

"This is all officers' country, sir," Pettengill explained to the commodore. "The master carpenter says we'll have the partitions and fittings tomorrow or next day. I can offer you Madeira or Burgundy —or perhaps a touch of West Indian rum?"

"Madeira, if you'll be so kind," murmured Mrs. Harrifield. Her eye caught Pettengill's: she blushed, ever so faintly. "Madeira for me," the commodore said. "And for me," chimed in Turner.

"Why, Tom," wheezed the commodore, "what's come over you? Never knew you to touch wine before. Rum's more your style."

"I've a fancy for Madeira this afternoon."

"Your taste's improving," the commodore told him.

Mrs. Harrifield divided a smile between them: Turner lifted his glass to her.

The woman's an artist, thought Pettengill. She's handling these old boys perfectly. She had been very ready to help when he had told her that he wanted to avoid inspection this afternoon if he could because his ship wasn't ready for sea and he was afraid he would be blamed. He had said nothing about unofficial improvements, for he had no idea what Mrs. Harrifield's current relations with Crossmore might be, though she had hinted she was back in Philadelphia for good. The one point she had been very definite about was that Pettengill was having supper with her tonight, at her house. With Madeira to wash it down.

She was talking in a low voice to Turner. No, she wasn't talking; she was listening, her hazel eyes soft with understanding and interest.

"Tidy little ship you have here, Captain Pettengill," the commodore observed. "Not much in the way of sails, though, judging from the matchsticks they've given you for masts."

"They're only meant to be insurance against engine breakdown, sir," said Pettengill. "I expect I could lie to in heavy weather, but of course, sir, she's really meant for inland waterways where a ship dependent wholly on the wind might find herself in trouble." The commodore scowled, and Pettengill added hastily, "Anyway, sir, my chief engineer tells me he has a mighty reliable engine down below and I needn't trouble myself about its failing me in a pinch."

"That's correct, Commodore," chimed in Pete Hewitt. "I must say, sir, your Yard has performed miracles. That's the only word for it—miracles."

"Your engine wasn't built at this Yard, Mr. Hewitt," said the commodore tartly.

"No, sir, of course not, it was built by Merrick and Sons. But civilian contractors don't do work like that without careful supervision, Commodore. I consider that the splendid machinery of this ship reflects the greatest credit on the organization of the Philadelphia Navy Yard. And it's been my experience, sir, that good organization stems from the man at the top. Your health, Commodore. With profound respect."

Pettengill stifled a grin. You'd think Pete'd been a chief engineer for twenty years instead of twenty days. He was as tactful as Emma, in his way. Look at the old boy beam.

Turner was beaming, too. Pettengill tried to catch what he was saying to Mrs. Harrifield, but the junior officers were making too much noise. They were all enchanted to have a pretty woman aboard, they all wanted to talk to her. But they didn't dare cut in on Turner, so they were talking loudly to each other.

Mrs. Harrifield lifted her hazel eyes to Turner's face, looking just a trifle startled and shocked; she shook her head, her lips moved. Turner bent closer, obviously insistent.

"I thought, Captain," remarked the commodore, "you were supposed to have a nine-inch pivot gun aft. Seemed to me the brass turning-circles they've let into your deck planks look big enough for an eleven-inch pivot mount."

"Yes, sir," said Pettengill. "I understand the Bureau of Ordnance is reconsidering the *Lycoming*'s battery. You know they've had second thoughts about my broadside guns and now there's an idea I ought to have a heavier pivot to make up for 'em."

"If Chiefs of Bureau wouldn't change their minds so often, my life'd be easier," the commodore muttered. "Eh, Tom?"

Turner, even redder-faced than before, was at the commodore's elbow.

"You're very right, sir," Turner agreed. "And that's just what I wanted a word with you about," he went on. "There's a fresh squall blown up over the horizon about the *New Ironsides*' steam machinery. Isherwood's insisting she's underpowered. Wants to redesign her boilers."

"Nonsense!" exclaimed the commodore. His voice shifted to a wheeze of angry excitement. "I'll not have any more changes! I'm getting almost daily letters from Secretary Welles himself: speed, speed, get that ship finished. Turner, you go right down to Cramp's and—"

He drew Turner aside, glancing at Pettengill, who went over to Emma Harrifield.

"You'll be disappointed, Caleb," she purred. Pettengill could almost see her licking cream from her lips. But he didn't like that word "disappointed."

"Captain Turner's insisting that I have supper with him tonight," she explained. "We might be—late."

"You mean—"

"I'll write you a note, Caleb. Our supper's only postponed, I promise."

"Sorry I can't carry on with the inspection this afternoon, Pettengill," interrupted Turner's gruff voice. "Another duty—I have to get along to Cramp's shipyard for an hour or so. Mrs. Harrifield, I might just have time to see you to your door first, unless you and Captain Pettengill have made other arrangements?"

"It's very kind of you, sir. I've plenty to do here." Pettengill was astonished to discover that his annoyance was quite genuine.

"I'm sure of that," Turner replied testily. "Very well, Captain. The inspection ordered by the commandant will be postponed until tomorrow or next day. I'll notify you. Congratulations on your command, sir."

Pettengill, bowing over Mrs. Harrifield's hand, mumbled something about the honor of her visit.

He ushered his guests up the ladder to the quarter-deck. There were side-boys at the gangway, the guard of the day—six gawky hands and a petty officer—was drawn up at attention. Casson had been up there attending to the details.

"Good luck to you, Captain Pettengill," said the commodore, touching his hat to the *Lycoming's* colors. He went down the brow to the dock; Turner was making a ceremony of helping Emma Harrifield over the waterway. She gave Pettengill a gleaming look from the hazel eyes—no, they were tawny now. Those queer inner fires of hers were alight again, but not for Caleb Pettengill. She was clinging to Turner's elbow in a way that Pettengill remembered very well. He jerked his angry gaze away from them just in time to see a grin disappear from Pete Hewitt's freckled-rimmed countenance.

"You might get out of that regalia and give some attention to your department, Mr. Hewitt," he said tartly. "We're under orders for sea, in case you've forgotten."

"Aye aye, sir," said Hewitt.

"Mr. Casson," Pettengill went on, "now that the ship's clear of visitors, there's no reason for all this delay in letting the Yard workmen back aboard. We've wasted too much time on folderol as it is."

"Aye aye, sir," said Casson, looking hurt.

Pettengill, having done what he could to share his unhappiness, jerked open a door under the break of the hurricane deck, a door he was glad the commodore and Turner hadn't noticed. It was another innovation—one which violated all naval tradition—to have the captain's cabin up here, opening directly on the quarter-deck where he would have no ladder to climb when he had to be on deck in a hurry. The cabin was still as bare of fittings as the wardroom space below, but it served well enough as a place to shift into working clothes. The steward was already fussing with the gear that hung behind a strip of canvas in one corner.

"Never mind that frock coat, Williams," Pettengill said. "I'll have the jacket and the old blue pants."

"Yassah," said the steward. "I thought you said—"

"Never mind what I said. Do as you're told."

"Yassah."

Pettengill slid his lanky legs into the old blue pants and reflected with bitterness on the female sex in general and Emma Harrifield in particular. Casting him aside like that—on a moment's notice. "I'll write you a note—our supper's only postponed."

Suddenly he began to chuckle. He was blaming Emma for faithlessness, when in fact she had done exactly what he'd begged her to. She had taken care of Commander Thomas Turner very neatly. There would be no inspection of the U.S.S. *Lycoming* that afternoon.

Pettengill chuckled again as he buttoned his jacket.

Tomorrow or next day was as good as next week or the week after, with the Yard in its present turmoil. He had no doubt that Turner's statement about proposed changes in the *New Ironsides'* steam plant was perfectly genuine, though of course Turner had brought it up to give himself a sound reason for putting off the inspection and getting away from the *Lycoming* in a hurry—and a plausible excuse for seeing Emma Harrifield home at the same time. There would be other pressures on Turner's time, and the commandant's, new pressures every day.

Considering the peremptory character of Pettengill's sea orders, it was possible he might get the *Lycoming* ready for sea and get out of this Philadelphia Yard without ever being inspected at all.

Good humor completely restored, Pettengill strode out to the stir and bustle of the quarter-deck.

"Where's that master carpenter, Mr. Casson? He's got to look alive about those cabin and wardroom fittings!"

"He's below now, sir," Casson announced.

"That's well. Now see here, Casson—" Banks' old trick of dropping the "Mister" on occasion always worked. Casson brightened perceptibly. "You and I've been too easy with these receiving ship people. We need a full crew, including at least a few hands we'll have some hope of making petty officers of, to say nothing of three or four first-class firemen. We'll have a look at the station bill after supper, and tomorrow morning—"

He went on talking happily. Tomorrow's mail would certainly bring Terry's letter, and he could open it with a clear conscience.

Chapter Eighteen

Acting Lieutenant Pettengill, standing on the *Lycoming*'s hurricane deck beside the for'd pilothouse, eyed the roofs and church spires of the little city of Annapolis with distaste. It wasn't the Naval Academy that bothered him—not now. Anyway the academy and all its works had been safely hauled off to Newport in May, right after the war began, to keep clear of the uncertain temper of Maryland secessionists. What Pettengill didn't like about Annapolis was the telegraph line to Washington.

He had gotten away from Philadelphia at last, after every maddening delay that one foul-up after another could produce. There had been no further inspection, though some queer tales about the innards of the U.S.S. *Lycoming* were beginning to circulate around the Navy Yard. Pettengill had not really breathed freely until he had cleared away from New Castle after taking aboard his shells and powder, and had dropped his pilot off Delaware Breakwater, the last place at which he could be recalled by telegraph.

No telegraph was working to Hampton Roads from Washington. And Du Pont was reported on the point of departure for Port Royal —and the *Lycoming*'s battle-trial.

She was ready for it, bless her. She even had a full crew—of sorts. The great majority were youngsters who had enlisted at the Navy rendezvous in Philadelphia "for the term of this rebellion or three years." They had joined up to fight a war, and they'd chosen the Navy because they had heard the grub was better, or because the sad tales of slaughter and mismanagement at Bull Run had made them wary of the Army, or because of some romantic notion about sea service. There were perhaps twenty men who had made a cruise or two in merchant ships, some of these were petty officer material. Hewitt had laid hands on half-a-dozen competent firemen; the carpenter's mate and the armorer were skilled in their trades; the ship's cook, thank heaven, knew his business. But of old Navy hands there were almost none. Pettengill had snatched one seaman who had been captain of the fo'c's'le in the *Colorado* frigate from under the noses of half-a-dozen eager seniors by chancing to be on hand when the man reported aboard the receiving ship, and had rated him bo's'n's mate. His fat friend the paymaster had procured a capable yeoman. That was all—except that Quarter Gunner Jackson had reported aboard, having contrived to get himself transferred to hospital from *Valiant* and then undergoing a miraculous recovery. He was now Gunner's Mate Jackson as reward for his ingenuity.

The morning before his arrival at Annapolis, on October 27, Pettengill had happily reported himself to Flag Officer Du Pont aboard the flagship *Wabash* in Hampton Roads. He was nine days overdue, but the delay was no fault of his, as Du Pont readily understood. He had received Pettengill very cordially, despite his many cares. But to Pettengill's consternation Du Pont had almost immediately sent him a hurry-up order to make all speed for Annapolis to provide escort for a convoy of Army supply vessels.

Pale cloud-filtered sunshine warmed Pettengill's pock-marked mahogany face. A brisk easterly breeze whipped the skirts of his shore-going frock coat around his long legs. But neither sun nor salt air could erase the warning signals that flew as plain as a string of flags at a consort's yardarm. Nor could they erase the ache in the secret corner of his heart.

"Stand by the port anchor!" he roared. "Slow!"

He felt the beat of the great paddle wheels slacken. The *Lycoming*'s slim hull crept toward the anchorage off the railroad dock.

"Stop! Slow astern!" The paddles thrashed madly: the gunboat lost way. "Stop! Let go the port anchor! She's yours, Mr. Frye: get my gig in the water and bear a hand about it!"

The chain cable was still roaring out through the hawsehole as Pettengill galloped aft and down the ladder to the quarter-deck. If that hook was in the ground more than half an hour, it would be because the damned convoy wasn't ready. It probably wasn't, being an Army convoy and a pack of windjammers at that.

Luckily there were only three of them, the two ships that were anchored near the *Lycoming* and the bark that was taking in cargo alongside the dock. The ships were deep-laden: the bark was the immediate problem. Pettengill's orders were peremptory. These three vessels were carrying the first-line ammunition, guns, engineer stores, and tentage for Brigadier General Thomas W. Sherman's army, the troops that were to take over the forts at Port Royal after Flag Officer Du Pont's squadron had battered them into submission. Pettengill was directed to escort the three ships down to Hampton Roads to join the squadron without delay.

Reading between the lines of his orders, Pettengill guessed that the real reason he had been sent to Annapolis was to hurry the convoy along: the general was probably waiting for it, and Du Pont didn't want to be delayed by army excuses if he got a favorable break in the weather. In the Flag Officer's book, any more delay would be charged up to Pettengill, regardless of the fact that he had no real authority over chartered Army supply ships except when they were actually underway as a convoy. This was cause for worry enough, without the fear of Philadelphia at the other end of the telegraph wire.

The gig was being swung out smartly enough.

"Shore boat coming off, sir. Mail flag," reported the quartermaster of the watch.

All the mail for the squadron went through Annapolis, the base of operations. Someone in the post office had had the wit to sort out *Lycoming*'s pouches when the signal station had reported her standing in.

"Tell Mr. Frye I'll just have a look at the mail before I shove off," said Pettengill. He went to his cabin, slamming the door as though to drown out the sharp protest of his conscience. He had no business wasting time on the mail; his business, his only business, was to get that convoy under way and out of here. But maybe this time—

He flung himself into his desk chair and glowered at the dancing pattern of reflected sunlight on the white paint overhead. The ports were open; the breeze swept in, fluttering the green baize curtains.

The breeze was freshening and showing signs of hauling round to the north. That meant that Du Pont's squadron, weather-bound by easterly gales in Hampton Roads for the past week, might be able to put to sea—maybe tomorrow. Du Pont might not wait for the convoy if he got a fair wind for Port Royal: he couldn't afford to, with all the weak steamers and sailing vessels in his motley fleet. Pettengill's orders covered that possibility. He would have the miserable job of shepherding his three windjammers all the way to Port Royal. At this season the easterly storms rarely blew themselves out until the wind hauled round by the south into the west: a northerly shift one day was quite likely to shift back easterly and rise to gale force the next. Pettengill could picture himself off Hatteras with a paddle-wheel gunboat built for river service and rolling her guards under in any kind of seaway, trying to help an undermanned, overloaded square-rigger claw off Hatteras in a real buster. He pulled a chart toward him.

Bang-bang on the cabin door. The ship's writer poked his head around the edge of the doorframe.

"Mail, sir."

"Leave it there on the transom," Pettengill said, barely glancing up from his chart. The door clicked behind the departing sailor. Pettengill was out of his chair and across the cabin in two long strides, burrowing into the pile of envelopes and packages like a diver looking for a pearl in a heap of oyster shells.

His stomach knotted. He went through the pile again, item by item. Still nothing. Personal letters were sometimes forwarded to ships under official cover. He ripped open envelopes, flinging aside the contents after a glance at the weary lines of type: Bureau of Construction, Equipment & Repair—Coal Depot, Philadelphia, Pa.—Laws Relating to the Navy and Marine Corps Enacted by the 1st Session of the 37th Congress, to and including August 6, 1861—Changes in Ordnance Instructions—Navy Department General Orders—

So she wasn't even going to answer his letter. It had been three weeks since he had mailed it. Plenty of time—

The door clicked open. Pettengill jerked his head around, mouth open to blast the intruder.

"I knocked twice," Pete Hewitt said. "Guess you were too busy to hear me. I'd like permission to haul fires under number one boiler, those flues are still getting choked. I figure a couple extra rows of firebrick on the bridge—"

"No!" cut in Pettengill. "I want the engine room kept on short notice, Pete. This is no time for any damn tinkering."

Hewitt took off his battered steaming-cap and ran his fingers through his shock of red hair. His habitual grin didn't show up on his round freckled face.

"You better blow off some of that pressure, Captain," he advised. "You're as jumpy as a minister's daughter on her first moonlight hayride."

"For God's sake, can't you say three words without dragging in women?"

"For God's sake, can't you stop fretting yourself into the looney house over that little Rebel blonde?" Hewitt retorted, his eyes flickering toward the tattered mail. "Let her go South and sleep with Jeff Davis if she wants to. Get yourself another one—half-a-dozen other ones. You'll be no good to yourself or the ship until you get her out of your half-baked mind."

The words bit through the red mist of Pettengill's rising rage like a shaft of cold revealing light. He couldn't think of anything to say. The fire of his fury was cold ashes now. He stood there staring at the angry little engineer.

"I'm sorry, Cal." Since he'd been aboard *Lycoming*, Hewitt had never used Pettengill's first name before. It was always "captain" and "sir." Even when they were alone. That "Cal" was born of pity.

"I—I've got to get ashore. See about the convoy," Pettengill managed to say.

Hewitt nodded, half-turned to leave the cabin. Then he swung back to Pettengill:

"All you need," he said in exactly the tone he would have used in reporting an engine-room deficiency, "is a brand-new exciting gal. I hear this town's full of lovely ladies from Washington and Baltimore since the Army base started."

"Don't talk like a fool, Pete. I won't have time to go traipsing after women. Anyhow, what lovely lady's going to take a second look at this ugly mug of mine?"

"Now you're being sorry for yourself," Hewitt said. "Your trouble is, you don't try. You fiddle around and act meeching, so the gals treat you like a deck swab—not because you're ugly, but because they think you don't appreciate 'em. Remember John Paul Jones—grapple 'em, give 'em a broadside and board 'em through the smoke! It never fails."

"The hell with women," muttered Pettengill. "They're the curse of the Navy."

"Try it," begged Hewitt, ignoring his captain's remarks. "Try it just once—next chance you get. It's the only cure for what ails you." He reached for the door knob, saying over his shoulder: "Very good, sir. Engine room on short notice until further orders."

Pettengill picked up his cap and stepped out on the quarter-deck.

"Gig's alongside, sir," reported the officer of the watch.

"I'll have a boat officer in her, Mr. Frye," Pettengill said. To Casson, hovering by the gangway to see the captain over the side, he added: "I won't be ashore long, Mr. Casson. I'd be pleased to have the ship ready to get underway immediately on my return."

"Aye aye, sir." Casson's dark eyes lost some of their sparkle. He'd been counting on a night on the town, Pettengill guessed. Women again!

Pettengill swung himself down the ladder and dropped into the stern sheets of the waiting gig.

"Railroad dock," he said to the boat officer. He pushed Hewitt out of his mind and concentrated on practical problems. The Army had a big establishment at Annapolis, which was the southernmost railhead in Union hands except for Washington City itself; consequently it formed the base for expeditionary operations against the Confederate coast line. His orders informed him that a Colonel Brean was representing Brigadier General T. W. Sherman, Army commander for the Port Royal expedition: so Brean was the man he had to see. He eyed the two ships at anchor—*Cassandra* and *Ezek Powell*. They appeared to be ready. The bark alongside the dock would be the *Norwich City*, Sheldrake master. Looking at her water line, Pettengill guessed she was only about half laden and it was already after three o'clock in the afternoon. Now the tide—

"Sir," said the boat officer in a low voice. He was the last-joined of the volunteer officers; he had reported aboard just before sailing from Philadelphia. Pettengill didn't know much about him yet. His name was McAndrew, Master's Mate Ronald McAndrew.

"Well, Mr. McAndrew?"

"I—I've got to have twenty-four hours' leave, sir. To go to Washington. I've *got* to, sir." He was still keeping his voice down, almost whispering, so the hand pulling the stroke oar couldn't overhear.

"That's impossible, Mr. McAndrew. The ship's under sailing orders. That means no liberty for the crew and no shore leave for officers beyond signal distance, maybe not even that. I don't know yet whether we'll be here another hour. Leave to go to Washington's out of the question."

McAndrew swallowed, flicked a quick look at Pettengill. In his deep-set eyes desperation glittered.

"This is an emergency, sir," he insisted. "I—it means a lot to me. I'll join the ship at Hampton Roads at my own expense, sir. I've just got to get to Washington."

The dock was close ahead; McAndrew broke off to snap orders at the gig's crew:

"Trail bow—way enough! Toss! Hook on, there, bowman."

The boat eased up to the foot of the landing steps, bumping gently alongside. Pettengill hopped ashore, conscious of McAndrew's despairing eyes.

[241]

"Just step up here on the dock a moment, Mr. McAndrew," he said, furious at the delay but unable to walk off and leave the boy without another word.

"Now then—just what's this emergency you speak of?" Pettengill demanded.

McAndrew hesitated, gulped, then words burst from him like a flood:

"It's my wife, sir. She's a Washington girl; she lives there, works in a Government office while I'm at sea. I've just had a letter from her in this mail. She says it's all over between us, she doesn't want to see me any more. I've heard she was running around with some Army officer, but I didn't believe it—now I don't know. All I know is I've got to see her, talk with her. I love her, Captain, I can't bear just to let her go like this. Won't you please grant me leave, sir?"

"I'm sorry, Mr. McAndrew," Pettengill said. "The ship's on active service and your country's at war. Personal troubles can't be allowed to interfere with the performance of duty. I can't grant your request. You'll wait here with the gig till I return. Keep the hands in the boat."

McAndrew took a step forward: for one instant Pettengill thought the lad was going to take a swing at him. Then he muttered something that might pass for "Aye aye, sir," turned and half-stumbled down the steps to the landing. Pettengill turned sharply away and strode down the dock. He wasn't pleased with himself. He had sounded off like a pompous ass. Worse, he had allowed his own bitterness to prejudice his decision. By strict regulation he hadn't the power to grant an officer leave, because here at Annapolis he was in telegraphic contact with the Navy Department, but he could at least try— No! He was certainly not going to remind the Navy Department of his presence at Annapolis by sending any silly telegrams. His sole business at Annapolis was to get the convoy moving down the bay, not to worry about women.

He stared fiercely ahead of him along the dock. The first person he saw was a woman. She was standing with her back toward him, near the end of a string of boxcars, talking to a thick-bodied man in Army uniform; straps glinted on his shoulders. He appeared to be arguing with her. Anyway he was waving his arms. She just stood there and listened.

Even with her back turned, there was something familiar about her tall slender figure and the mass of brown hair coiled at the nape of her neck—something about the way she held her head, chin up as though defying the world. The reddish dress she wore was full-skirted, but the upper part of it did nothing to disguise the lines of the body underneath. Pettengill could recognize the cut of a ship's royals twenty miles away if he had seen them once before, but ships were different from women.

Something else was very wrong on the dock. The boxcars stood on the spur track of the Annapolis & Elk Ridge Railroad, the track which Major General Ben Butler had built to the dock, right across the Naval Academy grounds. Beyond the cars, a small locomotive simmered. Beside each of the cars was a heap of stores: two gangways sloped up from the dock to the deck of the *Norwich City*. Tackle dangled idly from the bark's main yardarm; cargo nets lay limp underneath. Some fifty-odd colored roustabouts sprawled on the planks of the dock or sat along the stringpieces, laughing and jabbering in idle glee. A man in a peaked cap and a dirty sweater paced nervously back and forth, slapping the back of one hand against the palm of the other. Clearly the lading of the *Norwich City* had been going ahead full blast, when suddenly it had been interrupted. Pettengill quickened his step.

The Army officer's plump pinkish face brightened as he took in the details of Pettengill's uniform. Pettengill lifted his cap to the eagles that adorned the man's shoulder straps.

"Lieutenant Commanding Pettengill, sir, in charge of convoy," he said, introducing himself. "I expect you're Colonel Brean?"

The colonel nodded, but before he could say a word—

"Why, Captain Pettengill!" murmured a well-remembered voice. "This is really unexpected."

She was looking at him over one rounded shoulder, her dark-blue eyes alight with amusement. She had found him amusing once before, Pettengill recalled bitterly. He gave her a jerky bow.

"Your servant, Miss Pryor," he rumbled. He knew now who was holding up the lading—Prudence Pryor, agent of the United States Treasury Department, specializing in the detection of illegal trading with the blockaded Southern States.

She wasn't going to tangle this convoy up in her infernal red tape. . . .

"My orders, sir." Pettengill whipped the document from his pocket. "You'll see they call for the utmost dispatch in getting the convoy down to Hampton Roads. I'd be glad to be underway by sundown, if your ships are ready."

This was fairly strong meat for a Navy lieutenant to feed an Army colonel, but Pettengill had thrown half-measures overboard the minute he recognized Prudence Pryor.

"Two of them are ready now, Captain," said Brean. "Unhappily, Miss Pryor here—whom you seem to have met before—has some misgivings about the cargo that's going aboard the *Norwich City*. She's got an order from the Secretary of the Treasury to make a full inspection."

He paused, his eyes shifting from Prudence to Pettengill and back again.

"I met Miss Pryor last month, down South when I was on the blockade," Pettengill explained. "She's only doing her duty as she sees it, I'm sure. But this is a matter of military necessity, as I see it—and I'd guess, Colonel, as you see it. I'm responsible to Flag Officer Du Pont, who's no man to take excuses for delay. You're responsible to General Sherman. From what I know of him—" Pettengill had never laid eyes on Sherman—"he's pretty tough with dawdlers too."

"Hell, yes," put in Brean. "Uh—your pardon, Miss Pryor."

"Neither of us," Pettengill went on, "is responsible to the Secretary of the Treasury. So what are we waiting for?"

"But—"

"Excuse me, sir, is this a time for buts? Let's get that cargo moving. Miss Pryor and her Secretary can sort out the buts in Washington."

"You're right, Captain!" cried Brean. "Captain Sheldrake! Get those lazy roustabouts on their feet!"

"You gentlemen," said Prudence Pryor softly, "seem to think you've settled this whole business between you." The amusement was all gone from her eyes: they were hard as the blue steel of a Navy pistol. She turned them full on Pettengill. "You're making a very serious mistake, Captain Pettengill," she told him. "I don't know what Colonel Brean's part in this matter is, but I do know the sort of cargo that's being put aboard that bark. The colonel says I have misgivings. I have more than misgivings, now. I've seen the thing for myself. Look at those stores. Salt—tons of it—ten times as much as Sherman's little army can use in a year, but desperately needed by the Rebel army to cure meat. Rolls of dress goods—Southern ladies are paying ten prices for cotton prints like those over there, since the blockade's cut 'em off from New England. There's a crate full of brass fittings and valves. Coils of wire. Sheet iron." Her finger stabbed at each item. "Are those military supplies for an army in the field, Captain Pettengill? Or do they add up to the stock of an illegal trader, a scoundrel raking in dirty dollars by supplying the enemy's needs while his countrymen are shedding their blood to put down this rebellion?"

There was certainly something queer about that cargo. But if it stank to high heaven it wasn't going to keep Pettengill here in Annapolis a minute longer than necessary. . . .

"That's not my problem," he said. "I take my orders from Flag Officer Du Pont. He wants that ship and the other two at Hampton Roads, and I mean to take 'em there as soon as Colonel Brean gets this one laded."

He glared at Brean, who looked scared.

"You gonna argufy all night?"

It was the man in the peaked cap: how long he'd been standing there listening, Pettengill didn't know. He was a mean-looking character, with close-set bloodshot eyes, a tobacco-stained beard, and bad teeth.

"No, no, of course not, Captain Sheldrake," Brean assured him. "Get on with the work." He seemed to be scared of Sheldrake too.

Sheldrake spat explosively on the planks.

"'Bout time," he snarled, with a venomous glance at Prudence. He swung away, bawling: "Hump yerselves, y' black bastards! Git that cargo movin'!"

The roustabouts leaped to obey; on the *Norwich City*'s deck a loud voice began yelling orders.

"Very well, gentlemen," said Prudence Pryor. "You leave me no choice save to send a telegram to the Secretary of the Treasury, reporting that this ship is carrying illegal trade goods. And that you both have been warned of the fact. Good afternoon."

She spun on her heel and marched off down the dock, head high and slender back ramrod-straight.

Brean's face went sickly white.

"Maybe we'd better—" he began.

"Go ahead with the job," interrupted Pettengill. "I'll take care of Miss Pryor. I'll tell her I'll cover us all by making a full report in writing about this cargo to the flag officer the minute I get within hail of the old *Wabash*. That ought to satisfy her."

Brean managed a sickly grin.

"You think she'll believe that?"

"Believe it!" snapped Pettengill. "Of course she'll believe it. She knows my word's good."

Brean thought he meant to lie to Prudence: that was what Brean would do in his place. But he had no time to waste on indignation.

At all costs he had to keep Prudence from sending that telegram, for it might mean the Navy Department would hear that the *Lycoming* was at Annapolis. He had to keep Prudence from reaching the telegraph office. . . .

Brean seemed to be searching for words and not finding any that were suitable.

"I've got to hurry, sir," Pettengill told him. "One favor—please ask my boat officer at the steps there—his name's McAndrew—to go back to the ship and say that I'll be off later in a shore boat. I'll see to Miss Pryor now. Don't worry about her."

"Look!" squalled Brean, pointing past Pettengill's shoulder. The blast of a locomotive's exhaust told Pettengill what he would see even before he turned—and as he turned he was already running.

Chapter Nineteen

The little yard engine was starting to move, smoke belching from its bell-mouthed stack; Prudence Pryor, waving mockingly at Pettengill, stood in its gangway.

He ran as he had rarely run in his life, in long bounding strides, his frock coat flapping about his thighs. The engine's exhaust quickened, but the wheels were spinning on the slippery rails. He was closing the gap. Another couple of jumps and he would be able to reach the handrail on the tender. The exhaust roared, the engine leaped forward.

He might have stopped if Prudence hadn't turned suddenly as though to say something to the engineer; the exhaust had slackened to a slower beat. He drove his long legs ahead in one final effort as the engine wheels clicked over a switch. He could hear Prudence screaming angrily above the clamor of the locomotive. As his fingertips touched the handrail, he flung himself ahead, his hand closed on the iron bar, and with a final bound he felt his feet hit the step.

He clung there, heaving in long breaths while the engine clattered over the switches and gathered speed again. Presently he clambered up the rungs on the rear of the tender and slid down over the load of firewood into the cab.

The colored fireman gaped at the sudden appearance of a naval officer in full uniform. Pettengill brushed the man aside, laughing at the anger that flew its scarlet flag on Prudence's cheeks.

There was anger in her eyes, too; but there was something else, far back in the dark-blue depths, a queer sort of excitement that puzzled Pettengill even as it stirred some deep response within him. Once before he'd seen a glow like that in a woman's eyes.

Across the cab, the engineer turned his head and yelled:
"Who are you, mister?"
"Mind your business!" Pettengill rasped. He stood there looking

at Prudence, trying to catch hold of that elusive thread of memory. Somehow it seemed important.

"All right, here's West Street depot!" the engineer sang out. "Get on them brakes, you, Mose."

He slammed the throttle shut; the exhaust ceased. The fireman twisted at the tender's brake-wheel. Iron shrieked on iron; the engine slowed. The end of a rickety wooden structure slid past the cab. The fireman gave one final heave on the wheel, and the engine shuddered, panting to a stop.

"Here y'are, miss," announced the engineer, coming across the narrow iron floor. Prudence was fumbling in her handbag: she handed him something with a golden glint, and he said: "Thank y' kindly, ma'am." He looked hard at Pettengill, already on the platform holding up a hand to Prudence. She let him help her down without protest: the engineer snorted and went back to his seat. Steam hissed viciously from the cylinder cocks as the engine backed away.

From an open bay window a few feet down the platform, there came the intermittent chatter of a telegraph sounder, as unwelcome a noise as Pettengill had ever heard in his life. His hand tightened on Prudence's arm.

"Let's sit down a minute," he said. Half-a-dozen depot loungers were staring with interest at the unusual spectacle of a Navy lieutenant and a pretty girl arriving on a switch engine. Pettengill swept them with his best quarter-deck glare as he propelled Prudence toward a slatted bench.

"I must look a sight," said Prudence. She took a mirror from her handbag and began patting at her hair and adjusting her bonnet.

Pettengill cleared his throat.

"Miss Pryor," he began, "I want to explain something."

"There," said Prudence, giving a final pat to her hair. She sat up a little straighter. "Now I must get along."

"Wait just a minute," begged Pettengill. "You needn't send that telegram. Listen to me—"

"You're suggesting I compromise with my duty, Captain Pettengill?"

"No! I agree with you there's something wrong with the *Norwich City*'s cargo. I don't trust Brean, and Sheldrake looks like a bilge-rat to me. But my flag officer's in no mood to listen to excuses; he'll hang me if I don't bring him that convoy and do it fast. What's wrong with this idea: you write a letter to the Secretary instead of sending a wire. I take the convoy down tonight, get to the Roads tomorrow.

On the way down the bay I'll write a full report to the flag officer about the *Norwich City*'s cargo. I'll take it to him personally the minute I get within hail of the flagship."

He tried to sound confident and persuasive. Deliberately he ignored the thought that he ought to warn her the flag officer might not be in the Roads when the convoy arrived, and then he would have to take it all the way down to Port Royal by himself.

Prudence was looking at him with skeptical eyes.

"You've got just one idea in your head, and that's to get out of Annapolis as quick as you can," she said. "Suppose I go along with your suggestion. How do I know your report won't be buried and forgotten until it's too late? Your flag officer has plenty to worry him besides illegal trading. Especially when it's really the Army's responsibility and not his."

"The General's quartered in the flagship. Du Pont can pass it along," urged Pettengill. "I told Brean what I was going to do; he'll have to cover himself by reporting to the General, too."

"You told Brean!" cried Prudence, sitting up very straight. "I don't like that! If Brean's in this dirty business as deep as I think he is, he'll be more scared of your report to Du Pont than of mine to the Treasury, because he'll be right there to be put on the griddle. He'll spend all his time between now and then figuring out how to undermine you."

"What do you mean—'he'll be right there'?"

"He's on Sherman's staff, he's going back to Washington tonight and on to Hampton Roads in a steamer tomorrow morning."

Pettengill closed his mouth just in time to bite off a four-letter word.

"You needn't snarl at me like that," Prudence said. "All right, Captain Pettengill. Since it means so much to you, I'll—"

"Did yo' say Pe'engill, ma'am?" inquired a plaintive voice. A very black urchin stood beside the bench, clutching a sheet of yellow flimsy. Pettengill's stomach slowly turned over.

"I'm Captain Pettengill," he admitted.

"Message for yo', suh. Done come on de Ahmy wiah f'om de base."

Pettengill grabbed the paper, ran his eye over the operator's neat penciling:

Captain Pettengill: Can you meet me at the Maryland Hotel in half an hour? Urgent and confidential. Brean.

"Don't go," advised Prudence quickly, reading the message over his shoulder. The faint perfume of her hair disturbed him.

"Of course I'll go," he snapped. "I've got to. Something must've happened about the convoy."

"Op'ratuh says the ge'man's waitin' foh an answeh if'n we find yo'."

"Tell the operator to say Captain Pettengill will be there," Pettengill ordered.

"You're being plain pig-headed," cried Prudence as the boy scampered away. "Brean's laying a trap for you. I'm sure of it!"

"Woman's intuition?" Pettengill said, getting up from the bench. "Don't you worry. I'd like to see that fat boy catch Caleb Pettengill in any trap."

"I ought to send that wire right now. You're such an idiot, I oughtn't to trust you."

Pettengill caught a glimpse of the station clock from the corner of his eye.

"It's after five," he pointed out. "You're not likely to get much action in Washington any more tonight—not from the Treasury, anyway."

"So you kept me here with your fine promises and one eye on the clock!" she blazed at him. "You should be very proud of yourself, Captain Pettengill. Tricking a woman. Go meet your dear friend Colonel Brean. You're birds of a feather."

She was gone around the end of the station in a swirl of petticoats. Pettengill ran after her, reached the street side of the platform just in time to see her jump into a carriage and hear her cry "Custom House" to the driver.

She couldn't send any wires from the Custom House. Tricking a woman! All tough and self-sufficient as long as things went well for 'em, but if you outsmarted 'em anywhere, then you were tricking a woman. . . .

Clutching this bit of male illogic, Pettengill climbed into a creaking carriage and bade the Negro on the box take him to the Maryland Hotel.

All he wanted from Brean was word that the *Norwich City* was ready to cast off her lines. He was even glad to find the *Norwich City*'s hang-dog skipper, Sheldrake, lounging against a hitching rack in front of the hotel.

Sheldrake slouched along the brick sidewalk as Pettengill got out of the carriage.

"Colonel says go right up to Parlor Two," he announced. "Head o' the stairs."

"All right," Pettengill nodded. Sheldrake turned away before Pettengill could ask any questions about the *Norwich City*.

He pushed his way through the crowded little lobby, full of women and Army officers, and went up the carpeted stairway to the wide hall on the next floor. A large metal figure "2" adorned a pair of double doors. Pettengill knocked, someone inside called "Come in." It sounded like—

Pettengill opened the door. It *was* a woman—a young woman in a tight-fitting black bodice and a billowing hoop skirt of black and silver. She beamed at Pettengill.

"Come in, come in," she invited hospitably.

"I was expecting to find Colonel Brean here."

"He'll be along pretty quick," she assured him. "Come on in and rest yo' feet. Don't stand there with the do' open."

There was a touch of Dixie in her husky voice, more than a touch of invitation in her smiling black eyes. She patted the cushion beside her on the fringed couch where she sat.

Pettengill closed the door and walked across the tawdry, overfurnished parlor, embarrassedly aware that he could see a broad canopied bed through the open doorway of the next room.

"Pour yo'self a glass of wine before yo' sit down," she urged. "One for me, too."

A silver bucket holding wine bottles stood on a marble-topped table. Pettengill poured wine into two glasses, carried them over to the sofa, and sat down beside the girl. She used a heady perfume, quite unlike the delicate scent of Prudence Pryor. But this girl looked at him as though he were a male human being.

She laughed gently into his eyes and said:

"Here's to fun and games."

They both drank to fun and games. It was good wine. Even if it wasn't nutty old Madeira.

"May I ask your name, ma'am?" he ventured. "Mine's Pettengill—Captain Pettengill. Navy."

He was beginning to hope Brean wouldn't get there too soon.

"Pleased to know yo', Captain," the girl said. "Yo' just call me Susie."

"Here's to you, Susie," grinned Pettengill, lifting his glass.

He heard the door open—and saw all the color drain from Susie's face, leaving her great black eyes staring in horror from a dead-white mask.

He was on his feet automatically, swinging around.

Master's Mate Ronald McAndrew was in the act of kicking the door shut behind him. His eyes were fixed on Pettengill, twin points of flame glowing in their deep sockets. In his right hand, a double-barreled derringer pointed unwaveringly at Pettengill's stomach.

"So this is why you wouldn't give me leave," he grated.

"Ronnie! Oh, Ronnie!" Susie wailed from the sofa.

McAndrew had no attention for anyone but Pettengill.

"I'm going to kill you," he announced. "And let her watch you die."

Pettengill gauged the distance. There would be one bullet in him, maybe two, before he could get across the parlor floor. McAndrew was sidling to the left—to get Susie out of the line of fire, Pettengill guessed. But he was coming no nearer to Pettengill.

"You're making a mistake, Mr. McAndrew," Pettengill said quietly.

"A mistake! When I find you in a room with my wife—registered C. Pettengill and wife?"

"That's a lie, McAndrew!"

"It's a lie you'll die for," McAndrew told him.

Pettengill shifted his feet slightly, muscles tensed for a leap. He could see McAndrew's knuckle whiten as his finger began to squeeze the trigger.

"What's wrong, Cal? What's this man doing here with a gun?" demanded Prudence Pryor. She was standing in the doorway of the bedroom, hatless, hair a little disordered, her eyes wide with anxiety—the picture of a lady aroused from a catnap by alarming sounds. For once Pettengill did not fumble a fast cue.

"He's Mrs. McAndrew's husband, honey," he said. "I think he has a mistaken idea as to why Mrs. McAndrew is visiting us."

The derringer slid from McAndrew's nerveless fingers and thudded on the carpet.

For an instant there was no sound in the room except Susie's sobs. Then Prudence murmured "Poor lamb" and went to sit by her.

Pettengill took charge.

"I'll thank you not to drop loaded firearms on the deck in that careless fashion, Mr. McAndrew! Pick the thing up and put it on the table. Now then—I left you on duty in charge of my gig, at the railroad dock landing. I'd be glad to have some explanation of your presence here."

McAndrew squared his shoulders.

"A colored boy brought me a note, sir. Down at the landing. The note said if I wanted to see my wife I'd find her in Parlor Two of the Maryland Hotel with a naval officer. I guess I just went crazy, Captain. I had to come. I couldn't think of anything else but getting here to see— Then when I asked who was registered in Parlor Two and they told me— Well, sir, I went across the street and bought this gun and came up here to kill you."

"How long ago did you get that note?" Pettengill demanded.

"Maybe twenty minutes or half an hour, sir. I came directly here."

"Hadn't Colonel Brean passed my order along to you to go back to the ship long before that?"

"Colonel Brean? You mean the Army officer on the dock, sir? No, he never said a word to me."

"The boat's still there, then?"

McAndrew flushed.

"No, sir. I ordered the cox'n to return to the ship."

"Cutting off my retreat, eh?"

"I—can I have a word with my wife, Captain? Before you order me under arrest?" McAndrew begged.

"Who said anything about arrest?"

"I should think not," spoke up Prudence Pryor. "This poor child's been through enough without that. Go tell your husband what you just told me, dear."

"Oh, Ronnie!" Susie was on her feet, her tear-stained face aquiver. "I heard Captain Pettengill was here. I came to ask him if you couldn't get off that awful ship and be stationed in Washington— where—where we could be together."

"Susie! Then you didn't mean what you wrote."

They were in each other's arms and Susie was weeping her heart out on her husband's shoulder.

Pettengill was conscious of a couple of loose ends—like Irish pendants in the rigging.

"Mr. McAndrew, did you keep that note?"

"No, sir," said McAndrew, his voice somewhat muffled by Susie's hair. "I tore it up and chucked it overboard."

"I don't suppose we'll ever find out what busybody sent it, then," Pettengill went on. "No matter. Do you suppose you could find a shore boat to take you off to the ship—in an hour's time, Mr. McAndrew?"

"Yes, sir!" McAndrew cried.

"Then perhaps you'd better employ that time in seeing your

wife—er—safely bestowed for the night. I'll expect to find you logged aboard in one hour from now, Mr. McAndrew."

"I'll be there, sir! And—thank you, Captain. Thank you, Mrs. Pettengill."

He was half-dragging Susie toward the door. Susie, eyes demurely on the carpet, murmured her farewells. The door clicked shut behind them.

"You really need a guardian." Prudence sounded half-angry, half-amused.

"I—had one. Just in time," he muttered.

"I couldn't leave you to your own devices, you great lummox," she told him. "I *knew* Brean was laying some sort of trap for you."

He managed to lift his eyes to meet hers—and saw in the dark-blue depths that same queer excitement glowing behind the laughter. An answering excitement began to move in his own veins.

"But how did you find me?" he asked.

"I can read hotel registers, too," she informed him tartly. "C. Pettengill and wife, forsooth. I wanted to see just what that might mean. That's why I came in through the bedroom. Don't you ever lock a door when you're meeting a lady under such ticklish circumstances?"

"I wasn't meeting a lady! I never saw her before. I didn't know she was here till I opened that door! Sheldrake met me on the sidewalk; he said Brean was waiting for me in this room, for me to go right up. I never signed any register."

He was walking toward her, scarcely knowing what force impelled him. It was suddenly of vital importance that she should believe what he was saying.

"So that was it! And I'd warned you already!" she jeered. "The oldest snare since the serpent and the apple—the erring wife and the suddenly appearing husband. The badger game. Oh, you booby!"

She was lovely, standing there making fun of him. Lovely and maddening. The blood hammered at Pettengill's temples.

One long stride and he had her in his arms. He felt her body stiffen, her elbows dug into his chest: she struggled to break the iron ring of his embrace. He pulled her to him, and turned her desperate face to his. His lips went down hard on hers, crushing her soft mouth—she whimpered like a hurt child—then her mouth moved under his, her lips relaxed, her body flowed up against him.

Chapter Twenty

Into the Elysian darkness, disturbing sound penetrated and would not be denied.

"Let 'em knock," Pettengill muttered. He had locked the door—both doors.

"No, darling!" whispered Prudence against his ear. "See who it is first. Maybe the convoy's ready."

Pettengill sat bolt upright. He had forgotten about the convoy—about his duty, his orders, his ship—and the sword that hung over him at the slender end of a telegraph wire.

It was dark outside.

Whoever was hammering on the door of Parlor Two wasn't going to give up.

Pettengill rolled out of bed, felt his way around the end of it, padded into the parlor, carefully closing the connecting door behind him. There were matches on the marble-topped table; he lit one, applied the flame to a gas jet in the overhead fixture.

"Be right with you," he called out, sliding into shirt and pants. He stuck his feet into his shoes and turned the brass-tagged key in the hall door.

"Took you long enough," grumbled Pete Hewitt. "We got trouble, skipper. Take a look."

He pushed a blue official telegram at Pettengill, who read it under the gaslight, his lips forming the words as though he were unsure of the meaning.

> Senior Officer Present, Annapolis Harbor. Subject imperative military necessity, detain U.S.S. *Lycoming*, Lieutenant-Commanding Pettengill, at Annapolis until arrival Assistant Secretary Fox and party leaving Washington special train tonight. Faxon, Acting.

The Honorable Gustavus Vasa Fox, Assistant Secretary of the

Navy since last July, was just about the last individual in the world that Pettengill wanted to see aboard *Lycoming* right now. Fox had been responsible for the original double-ender design. They must have become suspicious in Philadelphia, and Fox had heard of it. Pettengill could see himself relieved of command and waiting trial by general court-martial with a list of charges and specifications that would keep ten clerks busy for ten days writing out.

He reread the telegram. Faxon, who had signed it, had succeeded Fox as chief clerk of the Navy Department, and frequently acted for Fox or Secretary Welles in routine matters. But like many chief clerks, he was cautious and precise. His caution might save Pettengill now: he had put in those words "Subject imperative military necessity" to cover himself in case Flag Officer Du Pont didn't take kindly to the Department's giving direct orders to a ship under his command. In that case the blame would be passed to some unknown "Senior Officer Present," who happened to be Pettengill himself, since the *Lycoming* was the only naval vessel then at Annapolis.

Pettengill decided that "imperative military necessity" required the immediate departure of the U.S.S. *Lycoming* and convoy from Annapolis Harbor. By the time that decision came to be questioned, many things might have happened.

"When did this come?" Pettengill demanded.

"Shore boat brought it off to the ship just after young McAndrew reported aboard. McAndrew told us where to find you, and I persuaded Casson he'd better let me bring it to you myself instead of sending one of the volunteer officers."

Pettengill looked again at the blue flimsy.

"Sent from Washington seven twenty-five," he noted. He grabbed his vest from a chair-back, pulled out his watch. "It's eight-forty now. High water an hour ago. Where's the wind?"

"Hauled northerly and freshening."

"Then we've got a chance—if we can get the convoy underway before that damned train gets here. No telling what time it left Washington." Pettengill was thrusting his arms into the sleeves of his frock coat as he talked.

"That's the stuff, Captain!" applauded Hewitt. "That's the old Pettengill stuff!" He jerked his head toward the closed bedroom door, grinning. "Took my advice, eh? Just what you needed. I can tell you've got that blond Rebel firecracker clear out of your noggin!"

"Shut up, dammit! How'd you come ashore?"

[256]

"Boat's waiting at the railroad dock," said Hewitt, still grinning.
"Has *Norwich City* cast off yet?"

"No. She's finished lading, but she's still fast to the dock. Casson took the liberty of sending orders to her and the other two to be ready to get underway, but she hadn't moved when I came ashore."

"Right," Pettengill snapped. "Wait for me downstairs. I won't be two minutes. Have a carriage standing by."

"Aye aye, Captain. Love 'em and leave 'em, that's for sailors."

Pettengill cursed his chief engineer's departing back, strode to the connecting door and flung it open.

He had left the room in complete darkness: now a faint blue flame at a wall-bracket showed him the empty bed. And a note on a pillow: "Brean went to Washington evening train—be careful. P."

Underneath, in very evident haste, she had scrawled something else: "Luck with the blond Rebel."

Pettengill ran back through the parlor and out into the hall. No one was in sight. He raced down the stairs. There were many people in the lobby, many women—but no Prudence. She must have dressed faster than a midshipman turning out for the twelve-to-four watch on thirty seconds' leeway.

But Pete Hewitt was in the vestibule.

"Come on, Pete. Naval Academy gatehouse, driver. Scott Street."

He must get away from Annapolis with the convoy before the Assistant Secretary arrived or some further message was delivered that had no loopholes in it. And now that he knew of the *Norwich City*'s highly suspicious cargo, a serious responsibility attached to him until he had passed on the information to his superior.

On the blockade it would have been Pettengill's duty to sink any ship which was so engaged and refused to heave to on demand. But breaking the blockade under cover of the Army's supply system was another thing; there might be politics in it somewhere, someone "higher up" who could make or break acting lieutenants.

Brean had gone to Washington. Could Brean have stirred up the sudden excursion of Assistant Secretary Fox to Annapolis? No. Brean knew nothing whatever about Pettengill's alterations to the *Lycoming*. But it was Brean who had asked Pettengill to come to the Maryland Hotel. It was Brean's message, through Sheldrake, which had sent him up to Parlor Two, to find Susie McAndrew waiting there. And it was also Brean who had neglected to pass on the order to McAndrew to go back to the ship. Brean had undoubtedly sent the note to McAndrew that had brought the youngster to Parlor Two to find Pettengill with his wife. "I hear she's running around with some Army officer," McAndrew had said. Brean, of course!

Pettengill had mentioned McAndrew's name when he had asked Brean to pass the order to him and Brean had heard that name before, from Susie. He had forged Pettengill's name on the register to discredit Pettengill. Prudence had said: "He'll be more scared of your report to Du Pont than of mine to the Treasury. He'll spend all his time . . . to undermine you."

"Halt—who goes there?"

It was the sentry at the gatehouse, a raw-boned volunteer who didn't even ask to see a pass; uniforms with gold lace on them were all he needed. Pettengill strode with Hewitt through the darkness along the rutted road the Army had built across the Naval Academy grounds.

Planks underfoot, and the tracery of spars and rigging against the night sky: the *Norwich City* was still alongside the dock—no sign of life on her dark deck save a single glowing cigar-end.

"Anchor watch, there!" called Pettengill. "Rouse out your captain!"

"I'm the captain," answered Sheldrake's surly voice.

"Then why the hell haven't you cast off your lines and warped out to your anchorage, ready to get underway?"

"Colonel Brean's orders—I ain't to move this here ship till he tells me."

"Boat's at the landing?" Pettengill asked Hewitt.

"Right. Frye's boat officer."

"Mr. Frye!" called Pettengill.

"Aye aye, sir!" came a prompt answer.

"Lay ashore here with your boat's crew! Lively does it!"

He could hear Frye giving orders, hear the thump of feet on the landing-steps. He could also hear other footsteps, coming down the gangplank on the run.

"What y' figgerin' on?" panted Sheldrake's voice at his elbow.

"Since you won't do your duty, I'll put my own people aboard your ship and take her out of here myself."

"You wouldn't dast! She's an Army ship," stuttered Sheldrake.

"You better not take chances on what he'd dast," Hewitt advised.

"On the double, lads—follow me!" called Frye's voice. The planks rumbled under the oncoming feet.

Sheldrake turned and ran up the gangplank screaming orders:

"All hands! All hands loose sail! Mister Engle! Bo's'n! Turn up all hands! Single them lines!"

However high the regard Sheldrake might have for Colonel Brean's orders, the last thing he wanted was a Navy crew aboard his vessel. Pettengill had been sure of that.

Men were boiling out on the *Norwich City*'s deck.

"Jib 'n' fore-topmast stays'l, Mr. Engle!" howled Sheldrake. "Stand by to cast off for'd!"

"Captain Sheldrake!" shouted Pettengill. "You'll follow *Cassandra* out of the harbor. Order of sailing's *Ezek Powell, Cassandra, Norwich City, Lycoming!*"

"Aye aye, Cap'n."

"You sure made a Christian out o' that feller in a hurry," Hewitt said.

"I'll make something else out of him when I get him down to the Roads."

The gangplank, cast off from the bark's deck, crashed on the stringpiece of the dock: the gray triangles of the headsails rose in her fore-rigging, her bow began to pay off from the dock as the wind took hold.

"Lantern moving over there, sir," said Frye suddenly. "Coming this way."

"Get your men back in the boat, Mr. Frye."

As the boat shoved off from the landing, Pettengill could see the *Lycoming*'s riding lights out across the dark surface of the harbor. Suddenly he desired, more than anything else in the world, to stand on her deck again.

"Put your backs into it, bullies!" he called.

The beat of the oars quickened. The dark mass of *Cassandra*'s hull loomed up ahead. Pettengill hailed her:

"*Cassandra* ahoy! Underway in five minutes!"

"Aye aye," somebody answered.

From the *Ezek Powell* came equally ready assurance.

"Boat ahoy-y-y!" That was his own quartermaster, hailing from the gunboat's gangway.

"*Lycoming!*" yelled Frye in answer.

It was the first time Pettengill's presence in a boat had been announced in the Navy's time-honored fashion for a captain coming aboard. Pride warmed his heart.

He went up the ladder two steps at a time. His executive officer was waiting for him.

"Is the signal for getting underway bent on, Mr. Casson?"

"Yes, sir. One red lantern at the peak is what I told 'em."

"Hoist it. Call all hands. I'd be glad to see how quick we can get that hook out of the mud."

"Aye aye, sir!"

"You can give me steam, Chief?"

"Yes, sir," chuckled Hewitt. "All you can use—now you've blown off your own."

He trotted off toward the engine-room hatch.

The pipes were shrilling through the ship: "All-l-l hands! All hands up anchor!" A rush of seamen, lashed by hoarse commands, came charging past Pettengill to man the falls and get Frye's boat out of the water. All about him swirled the orderly confusion of a man-o'-war preparing to leave her anchorage: "Rig in that ladder, afterguard! Jump to it!" "Steam on the windlass, sir!" Pettengill went for'd over the hurricane deck to stand beside the pilothouse. He'd let Casson take her out.

On the fo'c's'le, steam hissed at the windlass. Pettengill took nightglasses from the rack, raked the shore line with anxious eyes. The *Norwich City* was well away from the dock: they were loosing her fore-tops'l, he could see it against the sky. Here came *Ezek Powell*, under jib, tops'ls, and spanker, standing bravely down the channel. *Cassandra* was moving too. The convoy was on its way.

But there was something else: a dim light, low down on the water, over toward Fort Severn. It could be a boat lantern.

A bell clanged in the engine room, the paddles thrashed as Casson brought *Lycoming* up over her anchor.

"Heave round!" Casson's voice was right at Pettengill's shoulder.

Steam hissed again. Ker-lunk, ker-lunk—the links of the chain cable began revolving around the wildcat and paying below into the cable tier. A steam windlass was certainly handier than the old-fashioned capstan. Hewitt had noticed this one in Philadelphia, waiting to be put aboard a store ship.

"Up and down, sir!" came a hail from the fo'c's'le.

Pettengill's glasses were on the dim light again; it was certainly moving, moving toward *Lycoming*. And closer than he had thought. He held his breath, listening. Ker-lunk, ker-lunk.

"Anchor's aweigh, sir!"

Bright scarlet flashed in Pettengill's eyes: a seaman was lifting the port running light into place. Automatically Pettengill's head jerked around in time to see the green starboard lantern settle behind its screen. Smartly done, Navy fashion.

And just barely in time.

Across the water came a distant high-pitched hail:

"Ahoy-y-y! *Ly-co-ming*—ahoy-y-y!"

"Bridge there!" squalled an after lookout. "Boat's hailing!"

Cassandra was slipping past, foam boiling at her cutwater, and *Norwich City* was coming along behind her.

"Half-speed, Mr. Casson, if you please," said Pettengill. "Course sou'east a half east. And you might send a hand aft with a speaking trumpet. Tell that lubber in the boat that we're underway with a convoy and can't wait for him."

The paddles churned water, and the *Lycoming*'s long sharp prow came round under the pressure of the rudder. Forward, they were catting the anchor; aft, Pettengill caught an echo of a voice that bellowed his message, and a faraway wail of protest.

Let 'em wail. No one could blame a captain for not heaving to when he was responsible for the safety of a convoy of windjammers and was already under way, following his charges out of harbor at night. . . .

Chapter Twenty-one

"By the mark, three!" intoned the leadsman in the chains.
That meant there were still eight good feet of water under *Lycoming*'s keel, better than Pettengill had hoped for in this treacherous green-hung channel. He swept the gnats out of his eyes and glared at the sketch pinned to the chart-board.

A hell of a thing to navigate a ship by, but there weren't enough reliable charts of these tangled South Carolina inlets to go around. . . .

According to the sketch, he should open up a broad reach on the port hand very soon, a reach that would bring him right up to the wharf at Burrell's plantation, where he was supposed to find the Army detachment he had been sent to support.

He cursed the Army, the gnats, the idiot with three thumbs on each hand who had drawn that sketch, the war, and Flag Officer Samuel Francis Du Pont. He remembered the last words Du Pont had spoken to him in the great cabin of the *Wabash*.

"I'm not pleased with you, Captain Pettengill. Not pleased at all. If I had anyone else to put in command of your ship, I'd send you North. As it is, you'll do well so to conduct yourself that the next time I hear of you it'll be in a fashion to alter my present opinion of your worth."

Pettengill peered ahead along the sun-dappled water. What if he *had* parted company with one of his convoy? *Cassandra* had come in safely, and Pettengill had put a towline aboard *Ezek Powell* and brought her in too, after she'd lost her foremast and main topmast in one of the worst gales Pettengill had ever encountered. That wasn't bad seamanship—not with a slim-waisted paddle-wheel gunboat rolling so hard that one paddle wheel was buried deep half the time, while the other beat the air. It wasn't his fault that he had lost sight of *Norwich City* while he was taking the *Powell* in tow and that nothing had been heard of her since. No captain could have done better in that storm.

Du Pont had received a bitter complaint from the commanding general, Thomas W. Sherman, that *Norwich City* was carrying the most vitally needed stores of ammunition for his troops and a full half of his field artillery. Du Pont wasn't the man to let any one-star general walk over him, but it hadn't made him feel any kindlier toward the officer whom he held responsible for his embarrassment.

Du Pont saw the report about *Norwich City*'s illegal cargo which Pettengill had sent aboard the flagship, along with his report of the voyage down from Hampton Roads, as a faked-up excuse. "A tissue of miserable insinuations unsupported by a shred of evidence" were his exact words. In the face of what General Sherman had said, Pettengill could hardly blame the flag officer for jumping to this conclusion; it was true he had no evidence that would stand up against the flat assertion of a general officer. The evidence was probably settling into the ooze of the ocean bottom by this time, along with that rat Sheldrake.

If Pettengill had got away from Annapolis a couple of hours earlier he would have reached Hampton Roads in time to join the tail of the squadron as it put out to sea, and he might have been able to make the report to the flag officer about the *Norwich City* while she was still afloat. As it was, on his own, he had taken the convoy well out to sea to keep clear of Cape Hatteras and Frying Pan Shoal. Then the wind began to rise, the storm had hit him—and in the end he had arrived to find the battle over, Du Pont and Sherman in full possession of Port Royal Harbor, and trouble waiting for him.

God only knew what the Department had heard from Philadelphia by this time, or why Assistant Secretary Fox had made the vain dash to Annapolis, but it would mean more trouble when the first mail steamer arrived from the North, and Du Pont would be in no mood to shield Pettengill.

"Eight bells, sir," said a cheerful voice. "Pipe to dinner, sir?"

It was McAndrew, who had the forenoon watch.

"Make it so," Pettengill said gruffly. The youngster looked as though he hadn't a care in the world. "One watch at a time, Mr. McAndrew," Pettengill added quickly. "Keep the watch on deck at their quarters."

This was enemy country. At any moment, the greenery might vomit flame and iron. Pettengill looked down at the gun crew of the 100-pounder rifle on the forecastle, skylarking half-naked in the baking heat. In ten seconds they might be pivoting that gun around to fire *Lycoming*'s first shot in deadly earnest. His *Lycoming* was the best-constructed gunboat in the world for river fighting; she would survive. They might court-martial Pettengill for making her so, but some of those men down for'd there, others below in the engine room, would live through that first fight—when it came—who otherwise might be torn to bloody shreds or die miserably in the scalding steam of a broken boiler.

This wasn't a crew in the Navy tradition, with a hard core of old-timers to whip the green hands into shape. It wasn't the *Sheboygan's* mixed bag of nationalities, either. The *Lycoming* was manned by American boys, mostly Pennsylvania-born, and they were Pettengill's to mold. All he knew so far was that they were quick to learn and possessed of a devouring curiosity about matters concerned with guns or steam machinery. They had done well handling the ship in heavy weather, better than he could have expected. How they would stand up in battle, he had yet to find out.

"Seems to me there's open water ahead to port, sir," called Casson from the pilothouse window.

This might be the reach shown on the sketch. Frye, who had just relieved McAndrew, was looking inquiringly at Pettengill.

"Slow," said Pettengill.

"And a half two," announced the leadsman.

Shoaling a little. Here was the reach.

"Conn her around handsomely, Mr. Frye. No telling where the channel is. Either they've taken up the buoys, or there never were any."

The Negro pilot who had come aboard the flagship while he was there had sworn you could carry twelve feet right up to Burrell's wharf, which left *Lycoming* two feet to spare. Not enough for comfort, but enough maybe to scrape by.

"Smoke ho!"

Pettengill had seen it already, a smudge of drifting gray smoke perhaps a mile ahead, to starboard, where there seemed to be open ground. Through his glasses it looked like a burning house or like smoke still rising from the embers of a house that had already burned down. Other smoke rose a little farther inland: this was a thick column, climbing into the sky.

But no one had set fire to the wharf, a rickety-looking thing made of palmetto logs. Burrell's plantation wasn't where the sketch said it ought to be. There were people on the wharf. Pettengill focused his glasses more carefully, took another look—they were wearing blue and the sun glinted on steel. For once the Army had turned up where the Navy had been told to look for it. If General Wright was available near the wharf instead of off on some wild-goose chase, Pettengill could find out what the situation was and get on with his work while he still had six hours of daylight.

Du Pont's orders had read:

> You will proceed with the U.S.S. *Lycoming* to Burrell's plantation on the Manasto River and co-operate with Army forces commanded by Brigadier General Wright, for the purpose of clearing away enemy obstructions to navigation and reducing works protecting the same. The destruction or capture of enemy gunboats reported operating in this vicinity will be your first consideration if any such vessels are encountered.

That was just the sort of work *Lycoming* was meant to do.

"There ought to be deep water leading up to that wharf, Mr. Frye," Pettengill said. Those were certainly Army people on the wharf; he could see an officer or two moving about. A couple of wagons coming along past the smoldering ruins of the house were piled high with cotton bales. There was quite a heap of bales near the wharf, too. There seemed to be many Negroes around the place. A horseman left the wagons and galloped hell-for-leather back along the road.

A far-off spatter of musketry came to Pettengill's ears. He swept the open ground beyond the house with his glasses. A few blue dots were moving across the field, and a clump of blue in one spot—half a regiment of infantry, Pettengill guessed, with one company deployed as skirmishers—was advancing toward the woods where the other smoke column was rising.

An officer on the wharf was waving his arms. Washington had never worked out a simple system of signals for joint operations. If there was a fight going on it was a waste of time to bring *Lycoming* in to the wharf to be told verbally what a single flag message might have conveyed.

"Keep her under way, Mr. Frye." Pettengill picked up a speaking trumpet as the *Lycoming* eased inshore.

"Is General Wright there?" he called.

The Army officer, a young man with long silky sideburns, pointed off toward the distant troops. He cupped his hands over his mouth and his words came clearly enough as the beat of *Lycoming*'s paddles died:

"The general's compliments, sir. He's driving the enemy back toward their entrenchments. He'd be glad of the support of your guns. First turn on your right brings you up to their fort."

"Any sign of Rebel gunboats?" called Pettengill.

"No. But the woods are full—"

A heavy gun, heavier than a field piece, sounded over beyond the woods. Wright's troops must have come within range of the Johnnies' fort. There was no time for more talk.

"Tell the general we're on our way," shouted Pettengill.

The engine-room bell clanged, the paddles went to work again, and the *Lycoming*'s prow nosed into the sluggish current.

The blue dots were out of sight now. So was the galloping horseman. The larger patch of blue, the supporting column, was at the edge of the woods. The cotton wagons puzzled Pettengill. Why would the Army be collecting cotton when a fight was going on? There were men in blue helping the Negroes unload the wagons, as well as a couple of white men who were not in uniform. An officer seemed to be directing the work; he turned toward the *Lycoming* as she gathered speed, and into the field of Pettengill's glasses leaped the round pink face of Colonel Brean.

He couldn't have got here ahead of Pettengill—or could he? It was just possible—if he had got aboard a fast steamer and gone down the Potomac to Hampton Roads that same night. The hell with him.

Pettengill examined the sketch which was supposed to serve him as a chart. There should be a channel leading from the Manasto River over toward the Coosaw, connecting with St. Helena Sound and deep water. It made sense for the Johnnies to try to block that channel; the Union troops couldn't operate without naval support and water transportation, but once the Union grip was firm on all this network of inland waterways, both Charleston and Savannah would be wide open to attack. The Southern commanders must be desperately trying to gain time in order to bring more troops for the defense of their great seaports.

There was the opening of the channel, just about where Pettengill had expected to find it. It was narrow, but there seemed a good volume of water swirling out of it into the broad reach; it might be fairly deep.

The gunfire was nearer now.

"Beat to quarters, Mr. Casson."

The *Lycoming* was already partially cleared for action: the guns were provided, boats prepared for hoisting out, ground tackle ready for instant use, shell-whips rigged and ammunition-scuttles open, small arms distributed. Now, as the spring-rattle roared, the guns were cast loose: the 100-pounder for'd, the big 11-inch Dahlgren shell-gun aft, the two howitzers on each broadside. Master's Mate McAndrew, officer of the powder division, came to get the magazine keys from Casson. The quick glance he gave Pettengill seemed to say: "Try me now, Captain. Let me prove what I'm ready to do for you." The master-at-arms was reporting the galley fire out; an assistant engineer was directing some of the black gang, connecting fire hoses and leading them along the deck; another came up to stand by the engine-room bell, a duty which in action required engineering ability in the view of whoever had written that regulation.

"Cleared for action, sir," reported Casson, who had automatically taken over the deck.

Pettengill scarcely heard him. His attention was completely absorbed in watching the water ahead of the *Lycoming*. The chant of the leadsman echoed in his ears every few minutes; there was still enough water under *Lycoming*'s keel as she breasted the quick-flowing channel, which turned and twisted amid sand spits and patches of thicket so that he could never see clear water ahead for more than two hundred yards. There were other channels leading into this one, both sides.

The *Lycoming* sloshed along, her wake washing up against the swampy banks on either hand. Another bend, and the channel was shadowed by overarching trees. In the deep greenery nothing stirred save a flight of birds and the eternal gnats and mosquitoes. There was still another bend ahead. Pettengill couldn't see around it for the foliage.

Without an instant's warning, the green barrier before him vomited flame and thunder. The *Lycoming* reeled under a blow that shook her slender frame. Pettengill heard the rush of a second heavy shot just overhead at the same instant that he heard the sharp voice of Frye at the 100-pounder: "Point-blank! Ready! Fire!" The deck shuddered with the roar and recoil of the great gun. Each division officer was under orders to return fire instantly. All guns had been loaded with shell and five-second fuzes. The double crash of the forward pair of 24-pounders, fired almost together, smacked on Pettengill's eardrums as he yelled:

"Slow astern, Mr. Casson!"

Once more twin lances of flame leaped out from the masked battery. Once more he felt and heard the splintering crash of a hit somewhere below. Those were 32-pounders, firing solid shot—no shells were exploding. They were trying to rake him, puncture his boilers. How would they know about those two-inch iron-plated bulkheads, fore and aft, that guarded *Lycoming*'s machinery space?

The *Lycoming* heeled over as the 11-inch shell-gun on her poop let go. Pettengill whirled. The big gun was pivoted to port, smoke swirled from its muzzle. He realized that there was smoke along the bank of the channel too—hidden riflemen. A bullet hit the pilothouse, whined away viciously just clear of Pettengill's shoulder. He ran aft to the break of the hurricane deck, shouting: "Howitzer crews, sweep those bushes with canister!" There were three men down and bleeding on the quarter-deck.

The 100-pounder on the fo'c's'le crashed again, but this time only one enemy gun answered, and that one missed. Pettengill saw the shot ricochet from the water and disappear in the thicket. The infantry fire from ashore was increasing. It would be safer to run past the hidden battery now that its fire had been beaten down a little than to stay here and slug it out while that damned musketry decimated his gun crews. So far, Pettengill hadn't seen a single enemy soldier.

The hammering of bullets on the for'd pilothouse, as Pettengill came back to it, sounded like a gang of Navy Yard riveters hard at work; the brass sheathing and shutters were starred with lead.

"Stop! Ahead slow!" Pettengill shouted above the thunder-echoes of the howitzers. He wanted to bring the 11-inch to bear on what might be left of the Rebel battery. "Ahead half!" The *Lycoming* was forging back toward the bend; no damage to engine or boilers so far, thanks to the stout foundrymen who had turned out those iron plates.

"Captain! Get inside here!" Pettengill waved Casson's plea away. His eye was on the channel as the *Lycoming* came around the sand spit.

"Full astern!" he yelled suddenly.

The channel was blocked by a double row of thick piles, deep-driven all the way across it. At that instant, the blast of the 11-incher, fired at its maximum forward train, almost knocked Pettengill off his feet. This time he saw the thicket swept away as by a giant scythe. Gray figures, two or three of them, bounded through the smoke like marionettes, past an upended gun muzzle. There was no answering fire. The masked battery was dead. But the riflemen weren't, and there was no getting through those piles.

"Shift the conn aft!" Pettengill shouted.

The *Lycoming*, like all double-enders, had rudders and steering positions both fore and aft. One of Pettengill's innovations had been to carry the heads of both rudder posts through on deck, so that a tiller could be shipped; this enabled the inactive rudder to be more firmly and quickly secured in shifting from one end to the other and also provided an emergency steering position which was much handier than relieving tackles, at least in smooth water.

In repeated drills, Pettengill had succeeded in shifting the conn in just under three minutes. Now the hours spent at drill paid off, the double blast of the steam whistle which signaled the shift had barely sounded when Casson and the quartermaster were racing aft, followed by the helmsman as soon as the quartermaster reached the after pilothouse; down on the quarter-deck the "old rudder" was being lashed fast. Two and a half minutes, Pettengill guessed, trotting aft heedless of whining bullets. Any ordinary gunboat, trying to go astern in a narrow channel like this, stood an excellent chance of getting aground—a double-ender was different.

Lycoming was backtracking away from the barrier, her howitzers blazing as fast as they could be served. The musketry fire was slackening; canister at that range was no joke. The 11-inch let go another blast—Master's Mate Stevens, in charge on the quarter-deck, was doing all right for his first action; more than likely that was canister too, enough of it to sweep away a whole company with a single round.

Respite now for a minute. Time to check on damage and casualties, decide what to do next.

Through the smoke that drifted along the surface of the water Pettengill saw a dark shape shove out into the stream from one of the side channels, right across *Lycoming*'s course and not more than two hundred yards away. The next instant he was flung to the deck by an impact that knocked the breath from his body; his eyes were blinded by a wicked flash of fire. Iron fragments clattered all around him. The faint sound of someone's screaming filtered through the roar of the exploding shell to his deafened ears.

He found himself on his feet, clinging to the rail above the quarter-deck. Someone was giving orders.

"Load with shell, Mr. Stevens! Fire at her water line 'midships!" Pettengill scarcely recognized his own voice.

He blinked his eyes, trying to focus them on the Confederate gunboat that had leaped so suddenly from that side channel to cut off *Lycoming*'s withdrawal. She was a small black steamer; no paddles— a screw steamer, then—low in the water, one big gun for'd—

"Howitzers! Use grape on that gun crew! Dead slow on the engine." *Lycoming* wasn't built for ramming.

Fire stabbed at Pettengill from the enemy deck: this shell burst low, close alongside the *Lycoming* and just for'd of the port paddle-box. They were trying for his wheels. The 11-inch let go. Its crew leaped to reload, their naked torsos swaying and bending in the smoke like devils dancing in hell. Pettengill braced himself for the next enemy shell. His own 11-incher beat the Johnnies to the punch. Smoke hid the enemy ship again, smoke and something else—a vast white cloud of steam. That shell had burst in her boiler.

Through the fiendish howl of the outrushing steam came the thin shrieks of scalded men.

"Cease firing!" bellowed Pettengill. "Stop her! Away both quarter boats, Mr. Casson. Pick up as many as you can."

The breeze was pushing back the clouds—gray smoke and white steam—that veiled the shattered gunboat. She had rolled far over to port and was down by the head, the current was taking her round. Her bow would be clear of the channel before she hit the bottom. She was going down fast. A burst boiler couldn't have done all that damage; some of it was the effect of shellfire. Men were still jumping from her into the water. Pettengill could see a dozen heads bobbing about on the dark surface, and one stripped white corpse floating belly up. But there were live enemies to think of.

He ran back to the other end of the hurricane deck.

"Any more firing from those bushes, Mr. Frye?"

"Not for the past few minutes, sir." Frye's face was black with powder and the thick grease that was used to coat the rifle shells, but he was grinning happily. The gun crew were waving their arms and cheering. The howitzer crews were cheering too, so were the fire parties. The whole ship's company took up the chorus.

"Hurray-y-y! Hurray for the old *Lycoming!* Hurray for Cap'n Pettengill!"

The cheers of his crew after a hard-fought action are a heady wine for a young captain. Pettengill savored it, then thrust the cup from his lips.

"Belay that noise!" he roared. "Mr. Casson, I'll thank you for a report of damages. Get the decks cleared up and strike those wounded men below. Tell the surgeon he'll have his hands full presently."

His boats were pulling men out of the water—some who were able to help themselves over the gunwales, others who weren't.

Pete Hewitt came out of the engine-room hatch and along the gangway of the hurricane deck. He lifted his cap formally.

"No casualties in the engineer department, sir," he reported. His eyes were shining. "Damage minor—condenser tubes leaking, bracing of number one boiler'll need some going over. A solid shot started the armored bulkhead behind it, but it didn't come through. Bilge pumps are choking up—that's because they rushed us off from Philadelphia without the strainers. I'll have 'em cleared in an hour, and we'll make our own strainers first chance I get. That's about it, Captain. Congratulations, sir. From the heart."

"Thanks, Pete." *Lycoming* had taken her beating and walked away with it.

Assistant Surgeon Mawley was climbing the ladder.

"Two men killed, sir. Eight wounded, one fatally. One officer wounded, not serious. Master's Mate McAndrew, splinter in deltoid muscle."

Eleven casualties, only three fatal, out of 130-odd officers and men.

"McAndrew refuses to go off duty, sir. I told him—"

"Never mind what you told him, Doctor. Get below and see what you can do for those wounded Johnnies." The first boat with the survivors of the Southern gunboat was coming alongside. The gunboat herself was on the bottom now, lying over on her side, with steam and smoke still rising from her broken hull.

The distant guns were sounding again. The troops were assaulting the Confederate fort—and the *Lycoming* wasn't there to support the Army. The sunken gunboat had come out of a very narrow channel, but a screw steamer of her size would certainly draw as much water as *Lycoming*. Maybe that channel might offer a way around the obstruction. It looked so on the sketch. If not, he could always back up.

"Bear a hand with those survivors!" he called out. "Mr. Stevens, as soon as your boat's clear of casualties, see if there's enough water so I can get past that wreck into the side channel. Mr. Casson, I'll want the ship ready to go into action again immediately."

There was water enough—just enough—to let the *Lycoming* scrape past her sunken foe. She was still going stern first—there was no room to turn her around—but that didn't really matter. This channel was even narrower than the one Pettengill had been following when he was fired on, and had just as many bends, sharper ones, too; twice the *Lycoming*'s paddles beat up thick mud as Pettengill conned her around a hairpin turn. The trees were thicker; the afternoon sun filtered through them only fitfully.

"By the deep, four," chanted the leadsman.

Four fathoms in this ditch? But the channel was widening right beyond the next bend.

"And a quarter, four," the leadsman announced.

There was a connection with the Coosaw River and St. Helena Sound. Maybe this was it.

Pettengill couldn't hear the far-off guns any longer. He shaded his eyes against the trickling sunbeams and tried to peer through the tangle of green on the shore.

"Slow!" he said sharply. He had seen something that certainly was no tree—unless a tree had shrouds and ratlines attached to it.

"I'll have all hands at quarters, Mr. Casson," he ordered. "Pass the word quietly. No rattle, no pipes."

Another bend. The *Lycoming* crept slowly around it. Just ahead, the channel divided: the left branch was the wider, and had fewer trees on its farther bank; the right-hand branch seemed to lose itself immediately in a mass of foliage.

A mass of foliage triced up around the masts of a ship and intertwined with her rigging. Pettengill had spotted her shrouds by sheer accident; he might have steamed by and never noticed anything. His heart was beating a little faster as he edged the *Lycoming* into the narrow channel. Soon he could make out the shape of the hidden vessel's stern; there was something familiar about it. All at once he knew. She was the bark *Norwich City*.

"Arm and away—" he began.

The deck smacked upward beneath his feet as though some huge submarine monster had suddenly risen under *Lycoming*'s keel. He felt the jar of a muffled explosion; water leaped skyward in a foaming column close alongside—just abreast the engine room.

"Torpedo!" yelled Casson from the pilothouse window.

"Stop her!" shouted Pettengill. He pushed past Casson into the pilothouse, blew into the engine-room voice tube.

"Engine room," said Hewitt's voice, not a trace of excitement in it.

"What's the damage, Pete?"

"Can't tell," said Hewitt. "There's water coming over the footplates already. Oiler's dead, two men hurt. I need more hands. Those damn bilge plumps— Better beach her."

The tube snapped shut.

"Send twenty hands to report to Mr. Hewitt," Pettengill ordered. "More if he needs 'em."

If the water got into the firerooms there might not be steam on the engine much longer.

Pettengill turned away from the white strained faces of Casson and the quartermaster—looking to him to save the ship from this peril as he had saved her in the hour of battle. He closed his ears to the shouts of alarm, the feet that hammered along the decks, the sound of inrushing water down below. He focused his mind on the sand-bar where the channel divided. If he could beach her there, stern first, at least she wouldn't sink; the tide was running out. The rise and fall here would be about seven feet; at slack water he might be able to get at the hole in her bottom.

Of course moving her at all meant he might run smack on to another torpedo. But letting her drift meant the same thing.

"Slow ahead," he ordered. Since the *Lycoming* was steering by the stern, this amounted to backing away, out of the narrow channel toward the wider reach. The paddles responded to the bell. Leaning over the rail, Pettengill conned her; no time to shift to the other rudder; the list was getting worse, and that wouldn't help when it came to getting at the damage.

"Stop. Astern slow. Starboard a half point." Now her stern was moving toward the sand-bar. Pettengill tried to calculate the best angles of fire for his guns in case the Johnnies found her and attacked before he was through with his repairs. "Starboard another point."

The list hadn't increased the last few minutes.

Pettengill heard the squealer of the voice tube, and checked his next order instinctively.

"Captain!" yelled Casson. "The chief says the pump's holding its own; he thinks it's starting to gain on the water."

"Stop. Slow ahead." The *Lycoming* drew off a little from the sand-bar into deeper water. "Stop. Take her a minute, Mr. Casson."

The engine room was full of steam and coal gas as Pettengill clattered down the long iron ladder past the inclined frame on which the crosshead worked. It was full of sound, too: the hiss of water on hot coals, thudding of hammers, and the steady throb-throb-throb of a steam pump. As he hit the foot-plate the water sloshed around his ankles.

Pete Hewitt grabbed his arm.

"You beach her yet?"

"No."

"You won't have to now. I just cut in the other pump. They're both sucking. It's your watertight bulkheads that did the trick—and young McAndrew here."

McAndrew leaned against a stanchion, looking like a drowned rat. He was covered with bilge slime from head to foot: one arm was in a sling, the other hung limply at his side.

But his eyes were on his captain's face: they seemed to beg for approval.

"This kid," said Hewitt, "got down in the water up to his neck and kept the pump intake clear of weeds and dirt with his one good hand till I could spare a man to spell him. Now I've got two men at it, working quarter-hour shifts. But if it wasn't for McAndrew you'd've had to stick her ashore to keep the water out of the fires, bulkheads or no bulkheads. It's in the ash-pans as it is, but we're getting rid of it fast."

Pettengill laid a hand on McAndrew's shoulder.

"Thank you, Mr. McAndrew," he said. "Not many wounded men would've done that. I won't forget it in my report to the flag officer."

McAndrew lifted his head and tried to grin. "It's nothing, sir," he said, "to what I owe you."

"Turn in at once," Pettengill added. "I'll see the surgeon serves you out something to warm your innards."

"Thank you, sir."

Pettengill was already running up the ladder.

"Mr. Casson!"

"Sir!"

"As I was about to say when that damned Rebel torpedo interrupted me, I'd be glad if you'll arm the first cutter and send Mr. Stevens to take possession of that ship in there under the leaves. She's our missing friend from the convoy, the *Norwich City*. We'll give her back to the Army with our compliments."

Chapter Twenty-two

The bright rim of the morning sun appeared above the sandhills behind Fort Beauregard, its first rays gleaming on the quiet waters of Port Royal Harbor. To Pettengill, the dawn of the new day held no promise as he leaned on the *Lycoming*'s taffrail.

The starch had gone out of him in the course of writing his report to the flag officer on yesterday's proceedings. It didn't look well, set down on paper, to admit that he had run his ship on a torpedo and damaged her so badly that he had to abandon his mission and come limping back to Port Royal with a thrummed sail hauled taut under her bottom, like a baby with its backside in a sling. The Army might have suffered a bloody repulse which the General would be only too happy to blame on Pettengill for not being there to support him.

And for this miserable result, four of his men had died. The four pine boxes which the carpenter's mate had hammered together were ranged in a row on the quarter-deck, an ensign secured across them. A sentry with bared cutlass paced back and forth to do them honor, as though that mattered now to Ordinary Seaman Kennedy and Landsman Uhlinger, who had been shot down during the fight in the channel, or to Landsman Onslow, who had died of his wounds on the way to Port Royal, or to First Class Fireman Rafferty, who had been standing oiler watch in the engine room when the torpedo explosion hurled him against the cylinder head and smashed his skull.

As soon as the anchor was down, two other wounded crewmen and several wounded prisoners had been sent across to the *Wabash*, where there were better sick-bay facilities than the *Lycoming* could provide. The rest of the wounded weren't in bad shape. Doctor Mawley thought all of them would be fit for duty in a few days. Pettengill had talked with them as best he could; they made light of their hurts, seemed to be thinking only of the fight they had helped to win. What a mockery! A miserable little success in a swamp-bordered inlet, gained at the cost of failing in the mission the ship had been sent to perform. They apparently regarded him as a hero.

Pettengill stared miserably across the harbor at the big *Wabash*, lying off Hilton Head with Du Pont's square blue flag fluttering at her mizzen. If the Old Man had finished his breakfast, he might be reading Pettengill's report by this time. Pettengill had been up most of the night writing it; it had gone over to the flagship at 3 A.M. Pettengill pictured the stern mouth tightening under those magnificent whiskers. He could hear the leonine roar: "Pettengill again! This time, by God—"

There had been a mail steamer in the night before, the first mail from the North since the taking of Port Royal. She might have brought the flag officer news of Pettengill's other crimes, like rebuilding the U.S.S. *Lycoming* to his own design and running out of Annapolis in violation of a direct order from the Department to await the arrival of the Assistant Secretary of the Navy.

There hadn't been a soul aboard *Norwich City* when Stevens' men had boarded her, just her cargo, apparently intact. The bark lay now a cable's length away, in the same state as Pettengill had found her, topmasts housed, rigging all tangled in withering tree branches. An Army boat was alongside; the Army people had been coming and going all during the morning watch, but none of them had come near the *Lycoming*.

Any minute, a string of flags might go climbing up to the *Wabash's* to'gallant yardarm—*Lycoming's* number, followed by the ominous order: "Commanding officer report aboard flagship immediately." Well, he could at least be properly dressed for the occasion.

He was still wearing the crumpled service whites he had worn all the day before and all the night spent picking his way through the channels, dragging the deadweight of the *Norwich City* astern, and sweating over the interminable pages of his report.

As he went into the cabin his steward popped through the pantry door with a tray; the odor of steaming coffee was welcome. Pettengill was still glad of small comforts: coffee, a shave, a clean shirt and his summer-weight frock coat. He turned his eyes away from the shoulder straps with their silver foul anchor, the single gold sleeve stripe of which he was so proud. They would never send his name to Congress now.

He gulped his coffee, poured another cup, sitting slumped in the chair before his desk. He sat there a long time, looking straight ahead. The coffee grew cold in the cup. Around him were all the familiar sounds of the ship's routine, he heard six bells strike, then seven. The hands were piped to breakfast. The officer of the watch reported eight bells. Pettengill muttered, "Make it so." He sat on.

Someone knocked on the cabin door.

"Come in."

"Mr. Frye's respects, sir," said the quartermaster. "Boat's standing this way from the flagship. Flag officer's barge. Flag in her bows."

Pettengill was up and out of the cabin as though propelled from his own 11-inch Dahlgren. He snatched the quartermaster's telescope, put it to his eye.

"Damn and blast it, Mr. Frye! What are you lolly-gagging there for? You've got five minutes to get every officer on deck in undress uniform. Six side boys, well scrubbed. I want the ship's drum on the quarter-deck, and a guard of twenty men with muskets and cutlasses."

Frye was squalling panicky orders; he should have had these things in train already. The barge wasn't coming too fast, he'd just about make it.

Beyond the barge, Pettengill's eye noted something else.

The flag had disappeared from the mizzentruck of the *Wabash*; which meant that the *Lycoming* was to hoist it at her own truck and salute it as the Old Man came over the side. That was the sort of compliment a flag officer on a disciplinary mission would ordinarily omit.

"Have a blue flag bent to the main truck halliards, Mr. Frye. Saluting gun's crews to quarters. Here, Mr. Casson, get the keys to the magazine and pass 'em to the gunner's mate. Quick's the play, that barge is almost alongside."

He dashed back into his cabin, buckled on his sword belt, dragged his cocked hat and epaulettes out of their tin case, and ran out again into the sunshine of the quarter-deck just in time to hear the barge's coxswain crying: "Way enough! Toss!" He took a quick look around —everything was ready.

A cocked hat so resplendent in gold lace as to show barely a patch of black here and there was just rising above the starboard hammock nettings: under it, the famous Du Pont whiskers came into view. Pettengill moved toward the gangway: his heart was sick, but he set his jaw firmly.

The pipes squealed, the drum beat two ruffles, the blue flag soared aloft; somebody barked "Present arms!", the side boys tugged at their hat brims.

Pettengill lifted his own hat and stepped forward to receive the Flag Officer Commanding the South Atlantic Blockading Squadron. Bang! went the first gun of the salute.

Du Pont towered in the gangway; he seemed to dwarf every other figure on the crowded quarter-deck. His eyes were stern, and they were looking straight into Pettengill's. He lifted his hat to the colors, took a step forward and held out his hand.

"Good morning, Captain Pettengill!" he said. "I'll be glad if you'll present your officers, after which I'll make an inspection of your ship."

Pettengill made the presentations in a daze of misery. Casson first, then the watch officers, the doctor, the paymaster, and the engineers. Du Pont found a kindly word for each. He reduced McAndrew to stuttering confusion by asking about his wounded arm and saying he would be mentioned in dispatches for what he'd done down in the flooded compartment. He stood with bared head before the flag-draped coffins on the quarter-deck, and announced his intention of being present when they were buried over on Hilton Head that afternoon.

Then he glanced at Pettengill.

"You may dismiss from quarters, Captain. Let your officers and men go about their morning duties during the inspection, which will not include the crew."

As the inspection proceeded, Pettengill's astonishment increased at every step. Du Pont asked questions; he wanted to know something about every detail, but he offered no criticism, no scathing remarks.

He examined with interest the dented plate of the for'd engine-room bulkhead where the enemy ball had hit; the splintered holes in the bows, with the carpenter's gang hard at work on them; the iron coaming that slanted inboard all around the engine-room hatch, scarred now with bullets and shell fragments; the low-hung iron guards on the paddle wheels, one of them bent so badly as almost to touch the paddles. Then he was going down the ladder into the engine room, and nothing would do but he must be on his knees peering into the bilges where the torpedo had opened a hole in *Lycoming*'s bottom.

"This is where young McAndrew distinguished himself, I take it?"

"Yes, sir."

"H'm. Don't understand how your ship kept afloat with all that water in her, Captain."

"It was mostly between those two bulkheads, sir. We were all right as soon as we'd closed off the other compartments."

"Compartments?" said Du Pont sharply, looking up.

"Yes, sir. The whole—"

"Later!" Du Pont got to his feet. He looked around the engine room.

"These are your forced-draft blowers, chief?" he asked.

"Yes, sir," said Hewitt.

"H'm. I've got smaller ones in the *Wabash.*"

Back on deck, he looked over the pilothouses, the battery, the masts and rigging, the boats, and the rest of the gear with equal interest and the same curt comments:

"Brass plates and shutters on both pilothouses." He fingered a bright bullet-splash. "Steam windlass. Foremast stepped pretty well aft, Captain? Better field of fire for your forward pivot gun, of course. H'm. I see you've an eleven-inch Dahlgren for a stern-chaser; seems to me I was told these double-enders would have nine-inch stern guns. Very well, Captain. I've seen all I desire. Now a word with you in your cabin, if you please."

Pettengill ushered the flag officer through his cabin door. He wasn't reassured by Du Pont's curt order to the flag lieutenant to remain outside. Du Pont took off his cocked hat, mopped his high forehead with an enormous silk handkerchief, and looked around the cabin.

"I hope you'll find this chair comfortable, sir," Pettengill offered. "Would you care for a cup of coffee, sir?"

Du Pont sat down, still mopping. It had been hot in the engine room.

"I should enjoy some coffee very much, thank you."

Flag officers didn't drink coffee with captains they were about to break. Pettengill's offer had been purely mechanical.

He croaked the order to his hovering steward.

Du Pont was still surveying the cabin.

"Very comfortable quarters, Captain Pettengill," he said. "But isn't it a trifle unusual for the cabin to be up here under the break of the superstructure, opening directly on the quarter-deck?"

"Yes, sir," Pettengill agreed. "But it's handy. I've got rooms for my executive officer and chief engineer on the port side of this one. That way, Mr. Casson and I are both practically on the quarter-deck all the time, and Mr. Hewitt's only two jumps from the engine-room ladder."

"H'm." Du Pont sipped his coffee.

"I suppose you know," he remarked severely, "that there is no more sacred tradition in the Navy than that which regulates the position of officers' quarters aboard ship? How on earth did you induce the Department to allow such a wholesale heresy?"

Pettengill looked straight at him.

"I didn't, sir," he said. "I did the whole thing myself."

"Just how did you contrive to do that?"

"The Philadelphia Navy Yard was so overworked when this ship was under construction, sir, that there wasn't much supervision. Everything was pretty well left to the master workmen. I had some back pay coming, sir—and I—sort of arranged things."

Du Pont set down his coffee cup.

"And those armored bulkheads? The iron coaming on the engine-room hatch? The plates on the pilothouses? The armored guards on your paddle wheels? The watertight compartments? The eleven-inch gun? The steam windlass and the frigate-size blowers? All these were obtained by you in this same highly informal fashion, Captain Pettengill?"

"Yes, sir."

Flag Officer Du Pont leaned back in Pettengill's chair and allowed the explosion of his mighty laughter to shake the cabin.

"I've never heard the beat of this one," he gasped between bellows. "When I was a lieutenant, Frank Du Pont was counted a damn clever Navy Yard thief, but, by God, I never aspired to such magnificent audacity as this. Oh, it'll be the death of me!"

He wiped the tears from his eyes at last, ran a finger round inside his collar.

"You realize what you've done, I hope?" he asked. "You've virtually thumbed your nose at the august authors of the double-ender design. Including the Assistant Secretary of the Navy. I'm going to have to take a very high line with 'em to save you from their wrath."

"To—to save me, did you say, sir?"

"What else? D'you suppose I'd let the land sharks get their teeth in any captain of mine who can fight his ship as you fought yours yesterday?"

He slammed a fist down on Pettengill's desk.

"The Rebels thought they had you in a trap! The whole Rebel army was gloating over the Yankee gunboat they were going to sink. They surprise you with raking fire from a hidden battery, but your armored bulkheads surprise *them,* damn them, and you give back better'n you take. Their riflemen in the bushes can't pick off your helmsman; plating on your pilothouses takes care of that, while your guns take care of the riflemen. D'you know the Army found more than seventy dead Rebels in those bushes, Captain? They have the channel blocked, and a gunboat pops out to cut off your retreat; you cut her down instead, she can't win against an ironclad. Captain Pettengill, you took that enemy trap apart, piece by piece, and threw the pieces back in the enemy's face! A fact which I'll take the greatest pleasure in throwing in the Department's face in reply to their whimpering complaints about your suspected irregularities in the Philadelphia Navy Yard! Irregularities indeed! I wish I had more captains who could produce such irregularities! If there was anything irregular about what you did to this ship, you proved yesterday you were right in every detail of it, even to walking off with a torpedo hit in your bottom that'd have sunk the *Wabash!*"

"But—but, sir—a trap, you say? I didn't realize—"

"Of course it was a trap, Captain!" thundered Du Pont. "A well-laid trap, baited by a damned traitor who betrayed your coming to the enemy as soon as he saw you steaming up to Burrell's wharf!"

"Colonel Brean!" Pettengill remembered the galloping horseman.

"That's his name. He was behind this dirty affair of the *Norwich City*. He stood to make a cool quarter of a million by trading her cargo for cotton that he could sell in Boston at eighty cents a pound. Oh, he had the wool pulled over General Sherman's eyes in fine fashion, I can tell you. Just before I left the flagship, I had a most handsome apology from the General for his attitude when he thought you'd lost his precious supply ship. A written apology, Captain Pettengill!"

"I hope Brean didn't get away," Pettengill remarked.

"He's over at Hilton Head in close arrest. General Wright caught him trying to desert to the Rebel lines right after the Army took that fort up the river. By the way, you'll be glad to know General Wright gives you full credit for that."

"Sir?" Pettengill said in a choked voice. "He gives *me* credit?"

"Wright tells me the fugitives from your victory on the river had spread such panic that the Rebels in the fort just fired a few shots and ran when they saw our troops coming. He's saying so in his official report to General Sherman, too. H'm."

Pettengill's four men had not died in vain. Victory, Du Pont had said. Victory! A magic word, even in the face of death.

"Brean's made a full confession," Du Pont went on. "Hopes to save his treacherous neck, I suppose. I've read it. He seems very bitter against you—and against some young lady he says was working for the Treasury." There was a question in his voice.

"That'd be Miss Prudence Pryor, sir," said Pettengill carefully. "She's a Treasury agent, all right. She had her suspicions about the *Norwich City's* cargo. I begged her not to delay the convoy, promised I'd report the circumstances to you for proper action. She seemed satisfied, but I guess it didn't suit Brean."

Du Pont chuckled.

"That's not quite the way Brean tells it," he said. "No matter. You appear to have a way with young ladies, Captain Pettengill, to be able to satisfy a Treasury agent so easily. A dangerous gift for a sailor. It runs in my mind that I once warned you the sea's a jealous mistress."

Du Pont was getting out of his chair; Pettengill got up too.

"There's no chance of putting you in dock here," Du Pont said, and now his tone was again that of the commander in chief speaking to a junior. "How soon can you make your ship ready for service?"

"By tomorrow morning, sir," Pettengill told him. "It'll be a patchwork job, but she'll answer, if I can get—"

"Let me know within the hour what you need," Du Pont cut in. "Yesterday's fight opened up further possibilities for the Army—with naval support, of course—that must be exploited before the enemy recovers from the shock. I'll give you another gunboat besides this one, and you'll act as senior naval officer in the Manasto River, supporting General Wright's operations. Keep me fully informed: I'll expect written reports at each opportunity."

Senior naval officer! An independent command! There were commanders grown gray in the service, let alone lieutenants, who'd give their eyeteeth for an assignment like that. . . .

The flag lieutenant was at the door.

"Flagship's signalizing, sir. Urgent message for you from General Sherman."

"Back to the treadmill," grumbled Du Pont. He held out his hand. "Good luck to you, Captain Pettengill. I'll send you over your written orders this afternoon."

Pettengill mumbled something that could pass for thanks. He followed the flag officer out to the sun-scorched quarter-deck.

"That's a wonderful place for a cabin," Du Pont murmured. "I remember when I was in the old *Ohio* seventy-four, they stowed me down on the orlop to make room for the commodore's wife up above. No air. Three ladders to climb when they beat to quarters. Rats. Women are the curse of the Navy, Captain Pettengill. At times. But they also have their points. At other times." He chuckled and turned away.

The drum rolled, the guard presented arms, the pipes shrilled, and the flag officer went down the ladder to his waiting barge, still chuckling.

Pettengill stood with lifted hat until the barge was clear of the side. Then he walked slowly into the cabin, still moving like a man in a dream.

A report of his fight in the channel would go to Washington couched in such language that there would be no question about his permanent commission. For the Department to take any other view, especially after Du Pont had appointed him to an independent command, would be an intolerable reflection on the judgment of the Flag Officer Commanding the South Atlantic Blockading Squadron, the officer whose great victory at Port Royal had earned his country's gratitude.

Banks had been right. Give Du Pont loyalty, and he'd give you loyalty in turn until the last cat was keel-hauled. In his proud way, he was apologizing for having entertained any doubts.

There was a heap of mail on Pettengill's desk. He spread it out, stared at it. The flag lieutenant must have brought it along in the barge.

There was a white envelope with a Washington postmark; it was addressed in a sprawling, girlish hand that he recognized more by instinct than long familiarity. Terry had answered his letter, after all. And there was another—a small square thing with the initials P.P. on the back. And another from Philadelphia.

"Morning quarters at three bells as usual, sir?" Casson asked from the cabin doorway.

Pettengill snapped out of his daze.

"Good God, no, Mr. Casson! Keep every man at work to get the ship ready for service by daybreak tomorrow! You've got the carpenter's report there? What does he need in the way of planks and timber? Send the list over to the flagship at once. The boat officer might say to the fleet surgeon, with my respects, that I'd be glad to be relieved of the care of those wounded prisoners at his early convenience. Messenger! Ask Mr. Hewitt if he'll kindly step up here."

He was out on the quarter-deck by this time, leaving his mail unopened and forgotten. His ship—his *Lycoming*—his gold-plated gunboat—had not failed him at Annapolis in his hour of trial. She had not failed him in battle. She would not fail him, he knew as he stood there, in the trials and battles that were yet to come. A sudden thought darted into his mind.

"Mr. Casson!"

"Sir!"

"Have the sailmaker's mate make up a senior officer's pennant. We'll be needing one tomorrow morning."

He would have an ornament to bedeck his love when next they sailed together.

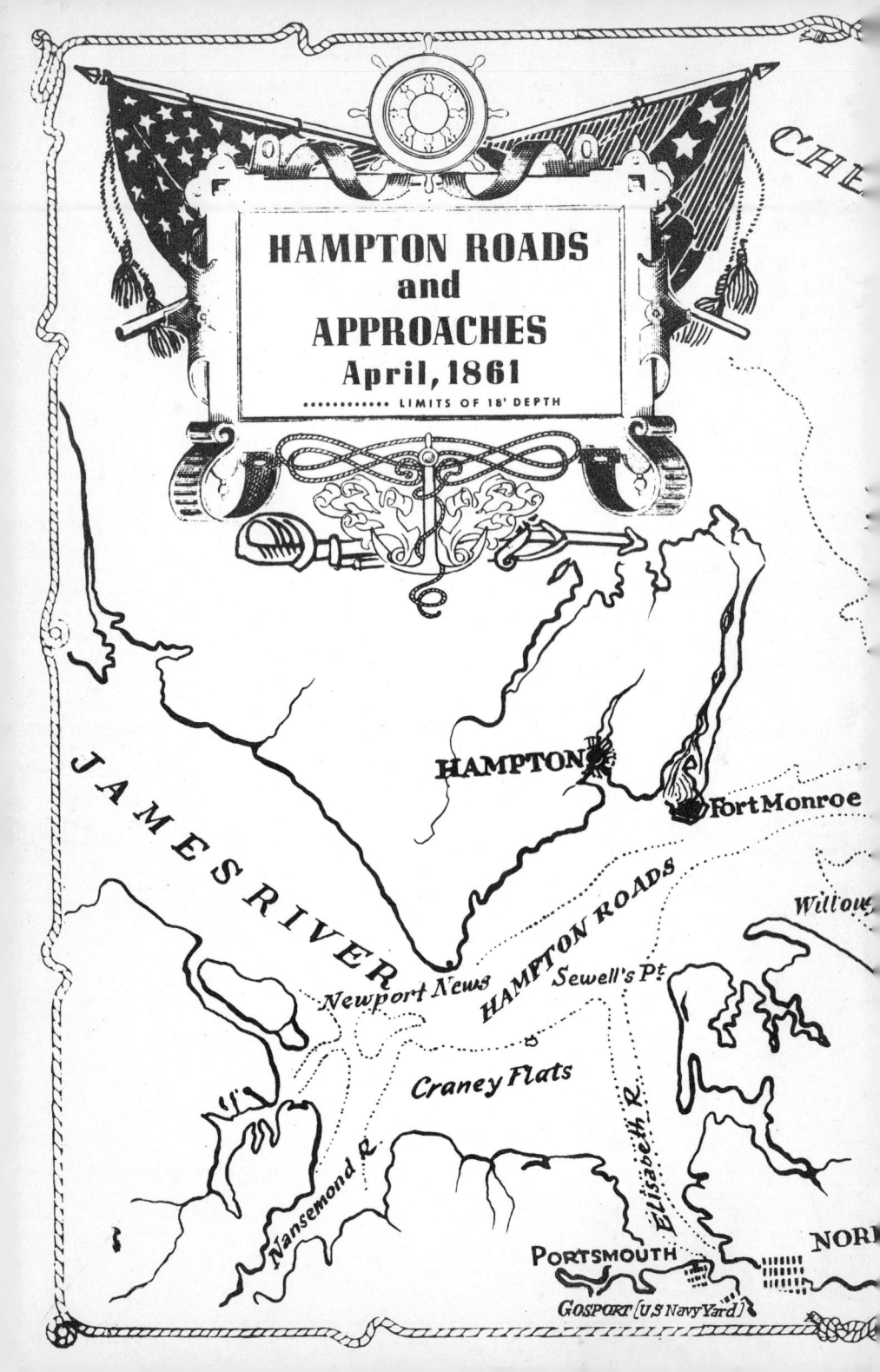

HAMPTON ROADS and APPROACHES
April, 1861
.... LIMITS OF 18' DEPTH

HAMPTON

Fort Monroe

JAMES RIVER

HAMPTON ROADS

Newport News

Sewell's Pt.

Willou[ghby]

Craney Flats

Nansemond R.

Elisabeth R.

PORTSMOUTH

GOSPORT (U.S Navy Yard)

NOR[FOLK]

CH[ESAPEAKE]